FRAMEWORK FOR DEATH

A MYSTERY

BY
AILEEN SCHUMACHER

A Write Way Publishing Book

This book is a work of fiction with references to real places, fictional places and real places with which the author has taken fictional liberties. The characters and incidents are the product of the author's imagination.

Dedication

*To Dominique Raye, Golden Child, my favorite Knick-Knack:
This one is for Nicky because I told her so. I love you, sweetie!*

Acknowledgements

I would like to acknowledge the following people:

Bobbye Straight, Jan Kafka Skipper, and JoAnne Bowers for being my own personal support group (which involves enough it could be a book in itself); Irene and Duffy Stanley for allowing me to visit their Rim Road residence; Carol Wood for taking me there, Lilly Aguila for her outstanding expertise in Spanish profanity; Ana Reyes for proofing the same (and the regular Spanish, too!); Donna Eckel for allowing me to exploit her husband; David Eckel for medical advice; Charles Stubbs for telling me "Brazilian cherry wood" as many times as it took; Bruce Hoffman for legal advice, Jim Skiles for insurance advice; Bill and Melba Schumacher for helping with "The Great Southwestern Book Tour" and providing local details; Kevin for being my trainer and murder consultant; Richard for being my number one groupie and the love of my life; and the following people for their help and encouragement: Richard D. Blum, Les Standiford, Rangeley Wallace, Elroy Bode, Meg Chittendon, Beth Kane, Marilyn Haddrill, Patricia Morris, Jane Rubino, Rollie Steele, Pat Steele, Glenn Calabrese, Betty Davison, Joyce Hunsucker, Leslie Collins, Judy Flanigan, Jane Gaboury, Joseph A. Derie, Sanne Poulin, Dorrie O'Brien, Barbara Clay, Kate Derie, Denise Stybr, Patti Cheney, Jeri Wright, Kate Buker, Sharon Salinger, Sally Fellows, Barbara Franchi, Dina Yagodich, Calvin Branche, Janise Ross, Lou Anne Jaeger, Mary Miller, Sandie Herron, the late Don Sandstrom, Suzanne Saunders, June Maxwell, Kerie Nickel, Lillian Roberts, Heather Campbell, Rhonda Welfare, Harriet Klausner, Lucy Neighbors, Janet Williams, Virginia Conn, Joanne Marshall, Leslie Ann Duncan, Beverly Connor, Chuck West; the Rim Area Neighborhood Association, the subscribers to DorothyL Mystery Digest, and all who read my first book and encouraged me to write this one. You know who you are!

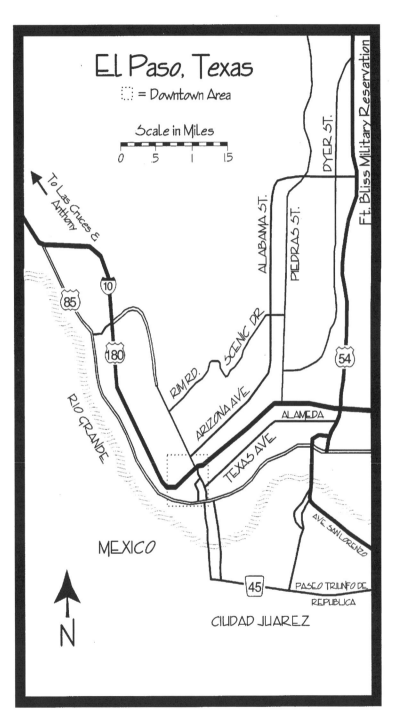

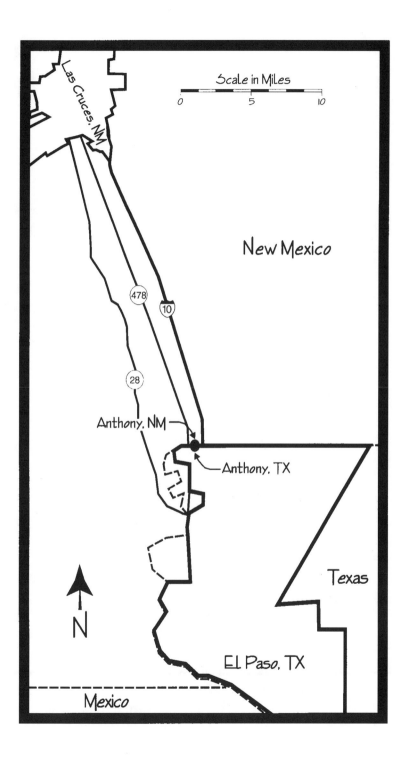

PROLOGUE

Omaha, Nebraska:
Thursday, December 28, mid-afternoon

It took Alicia Boyce a minute to realize that she was actually awake, because she hadn't been aware of falling asleep. Waking and sleeping seemed the same lately, both filled with a sense of anxious waiting. She looked at her watch. She had dozed for less than an hour, and she didn't hear any sounds from the next room. With any luck, the baby would sleep on for a while.

One more day. Only one more. Alicia turned on her back and surveyed the room that had become her prison, reaching into her nightstand to pull a cigarette from its hiding place. She had started smoking when she was sixteen, as a way to control her weight and nerves. Raymond didn't allow her to smoke. He said it wasn't in keeping with her image as a former Miss Nebraska, but after tomorrow, what Raymond liked or didn't like wouldn't matter.

Alicia remembered when a cigarette had been a handy substitute for an overwhelming urge to eat, but now, the need to control her weight was like a forgotten dream. Eating was just a means to an end, a way to stay strong, strong enough to get away from Raymond.

Her hands shook as she lit the cigarette. She sometimes thought that she had been shaking from the moment she made the decision to leave, but surely no one could shake for that long. Luckily Raymond was too busy to notice—too busy with his business deals, his colleagues, his other women.

The details of the arrangements swirled in her mind, an endless pinwheel of anxiety. She reviewed one part of the plan and let it go, only to pick up another part and look for possible flaws. She had decided that they would leave tomorrow, just before the New Year. Much more waiting and she would lose what little sanity she had left.

It was abnormally quiet in the house. Raymond had left on a business trip the day after Christmas and wouldn't return until New Year's Eve. He hadn't questioned her decision to remain behind and give the household staff a week of holiday leave. He was so sure of her, so certain he'd eliminated every vestige of free will and courage. For a long time, she had feared he was right. But that was before she found the video tape.

Of course Raymond would never leave her totally alone. The chauffeur lived over the garage, the groundskeeper and his wife were in their house down by the electronic gate, and her stepdaughter, Patty, came and went at will. But as long as the groundskeeper stayed at his house, and the chauffeur would drive her and the baby anywhere they wanted to go, everything would be fine.

And with only one more day to wait, it was unlikely she would see Patty again, which was just fine with Alicia. This was the height of the party season, and if Patty excelled at anything, it was parties. Alicia had always been intimidated by her husband's fashion-model daughter, only two years her junior, but now the feelings had intensified and grown more complicated. She feared and loathed Patty, but she also felt small stirrings of pity toward her stepdaughter. Altogether too many emotions to try to keep off her face.

Patty would have to deal with her own problems; Alicia had enough of her own. She took one last drag on the cigarette and snubbed it out, running her hands through her dark shoulder-length hair as she looked at the room one more time. She remembered when the luxury of her surroundings had filled her with delight, when she would wake up every morning, look around, and feel like a princess living in a fairy tale come true.

That stage hadn't lasted long, but the memory was enough to bring a bitter taste of self-loathing up the back of her throat. What a fool she'd been, a young girl with no experience at anything but farm chores and sweet young boys, as tongue-tied and shy as she herself had been. Alicia was ripe for the taking in the glittering tinsel world of beauty pageants, strutting the catwalks unprotected by any street smarts, thinking the best of everyone, just happy to be winning, with nothing whatsoever going for her but her long legs, slim body, and sleek dark-haired beauty.

Raymond had swept her right off her feet, with his own dark good looks and his money, which bought *entrée* to a world Alicia hadn't known existed. The first time Raymond cupped one hand over her breast as he smoothly unzipped the back of her gown with the other, there in the back of his limousine, he didn't pause to raise the tinted glass window that separated them from the driver, and Alicia thought that she would die of embarrassment.

Raymond touched her like he had a right to, with none of the whispered entreaties of those other suitors, and it never occurred to Alicia to question what was happening. Then a wedding ring joined the five carat diamond engagement ring on her finger, and it was too late to get out.

Five long years she lived with Raymond, four of those with the knowledge that she was now a caged possession in the luxury that she had lusted after, a possession who knew too much to ever be set free. She hadn't wanted the baby, but Raymond had, and Raymond usually got what Raymond wanted.

For a while after Hannah was born, Alicia thought that she could make a go of it, closing her eyes to the things that went on around her and concentrating on Hannah, the love of her life. But that was before she found the video. She couldn't let herself think too much about the video, or she would go mad.

She thought about lighting another cigarette to still the growing symptoms of a full-blown panic attack, but she fought against the urge. A good mother didn't smoke, and she planned to quit just as soon as they were safely away. When she felt like she was losing her mind, like she couldn't stand one more minute without screaming, she had found something that worked almost as well as a cigarette. She would go into the nursery and look at the sleeping Hannah.

Hannah meant everything. Hannah was more important than Raymond and his business dealings, more important even than her all-consuming fear. She would do anything for Hannah. Alicia could be brave for Hannah; for Hannah she would take risks that she would never have dared contemplate on her own. She would die for Hannah, if need be.

And right now, she would go look at Hannah, and let the sight of her sleeping daughter calm her fears and strengthen her intent. She would think about how, after tomorrow, she and Hannah would never come back to this place. Alicia smiled to herself, as she pulled back the covers and swung her legs to the side of the bed. She reached for her designer robe, the one that matched her designer gown, the two together costing more than her father earned in a month of farming. Tomorrow, she and Hannah, free.

CHAPTER ONE:

COLLAPSE
El Paso, Texas:
Sunday, January 1, early afternoon

Second quarter, eleven minutes to go, the underdogs just scored a touchdown, and his damn beeper went off.

David Alvarez didn't put much credence in statistics that correlated crime with natural phenomena. Some studies claimed more murders were committed in hot weather, others purported that crimes of passion increased during the full moon, and still others linked incidences of violence to snow storm cabin-fever. As a detective with the El Paso Police Department Special Case Force, Alvarez had reached the unshakable conclusion that crimes were invariably committed, or discovered, whenever he was attending a major sports event. So it was no surprise to hear his beeper go off after a spectacular touchdown at the Sun Bowl game in the football stadium at the University of Texas at El Paso.

The crowd surged to their feet in the clear cold air that characterized winter in this Southwestern part of Texas. At two o'clock in the afternoon the sun was steady and bright, but every breath or utterance from the crowd puffed steamy white into the cold, dry desert air.

Alvarez glanced at his partner, Scott Faulkner, when they sat back down. Scott's wife, Donna, had provided Alvarez with the perky blond sitting next to him.

Donna, like Scott, was from a wealthy El Paso family, and had relatives and connections to spare. Alvarez was of mixed Hispanic and Anglo heritage, had grown up in near poverty, and didn't relate well to perky. He didn't really relate all that well to Donna, either.

Still, the blond next to him was young and supple and seemed eager for whatever other contact sports activities that might follow the football game. Being tall, never married, and undeniably good-looking didn't hurt Alvarez's appeal to the opposite sex, but his relationship with the blond hadn't progressed that far yet. They were still in the happy-happy stage of a blind date, where one was simply grateful to learn that the provided companion had neither limb nor substantial IQ missing. However, this gratitude hadn't kept a familiar sensation of boredom from circling around the edges of his consciousness before his beeper went off.

Having spent close to two decades of his 38 years involved in law enforcement, youthful enthusiasm sometimes made Alvarez weary. But that didn't mean he would rather be at a crime scene. Surely he hadn't become that jaded. Or had he? He glanced at the blond next to him, noting her flawless complexion and the freckles scattered across her nose before he turned his attention to his partner.

Faulkner and Alvarez looked at each other while the beeper issued its insistent call for attention, neither willing to be the first to acknowledge its existence. As the cheering died down the beeper seemed to get louder.

It was Donna Faulkner who spoke first. "Not now, Scott," she said. "Tell me that isn't what I think it is."

"What?" asked the perky blond. "Is that the police department? It must be something really important for them to try and get in touch with you here, right? This is exciting!"

Alvarez decided to make his exit. "I'll make the call," he offered, standing up.

Faulkner stuck to him like they were glued together at the shoulders. "I'll g-go with you," he said.

"What's going on? Are you coming back?" the blond asked.

"Fat chance," Donna said tersely.

"If we don't come back, we'll take my car," Alvarez offered, which didn't seem to make Donna feel better.

"I'll see you l-later back at the house," Scott chimed in. "I'll c-call if it's going to be late." He leaned over and kissed his wife before he started moving toward the aisle.

Alvarez turned to his date. "It was nice to meet you," he said. "Enjoy the game."

"Wait—can't I come with you?"

Alvarez didn't bother to turn back. "I don't think so," he tossed over his shoulder. He winked at Donna as he passed in front of her. "Catch you later."

He and Scott headed for a pay phone on a wall next to a massive column. Ever since the homicide case involving the construction of a stadium like this one, Alvarez was conscious of the structural parts holding everything up. An engineer involved with the case had told him that if the case hadn't been solved, the problems with the construction could have resulted in a structural collapse at a later date. Police work was like that, affecting things that normal people took for granted and turning them into something forever to be viewed askance.

It had been months since that case, and he hadn't been able to get the engineer out of his mind. All five-feet ten-inches of her, and the way she managed to look down her nose at him, in spite of the fact that he was six-foot-two.

Alvarez reached in his pocket for some change to feed the phone. Faulkner stood leaning against the wall, waiting patiently. There was an unspoken agreement between the two about who would make the call—dispatchers at headquarters actually preferred to talk to Faulkner, who was more easygoing than his partner. But, with Scott's stutter, it was sometimes difficult for him to be understood.

"You didn't have to leave the game, man," Alvarez said, dialing the number. "I could have made the call and gotten back to you."

Scott shrugged. "It was getting pretty uncomfortable," he said, stutter-free.

Alvarez had made a practice of studying the circumstances under which Scott's stutter appeared and disappeared. It was merely an intellectual exercise for personal entertainment, since he knew from experience that Faulkner could yell "Watch out!" or "Get down!" as clearly and quickly as anyone.

"She's Donna's cousin and she's a nice person," Scott continued, "but she's really ..."

"Perky?" Alvarez asked, feeding coins into the phone.

"Yeah," Scott said. "She's short, too," he added dismally, as if he felt personally responsible for the fact. Scott was well aware of Alvarez's preference for tall women.

"Tell Donna to give it a rest," Alvarez suggested while he waited for someone to come on the line. Maybe it would be faster to dial 911 and ask to be patched through, he thought.

"She thinks you don't like her," Scott answered. Alvarez knew he was referring to Donna.

This was an old conversation. "It's not that I don't like her. I think she's great for you, man. I just don't want one *like* her," Alvarez said. "And she doesn't like that."

Scott shrugged again. Their relationship pre-dated his marriage, so Alvarez didn't have to tiptoe around the difficulty he had in dealing with his partner's wife. The bottom line was that David Alvarez and Donna Faulkner had to share Scott. Donna didn't particularly approve of Alvarez, and Alvarez didn't especially like her or the fact that his partner had married her. But, unlike Donna, Alvarez was willing to live with the situation without trying to fix it. In his opinion, it was about as good as personal relationships got for law enforcement types.

Hell, it worked for the three of them. Donna just hadn't
realized it yet. Maybe when she did, there would be an end to
the continuous stream of eligible female relatives and friends.
Maybe he could suggest a height criterion—go over to Scott's
house and make a mark on the door jamb and have Donna
line up potential candidates to see how they measured up.

Where he'd grown up, he and his sister Anna used the walls
in the bedroom they shared to mark heights and dates and things.
But that didn't mean his household had been without standards:
a sheet had served as a divider in the bedroom the two siblings
shared, and only pencil marks were allowed. Further, no mark-
ings were tolerated in the bedroom shared by Alvarez's Kansas-
bred mother and his paternal grandmother, a wizened Hispanic
woman who spoke minimal English. There, the wall art had
consisted only of crucifixes and religious pictures.

Alvarez cupped his hand over his free ear to better hear
the dispatcher who had finally fielded his call. Then, lifting
his shoulder to cradle the phone and leave his hands free, he
searched in his pocket for a notebook and pencil.

The one-sided conversation would have piqued most
people's curiosity, but Scott Faulkner waited patiently, knowing he would get the whole story as soon as Alvarez got off the
phone. However, even by their standards, the conversation
was unusual.

"He what? ... I hate it when a cop falls into the middle of
a crime scene, it makes our job so much harder... No lead on
the call? ... There was what in the bedroom? ... Yeah, I'm happy
the kid's okay, I've still got a cop falling into the middle of a
crime scene, man, it makes us all look bad ... Yeah, that is
strange. Maybe there's a couple more bodies to go with the
extra IDs ... it was a joke, man, simmer down ... Give us thirty
minutes—hey, we're in the middle of the damn Sun Bowl,

okay? ... No, I'm not allowing for time to stay and watch the rest of the game."

Alvarez hung up the phone and looked at his partner. "We're headed to your old stomping grounds—Rim Road. Maybe we can stop and chew the fat with your folks. I know how much they love to see you on the job. Come on, I'll fill you in on the way."

Alvarez heard another cheer go up from the crowd, remembered that this would be another football game he would never see completed, and cursed in Spanish under his breath.

"*Creo que sí también*," said Scott, which loosely translated as "Yeah, I feel that way, too." When Scott started working with Alvarez, he had had virtually no knowledge of Spanish slang and profanity, a void in his education that Alvarez took great pains to fill. "L-look at it this way. We'll b-b-beat the rush out of the stadium."

"And everyone keeps telling me you have no sense of humor."

Literal, methodical, and detail-oriented, Scott Faulkner did in fact have a reputation for being humorless. Alvarez found his partner's single-mindedness itself to be a source of comic irony. Alvarez was thankful for whatever had led Scott into police work, even though it had alienated him from his wealthy family.

And Scott Faulkner had the benefit of the best secondary education that money could buy. A background like that was good for an endless store of quotations; today was no exception. As they walked out of the stadium, Scott grinned at him and said, "Let the games begin."

The two detectives referred to their work as story-telling. Starting with whatever facts were known, the goal was to relate a story that best filled in the information that was missing. A good story could trigger investigative efforts that would yield facts, allowing the hypothesis to be refined until it was no longer a hypothesis.

Alvarez and Faulkner set no limits on the plausibility of their stories, even though both were familiar with the theory that claimed simple explanations were the most likely to be true—they'd been detectives too long to believe that all the answers were simple ones. Some of their cases had been solved by an idea embedded in a story initially told as a joke. One or the other would take it seriously, look into it, and suddenly a fantastic explanation of how a crime was committed and who did it was no longer fantastic, but as close to the truth as they were likely to come.

Some cases started out simple and got complicated. Some cases started out complicated and got bizarre. The one phone call had already told Alvarez which type of case they had on their hands.

He had plenty of time to tell Scott about his conversation with the dispatcher as they walked to his car. Alvarez had been too cheap to ante up for the prime parking area. Instead, he had opted for general parking and hitched a ride with the Faulkners and the perky blond to the expensive parking closer to the stadium.

"What we have is a structural collapse in a residence, apparently resulting in two fatalities."

Scott was unimpressed with his technical description. "Before that c-c-case last summer, you would have said the roof fell in," he observed. "I remember how you couldn't get the difference between c-c-c-concrete and cement straight."

"Police work gives you a chance to associate with and learn from so many different types of people," replied Alvarez, generously not taking offense.

"Yeah, I've wondered about that," Scott's breath puffed white into the clear afternoon air as they walked past what seemed to be acres of cars. "Every time we flip a coin over something, you win," Scott continued. "Every t-t-time we play pin ball, you win. Every time we play c-c-cards, you win. Considering the people we come across, maybe you should be more s-s-selective about what you learn and who you learn it from."

"Have you ever noticed that you stutter more when you're bitter about something?" Alvarez countered. "That, and having your in-laws around. Anyhow, the roof didn't fall in, as you so simplistically put it. The floor did. But the floor happened to be the ceiling to a room in the basement, so you're partially right."

"Where is this? Don't tell me we're going to be next door to my p-parents."

"No, it's on the other end of Rim Road from your ancestral abode." Alvarez consulted his notebook while his partner shaded his eyes and looked in vain for Alvarez's vehicle, a shockingly purple rental car that Alvarez was tolerating while his cherished bronze Corvette was in the shop. "The house belongs to one Lenora Keaton Hinson, who is assumed to be one of the deceased."

"Hinson," Faulkner repeated to himself, as Alvarez took off in the opposite direction. "I know who they are. The son was a f-few years younger than me, and he had a younger sister, too. Their father died years ago; he was a p-p-partner in the original development of Rim Road. Left a lot of money. I remember my parents saying something about a disagreement over the will— Where the hell is your c-c-c-car, David?"

"See, you get upset, you start to stutter. I didn't plan on having to find the car. You were supposed to drive me to it, remember?"

"If we have to hike around much longer I'm going to need s-some sun screen."

"See what I mean about your stuttering? There." Alvarez pointed at the distance and took off with purpose. "You're wrong about the original development of Rim Road—typical Anglo tunnel-vision perspective. You and your family probably think the land just sat there in pristine condition, all those years, waiting for rich Anglos to come live on it. My old *abuela* used to dandle me on her knee and tell me stories about how the people of *La Raza* used to live there in their own little *barrio* they called home, until the Anglos wised up."

"You're kidding," Scott said flatly.

"No, I'm not kidding," answered Alvarez. "The settlement was called Stormsville, a nice Anglo name, filled with lots of little brown people and no utilities. The city condemned it for sanitary reasons and relocated the inhabitants. How the property then came to be in the hands of people like your parents is a story likely too complicated for my simple *pachuco* mind to grasp."

"I m-m-meant you were kidding about your grandmother dandling you on her knee. Didn't she think you were a juvenile d-delinquent on the road to ruin?"

"Do you want to hear about this case or not? Emergency dispatch got an anonymous phone call reporting an accident at the Hinson house. When the uniforms couldn't get a response, they went on in. One of the officers fell through some kind of entry hall into the room below. Some kind of fancy rug had been stretched and tacked to the baseboard in the entry hall, so it stayed in place when the floor under it fell in. Pretty weird, huh? Some poor cop thought he was walking into the living room when the rug came untacked. He fell through it into the basement, right on top of a bunch of debris covering two bodies, one of whom might be the owner of the house."

"I don't remember ever going d-down to the basement when I was in the house."

Alvarez looked at him. "Yeah, I'll bet you don't."

"So what does all this have to do with us? How do we even know that a crime has b-b-been committed?"

"We don't. But we've got lots of questions. Did I mention that a live female infant was discovered in an upstairs bedroom? No, don't get all sentimental on me—it looks like the kid is going to be okay."

"That's not g-g-good enough," Scott said flatly.

"I'm with you, man. But the cop who fell into the room brought out a purse to try to ID the second body, and maybe get a handle on who the kid is."

"What did they find?"

"Three different sets of IDs with three different names, all for one single person—presumably the second body."

Scott let out a low whistle of appreciation.

"And there's more. Seems there was a reason Mrs. Hinson never let you into her basement. It's been refinished, all right, into a big rec room or den or something."

"So? Sounds like someone didn't do a very g-good job of it."

Alvarez rounded a van, blinked at the glaring shade of purple which still managed to surprise him, and unlocked the door to his rental car.

"So what else about the b-b-basement?" Scott asked doggedly.

Alvarez grinned. This was almost as good as telling a story. Scott might have read the complete works of Shakespeare at Harvard, but Alvarez had read all of Dame Agatha Christie. "We're doing one better than a locked room investigation," he said. "If that poor cop hadn't fallen through the floor, they'd have had a hell of a time finding the bodies."

"Why's that?"

"There's no visible entrance into the room where the bodies were. From all outside appearances, the basement is unfinished. It looks like what we've got is a real, genuine secret room."

Scott thought about that as Alvarez drove out of the congested parking area. "Now you see it, now you don't," he commented sagely.

Alvarez groaned and accelerated. He needed to make up for lost time.

CHAPTER TWO:

REVERBERATIONS
Omaha, Nebraska:
Sunday, January 1, early afternoon

Derek Dowling was not having a rip-roaring New Year's Day himself, but had he known about David Alvarez missing the Sun Bowl game, Dowling would have had little sympathy. Shifting a wad of gum to one side of his mouth, the DEA agent would have said something like, "Suck it up and get over it." Tact had never been his strong point.

Dowling had known for almost a week that he was going to have to cut his losses, but the current administrative screw-up was enough to make him feel like punching some holes in the wall. Hell, it was enough to make being stationed in Omaha, Nebraska, not seem like such a bad thing, and that was a scary thought.

The middle-aged, gray-haired judge looked up from the papers in front of her and shook her head, like she really regretted the sentence she was about to pronounce on Dowling's operation. The other assorted state officials sitting around the conference table leaned forward, waiting to hear the words that would officially send eight months of work down the toilet.

The number of people present in the room was a joke in itself—an emergency meeting, a top secret meeting to boot, with twelve people present. What did they expect? With thirteen they could have re-enacted the Last Supper, because Dowling for sure knew that at least one Judas was in the room, maybe more.

Since Dowling already knew what was coming, he concentrated on counting the flakes of dandruff on the judge's black blouse to distract himself. This was not the New Year's Day that he or his DEA task force had envisioned. This was not going to be the day that Raymond Boyce went down for the big fall.

"What we have here," the judge said primly, "is an unfortunate case of miscommunication between SOU and SIU and the DEA."

Dowling still had trouble remembering that SOU stood for the Special Operations Unit of the Nebraska State Prosecutors Office, and that SIU stood for Special Investigations Unit of the Omaha Police Department. He should have known from the beginning that something involving SOU and SIU would be doomed—the two acronyms used in the same sentence reminded him of calling hogs.

What they had here, in simple terms, skipping the legalese thank you very much, was a royal fuckup, which was what you always got when there were too many players. The DEA had been forced into sucking up to the local enforcement agencies, because one of their own had originally turned up the stool pigeon. But then the operation had become Dowling's, and the pigeon had become Dowling's pigeon, and he sure as hell hoped this royal fuckup wasn't going to effectively turn his little pigeon into dead meat.

"Mr. Dowling, are you still with us?" The judge was now talking to him, because Dowling had stretched out his long legs, folded his hands over his flat stomach, and closed his eyes. "You represent the DEA in this operation. I wouldn't want anything discussed here to be misconstrued or miscommunicated to your agency. Are you paying attention?"

"Your honor," said Dowling, without opening his eyes, "I make it a practice to close my eyes whenever I'm being screwed." He continued chewing his gum with his eyes closed. There was an uncomfortable silence in the room.

"Mr. Dowling," the judge's voice took on a shrill tone, "your attitude is inexcusable."

Dowling opened his eyes and looked straight at the judge. "Your Honor," he said evenly, "if you're so interested in my participation, I'll be happy to tell you exactly what's going on, and why it's happening. Then, what I'd be really interested to know, what I would snap to attention for, and stand up and salute, is to hear you tell me what you and the State Prosecutor's Office plan to do about it."

"Mr. Dowling," the judge started, but Dowling steam-rolled right over her.

"What we have is one Raymond Boyce, proud citizen of Omaha, Nebraska, and one of the major connections for heroin trade in the *world*. Not in this godforsaken state, not in the US, but in the world. He's smart, he's connected, he's our worst nightmare, a high-tech Godfather, if you will. His specialty is stealing credit. Suddenly five grand is run up on your credit card by someone who knows your mother's maiden name and the name of your kindergarten teacher. You report it, the credit company eats the loss, and Boyce has five grand toward his next drug deal. Try multiplying that by ten to twenty hits a day, every day, three hundred and sixty-five days a year, and you'll know how he manages to buy in mind-boggling quantity."

"Mr. Dowling," the judge interrupted him. "Don't patronize us. We all know who Raymond Boyce is, and we all know we need to stop his activities. But we need to do it legally."

"I haven't finished," said Dowling. The judge opened her hands wide in exasperation, but didn't say anything else. "What Boyce does is steal and use information. He says the word, and somewhere, somehow, in some goddamned government office like this one, all records of your social security benefits disappear. He says the word, and suddenly your discharge from the military isn't honorable anymore. Hell, your honor, have you checked lately to see if you have any overdue library books?"

"Really, Mr. Dowling, histrionics are neither necessary nor constructive—" the judge might have thought she could stare him down, but better individuals had tried. And to Derek Dowling, the pursuit of Raymond Boyce bordered on a religion.

"Histrionics?" Dowling rolled the word on his tongue like he was tasting it for the first time. "Kind of sounds like history, doesn't it? And we sure have some history on this guy, your honor, we certainly do. Every time we get close to busting this creep, something happens, something goes wrong. Then we finally get someone on the inside, really on the inside, to cooperate with a wire tap, and we record enough conversations to put Raymond away forever. We plan to start the New Year by finally seeing the results of all our diligent efforts. There's just one problem—the wire tap application that you approved turns out to be, what is the word of the hour, 'invalid'?"

"I was not aware of the change in state law when I approved the application eight months ago. Neither were the participants seeking the application. It's not anyone's fault, Mr. Dowling, it's just one of those things," the judge said to him, but she did have the decency to look uncomfortable while she said it.

"Yeah," said Dowling, getting to his feet. "It's never anyone's fault. That's why you and I are the only ones talking at this meeting—no one else has anything to say. Somehow the assistant state attorney signed the wire tap application, and it was approved on the basis of that signature. Somehow no one noticed that there had been a change in state law, and that the application had to be signed by the chief prosecutor, not the assistant state attorney. We get ready to move, and all these details magically come to light. The wire tap application is no good, the tapes aren't admissible, and Boyce skates again."

"A personal vendetta does not justify bending the law to your own purposes," the judge admonished him.

"That's rich," said Dowling. "I'll tell you what's personal about this—our inside contact may die because of this screw-up. *That's* personal. I have to explain to my people why they should even give a fuck about starting over on this case. *That's* personal. Boyce brings more heroin into the country, and with it more junkies, more drug deaths, more organized crime. If that's not personal to you, your honor, maybe you should re-think the office you hold."

"Mr. Dowling, I must insist—"

"But I've saved the most personal thing for last, your honor. It's the only goddamn thing that's important right now, since you've established that those papers sitting in front of you don't mean a damn thing. I take it real personal that someone, maybe more than one, hell, I don't know, maybe the whole lot of you, are in Boyce's pocket. When you tell me what you plan to do about that, your honor, then I'll be standing there paying attention. I think until then I'd rather spend my time doing damage control."

"Mr. Dowling," the judge's voice was shrill again, "you're lucky this isn't a court of law or I'd lock you up for contempt and throw away the key."

The gum had lost its flavor. Dowling fished it out of his mouth and deposited it under the conference table, sketched a salute at the judge who was still railing at him, and walked out of the room. The commotion that followed his exit was of no interest to him.

Screw the locals. There were loose ends in this fiasco that were making him nervous. Witness Protection had yet to give him an update on his stool pigeon. It was time for a new plan. It wasn't any use crying over spilled milk, especially when he could smell the threat of spilled blood in the air.

CHAPTER THREE:

SITE CONDITIONS
El Paso, Texas:
Sunday, January 1, early afternoon

There were three police cars, lights flashing, and one ambulance parked on the street in front of the Rim Road house. The presence of so many authorized people at a crime scene was a detective's nightmare in itself. A parked police car with its lights flashing was enough to draw a crowd of curious onlookers, and the press was never far behind. Preserving a crime scene intact was hard enough; with a crowd of curious people and reporters eager to get the first jump on a story, it was often impossible.

So far they were in luck, it seemed. This was probably one of the few neighborhoods where it would be considered an unthinkable breach of manners to show any evidence of curiosity about a neighbor. Alvarez was genetically predisposed to a healthy distrust of those born to riches, but he was pragmatic enough to be grateful for any breaks that came his way. And the local press was probably stretched thin, covering the pomp and circumstance of the Sun Bowl. Still, the first priority was to get some of these vehicles off the street.

It was a long walk up a winding sidewalk to the imposing, ornately carved double doors which served as the front entry. The house itself was a stately, two-story red brick structure with a large, white, wooden porch, complemented by white shutters and trim.

Rim Road was actually an extension of the end of Scenic Drive, a road that ran from one side of Mt. Franklin to the other. In the middle was an outlook where drivers could park and enjoy the panoramic view of the city stretched out below, or the charms of their companion, depending on the focus of the evening.

Only the side of the road against the mountain had houses on it. Nothing would ever be built between those houses, many of which were over sixty years old, and their unimpeded view of the city, which rivaled that of Scenic Drive. An unmarked park lay behind the houses that stood above the city on a narrow bluff. Alvarez didn't know who ever went there, but the fact that the land behind the houses was owned by the City meant that nothing would ever be built behind them, either, and their terraced backyards would always overlook undeveloped desert land.

There were newer, larger, and showier residences in other parts of the city, but nothing could compare with a Rim Road address for a statement of belonging to a prestigious group that had more to do with one's heritage than one's annual income. Houses on Rim Road were rarely sold; they were more often passed down from one family member to another. There had been more than one squabble over the disposition of a Rim Road residence that had contributed to lining the pockets of the lucky lawyers involved in the fight. Alvarez figured that after his unpopular choice of occupation, Scott was out of the running for his parents' house for sure.

But there was one sense in which Rim Road belonged to all the community. Every Christmas, Rim Road surpassed its everyday stately grandeur with an absolute orgy of Christmas decorations. It was a Christmas tradition for El Paso families to take their kids to view the decorated plaza downtown and then the Rim Road extravaganza.

It was something Alvarez's own mother had done until he was too old for family activities, something he felt had occurred around age eleven, even if no one else had agreed with him. He remembered standing next to his mother one cold winter night, one hand grasping his little sister's and the other firmly engulfed in his mother's large, work-worn hand. His Hispanic grandmother was likely with them that night too, but she had never been much into hand holding.

It might even have been this house they lingered in front of that year. What would always stand out in Alvarez's memory was the sheer extravagance of the display—costumed people hired in shifts to stand unmoving in a living manger scene, with live donkeys, goats, and sheep staked out in strategic places on the lawn. The only thing missing were the camels.

That night, he stood as a child on the outside looking in, never supposing he would have the occasion to step inside one of these residences, at least not legally. His presence now was not so much a statement about equal opportunity for the poor and Hispanic, but more a statement that crime, violence, and death cannot be held at bay by money and family connections.

Hell, he even remembered the downtown plaza and the fenced pond area that had contained a healthy population of huge, somnambulant alligators, grinning their toothy grins at passers-by. Every Christmas the decorators would drape the concrete fence around the pond with lavish decorations and fill the trees in the plaza with spectacular light displays.

He remembered the year there had been a whole story-book display of fairy tale characters. But no matter how extensive the decorations, there were still those grinning alligators peering out at the holiday spectators, until someone got the bright idea to remodel the plaza and remove the carnivorous reptiles. Alvarez, realist that he was, had always preferred the plaza with the alligators. Now all the downtown reptiles occupied high-rise office buildings.

Alvarez was distracted from his recollections by a uniformed officer, hurrying to meet them before they could open the front door. "You don't want to go in that way," the cop told them in way of introductions. "There's a door around the side that opens into the kitchen, and there's a staircase that leads down to the basement. I'm Officer Kurita," he said as an afterthought, extending his hand.

"Alvarez," said Alvarez shortly, "and this is Detective Faulkner. Who's here?"

"Crime Scene has come and gone already. They don't want to go through any more of the house until the bodies have been removed and we get clearance that it's safe. The medical examiner is waiting for you to clear the bodies to be moved."

"And what are you doing here?" asked Alvarez.

"My partner and I were first on the scene—he's the one who fell into the room." Kurita swallowed audibly. Judging the young cop's experience from his apparent age, Alvarez surmised that his adrenaline level was probably off the scale.

"So who's here at the scene?" Alvarez asked again, making sure there was no edge to his voice. Police work was ninety-five percent asking the same questions over and over, except for the ninety-five percent that was paperwork.

"There are two other patrol teams here. They answered my call for backup after my partner—his name is Stan—after he fell into the room." It was almost like Kurita had to keep repeating Stan's experience to make himself believe it. "I went straight to the basement to try and get Stan out, so it was one of the other officers who found the baby in a bedroom on the first floor. The medics took Stan and the kid after they decided they couldn't do anything for the two in the basement."

Alvarez refrained from pointing out that had there been someone else in the house, he or she could have easily attacked

Officer Kurita and his partner while they were mucking around in the basement. He felt sure that Kurita was well on the way to figuring this out for himself. "Get rid of everyone except the ambulance driver and one other officer, then you show us around, and have the other officer keep away any neighbors or press. And turn the damn flashers off those cars."

"Yes, sir," said Kurita, and hopped to it, relieved to have something tangible to do and someone to tell him to do it.

"Wouldn't be hard for someone in the house to get away, with all the c-c-commotion going on down in the basement," observed Faulkner.

"No, but why would someone want to stick around?" asked Alvarez.

Scott shrugged and pushed open the front door.

Kurita called after them. "I *really* don't recommend you go in that way."

Alvarez wondered if Kurita had a low opinion of the IQ of detectives in general, but he didn't comment as he swung open one of the double doors. He certainly didn't plan on following Stan's path into the basement. He and Scott were content to look in from the doorway.

Ornate carpet still lined part of the entry hall, with half hanging down where it had pulled loose from two of the walls. Not much of the room below was visible from where they stood, but what they could see resembled a demolition scene. Debris covered what appeared to have been a furnished room.

"The ME wants to move the bodies, sir," said Kurita, joining them on the porch. "She's waiting for you to give her clearance."

"Since you don't want us to dive in from here," replied Alvarez. "what about that door around the side?"

"Yes, sir," said Kurita smartly, and led them around to a

side door, which opened into a large kitchen with a staircase that led both down to the basement and up to the second floor. Alvarez was distracted by the sight of a medium-size, fluffy white dog, tethered to a kitchen drawer. The dog started whining and lunging at Alvarez.

"Dog, sir," said Kurita smartly. "I secured it when I found it on the premises."

Alvarez refrained from saying that it was a relief the dog was in custody, and would not be free to pursue a cover-up of evidence while they were in the basement. The three of them left the dog whining and went down the stairs, Kurita leading the way.

The basement looked normal enough, with about half the unfinished floor space occupied by boxes and various domestic items obviously no longer desired for everyday use, but not yet discarded. Someone had cleared a path through the stored items to get to an unfinished interior rock wall. There was a massive wood wardrobe standing next to a door in the wall, which in turn opened into the room that Scott and Alvarez had seen from above.

"Stan helped us find this," Kurita explained. "He saw this door from the inside and banged on it 'til I was able to locate it from out here. That wardrobe was in front of the door. It's heavy, but it's on wheels, so it moved pretty easily."

Alvarez stopped to test it himself; he had to push hard, but then the piece of furniture moved smoothly on well-oiled wheels. "Did Stan say if he saw any way to move this from the inside?"

"No," answered Kurita eagerly. "I asked him that. There wasn't any way for him to get out until we moved this from out here."

"Interesting," said Alvarez to his partner. "If your parents had a room like this, they could have locked you up in it when you decided to become a police officer. Maybe this is the start of a new trend among affluent Anglos—Rim Road's answer to keeping kids out of gangs."

Faulkner, as always, took a factual approach to the conversation. "It would never be approved by the f-fire marshall."

As so often happened, his partner's dogged pursuit of facts provided a new line of thought for Alvarez. "That's a good point. Does the construction of a secret room have to meet Building Department requirements? Then, if the Building Department knows about it, is it still a secret?" he asked philosophically.

"If anyone at City Hall knows about it, you can b-bet it's not a secret," replied Faulkner. Alvarez wasn't about to argue with that. As he started to cross the threshold, Kurita barred his way.

"Sorry, sir," the young officer said, trying to achieve a balance between the authority he was trying to assume and the deference he was afraid to abandon. "The EMTs said anyone entering the room has to wear a hard hat."

Alvarez hated mandates, especially from people who, with no one to resusitate, had vacated the scene, having more exciting things to do, like watching a bowl game. "Kee-rist," exhaled Alvarez. He ducked past his partner and the uniformed officer and through the doorway.

Kurita started to protest, but Faulkner put a restraining hand on his shoulder. "Show me where the hard hats are," he told Kurita.

"You can give him mine—he's a family man," Alvarez called as they headed back up the stairs.

He paused as he entered the room to get a feel for the scene in front of him.

It was large and looked to be a combination bedroom and

sitting room, with a double bed at one end and a twin bed and a crib at the other. Alvarez filed the sleeping arrangements away for later consideration. The twin bed and crib were next to a door which opened into a bathroom. The wall across the room facing Alvarez had a small fireplace, complete with a stone mantel and raised hearth. These things were easy to discern, because they were along the walls of the room.

The middle of the room looked like pictures of bombed-out buildings in history books, and the one bomb scene he'd investigated. El Paso was big into knifings and shootings, but bombings, thankfully, were relatively rare. It was only because of his prior knowledge that he knew the devastation before him was not the result of an explosion.

Alvarez remembered the intent blue eyes of the structural engineer involved in that previous case, as she demanded access to restricted material she thought was vital to her search for structural flaws in the stadium under construction. He had tried to shake her up at the time by showing her pictures of the man murdered on the premises. She'd countered that the victims of a structural collapse looked worse and were more numerous.

It appeared that the middle of the room contained some chairs and tables, but it was hard to discern details. Everything four or more feet from the walls was covered with debris—portions of wooden trusses which had fractured and fallen; ragged sections of drywall that had been part of the ceiling; and fluffy yellow material that Alvarez assumed was insulation, since tufts of it hung from the parts of the ceiling that were still intact.

The most striking feature of the overall destruction was a large, dark, ornate wooden column, whose base was lying about ten feet from where Alvarez stood. The column stretched toward the opposite wall—large, impressive and massive, with two female bodies pinned under it.

A small, thin, mouse-colored woman stood up from where she was squatting next to the bodies, pushed back her hard hat to look up at Alvarez, and extended a latex-gloved hand. Her hair and skin were the same nondescript brown as her face, which was pock-marked from acne. She looked like she'd weigh 90 pounds soaking wet and would have to show ID to buy cigarettes.

"It's about time," she said.

Alvarez heard that so often he wondered if there was a new etiquette book out, distributed solely to medical examiners for use at crime scenes.

"I'm Pat Cornell," she added.

"You're kidding," he said.

"No, I'm not kidding. I've been down here cooling my heels, waiting for you to come. CSU has come and gone and I'm done here, so I'm waiting for you to okay moving the bodies."

"I meant, you must be kidding about your name."

"What about my name?"

"There's a famous author named Patricia Cornwell who writes forensic crime novels. Don't you think that's an amazing coincidence?"

Pat Cornell looked at Alvarez like she was waiting for him to admit to breaking into the house and killing the two women himself. She bared pointed little mouse teeth in what he supposed was a grimace, and for a moment he thought she was actually going to hiss at him. "I tell you what, Detective Alvarez," she said instead, "why don't we look at these two bodies, and then get the hell out of here? We can skip the introductions. I already know you and your partner's names, because dispatch sounded like they were sending God over to help us out. I was beginning to think you'd take as long as the Second Coming."

Alvarez was saved from having to reply by the arrival of Faulkner and Kurita, each wearing hard hats. Faulkner clapped the extra one he was carrying on Alvarez's head.

Pat Cornell held out a box of disposable latex gloves. "I don't want any excuses," she said, her remark primarily directed at Alvarez.

He and Scott meekly donned gloves.

"Okay, now that we have all the proper equipment and pass inspection, what do we have here?" asked Alvarez. "So we can get the hell out of here, as you said," he added pleasantly.

Faulkner rolled his eyes up, which reminded him there was no ceiling above them. "D-Do you think it's safe down here?" he asked.

This, Alvarez thought, from a man who had once faced down an armed assailant and eaten three cheeseburgers immediately afterward.

"I think just about everything that could come down already has," Alvarez said.

"Nothing else has come down while I've been here, and I've been here quite a while," added the ME. "Besides, the major damage looks like it came from this column. If one of those boards"—she gestured at the debris covering the floor—"hits you, there might be an injury, but I doubt it'd be fatal."

"Awfully convenient, both women happening to be in the way of the column when it fell," Alvarez said.

"No kidding," said Pat Cornell. "That observation doesn't exactly make you worth waiting for."

"No, it's other things that make me worth waiting for," said Alvarez.

"There's not much blood," Scott said quickly.

"There wouldn't be, if most of the bleeding was internal, right?" asked Alvarez, not because he didn't know, but because it would be a good idea to get on the mouse-woman's good side. "That's right," said the ME. "In any case, it's impossible to tell whether the blow from the column was fatal. We'll obviously know more after the autopsy. But I don't think this one"—she pointed at the younger of the two dead women— "died from being hit by the column."

The woman in question looked to be in her mid-twenties and had a dark-haired beauty that even death and the debris covering her couldn't disguise. She was on her side, with her head turned toward the floor. The column had caught her just under the shoulders. Alvarez knew it was likely her ribs and lungs were crushed under the load, but there was no sign of bleeding from her mouth or nose. Alvarez didn't think the mouse-woman was going too far out on a limb by guessing this one had been dead before the column hit her.

The woman had one arm outstretched above her head. Alvarez reached out, gently, and pulled back the sleeve of a sweater to expose her forearm. His effort was rewarded by the tell-tale sign of needle tracks.

Pat Cornell watched his actions intently. "Exactly, Hot Shot," she said tersely. "And she's cyanotic."

"Blue-tinged," said Scott automatically. "Indicative of d-death by heroin overdose. When?"

The medical examiner shrugged her shoulders, refusing to even estimate. "Look at the forearms of the other one," she told Scott.

He did the same thing Alvarez had done with the younger woman, exposing a nasty wound. "Defense wound?" he asked the ME.

"I've never seen a fall result in bruises with finger marks," she replied.

"The skin isn't just bruised, it's torn," said Alvarez.

"Warfarin is my bet," the ME answered. "Blood-thinning medicine," she added when Alvarez kept looking at her. "Lots of older people take it for various reasons. It increases the thinning of the epidermis that happens with aging."

"So how did she die?" asked Alvarez.

"I don't know," said Pat Cornell simply, "but I will later."

"It's Mrs. Hinson, I'm pretty sure," Scott said. Unlike the younger woman, the woman that Scott identified as Mrs. Hinson was face-down under the column, which lay across the middle of her back. Faulkner had gingerly turned her face toward him to get a better look.

"That's right," said Kurita from where he stood a few feet off, making his first contribution to the conversation. Alvarez imagined he'd seen all he wanted when his partner was rescued from the room. "The next door neighbors came over to see what was happening. We didn't let them down here, but they looked in from upstairs and said they were sure this one was the woman who owns the house. She lives here by herself, but they gave us her son's phone number. He's on his way over."

"What about the other woman?" asked Alvarez.

"They didn't know anything about her, or this room in the basement. I didn't mention the kid or the multiple IDs."

"Let's keep it that way for now," said Alvarez. Right now he couldn't come up with a scenario that resulted in two unrelated women, one unidentified, but with multiple IDs, dead in what appeared to be an honest-to-God secret room. And he hadn't even tried to throw in drugs or the child.

"Where was the purse, the one with the driver's licenses?" asked Alvarez.

"There," said Kurita, pointing at the double bed. "CSU took it and the suitcase they found in the closet, along with one of those things you carry around for baby stuff."

"A diaper bag," supplied Faulkner.

"Yeah," said Kurita. "One of those. Once the debris is cleared, we'll probably find some other things, but we didn't want to disturb the scene too much until you got here."

"What was in the suitcase?" asked Alvarez.

"Some clothes, some makeup, and ten thousand dollars in crisp, new, one-hundred-dollar bills."

"Now that's what I call traveling light," said Alvarez. That discovery must have been a cheap thrill for CSU, he reflected. Banking was the only other profession where you got to run your hands over money like that, if only fleetingly. "Shit, there goes simple robbery as a motive."

"You thought this would be simple?" asked Scott.

"*Creo que no, hombre.* But that doesn't mean I didn't hope."

Alvarez was interrupted by a commotion above. He looked up to see another uniformed cop and a dark-haired man looking down at them. The cop was trying to keep the man from getting any closer to the edge of the collapsed floor.

"That's her, that's my mother. Oh, my god," he said, peering down at them. Alvarez winced. Bullets and crazed criminals weren't the worst part of his job; it was dealing with bereaved family members. But, seeing as Scott was practically a neighbor, maybe he should talk to the bereaved son.

The man kept exclaiming as the cop pushed him away from the gaping hole above them. "This house is worth a fortune, goddamn it," Alvarez heard him tell the officer, true anguish in his voice. "What the hell has she done now? Wasn't it enough to ruin my life while she was alive?"

Alvarez revised his mental plan—this was someone *he* wanted to talk to.

CHAPTER FOUR:

AFTERSHOCKS
Las Cruces, New Mexico:
Sunday, January 1, early afternoon

Forty miles north of El Paso in Las Cruces, New Mexico, Tory Travers, a structural engineer and owner of Travers Testing and Engineering Company, battled with dinner. Tory looked dubiously in the oven to check on the turkey that her fifteen-year-old son Cody had persuaded her to roast. The bird looked, well, bloated. Trying to think positively, she told herself that maybe the adjective she was searching for was "plump."

A summer's employment at McDonald's had given Cody an interest in cooking, which he was trying in vain to pass on to his mother. Never more than an indifferent cook at best, Tory felt that by the age of thirty-five it was unlikely she was going to develop into a gourmet chef, galloping or otherwise, no matter how much she practiced positive thinking.

This turkey was simply going to have to suffice for dinner for six. Her friend Lonnie Harper, her secretary, Sylvia, and Jazz, her lead field technician, both long-time employees of Tory's engineering firm, were joining Tory and Cody for New Year's dinner. And, since Cody was leaving in the morning to visit his grandfather in Florida, Tory had let him invite his friend Cole over to have dinner and help him pack.

Assuming that a watched turkey never starts looking more savory, Tory wandered into the den, where the boys were camped out watching one of an endless procession of interchangeable bowl games. As Tory entered the room, they began to tussle in a friendly fashion over the remote control. Tango, the eighty-pound Transylvanian hound, watched them from his corner, thumping his tail in approval. Unaware of Tory's presence, the boys wrestled each other and finally rolled off the couch onto the floor with a resounding thump.

Cole's Atlanta Braves baseball cap came off his head, and handfuls of shoulder-length shining blond hair fell out. Cole was lying on his/her back on the floor, with Tory's son stretched out on top of him/her, laughing and still trying to wrest the remote control out of Cole's grip. Now that Cole's face was framed by that luxurious blond hair, Tory wondered how she could have mistaken the slight, elfin-featured teen for a boy.

Tory was beginning to wonder how she could have mistaken her son for a boy, too, since stretched out on top of the girl, obviously playing with her in order to let her keep the remote control out of his grasp, her son looked for a moment altogether like a man. It was like suddenly coming across a stranger in her house.

About as close as she ever came to being speechless, Tory managed the inane statement, "Cody, Cole is a girl."

Cody rolled off the girl and onto his feet in one easy movement, and faced his mother, his eyes even with hers.

When had he gotten so tall? Would she soon be looking up to talk to him? Suddenly, Tory felt like sitting down, so she did, sinking on to the couch. "Cody, Cole is a girl," she repeated, sounding as though she had about as much IQ as the turkey in the oven.

Cole grabbed her hat, stuffed her hair up under it, and scooted as far away from the couch as she could get.

"Of course Kohli's a girl," Cody said matter-of-factly.

"Kohli?" Tory echoed.

"Well, I usually call her Kohl," said her son in that matter-of-fact tone again.

"Cole?" she echoed him faintly.

"Kohl, like the stuff the Egyptians used to put around their eyes to make them darker," said the girl. "Do you want me to go home now?" she asked abruptly.

"Yes," Tory wanted to scream, "I want you to go home and never come back and never put your hands on my son again."

"Of course not," she said instead. "You just took me by surprise." She glared in Cody's direction, while he simply raised his eyebrows in acknowledgment of her surprise. When had he learned to be so facile? "Don't you live down the road, where the Mendez family used to live?" Tory asked.

"Yes, ma'am. We moved down here from Chicago right before school started. It was hard because I'm an only child and my parents work a lot. Cody was my first friend," she added.

"Kohl's parents are pretty famous attorneys," lover-boy threw in. "They do a lot of high-profile custody cases. They even got mentioned in *People* magazine a couple of times."

Now that was the height of fame, Tory thought. This wasn't the time to remind Cody that his own mother knew exactly what it was like to have her face plastered across the pages of popular publications. With a shock, she realized she hadn't been much older than this girl when all that happened.

"Why did your family move to Las Cruces?" Tory asked. Maybe this girl was only here temporarily ...

"My parents take cases from all over the country, and they consult to other lawyers, so it doesn't really matter where we live. Mom is from Chicago—that's where she met my dad, in law school there. But Dad is from Placitas, around Albuquerque, and he wanted to move to where it was warmer, so here we are."

The whole state to choose from, thought Tory, and your parents end up living a half mile down the road from me and my son.

"Kohli moved here just after all that stuff happened last summer, when that guy tried to kill you and you broke your arm, and you had to spend so much time going back and forth to El Paso to give statements and stuff," said Cody.

After Cody had gotten over his guilt at being away fishing with Lonnie when all hell broke loose, her son had taken the summer events in stride. Hell, he could even do a concise summary in one sentence, which was more than Tory could do. She still had nightmares about being trapped in a construction trailer while a madman tried to crush her to death with a crane and wrecking ball.

"Yes, I was pretty busy last summer," she replied.

"Kohli's going to help me start packing now," said Cody, as though there was absolutely nothing unusual going on. As though Tory needed to be reminded that Cody was leaving tomorrow to spend a week in Florida with Tory's father. The same father that Tory hadn't seen since she'd last seen her mother, who had long since departed for parts unknown.

The episode in the summer had forced Tory's hand in her search for information, desperate to figure out who was threatening her, her engineering business, and those close to her. She finally called her father in Florida to see if he knew anything, to see if he thought the threats had their origin in her checkered past, hopefully long forgotten.

The contact had been a wasted effort, but her father called back later to see if she and Cody were okay. He ended up talking with Cody, his only grandchild, while Tory dozed through the days of convalescence in a drug-induced haze. Never one to let an opportunity go by, Tory's father, a former state senator, parlayed those conversations into an invitation for his grandson to come to Florida over the winter holidays. Cody, always fascinated by anything new, had been happy to accept. Nonplussed, Tory hadn't been able to come up with a reason to refuse.

"Mom, come back to us. I asked if you needed any help with dinner."

Tory refocused on her son and his little companion. Amazingly, Cody going to Florida was beginning to look like a good thing. "No, go ahead and go pack. I'll call you when Lonnie and Sylvia and Jazz get here."

The two disappeared down the hall, talking quietly to each other, the cascade of blond shining hair nowhere to be seen. Tory wondered how this girl was going to help Cody pack without seeing his underwear.

She was saved from thinking too much about that by the doorbell. Tory opened the front door and joined her guests on the front porch.

"You won't believe what's going on in there," she said.

Lonnie Harper, a descendant of one of the wealthier ranching families in the area and related to at least half the people in the Mesilla Valley, at least by Tory's estimation, took Tory's comment in stride. "Hard day?" he asked.

He had been more than just a little surprised when Tory offered to cook dinner. Sylvia must have had some of the same misgivings, because she had come toting a huge tray of tamales. Jazz had come equally fortified, bringing a large bottle of malt whiskey.

"She's a girl," Tory said flatly.

Jesus Rodriguez, better known as Jazz, turned and looked at Sylvia critically.

Sylvia's flair for fashion heightened by the holidays, she was attired in a fire-engine red dress of gauzy material, which fell from a gathering under her ample bosom to barely graze the top of her thighs. Tassels hung from both the sleeves and the hem, giving the impression of a tapestry made into a baby-doll dress. Sylvia's legs were encased in black fishnet stockings. The outfit was topped off with six-inch stiletto heels the same fire-engine red as the dress.

"She's getting kind of old to be called a girl," Jazz said.

If Sylvia hadn't been holding the tray of tamales, she would have been more successful in elbowing Jazz in the ribs, but as it was, she only managed a glancing blow. "She doesn't mean me, *cabrón*," Sylvia said. "Who is a girl?" she demanded, turning her attention to Tory.

"Cole. Cole isn't Cole," she told them in leaden tones. "She's Kohli." When the three of them just stared at her, she spelled the difference.

Lonnie, at least, caught on. "So the kid Cody's been hanging around with is a girl, not a guy," he said carefully, feeling his way.

"That's right," said Tory accusingly. "What do you think about that?"

"Well," he said slowly, "I was thinking about taking them camping in the spring. Guess I'll think some more about it now."

Tory glared at him.

"I guess I could talk to him about it," he offered, wondering what he would say to Cody about having a girl for a friend. After all, the kid's mother was his friend. He just wished she was interested in being something more, which was obviously a subject best left undiscussed with Cody.

"What would you talk to him about?" Tory asked, as if she was reading his mind.

"Good God, Tory, I don't know. Cody's a good kid. He's got his head screwed on right, but he's growing up. It's a good thing, you letting him visit his grandfather, and letting me drive him down to the airport tomorrow. Maybe it's even good he has a girl for a friend, you know, broaden his horizons and that kind of thing."

Jazz and Sylvia were both looking at him, and he wondered if everything he was saying sounded as stupid as he thought it did.

Sylvia saved him. "I'm tired of standing out here on the porch holding these tamales," she said. "Let's go see this girl Cody's brought home." She went through the front door with a sense of purpose, deposited her tamales in the kitchen, sniffed dubiously at the kitchen aromas, and walked down the hall to Cody's room.

"Cody, you little devil," the group on the porch heard her call, "come show me this new friend of yours, the one your mom thought was a guy." They followed her into the house, hearing a full nanosecond pause between Sylvia knocking on Cody's door and walking into his room. Then there was a slightly longer pause, followed by "*Qué lástima, probrecita!* Why do you want to hide all this hair under a baseball hat? And your face—it's beautiful. You need to bring out your cheek bones, and maybe a little lip liner. You come with me; I'll fix you up before dinner so even Cody won't recognize you."

Sylvia backed out of Cody's room, dragging a stunned Kohli by one arm. She pulled Kohli back up the hall and said to her three friends: "Isn't she darling?" She had snatched Kholi's cap off her head. "We're going to freshen up before dinner, Tory. Can we use your bedroom?"

Dumbfounded, Tory nodded, feeling a sudden kinship with the girl; Sylvia was a force to reckon with where fashion and makeup were concerned. Even now, she was reaching into her large purse, pulling out a pale pink sweater with swirled white sequins and holding it up against Kohli, cocking her head thoughtfully and then nodding her approval.

"Do you always come prepared to perform a makeover?" asked Tory.

"My cousin gave me this sweater, and it just wasn't me; the color is too washed-out. I thought maybe it would look good on you, but it would be better on Ko-lay here. She's blond and has delicate features."

Sylvia said Ko-lay like it rhymed with *olé*. Tory wondered what was the opposite of delicate features. She resisted the urge to look in the mirror hanging in the hall, and for one crazy moment, she actually coveted the pink, sequined sweater.

"Kohli," the girl said distinctly, correcting Sylvia's pronunciation of her name. Maybe she had some guts after all.

"Ko-lee, Ko-lay, whatever. When I'm done with you, maybe you'll want to change how you say your name." Sylvia put her hand under the girl's chin, turning her face one way and then another. Tory wondered if she would inspect Kohli's teeth next. "And Cody," she called. "Don't think I've forgotten you. I brought you some sexy red boxers for your Florida trip. A late Christmas present."

"She should have been drowned at birth," muttered Jazz.

Sylvia turned on a dime. "What did you say?" she asked Jazz indignantly.

"He said Cody will really enjoy the surf—you know, in Florida," said Lonnie quickly.

Sylvia shot a suspicious parting glance at Jazz as she threw her arm around Kohli and disappeared into Tory's bedroom for the Sylvia Maestes New Year's Special Makeover Session. Maybe Kohli would think twice before she ventured into the Travers family household again, Tory reflected.

"I have the feeling a perfectly good table cloth gave up its life to make that dress," Lonnie observed. "I hope everything that's potential apparel in your bedroom is nailed down."

"I don't think you need to worry," replied Tory. "My tastes are far too tame for Sylvia's liking."

"With a few possible exceptions," said Lonnie. The remark was so unlike him that for a moment Tory forgot about the girl in their midst.

Something had changed in their relationship after the episode in the summer. She knew that Lonnie was more than willing for their relationship to progress from friendship to something deeper, but after her brush with death and the heady sensation of staring danger in the face and coming away the victor, she was somehow less open to the possibility.

She didn't want to admit that the shift in her feelings had anything to do with the arrogant detective she met during the summer. He had thrown down an invitation to continue their relationship like a gauntlet, and when she had neglected to pick up the challenge, he had disappeared from her life as soon as the details of the case were wrapped up.

"I came here to eat," Jazz said brusquely. "What is it I smell?"

"Turkey. One of those self-basting ones," said Tory.

They trooped into the kitchen to peer into the oven. After looking silently at the turkey, it was again Jazz who broke the silence.

"Looks bloated to me," he said.

Lonnie, as usual, tried to smooth things over. "It'll probably taste better than it looks. I think those self-basting ones are supposed to be idiot-proof."

"You know what they say about that," said Tory glumly. "Make it idiot-proof and someone will make a better idiot."

"Sylvia brought a lot of tamales," observed Jazz, as if he found that lone fact immensely comforting.

"You know," said Lonnie out of the blue, "sexual attraction can be a wonderful, heady thing. It doesn't really have a lot to do with having other things in common, sometimes, but it's just something you have to go with, and experience, to get it out of your system. I remember when Sherry and I couldn't keep our hands off each other," he said, referring to his late wife, who, seven months pregnant, had died in an automobile accident the same year Tory's husband had succumbed to cancer. "Was it that way with you and Carl?"

Tory tried to concentrate on a noncommittal answer. "No," she said. "I don't remember it ever being that way, exactly, between Carl and me. It was scandalous enough, after everything that happened in Florida, that I was nineteen and marrying a professor who was close to forty. Being with Carl," she said carefully, feeling her way, "was more like coming home. Finally belonging. Being with someone who made me feel safe."

"That's what I thought you'd say," said Lonnie, the man who up until now had never had a great urge to talk about feelings.

"Is there a point to this conversation?" asked Tory. "I thought we were discussing that girl in my bedroom with Sylvia, learning God-knows-what about how to make herself more attractive to Cody."

"Talking about me?" asked Cody, appearing in the kitchen as if on cue. "What's Sylvia doing with Kohli? When's dinner?"

"I'm talking about getting something out of your system, before you settle down and know what you really want," continued Lonnie, undistracted from pursuing their parallel conversation.

Jazz glowered at both of them. "I thought we came for dinner. I don't know what you're talking about, but you're sure not going to scare me into joining Sylvia and Ko-lay in the bedroom, *que sí?*"

What they were talking about, Tory thought, was permission from your best friend and one-time lover to pursue another man. A man with whom she had nothing in common. A man who had tried to save her life, but who had arrived too late, so she had saved herself. A man she hadn't seen in months. Tory fought an urge to follow Kohli into her bedroom and ask Sylvia for a make-over. Maybe she could stuff her dark brown hair into a baseball cap, drive down to El Paso, figure out where the guy lived, appear on his doorstep and ask, "Why the hell haven't I heard from you?"

Her train of thought was interrupted by Sylvia's and Kohli's reappearance. Kohli was wearing the pale pink sweater, and her hair was pulled back into an elegant French braid which reached halfway down her back. Sylvia had used a light hand with the make up, and the effect was enchanting. The girl had elfin features, elegant, arched eyebrows over large gray eyes, now fringed with mascara-darkened lashes. Her generous mouth was framed in a complimentary hue two shades darker than the rosy highlights that adorned her cheeks.

It was fortunate that Cody was leaning against the refrigerator, or Tory was sure he would have fallen flat on his face. He did manage to close his mouth long enough to utter one syllable: "Wow."

And she had always prided herself on raising an articulate child.

Sylvia surveyed her handiwork with pride. "Kohli told me how you're going to call her every day from Florida," she said.

Tory wondered how she would get through dinner without gagging.

"Makes you remember the initials for Sylvia Maestes are S and M," said Jazz darkly.

"What did you say?" asked Sylvia.

"He said you can always remember that Sylvia Maestes knows what's 'in,'" said Lonnie quickly.

Sylvia shot a dirty look at Jazz. Lonnie found himself glaring at Jazz, too. He didn't know how much longer he could keep up his diversionary tactics.

"Come on, let's get dinner on the table," said Tory, handing Jazz some silverware and Sylvia a stack of plates, since she didn't trust Sylvia with a handful of knives. Cody and Kohli stayed motionless, as if frozen in place, still staring at each other.

Lonnie glanced from Cody to Kohli and back again, looked at Tory across the kitchen, and raised his eyebrows as if to say "I told you so."

With a beginning like this, Tory could hardly wait to see what the rest of the year would bring.

"Let's eat," said Jazz.

CHAPTER FIVE:

THE OWNER'S REPRESENTATIVE
El Paso, Texas:
Sunday, January 1, early afternoon

As expected, Ryan Hinson identified one of the bodies in the basement as his mother, Lenora Hinson. While he didn't appear to be overwhelmed with grief, he did do a good job of seesawing between shock and outrage. He kept demanding answers that no one had.

"Who *is* that woman?" he kept asking, looking at the other body. "Where did this room come from?" He looked accusingly at Alvarez, who had nothing to offer but the standard condolences. "I grew up in this house," Hinson informed him. "How can there be a room like this in the basement of the house I grew up in? There was nothing here before. Look at the damage to the house. What in God's name has my mother done this time?" No one had an answer for that question, either.

After giving the mouse-woman permission to remove the bodies, Alvarez and Scott led Ryan Hinson upstairs to the dining room. Alvarez carefully explained that although there was currently no proof of criminal activity, the unusual circumstances surrounding the discovery of his mother's body warranted a full investigation. Further, maybe he would prefer talking to someone he already knew.

Ryan Hinson shrugged off recognition of Scott Faulkner by simply saying, "Oh yeah. You're the Faulkner boy who decided to become a cop." He seemed more distressed by the view from the dining room than he had been while looking at the bodies in the basement. Hinson couldn't seem to tear his attention away from the gaping hole in the floor of the entry hall.

For his part, Alvarez was distracted by the dog tethered in
the kitchen. It kept whining and fixing its soulful eyes on
him. At least, he *thought* it was fixing its soulful eyes on him;
the hair covering the dog's face made it impossible to tell if it
had any eyes.

"Is that your mother's dog?" asked Alvarez.

"Yeah," replied Hinson, still staring disconsolately at the
entry hall. "It's a Puli, a Hungarian sheepherding dog. They're
pretty rare, so it might have been worth something to breed it,
but my mother had it spayed."

The dog gave one last pitiful whimper and then collapsed
in a despairing boneless heap at the end of its tether, fixing
Alvarez with a baleful stare from invisible eyes. Alvarez found
this disquieting, but what was he going to do, ask for the dog
to be sequestered in another room because it bothered him?

"We know this must be a shock to you, Mr. Hinson," said
Alvarez formally, "but the sooner we can get some background
information, the better chance we have of figuring out what
happened here. Would you like some water or something?"

"What I'd like is a stiff drink. This is a nightmare. The
damage to the house is unbelievable, and I can just imagine
the publicity. It's just what I need in my life right now, another crisis. My God, what do you suppose has been going on
here? What if my mother was involved in some type of criminal activity?"

"Do you have any reason to think she would be involved
in something illegal?"

"My mother was a ruthless, domineering, controlling
bitch."

Alvarez resisted the urge to say, "But tell us what you really
think." Instead, he merely asked, "Why do you say that?"

"My mother was into control. She ruined my life and my

marriage. She ruined my sister's life, not that my sister didn't actively participate in the process, the stupid twit. Probably the real reason that my father died early was because it was the only way he could get away from my mother."

"How did your mother ruin your life?"

"My father died when I was twenty and my sister was thirteen. He'd founded Pinnacle Development, the firm that developed Rim Road, so when he died, he left a lot of money. Half went to my mother, half to Keaton and me. There weren't a lot of specifics in the will, just the general idea of where the money was supposed to go. But by the time my mother got done with my father's attorney, the money was tied up in trust until we each turn thirty-five years old. I'll be thirty-five next month. That means I've spent almost fifteen years waiting for that money, all because of my mother."

"And your mother controlled the m-money in the meantime?" asked Scott.

"Of course. How else could she control my life?"

Alvarez assumed the concept of getting a job and getting on with his life hadn't occurred to Hinson. "So you hold your mother responsible for withholding money that was rightfully yours?"

"Very bright, detective. Very on-target. To this day I wonder how she got my father's attorney to do something so outrageous, but Lenora had a way of getting what she wanted, and it isn't as if she didn't have resources she needed at her disposal."

"And she used control of the trust fund to control your life?"

"She had to approve every decision I made, or there wasn't any money. My mother insisted I become an accountant and take over my father's place in Pinnacle. I never had a choice."

"And how did your mother ruin your marriage?"

"She undermined me at every step. How would you like it if you had to consult your mother every time your wife wanted to buy something?"

No answers immediately came to mind. "So it would be safe to say that your wife didn't like your mother, either?"

"Marshay hates my mother's guts, and the feeling's mutual. It wasn't just the money. My mother never lifted a finger to get Marshay into the right groups. But she couldn't just leave it there, no, not Lenora. She made sure that Keaton, crazy Keaton, was inducted into every single organization that counts in this sorry excuse for a city."

"Who is Keaton?"

"His s-s-sister," contributed Scott.

"So there was Marshay," continued Hinson without a pause, "wanting to join these organizations and not able to, and then there was Keaton, who doesn't give a shit about anything, a member of every single club that means anything." Hinson grimaced at the memory. "On top of having to ask for money at every turn, it's no wonder our marriage went on the rocks."

"So is Marshay your wife, your ex-wife, or what?" asked Alvarez.

"We're legally separated," answered Hinson shortly.

"You said your mother ruined your sister's life, too. What do you mean by that?"

"Keaton wanted to go to medical school and marry her high school boyfriend. My mother wanted her to marry the son of my father's business partner and be a stay-at-home mommy. My mother got her way, but Keaton got even in the end."

"How?"

"Keaton's crazy. She's made a career of it. She's anorexic, bulimic, alcoholic, addicted to prescription drugs, depressed, bi-polar—whatever the affliction of the month, Keaton has it."

"Must be rough on her family."

"As long as her husband has enough money to send her away to whatever treatment center is in vogue, he'll hang in there. He's got to, to recoup his investment. Keaton's twenty-eight now, so he has seven more years to go."

It took Alvarez a moment to understand what Hinson was telling him. "Your sister's husband is waiting for Keaton to turn thirty-five so he can get his hands on her trust fund?"

"Damn right. Wouldn't you?"

This was another question that Alvarez decided to let go unanswered. "But the money will go to your sister, right?"

"Dale won't have any problem getting Keaton declared incompetent, not with her history. He'll probably get the money set up in trust for their daughter, naming himself as trustee."

"There's only one child?"

"Yeah, Keaton had her right after she got married, to get my mother off her back, but I don't think there will be any more. Even with the one kid, there was a big blow up when Keaton refused to name her after my mother. She named her daughter Hero. God, have you ever heard of anything so ridiculous, a little girl named Hero? You've got to give Keaton credit though, she dug in her heels, even when my mother threatened to cut her off. There must be some advantages to being crazy," said Hinson bitterly.

"There are no other grandchildren? Just Hero?"

"Right."

Alvarez thought over the implications of the trust funds. It didn't appear that Lenora Hinson's death would directly benefit Ryan, since he would supposedly get his money within a month, anyway.

"Who will administer K-Keaton's trust fund now that your mother is dead?" asked Scott.

"I don't know, and it doesn't concern me, does it?"

"How about the rest of the estate?" asked Alvarez. "Do you know who will inherit? Are there other family members?"

"There's no other family that I know of. I couldn't guess the content of my mother's will, she's threatened to change it so often. It's probably a toss-up between me, my sister, and my mother's beloved charities. Six months ago I would have given myself fairly decent odds, but we just had a fight."

"What kind of fight?"

"I wanted to move back in with her, and she wouldn't let me." Hinson didn't even look sheepish uttering the words.

"Why?"

"Marshay wanted me out of the house. I didn't see any reason to rent an apartment when my mother had all this room here."

"What'd she say?"

"She told me no," said Hinson. "She didn't even give me an excuse. She wouldn't let me draw any more money, either, so I'm still at my house, because I can't swing house payments and apartment rent both."

Killing Lenora Hinson did seem like a pretty extreme measure just to get a place to live, thought Alvarez.

Hinson was staring fixedly at the entry hall again. "And what about that other woman?" Hinson asked, as if he suspected her of being his mother's house guest when she'd turned down her own son.

"We'll contact every law enforcement agency that tracks missing persons, which is our best shot at identifying her unless someone steps forward and tells us who she is. You need to let us do the police work," Alvarez said firmly. He hadn't mentioned the infant or the multiple IDs so far, hesitating to give Hinson any more information than he had to. "Did your mother have any visitors who brought young children or infants with them?"

"No," said Hinson, looking at Alvarez like he was crazy. "My mother wasn't fond of children. Why do you ask?"

"Because we found a diaper bag in the basement room."

Hinson shook his head in bewilderment. "I don't know anything about that. I've got to look out for my own interests. I want to be prepared to deal with the liabilities."

"What liabilities?"

"The civil liabilities. If this was an accident, my mother's insurance will pay for repairs to the house, and for any claims from a third party. That woman down in the basement, whoever the hell she is, she's bound to have relatives, and relatives are always after money. If for some bizarre reason my mother is found to be even partially responsible for her death, the whole estate could be forfeit. Hell, there's even a slim chance a judge could throw in profit from the trust funds, since my mother was administering the money. You never know what will happen once something gets to court, and I plan to make sure it doesn't get there."

Hinson was way ahead of Alvarez in analyzing the legal implications of the situation. Alvarez was still stuck on the basic questions regarding the identity of the second woman and the baby, the purpose of the concealed room, and how Lenora Hinson died. No wonder Hinson had a trust fund and Alvarez didn't.

"Who do you plan to call?" asked Alvarez. "An attorney who's the opposite of an ambulance chaser, someone who makes sure the ambulance doesn't get chased?"

Hinson gave Alvarez a look of disdain, indicating that he realized Alvarez would never have access to a trust fund, regardless of his age. "No, I need to establish that this was an accident. Pinnacle has an engineering firm on retainer, and we give them a hell of a lot of business. I can have someone out here within an hour."

"Don't bother," said Alvarez. "No one's going to be allowed access to the house until it's cleared with the police department. Try checking with us tomorrow." He handed Hinson a card.

"I want someone to look at it as soon as possible."

"That would be tomorrow."

Hinson put Alvarez's card in his shirt pocket. "So am I free to go now?"

"A few more questions. What is your sister's married name?"

"Crandell. Her husband is Dale Crandell the Third. Our fathers started Pinnacle, and now Dale and I run it."

"How is Pinnacle doing financially?"

"Pinnacle is doing fine financially, not that I see any reason why you need to know."

Alvarez made a show of consulting his notes. "You said that you couldn't afford to move out of your house and get an apartment. If business is good, why is that a problem?"

"Everything is relative, detective. I'm sure the apartment that you envision is not one that would be satisfactory for me. When I tell you that I'm responsible for a mortgage, I don't mean payments on your standard tract house, I mean an estate home. Pinnacle and I both have some short-term cash flow problems, that's all. Which will soon be solved."

Alvarez didn't know how that long-winded explanation answered his question, but he decided to let it go for now.

"Where can we find your sister?"

"She and Dale live on the other end of Rim Road." Alvarez pushed his notebook across the table to Hinson and asked him to write down the address and telephone number.

"Would you prefer to be the one to break this news to your sister?"

"Not at all," said Hinson shortly. "Isn't that one of the things my tax dollars pay for?"

Alvarez imagined smacking Ryan Hinson upside the head with his notebook. "It might be easier for her to hear it from you," he said evenly.

"I'll call her from my car phone then."

Alvarez looked up at Hinson to see if he was being sarcastic, and decided he wasn't. "You haven't exactly characterized your mother in glowing terms. Do you know anyone who disliked her enough to harm her, or would profit from her death?"

Hinson let out a snort of laughter. "For me to list everyone who disliked my mother, detective, you'd have to get a bigger notebook. My mother had power, influence, and more money than God. She never hesitated to use any of it to get her way."

"Can you be more specific?"

"I disliked my mother, detective. So did my sister, my wife, my brother-in-law. I'm sure my sister's ex-boyfriend hated her, and then there's that poor attorney she duped into doing her bidding, if the old buzzard isn't dead by now. Right after the trust fund episode, I got a call from him, drunk as a skunk, apologizing all over himself. I told him to go to hell and hung up. As for who else would profit from her death ... I guess whatever charities my mother names in her will, but those would be limited to the ones that would let my mother tell them what to do and how to do it. All Souls Episcopal Church is bound to be in there somewhere. Father Sanchez might know about that. But I'm just guessing. Like I said, my mother's will was a constantly changing document."

"Write down her attorney's name, and do the same for the priest and church," directed Alvarez, and Hinson complied.

"Are you finally done with me?" asked Hinson. Alvarez nodded, and the man stood up. "I'll expect you to keep me posted on anything you find out."

Before Alvarez could reply, the dog in the kitchen sat up and resumed whining.

"C-can you take the dog?" asked Scott. "If you don't, it will end up at the Animal Shelter."

"Not my problem," said Hinson. "I told you before, it's not worth anything now."

"How about your sister?" asked Scott doggedly.

"Get real," replied Hinson. "My sister can't even take care of herself. The dog will be better off euthanized than living with Keaton. Remember, I want to know what you find out as soon as you have any information." He missed the glare Alvarez aimed at his back. He left through the back door.

"What an asshole," said Scott, stutter-free.

"I especially liked the part where he agreed to call his sister on his car phone to tell her their mother is dead. Talk about reaching out to touch somebody ..."

"It's a nice dog," said Scott. "Not its fault any of this happened." He walked into the kitchen, found a bowl, filled it with water and put it in front of the dog. It lapped up Scott's offering gratefully.

"You're contaminating a crime scene," said Alvarez conversationally. Scott just shrugged, which was about what Alvarez would have done in his position. The dog finished drinking and sat at attention, water streaming down its chin and onto the floor. "God, do you think that always happens when it drinks? Lucky this dog lives in a dry climate, or it would get mildew on its face." Every time Alvarez said anything, the dog wagged its tail and made little whimpering noises.

Scott bent down and scratched behind the dog's ears, and it wriggled in ecstasy. He consulted its collar. "It's a she. And her name is Cotton. I think she likes you."

"While you're busy interviewing the dog," said Alvarez, "I'm going to tell Kurita and the other officer to canvass the neighborhood. Unless somebody heard something, my bet is that the caller had inside knowledge about what went down. I'm going to arrange things so we can keep the kid under wraps until we have a better handle on this. Let's put a guard on the kid, too. If it's part of this, it could be in danger."

"Her," said Scott succinctly, still petting the dog. "The k-kid is a her. A c-concealed room, a woman no one knows, and multiple IDs. The b-b-baby has to be part of the whole deal. Maybe something like the Salvadorian Sanctuary m-movement."

Alvarez thought about it. That was pretty good for a first try. "No offense, *compadre*, but both bodies looked awfully white to me for anything related to Salvador. Maybe a drug deal gone bad in an underground distribution ring? And note, I use the term 'underground' specifically."

"Why would Lenora Hinson d-d-deal drugs? Her son already told us she had more money than God. Sounds like she was into causes, ones she could control."

"Well, I don't think that room was used to audition for the El Paso Symphony Orchestra. What's that thing where parents kidnap their kids from abusive spouses?"

"I don't know, but I like it better than a drug d-deal," said Faulkner, still petting the dog. "Let's take Cotton with us," he suggested suddenly.

"You've got to be kidding," said Alvarez. "That's a sissy dog. I wouldn't be caught dead with a dog like that. It looks like some kind of wind-up toy that you win at a carnival. For all I know, it has batteries inside."

"She," repeated Faulkner. "We're not going to make her p-p-part of a canine unit. I hate to see her go to the Animal Shelter. And besides, you're already driving a p-purple car, so what do you have to lose?"

Alvarez looked back and forth between his partner and the dog. Sometimes it was a pain in the ass having Scott Faulkner for a partner, even if he did have a point about the purple car. "You're going to owe me big time for this, *amigo*. And I'm not committing to anything, understand? Maybe the sister will take the dog if we show up with it, if not, we need to think of something else. Otherwise, it's off to the Animal Shelter."

"Sure," said Scott. Alvarez could imagine the lie detector reading on that one syllable.

"You think it's housebroken?" he asked dubiously as Scott untied the clothes line. "You don't think she'd like, piss in the car, do you?"

"I'm sure she would never do that," vowed Scott staunchly.

"Yeah, you've said the same thing about some of the women you've fixed me up with," grumbled Alvarez. "'I'm sure she would never do that,' you said, and you were right, she wouldn't. This would be a hell of a time for you to be wrong."

"We're going to talk to Keaton?" asked Scott, leading the dog toward the kitchen door.

"Sounds like a plan. Then I thought we'd stop by and see your folks, chew the fat, talk about trust funds and things like that. Them being in the neighborhood, and all."

"'Home is the place where, when you have to go there, they have to take you in,'" Scott said glumly. "Frost, *Death of a Hired Man*," he added for Alvarez's benefit.

"Yeah, and investigating a possible homicide should count, too," added Alvarez. He wondered if he could teach the dog to respond to a more macho sounding name, something like Bruiser, or Spike. Then a comforting thought occurred to him: He knew damn well Scott's father would know the outcome of the Sun Bowl game. With any luck, he might have even taped it. Alvarez felt better already.

CHAPTER SIX:

NEIGHBORS

El Paso, Texas:
Sunday, January 1, mid-afternoon

Alvarez wondered if he would feel claustrophobic when he finally returned to his own house. It took a while to get from where they parked on the street to the front door of Keaton Crandell's house. Whoever designed the walk through the landscaped grounds did not subscribe to the theory that a straight line was the best way to get from one point to another, and he could swear he heard an echo when he rang the doorbell.

They left Cotton in the car. Scott didn't want the dog to risk another face-to-face rejection if Ryan Hinson's sister declined to take her. Alvarez argued that "face-to-face" anything didn't apply when no eyes were visible, but Scott had been adamant. "She's been traumatized enough," he pronounced, and that was that.

Cotton had been perfectly satisfied to go with the two detectives, no questions asked, behavior that Alvarez wished more human subjects would display. After sniffing diligently at everything and turning around numerous times, the dog settled into the back seat of the rental car like she belonged there.

He told her sternly not to chew up anything in their absence, and she wagged her tail and panted in reply. Alvarez reserved judgment; he'd gotten the same answer too many times before, with dubious outcomes. Scott had to remind him to lock the car when they started up the winding sidewalk toward the palatial house. Alvarez only wished that there were some dognappers on the loose; it would be his first break in this case.

An exquisite little girl answered the door, frizzy dark hair floating around her face, eyes dancing with excitement. "Ooooooh," she said. "Mommy told me some policemen were coming. But you don't have uniforms," she added. She peered around Alvarez. "And there aren't any lights or sirens." She stared sternly at him, as if holding him solely responsible for these shortcomings.

"That's so the bad guys won't know we're on the job," improvised Alvarez. "Shouldn't you let your mother know we're here?"

"It's okay for you to come in," said the little girl, opening the door wide. "My name is Hero, and this is my house. Do you have any children?" she asked Alvarez. He wasn't even in the house yet, and the child was already directing the interview.

"No, but my partner has a little boy. When you're older, maybe you can babysit."

"You think?" The child stuck three fingers of her left hand into her mouth, which Alvarez took as a sign of interest.

"Maybe," he told her again. "But when you babysit, or even when you're just home by yourself, you should know who people are before you let them in. The way to make sure we're really detectives is to ask to see our badges."

"Okay," said Hero, giggling, "Show me your badges," she said, completely at ease with issuing commands, even with three fingers still in her mouth.

Alvarez and Faulkner were complying when a short woman with a shiny helmet of blond hair, dressed in black jeans and a black sweater, came down the staircase and put her hands possessively on Hero's shoulders. "That won't be necessary," the woman said. "Ryan told me you would probably come here. He called me from his car phone."

"I'm Detective David Alvarez," said Alvarez, extending his hand. "And this is my partner, Scott Faulkner. He used to be a neighbor of yours. I'm very sorry for your loss, Mrs. Crandell." He could see Scott shaking his head out of the corner of his eye.

"He's no neighbor of mine," said the woman shortly, ignoring Alvarez's extended hand. "I'm Marshay Hinson, and I'm not happy about you showing up here unannounced. There's a child to be considered, or don't you people think of things like that?"

"Marshay, whatever will we do with you?" said someone from the top of the stairs. Alvarez looked up to see a strikingly beautiful woman looking down at all of them, a faint smile on her face. "It's no wonder my mother despaired of you, Marshay. Always ask someone in *before* you start to insult them, dear."

Alvarez stooped and smoothly offered his hand to Hero, who shook it solemnly. The woman chiding Marshay came down the stairs to join them. She was tall and slender, with golden red hair that cascaded in ringlets around her face. She was wearing an ivory-colored jumper over a green satin blouse, and holding a glass with amber liquid in one hand. All she needed was a silver cigarette holder in the other hand to complete the picture of wealth and privilege that fairly oozed off her.

"I'm Keaton Crandell, Detective Alvarez," she said, offering him her hand. "And if it isn't Scotty Faulkner. I was madly in love with you when I was eight, but you were much too old to notice a scrawny little thing like me."

"Scotty" appeared unfazed by Keaton's appearance and demeanor. It must be his upbringing, Alvarez decided, checking to make sure that his own mouth wasn't hanging open, or anything uncouth like that. He was still trying to digest the information that Ryan Hinson's estranged wife appeared to be keeping company with his sister when a middle-aged, dark-haired man joined them at the door.

"Can I be of any help?" he asked. He was dressed in black

slacks and a black shirt, and Alvarez wondered if he could be the butler. Surely even butlers got New Year's Day off.

"The detectives have come to talk about mother's death, Rodney. I don't think you can be of any help, but when has that ever stopped you?" said Keaton. Alvarez was tempted to dig out his notebook and consult his notes. He didn't remember Hinson mentioning a Rodney.

The little girl tugged at his jacket. "It's okay," she told him solemnly. "Mommy already told me that Grammy Lenora is dead."

Alvarez looked down at the child. "I'm sorry about that," he told her. "It's our job to figure out what happened to her."

"I understand about dying," Hero told him. "We had a gerbil at school, and it died. The teacher found out that Calvin Vaughan fed him some of his wart medicine, and he got in a lot of trouble." She appeared lost in the memory for a moment. "I'm sad that Grammy Lenora is dead, but I'm not really sad, you know what I mean? I didn't like her all that much. I did like the gerbil, though," she added pensively.

"Hero, you know you don't mean that," said the aunt.

"Of course she means it, Marshay," said Keaton. "Just because my mother is dead doesn't mean we're all going to start pretending we liked her. Please, come in and sit down. There's no need for all of us to stand in the doorway."

Keaton let them into a living room that Alvarez figured was roughly the size of his house. Before they even sat down, the man in black introduced himself as Rodney Kiepper, carefully spelling his name before anyone asked him to do so.

"Rodney is a friend of the family," said Keaton. "He's a keeper, just like his name. Not his brother's keeper, mind you, but his sister's keeper." She laughed gaily at a joke that no one else seemed to get. "But then, Marshay is a keeper, too," she added.

Alvarez was wondering where to go with that when Scott

jumped into the conversation. "We're sorry about your mother, Mrs. Crandell. We'd like to ask you some questions, and it would be helpful to b-b-be able to talk to you alone."

"My, aren't we formal, Scotty? Is K-K-Keaton too difficult for you to say?"

"For God's sake, Keaton, don't be such an asshole," hissed Keaton's sister-in-law, looking like a blond warrior-goddess ready to do battle. "These aren't people you want to fuck around with."

Keaton looked directly at her sister-in-law. "Marshay, dear, you have absolutely no idea who I do or don't want to fuck around with," she said conversationally. She calmly turned her attention back to Alvarez and Faulkner. "I'm sorry, that was really rude. You'll have to forgive me, my medication and all ..."

"Mommy is sick a lot," said Hero, her eyes big at being part of all the grown-up excitement.

"I'll take Hero up to her room," said Marshay, glaring at Keaton. "But Rodney will stay with my sister-in-law." She issued the statement like an order.

"No, I want to stay," Hero cried, grabbing handfuls of her mother's jumper.

"Now Hero," said Kiepper soothingly. "Don't make things harder on your mother by misbehaving. I'll stay right here with her, and make sure she's okay."

"But I want to stay," wailed Hero.

"What if we come talk to you after we talk to your mother?" asked Alvarez.

Hero thought this over. "Should I have an attorney when I talk to you, like they show on TV? My daddy's an attorney."

Alvarez stifled a sigh. "We're just trying to get some information about your grandmother, Hero, so I don't think anyone needs an attorney."

"That means you don't think Mommy or me or Auntie

Marshay did anything bad, right?" asked Hero in triumph, and Alvarez knew he'd been had.

"No, we don't think that you or your Mommy or your Auntie Marshay did anything bad," he said. He crossed his fingers on the hand that was out of the child's line of sight.

"Okay," said Hero, trading the handfuls of her mother's jumper for her aunt's hand. "We'll go upstairs to my room and wait for our turn." She led her aunt out of the room and up the staircase, waving at the lot of them until she disappeared from sight with her frowning aunt.

Alvarez decided to let Rodney Kiepper stick around for the moment. He seemed harmless enough.

"Mrs. Crandell," said Alvarez formally, "I don't know how much your brother told you. He just identified your mother's body in the basement of her house. There appears to be a concealed room in the basement, and the ceiling to the room collapsed. This may have caused your mother's death. We won't know until we get the autopsy results. Another unidentified woman, in her mid- to late-twenties, was found dead in the basement with your mother. Do you know about any of this?"

"No," said Keaton simply. "If you weren't here telling me about it, I'd still be tempted to think that Ryan made it all up." She paused to take a drink from her glass. "However, my mother and I weren't exactly close."

"Do you know about any small children visiting your mother?"

"No, not ever. My mother wasn't fond of children. Why do you ask?"

Rodney Kiepper leaned forward, looking horrified. "Don't tell us there was a child killed, too," he said in horror. "Ryan didn't say anything about a child."

"No, the only fatalities are the two women," said Alvarez. "And please, sir, let us ask the questions."

"Your b-brother told us about your inheritance." This from Scott, who always liked to follow the money trail. "Do you know who administers the f-f-funds, now that your mother is dead?"

"I wouldn't have any idea."

"Do you know anyone who would want to harm your mother?" asked Alvarez.

Keaton laughed. "My mother was not a popular person," she said, "as I am sure Ryan explained to you at length. She was active in a great many causes and organizations in this city, and she stepped on lots of toes. But I don't think the people she associated with are prone to homicide, if that's what you're thinking."

"You mustn't belittle the good your mother did," piped up Rodney Kiepper, apparently trying to put a different spin on Keaton's words. "Keaton's mother was a well-known philanthropist in El Paso. I'm the headmaster at St. Michael's Episcopal School for Girls, which Keaton attended. Mrs. Hinson has been a significant contributor to our school for years."

"But that was only because she owed you, Rodney dear, for all those times you didn't kick me out, no matter how much you wanted to," said Keaton with a smile.

Alvarez got in another question before Kiepper could reply. "So you know nothing about the room in the basement?" he asked Keaton.

"Nothing."

"You don't seem exactly overcome with grief."

Keaton sighed as if disappointed in the question. "My mother was a calculating, controlling, bitter old woman, detective. The only thing that made her different from others like her is the fact that my mother is—was—very wealthy."

"Wealthier than your husband?"

"How would I know?" Keaton gave Alvarez another smile.

"I don't concern myself with my husband's financial affairs."
She lifted her glass and took another sip.

"Who will inherit your mother's estate?"

"I don't know."

"Your brother said something about an old boyfriend.
Does he still live around here?"

"Isn't that interesting? We've just found out that my mother
is dead, and already Ryan is stepping into her shoes. I'm twenty-
eight years old, detective, a married woman and a mother
myself. High school boyfriends are ancient history."

"Ancient history takes lots of time to research. Why don't
you give us a break and fill us in?"

Keaton sighed. "My mother sent me to St. Michael's, like
Rodney just told you. Not exactly a great place to meet boys.
When I was a sophomore I met a boy who went to public
school. He turned out to be the son of my father's doctor, but
I didn't know it when I met him. I was fifteen and he was
seventeen, and we were in love. Then he went away to college.
I've known Dale since I was born. Dale asked me to marry
him and I did. End of story."

"Boyfriend's name?"

"Such a juvenile phrase, detective. Gary Cabrioni is the name
of an old friend. And yes, before you ask your next question, he
still lives here. He took over his father's practice when his father
retired. And no, before you ask the question after that, we don't
see each other any more, except in passing."

"He wasn't your mother's doctor or anything like that?"

Keaton choked on the drink that she had lifted to her
lips. Alvarez thought he had startled her with his question,
but she was laughing again. "No, detective, he wasn't my
mother's physician. And in answer to your next question, I
really don't know who is. Or was."

"What is your sister-in-law doing here?"

"Even though she and Ryan are estranged, Marshay is very fond of Hero. She's very fond of Dale. We're all terribly fond of each other, detective. It's like living in *The Golden Bowl*."

"You're implying that your sister-in-law is having an affair with your husband?" asked Scott, stutter-free.

"Good God, Scotty," said Keaton in exasperation. "You always did have a way of saying whatever came into your head, didn't you? No, I'm not implying that Marshay is sleeping with my husband. I'm sure that Ryan told you all about my, shall we say, difficulties. Sometimes Dale gets concerned about leaving me here alone with Hero, and when he does, Marshay is always ready to play the loving auntie. And Rodney is ready to play the loving uncle, even if he isn't blood related. Aren't I lucky to have so many people looking out for me?" She drained the remaining contents of her glass and moved to the edge of her seat, indicating that the interview was at an end. But Alvarez wasn't ready to go.

"Where is your husband now?"

"He's with some friends at a Sun Bowl party. I don't care for football, so I didn't go."

A man entered the room from the back of the house, shedding his coat and gloves as he walked toward Alvarez and Scott. "I'm Dale Crandell, officers, and I don't appreciate finding you in my house interviewing my wife without me present." He couldn't have timed his entrance better if he'd been standing in the wings waiting for a cue. "I'm an attorney," he added.

Alvarez liked the way he worked that in early in the conversation.

Physically, Dale Crandell resembled Keaton's brother, dark-haired, tall, big-boned, but he moved with a vigor that Ryan Hinson lacked, and he was acting like a man with a mission.

He crossed to his wife and dropped a kiss on her head. "I'm so sorry about your mother, darling," he said.

Keaton appeared unmoved by the show of concern. "Don't tell me, let me guess. Ryan tracked you down and told you what happened."

"Ryan and Marshay both, dear. Everyone is very concerned about you."

"Your wife has been doing just fine in your absence," threw in Alvarez.

"My wife has a history of mental illness," said Crandell shortly. "I don't want you questioning her now." He glared at Rodney Kiepper. "I'm surprised you allowed this to go on, Rodney."

"Keaton didn't say it was a problem," Kiepper said defensively.

"No one's being accused of anything," said Alvarez. "We're just trying to get some information, and this seemed like a reasonable place to start."

"Start somewhere else. Keaton's had a terrible shock, and I want you to leave."

The two detectives stood up, but Alvarez wasn't about to go quietly. "Do you know anything about your mother-in-law's death?"

"Not a thing other than what I've been told. Please leave."

"You're an attorney. Do you know who will be administering your wife's trust fund now that Lenora Hinson is dead?"

"I have nothing else to say to you."

"You've got a cute little girl, Mr. Crandell. She was real anxious to talk to us, and I promised her that we'd interview her before we left. I don't want her to think I forgot my promise."

"I'll explain to her that I asked you to leave."

Keaton rose quickly and gracefully. She held her liquor

well, in Alvarez's opinion. "I'll see them out, Dale. After all, Scotty is an old friend, dear, even if he's a policeman."

Dale Crandell folded his arms over his chest and nodded in less-than-enthusiastic agreement. At the door, Keaton shook hands with Alvarez formally. Then, as Alvarez headed toward the car, she gave Scott a kiss on the cheek that seemed to take a rather long time.

Alvarez was halfway to his car when he realized what was waiting there. "Shit," he said, and turned around to wait for Scott.

"We didn't ask about the damn dog, and it's too late to go back and do it now. Shit, shit, shit. Look at what you got me into. What the hell took you so long?"

"Keaton was whispering into my ear," said Scott with characteristic equanimity.

"So what was she whispering? Did she give you all the answers?"

"She said that she was not as drunk or drugged as her brother told p-people she was, and that she noticed something about my good-looking p-p-partner that I should t-tell him."

"¿Qué?"

"She saw him cross his fingers when he answered Hero's question."

"But she did say 'good looking'?"

"I wouldn't make too much out of it. You still think we should t-talk to my parents?"

"Think they'd be interested in a dog?"

Scott didn't bother to answer.

Mrs. Faulkner answered the door in her usual distracted fashion, looking at the two of them for a moment longer than Alvarez would have thought necessary. "Scotty, dear," she said. "I do wish you would learn to phone ahead. Warren," she called to her husband as she let them in. "Scotty is here, and that nice Mexican man that he works with."

Alvarez had once tried explaining to Mrs. Faulkner that he was only half Hispanic, that his mother had come from good white Kansas farm stock. Scott told him later that to his mother, the idea of being half Hispanic was like being partially pregnant, it just didn't compute.

Scott kissed his mother's cheek and she said, "Jane Edgerton told me all about Lenora Hinson. No one on the Road was very fond of her, but I'm still sorry to hear she's dead."

"The Edgertons live next door to Lenora Hinson," said Scott, for Alvarez's benefit. "I'd like to talk to Dad, Mom."

"He's in his study, dear, exercising."

Scott led the way to his father's study, where Mr. Faulkner was pedaling on a stationary bicycle while holding a drink in one hand. "Hi, son," he said without stopping. "Don't mind me going on. Just got up to the required heartbeat range and all that, hate to stop in the middle, have to start all over," he puffed.

"Who won the Sun Bowl?" Alvarez asked, sitting in one of the overstuffed leather chairs that graced the room.

"UTEP. Field goal in overtime."

The required heartbeat range was obviously going to result in shortened answers from the senior Faulkner, which was fine with Alvarez.

With little prompting from Scott, Warren Faulkner verified much of what they'd already been told, including the fact that Lenora Hinson had a ruthless penchant for taking control. Scott's father had heard about the trust fund issue, and thought it strange at the time, but no more than that. Keaton's various problems were not news to him, either.

Scott's mother stuck her head in the study. "Scotty, dear," she said. "Donna's mother called me. Donna was very upset that you didn't stay to watch the ball game. She said that a friend of yours left in the middle of it and Donna was stranded with her cousin. That really wasn't very nice, dear. I hope you choose friends with better manners in the future."

Scott sighed. "That was David, Mom. We had to leave because of this case."

"Oh," said Scott's mom vaguely. "Well, Mr. Alvarez, I certainly hope that you and Scotty plan to make it up to the girls. I think they were very disappointed. I'm sure your parents didn't raise you to act like that."

"Yes, ma'am," said Alvarez, and mollified to some extent, Scott's mom disappeared again.

Warren Faulkner expressed the standard surprise and disbelief about the circumstances surrounding Lenora Hinson's death. Alvarez was beginning to think it was a wasted visit when Scott's father got on the subject of how the new generation of Pinnacle management had run a perfectly good firm into the ground, leveraged to the hilt to obtain capital for new developments. He didn't know for sure, he said, but he thought the recent slump in the real estate market was bound to be giving problems to a firm that was already overextended.

"Not that it's my worry," he puffed. "We haven't lent any money to them." Scott's father was a bank director, and had once advised Alvarez that if you didn't have cash in the bank for collateral, you shouldn't borrow funds. Alvarez had wondered why anyone with cash in the bank would need to borrow money, but after trying to discuss his racial heritage with Mrs. Faulkner, he had decided to let well enough alone.

Talking about money always got Warren Faulkner going. He climbed off his stationary bike, drained the rest of his drink, and threw himself into a chair opposite Alvarez. Then he told the two of them the name of every young, affluent, El

Paso matron that Dale Crandell had supposedly slept with. Alvarez was impressed in spite of himself.

He was just going to ask if Ryan Hinson's wife was included in the list when Mrs. Faulkner stuck her head in the study again. "Warren, I can't believe that you're repeating all those stories," she said in exasperation.

"Ruth," repllied the senior Faulkner, "the boys asked, and I'm telling them. It doesn't concern you."

"Well, it does too," said Scott's mother, "because Jane Edgerton just called. I told her that Scotty is over here, and she wanted me to ask him a question for her."

"The Edgertons who live next door to Lenora Hinson?" asked Alvarez for clarification.

"Well, of course," said Scott's mother. "We don't know any other Edgertons, do we, Warren?"

"I'm going to fix myself another drink," said Scott's father, and disappeared from the room. Alvarez figured the second drink was either a reward for finishing the exercise routine, or for not strangling Scott's mother. Maybe both.

"There's no need to be rude," Scott's mother called after him. "You didn't offer our guests a drink."

"We're working," said Alvarez, in spite of his resolve to let Scott handle the conversation with his mother. Talking to Mrs. Faulkner often left him befuddled for hours afterwards.

"What did Mrs. Edgerton want you to ask me?" inquired Scott.

She looked at him blankly for a moment. "Oh," she said, "I already answered her question, dear. I told her that you wouldn't mind a bit."

"Mind what, mother?" asked Scott. Alvarez could swear that good old imperturbable Scott was grinding his teeth.

"Mind if she asked the engineer at the Hinson house to take a look at the cracks in her garden wall when he's done."

"What engineer?" asked Alvarez, trying to match his partner's tone.

"The ones who work for Pinnacle. Who are they, dear?" she called out loud enough to make Alvarez flinch.

"Webb Engineering," called the senior Faulkner from wherever he had disappeared to.

"And Webb Engineering has s-someone at Mrs. Hinson's house?" asked Scott.

Mrs. Faulkner looked at him like he was very slow. "Where else would they be, on New Year's Day? I'm sure that they wouldn't come out on a holiday like this for just anyone."

"How d-does Mrs. Edgerton know that they're at the Hinson house?" asked Scott.

"Because there's a truck parked outside Lenora's house with the company name on it."

Now that was what Alvarez would call a bona fide clue.

"Good police work, Mrs. F.," he said. "We need to check this out."

"'Bye, Dad," called Scott, already heading for the door. Alvarez was right behind him. "Thanks for your help."

"Don't forget about making things up to Donna and her cousin," said Mrs. Faulkner, trailing behind them.

They waited until she shut the door before making a break for the car at an all-out run. It wasn't a good idea to do anything in a hurry in front of Scott's mom, as it brought out all kinds of maternal concerns for his safety.

"We've still got the damn dog," said Alvarez as they got in the car. Cotton put her front paws on the back of the front seat and licked his neck as he started the car.

"She likes you," said Scott, as Alvarez peeled away from the curb.

CHAPTER SEVEN:

INSPECTION
El Paso, Texas:
January 1, mid-afternoon

Officer Kurita was sitting on the porch of the Hinson house, but he rose to his feet when he saw Alvarez pull to the curb and park behind the truck with the Webb Engineering sign. Alvarez told Cotton to "stay" in a stern voice as he got out of the car, and slammed the door shut before she could follow him out. Maybe he was getting the hang of this dog obedience stuff.

Kurita came down the walk to meet them. "We finished the neighborhood canvas," he began without preface, "but we got zip. Lots of people are gone for the holidays, so we'll come back and hit it again tomorrow. Everyone else has finished up inside. I'm just waiting for the engineer to get done looking around down in the basement."

"What I'd like to know is how he got started," said Alvarez.

"He gave me your card, and told me he'd been asked to look around. I've got the card right here." He started fishing in his pocket.

Alvarez waved his efforts away. "Who did he say asked him to look around?"

Kurita looked dubiously at Alvarez. "It *was* you, wasn't it?"

"P-pretty smooth," contributed Scott.

"Stay here," Alvarez told Kurita. "Don't let anyone else in the basement, even if they wave my birth certificate in front of your face." Scott trailed after him to the side door, down the steps, and across the basement to the doorway that led into the room.

A short, dark-haired Hispanic man was standing in the room with his back to Alvarez, studying the fallen column at his feet. He wasn't wearing a hard hat. "Who the hell are you, and what are you doing here?" asked Alvarez.

"Who the hell are you?" countered the man, spinning around, and part of Alvarez's question was answered. He recognized Emmett Delgado, a structural engineer who, in a drunken rage, had once threatened Tory Travers.

Subsequently, Delgado became a long-shot suspect in a murder case, and in order to check his alibi, Alvarez had gone to see him in an alcohol abuse treatment center. It had been a brief encounter, since the visit quickly deteriorated into a shouting match between Delgado and the wife who had committed him. Alvarez didn't see any sign of recognition on Delgado's face.

He flashed his shield. "I'm Detective Alvarez, and this is my partner, Scott Faulkner." Scott had managed to find a hard hat somewhere, and was still adjusting it while he looked at the collapsed ceiling above them. "This is a crime scene, and you have no business being here."

"I'm Emmett Delgado, structural engineer, and I'm here at the request of Ryan Hinson," stated Delgado flatly, not backing off a bit. Scott stopped looking at the ceiling and raised his eyebrows. Alvarez could tell he recognized the name. "I told Mr. Hinson that no one would have access to the house until it was cleared by our department."

Delgado shrugged. "Ryan explained the situation to me. You're not by any chance an expert in structures, are you?"

"Is English your second language, or something? *Yo pregunto y usted contesta.* So what's it going to take to get you out of here?"

Delgado gave Alvarez a look worthy of a cockroach running across a dirt floor in a *barrio*. "I don't know what the hell *your* native language is, but I don't speak Spanish. Mr. Hinson is concerned about the possibility of further damage. Someone needs to determine if there's a chance that more of the ceiling will come down, and I'm that someone."

That had the effect of starting Scott looking up again, one hand firmly on his hard hat, to make sure it didn't fall off as he twisted his head into a ninety degree angle with his neck.

"You don't have the authority to make decisions like that," said Alvarez.

"And you don't know what you're talking about. I'm bound by ethics to ensure public safety."

"Christ, that sounds like a line you've been rehearsing. This isn't a public building, in case you haven't noticed."

"How many city employees have been in and out of here, including you and your partner? Or do you really think a thick skull makes you immune to falling objects?"

"You're way beyond any authority you may think you have, Mr. Delgado. You're interfering with a criminal investigation."

"Exactly what crime has been committed here?" countered Delgado.

Alvarez had an urge to answer, "That's for me to know and for you to find out," but he didn't think it would help. Instead he said, "You're trespassing. And that's just a start."

Delgado narrowed his eyes at Alvarez. Since his eyes were small and relatively closely spaced to begin with, it wasn't a pretty sight. "Webb Engineering is under contract to the city. Why don't you call the head of the Building Department and find out if he wants me out here or not?"

"If you're the expert, what have you f-found out?" asked Scott suddenly. Maybe he'd decided that playing the good cop would get them out of the room sooner.

Delgado looked at Faulkner, as if considering whether Scott rated the effort of an answer. "This is the result of faulty construction without benefit of engineering design or inspection," he said finally. "Ryan told me he didn't know about any of this. If there was no building permit, then no one reviewed the plans. There wasn't enough support for the ceiling, so it fell down." He looked at Alvarez. "Got it?"

Alvarez didn't get it by a long shot, but he decided to adopt Scott's strategy. If an asshole was standing in the middle of your crime scene, why not pump him for information? "Why wasn't there a collapse before?" he asked.

There was that look again. "There used to be a bearing wall down the middle of this room. It was removed so that the room could be configured in this fashion, for whatever reason. The column was obviously an afterthought."

"How can you tell that?"

"Listen, I've wasted enough time talking to you two, and it hasn't been a pleasant experience. I'll issue a report to my client. If he gives you a copy, you can read through it as many times as you need in order to understand what I'm talking about. I'm done here." Suddenly Scott was standing in the doorway, blocking Delgado's exit.

Alvarez was starting to get really pissed off. "Two people died down here," he said. "We don't know how they died, or why, but our job is to find out. We can take your word that you have business being here, or we can take you downtown while we check it out. If we do, we'll need to run your name, see if you have any prior offenses, stuff like drunken driving, assault, and all that."

Delgado stared hard at him, obviously trying to grasp something that was just at the fringes of his consciousness, but not succeeding. "What do you want to know?" he asked grudgingly.

"How do you know the column was an afterthought?"

"Because when you see a column smack dab in the middle of a room, someone screwed up. Unless there are six matching ones, and it looks like some architect's vision of something that will get him on the cover of *Architectural Digest*."

"So what happened?"

"The column collapsed and the ceiling fell in. Remember? I told you that already."

Alvarez took a deep breath. "I thought if something collapsed it would crumble, or break. The column looks in pretty good shape to me."

"Yeah, except for the fact that it's on the floor instead of supporting the ceiling, it looks great."

Alvarez wondered if a drink would improve Delgado's disposition. "So why is it on the floor?" he persisted.

Delgado gave an enormous sigh. "There's something called rolling. It happens mostly with beams, but it can happen with narrow columns. How can I explain this in terms that you'll understand?"

"Talk slow," said Alvarez. "I'll raise my hand if you start to lose me."

"When the load is too much, the column can become unbalanced. It starts to roll. If it rolls enough, it can begin to shift. Maybe you might understand it as kind of popping out of place. Any further questions?"

Alvarez would have liked to ask Delgado how colorful his hallucinations were in detox, but he restrained himself. "How could something pop out of place if it was attached?"

"Because it wasn't attached, another sign that it was a last-minute addition. The column was probably scavenged from somewhere—it sure as hell doesn't match anything else. Whoever built this room got worried about deflection in the ceiling. The column was put in to fix the problem, and cut to fit. That way, its position could be adjusted visually. The molding at the top and bottom was attached to the column itself, not to the floor or the ceiling." Delgado pointed with his foot to the intact molding at the bottom of the column.

"How would you have solved the problem?"

"What problem?"

"Constructing this room."

"I would never have removed the bearing wall."

"Then you couldn't have built this room the way it is, right? So how would you do it?"

Delgado looked at Alvarez in exasperation. "The answer to that question is too complex for you to understand."

"Try me."

"You'd probably need a total renovation of the framework that serves as the ceiling to this basement."

"Would that be a lot of work?"

"Yes, that would be a hell of a lot of work."

"The kind of work that would be hard to conceal from neighbors?"

"Yes. You'd be tearing out and rebuilding major portions of the existing house. Now, if you don't have any more questions, I'm leaving."

"I do have more questions. Is there any other possible explanation for the collapse?"

"Like what, a high wind? We don't usually see high winds in basements."

With an effort, Alvarez let that one blow right over his head. "Could someone have pulled or pushed the column out of place?"

"Why would anyone want to do that?

"Is it possible?"

"I already explained what happened here. If you want to engage in theoretical fantasies, do it on your own time."

"So you're absolutely sure that the column rolled and that's what made everything fall down?"

"I'm absolutely sure."

"You've been here, what, ten, fifteen minutes? And you know this for sure?"

"I'm an expert. This is not a complicated problem."

Alvarez reached into his memory of his discussion with Ryan Hinson. "And aren't your conclusions in Hinson's best interest?"

"I don't know what you're talking about."

"Isn't it beneficial to Hinson, from an insurance standpoint, to conclude that the collapse was caused by faulty construction?"

"I cooperate with you, and you question my professional ethics? I'm out of here. Shouldn't the two of you be out apprehending criminals?"

Alvarez didn't see much point in a discussion about professional ethics when there were more burning issues on his mind. "Don't ever use my name to get access to a crime scene again," he said.

"I don't see a crime scene."

"One more thing: We'd appreciate it if you didn't discuss this with anyone."

"You threaten me, insult me, and then you ask me to help you out? I'll talk to anybody I want."

"We're in the middle of an investigation here, Mr. Delgado. We cooperate with you, you cooperate with us. That way, you're being a good citizen, instead of a worthless *hijo de puta*, if you follow me."

"You can't talk to me like that."

"I thought you didn't *hablas Español*."

"I'm out of here, you SOB. I'm warning you that it's not safe for you to be in this room, and I'm telling the Building Department to salvage this site as soon as possible to prevent further collapse." Delgado gave Alvarez a triumphant glance that would have done a six-year-old proud, and pushed his way around Scott to exit the room.

"I always hate it when someone curses in acronyms," said Alvarez in disgust. "What a prick. A good Anglo Saxon description, *creo que sí*? I think he would have been better off staying soused."

"He was the structural engineer for the f-f-football stadium, right?"

"You got it. Do you think he has a leg to stand on with this public safety shit?"

"I don't know. He made it sound pretty good."

"You like standing in that doorway, *ese*?"

"I m-moved here to block his exit."

"Why didn't I think of that?"

"He said you shouldn't be in the room."

"I'm thinking."

"He said it was d-dangerous, remember?"

"I do my best thinking in dangerous situations. Christ, CSU is going to be really pissed off if they have to compete with a salvage operation."

"No kidding. I've already thought: I think we n-need a second opinion."

"Great idea."

"Do we know any structural engineers?"

"Nobody loves a wise ass."

"It's New Year's Day. We not only need a structural engineer, we need her home phone number. How will we ever manage?"

"Have you ever noticed how your stutter disappears when you're giving me shit?"

"So do you have her home phone number?"

"Yeah. I don't want to use the phone here; CSU would really have my ass. Don't even suggest your parents' house. I can't take your mother twice in one day."

"That m-makes two of us. Mrs. Edgerton will let you use her phone. She always liked me."

Alvarez followed Scott out and around the side of the house. A TV van was now parked behind Alvarez's car. Cotton was up on the back seat, barking madly at a blond reporter in a vibrant red sweater, who was pushing a microphone into Delgado's face.

"Fuck," said Alvarez. He could only hope that Cotton would screw up the background noise control. "I'd like to kill Delgado, but we don't have time for public service."

"Yeah. Probably wouldn't l-look good on TV, either."

"There is that," Alvarez admitted. "Think he realizes that's a concealed room in the basement?"

"I don't know, but if Ryan Hinson told him, it's not information that's going to be c-c-concealed for long."

"*No me digas*. It's too bad we didn't tell him about the kid and the multiple IDs. We could have watched it all on the six o'clock news."

"Come on, we'll go around the b-back way," said Scott, and Alvarez followed him over the wall into the neighbor's yard, hoping that the Edgertons didn't have a penchant for Rottweilers. They didn't, and were pleased to offer the use of their phone.

"I'll be back," said Scott, as Alvarez fished a worn business card out of the back of his wallet and began to dial.

"It's not like it's a private call, man," muttered Alvarez.

FRAMEWORK FOR DEATH 87

"I want t-to make sure Mrs. Edgerton meets Delgado," said Scott with a grin. "She's wants him to look at the c-cracks in her wall. Be a shame for him to turn d-down an old lady in front of a camera." "Good man," said Alvarez in approval, and gave him a thumbs up. He wished he'd thought of it himself.

Alvarez was just about to give up when someone answered the phone. "Travers residence. *Próspero Año*," a female voice said heartily above the background noise of people talking. Much too heartily for the owner of the Travers residence, thought Alvarez, dredging up a name from his memory. "Sylvia? Is Tory there?" "This is Sylvia. Who's calling?" "This is David Alvarez." Sylvia's joy at hearing his name literally vibrated through the line. Alvarez held the phone a few inches from his ear. "Dah-veed! *Cómo le ha ido, compadre?*" "*Puro dale dale.* Is Tory there?" "Tory's here. We're all here. There's even a girl with Cody. She was a boy before I got here, but I fixed that. No mistaking her for a boy any more, *ese.*" She began to giggle, and then to hiccup. Sylvia had obviously been celebrating the New Year for a while. "Sylvia, is Tory there?" he asked patiently for the third time. It didn't do any good to be anything but patient with Tory's flamboyant secretary, for in Alvarez's opinion, Sylvia Maestes rated as a force of nature right up there with hurricanes and tornados. But sex change operations? "Uh-oh," Sylvia switched to a whisper, "Lonnie's here, too." "I don't want to talk to Lonnie." "That's good, because I don't think he likes you too much."

"Sylvia, just put Tory on the line."

The phone clanked down on the other end. "Tory, you'll never guess who it is," he heard Sylvia call in a tone that would wake the dead. "David Alvarez is on the phone, and he wants to talk to you."

The background noise ceased.

Finally, he heard the receiver being picked up. "This is Tory." The voice was just as cool, cultured, and collected as he remembered it.

"Has Sylvia been drinking?" he asked.

There was another pause. "She's right," Tory said finally. "It really is you. Who else would call up after five months to ask if Sylvia's been drinking?"

"You know how long it's been?"

There was another pause. "I was in physical therapy after my arm got out of the cast. They told me it would be five months before it was fully healed."

"And is it healed now?"

"This is a funny time to call inquiring after my health, Detective Alvarez."

"David."

"I get out of the habit of using first names when I never talk to the person."

"If I didn't know you better, Tory, I'd say you sound pissed."

"You never called."

This time the pause was on his end. "I don't suppose it would have ever occurred to you to call me." There was no answer to that. He hadn't expected one. "Okay, fair enough. I thought about calling you, a lot. But your life is so nice and neat, wrapped up like a little package, and every time I started to call you, I knew that if I did, things wouldn't be simple any more. So each time I thought of calling you, I put down the phone." Alvarez was amazed that the words coming out his mouth were pretty close to the truth. He hoped they sounded as good as he thought they did.

He could feel her digesting that, turning it over in her head. "But not this time. Why?" She had always been one to come right to the point.

"I'd like you to come look at something for me."

"Some etchings, perhaps?" she asked drily.

"It's not like that." He heard how that sounded. "I mean, it could be like that, I'd like it to be like that, but it isn't like that. Right now it isn't like that. Maybe it could be like that later."

There was a pause. "You're right, this isn't simple," she finally said. "I have no idea what you're talking about."

He would have pounded the receiver against Mrs. Edgerton's antique table if he thought it would help. "I have a room. A room with a collapsed column and a collapsed ceiling, and two dead women. One was the owner of the house; we haven't been able to identify the other one. An engineer has been here, and he said the collapse was due to shoddy construction. But it doesn't feel right to me. I'd like you to take a look at it."

"Is the column big enough to hide a body in it?" she asked. Her voice wasn't quite so crisp now.

"No," he said firmly. "It's a rectangular wooden column, about six inches in width, maybe eighteen inches in length. Definitely not enough room to hide a body."

"Well, that's good, because I don't think I could do that again."

"You shouldn't have to. The bodies are gone, the place is secured, and all I want is a second opinion about what happened."

"Where is this house?" He told her. "Do you want me to look at it sometime this week?"

"Sooner."

"Tomorrow?"

"Today."

"Damn it," she said, anger finally overcoming the cool distance in her voice. "You call me up on New Year's Day after months of silence and expect me to drop everything and rush to answer your beck and call? You have a hell of a lot of nerve, David Alvarez. What makes you think I would do something like that?"

"Because Emmett Delgado was here trespassing on my crime scene, saying he had an ethical obligation to be here. He looked around for maybe ten minutes before he told me in no uncertain terms what had happened and that he's going to recommend the crime scene be turned over to salvage tomorrow, that's why."

"Jazz is over here. He's even mostly sober. I'll bring him with me. We'll be there in thirty minutes."

"Not thirty, Tory. It's New Year's Day and you'd have to speed to make it here in thirty—" He was talking to a dead line. And he hadn't even gotten a chance to ask about the sex change operation.

CHAPTER EIGHT:

MORE INSPECTION
El Paso, Texas:
Sunday, January 1, late afternoon

Alvarez, Faulkner, and Kurita sat on the porch while the blond reporter finished talking to Emmett Delgado. Fortunately the late afternoon sun warmed the air enough to make the wait comfortable, because it was a while before the reporter completed her interview. Alvarez sure hoped Delgado would be gone before Tory arrived. One homicide on New Year's Day was enough to deal with.

After Delgado finally drove off, the reporter headed toward the porch. She knew Alvarez and Faulkner, and was neither surprised nor daunted by Alvarez's repeated "No comment" in reply to her queries. From the questions she asked, it appeared that Emmett Delgado had spilled everything he knew, and then some.

"No comment is pretty bland for a situation like this." The blond favored the three men with a high-voltage media smile. "I've got a pretty good story going already, but it would sure help to get official verification."

Alvarez shook his head. "You'll have to decide all on your own whether that guy knows what he's talking about, or whether he just wants a little media attention." Sitting on the porch, surveying the vista in front of him, made him feel magnanimous. He rocked his chair back on two legs and wondered what it must be like to own a piece of property like this one. "Be a shame to be the only news service broadcasting facts that aren't true," he added.

The reporter's lips formed a pout, small enough to let them

know that a word from any of them could easily bring back the smile. "There's no way I'm going to keep a lid on this waiting for you guys to give me some answers. I've got enough right now to make the lead for tonight's news, unless somebody decides to spray the Sun Bowl revelers with an assault rifle."

"Now there's a thought, sunshine," said Alvarez. "Bet all the dead people would be happy to know they'd contributed to your career."

"Give me a break, Alvarez. If it wasn't New Year's Day, you'd have reporters crawling all over the place."

"*Es verdad, chica*," agreed Alvarez, bringing the conversation around to the question he wanted to ask. "So how come you're here?"

"Come on. I'm not so green that I'm going to tip my sources to you. At least, not unless there's something in it for me."

"Well, *chica*, my partner's a married man, and Kurita here, he's not dry behind the ears yet. But I'm always willing to consider trading my body for information." He gave her his most winning smile. She didn't even break her conversational stride.

"I'll be back, Alvarez. You and Faulkner catch some pretty high profile cases, and that's what this one looks like. I'll be keeping my eye on you." The smile was back now, looking more than a little predatory this time.

"*Es un favor que usted me hace*," Alvarez said cordially to her back.

"That view is just as nice going as it was coming," commented Scott, stutter-free.

"Wow," said Kurita. "Does she follow you guys around a lot?"

"You married?" Alvarez asked Kurita.

"No, sir," the young officer answered. "But I have a girl friend."

"That's too bad," said Alvarez. "I kind of thought the medical examiner liked you. While my partner is experiencing brain fade, let's talk over where we go from here." Kurita's face lit up.

"I want to know where the m-money goes," said Scott, never taking his eyes off the reporter as she climbed into the van.

"You'll probably have to jerk the attorney's chain to get him to cooperate."

"Maybe the lawyer's a 'she,'" said Kurita helpfully.

"What do you think we are, Officer Kurita?" asked Alvarez. "Sexist, insensitive, chauvinistic men?"

"Yeah," said Scott, eyes on the disappearing van.

"Note, Officer Kurita, the sign of a good detective. See how he keeps his eyes on the subject until she's out of sight."

"Kenneth Herneese," said Scott succinctly, without consulting his notes. "Lenora Hinson's attorney. Unlikely to b-be female."

"And what else can we get from Herneese?" Alvarez prompted.

"Information about the other attorney. The one who helped Mrs. Hinson take c-control of the trust funds."

"See, Kurita, there's hope for you yet. My partner is living proof that marriage doesn't totally rot the brain."

"The other money c-connection is Pinnacle," continued Scott, unperturbed. "We need to know if they're in trouble."

"So you cover the attorneys and the bankers tomorrow."

"And what will you c-c-cover?"

"You'll notice he stutters more when he gets resentful," said Alvarez for Kurita's benefit. "The boyfriend, *esse*. Never overlook the boyfriend, Officer Kurita."

"Especially if you get a chance to t-talk about the girl-friend," muttered Scott. "I don't know why you always g-g-get the sex angles."

"It's like spiritual gifts, man. We all have different talents."

"What can I do?" asked Kurita eagerly.

"Finish canvassing the neighborhood," Alvarez and Faulkner answered simultaneously as a shiny white RX zipped up behind Alvarez's car, coming to a squeaking halt inches behind his back bumper.

"Here comes the cavalry," said Scott.

"Wow," said Kurita.

Alvarez was already off the porch and walking toward the car. A wiry Hispanic man climbed out from the passenger's side as Tory, clad in blue jeans and a brown down jacket, emerged from the driver's seat. She pushed her sunglasses up into her dark hair as she surveyed the house, seemingly oblivious to Alvarez as he walked up, making a show of looking at his watch.

"*Más vale tarde que nunca*," said Alvarez.

Tory's dark shiny hair missed skimming her shoulders by a couple of inches as she turned to look at Alvarez. It was shorter than it had been five months ago. The light dusting of freckles just under her eyes was like he remembered, but there was no way to recall exactly how blue her eyes were unless you were looking at them.

Unlike the blond reporter, she didn't try a smiling approach. "Don't start with me," she said bluntly. "If you remember, my Spanish is fluent, and I understand every nasty thing you say."

"I remember all of it," he said simply.

She met his eyes for just a moment, then glanced toward the other man standing beside her. "Detective Alvarez, this is Jesus Alfonso Rodriguez. He's my lead field inspector."

Jesus Alfonso Rodriguez took Alvarez's hand in a firm grip. "Call me Jazz. I left a good bottle of whiskey to come see this, so let's get on with it, man."

"Not without hard hats," said Tory firmly.

Tory didn't want to start in the basement. Alvarez wondered why he was surprised, since she never did things the way he expected. Sure enough, she provided hard hats for everyone from the back of the RX, and there was even one hard hat left over. Then she started giving orders.

There were code books, surveyor tapes, callipers, cameras, clipboards, and calculators that she wanted carried to the porch. She started on the first floor, in a room adjacent to the entry hall. She lay on her stomach and got as close to the area of collapse as she could get, taking pictures and jotting down notes, asking Alvarez to measure things that didn't seem even vaguely related to the destruction below. Jazz took Faulkner and Kurita down to the basement and put them to work in a similar fashion, inspecting the outer part of the basement.

After twenty minutes of acting as a gofer and watching Tory skootch around on her stomach ever closer to the gaping opening in the entry hall, Alvarez asked if she wanted him to hold her ankles; he didn't want her to end up like Kurita's partner, Stan.

"No, I don't want you to hold my ankles. What I want you to do is go into the next room and get a measurement on that interior wall next to the entry hall. See if you can determine where the studs are located."

"*Estoy aquí, quierida.*"

She didn't even bother to turn and look at him. "The studs in the walls, Alvarez. You know, you pound on the wall and figure out how far apart they are."

"Call me David. You used to, back when someone was trying to kill you."

"Okay, David. Go measure the interior wall and tell me how far apart the studs are."

"You're so attractive when you're giving orders. Not to mention crawling around on the floor in tight jeans."

That got her attention. She scooted to a sitting position and turned to look at him. "My jeans are not tight. You called, I came. What's your problem?"

"Definitely not your jeans." She glared at him. "I want to ask you a question, that's all."

"Does it have to do with this?"

"I think so."

"Okay, ask."

"Were you in the bottom half of your graduating class?"

"What? I graduated with high honors, not that it's any of your business. What are you getting at?"

"Well, we've been crawling around up here with a tape and camera for almost half an hour, and you haven't even been in the basement yet. Delgado was here less than fifteen minutes, no books, no tapes, no cameras, no nothing. Not even a hard hat. After just ten minutes he was able to tell me what caused the collapse."

"Emmett Delagado is an asshole."

"You used to date him."

"Christ. Are we really going to do this? I went out with him a couple of times when I was a freshman in college. That's not exactly what I would call a significant relationship."

"He wouldn't agree."

Tory glared at him. "You wouldn't, you *couldn't* discuss me with Emmett Delgado."

"Never."

"Then what the hell is this about?"

"You also slugged Delgado in the face in front of a whole bunch of people. Then you broke into his office. That qualifies as some type of relationship, *que sí*?"

"What's your point?"

"I want to make sure you differentiate here. I'm not interested in your personal opinion of Emmett Delgado. I'm interested in your professional opinion."

"Then listen carefully. My professional opinion is that Emmett Delgado is a real, genuine, certified asshole. Emmett Delgado couldn't design his way out of a septic tank. He got his PE license in a cereal box."

"But how does he rate compared to all the other men you've kissed?"

She threw her clipboard at him, but he ducked it easily. "Do you know how much it bothers me that you did a deep background check on me?"

Alvarez wondered if they could hear her in the basement. "Just checking for a reaction."

"Oh, you'll get a reaction all right. I'm really into total humiliation."

"You don't need to be ashamed of your past."

"I'm not talking about my past. I'm talking about a certain hot-shot police detective, not following procedure, out of his jurisdiction, without backup, being held at gunpoint in a construction trailer. Does that sound familiar?"

"That does qualify for total humiliation," he conceded. "Isn't it nice we both have something to hold over each other?"

"Only a low life would think like that. I'm done here; I'm going downstairs into the room where the ceiling collapsed. Get the measurements for me, okay? And David?"

"*Sí, quierida?*"

"Don't fall into the basement while you're doing it."

After a repeat performance in the concealed room, they all gathered around Tory as she sat cross-legged with her code manuals and a calculator outside the door that led into the basement room. She reminded him of a crime scene technician, grousing about how she hadn't gotten a look at the collapse until after several other people had been on the scene.

"Kind of like sloppy seconds," Alvarez tossed off without thinking, earning a sharp look from Jazz.

"Hey, man, that's no way to talk in front of Tory."

"Sorry," Alvarez said immediately. Tory didn't even look up. She hunched over the clipboard in her lap, pushing buttons on her calculator and writing down numbers. Her hair fell forward and almost obscured her face. Alvarez felt like they were gathered around an exotic fortune-teller.

"It's okay, man," said Jazz in a low voice. "You work on the streets, you talk like the streets, I understand that. But not in front of Tory."

It took Alvarez a moment to remember what they were talking about. To cover, he sought Jazz's opinion on a man-to-man basis. "So, you think she's any good at this?" he asked, matching Jazz's tone.

"She's the best, man. Careful, but she's got intuition. Like detectives, *que sí?* Intuition is important to an engineer." Alvarez couldn't think of an appropriate reply. He personally thought the idea of engineering intuition sounded at least as scary as some criminals he had encountered.

"And she's been working with me for years, man," Jazz continued. "I taught her everything I know."

"So what's she going to tell me?" Alvarez asked.

"This wasn't no damn collapse, man."

Alvarez looked at Jazz in surprise just as Tory raised her head. "I don't see how there could have been a collapse," she said.

"Hot damn," said Scott.

"Wow," breathed Kurita.

"You're sure there weren't any high winds in here?" asked Alvarez. Tory frowned at him. "An in-joke," he said. "You had to be there."

"There is absolutely no reason, given the materials and the loads, to expect a collapse."

"You mean the column didn't roll?" asked Alvarez, trying out his new vocabulary.

"Give me a break. The column didn't roll. It had to have been moved out of place. Probably pulled."

"You're kidding."

"Do you think I would drive all the way down here and spend an hour crawling around this house, to be kidding about what I'm telling you?"

"And I left a good bottle of whiskey," Jazz reminded them.

"Okay, so you don't think the column rolled. What makes you think it was pulled out?"

"I'll show you." she told him. "But put your hard hats back on."

Everyone but Jazz followed her back into the room. Alvarez had a feeling that Jazz already knew what she was going to show them.

Tory walked to a point about three feet up from the bottom of the column. "Look," she said. Alvarez, Kurita and Faulkner took turns getting down on their knees to look under the column where she was pointing.

There was a faint pencilled x-mark on the floor, almost indistinguishable from a network of scratches. The difference was that the scratches were all parallel, while the x-mark was formed with two perpendicular lines.

"I think that indicates where the column was originally placed," said Tory. "The scratch marks are probably from the bottom being pulled out of place, somehow. But how could you do that and not bring the ceiling down on yourself?"

"P-probably with a rope," said Scott. Tory rewarded him with a smile fit for a stellar student. Alvarez figured Scott had come up with the idea faster than anyone else simply because he wanted the hell out of the room.

"Yeah," said Tory slowly. "If you put a rope around the end of the column, and stood outside the doorway," she pointed to where Jazz was standing, "you could pull the column down, but be outside the room when the collapse occurs."

"And after everything fell down, you c-could step inside just far enough to untie the rope," said Scott, thinking it out.

Alvarez had an sudden urge to kiss Tory, but since it wasn't the first time, he was accustomed to ignoring it. "Who would know to do something like this?" he asked instead.

"Whoever built the room," Tory answered with conviction. "Find the person who built the room. That shouldn't be too hard to do. Check with the Building Department."

"The Building Department has no record of this room ever being constructed," said Alvarez. "Delgado said that was the cause of the collapse, the lack of review of the design."

Tory looked at the three police officers. "I don't know how to break it to you guys, but the Building Department is not really in the business of catching design errors. They're far better known for taking bribes, but don't quote me on that. If every design error they missed resulted in a collapse, you wouldn't have time to investigate homicides."

"Wow," said Kurita.

Kurita seemed as mesmerized with Tory as he had with the blond reporter. It was not a trend that Alvarez liked. "Kurita, I want the column analyzed for rope fibers, first thing."

"You got it." This sounded a lot more exciting to Officer Kurita than canvassing a neighborhood where the median age was over sixty.

"I really appreciate your help," said Alvarez. "I'll see about getting you paid for your time. If your hunch about the rope fibers turns out to be right, there won't be a problem."

"It's not a hunch," said Tory, "and I'll probably end up getting paid anyhow."

"What do you mean?" asked Alvarez. So much for taking control of the conversation.

"I do work for most of the insurance companies that write homeowners policies in El Paso," she said. "I can guarantee you they won't take Emmett Delgado's report at face value."

"Wow," said Kurita. Alvarez was beginning to suspect that this was his favorite word. "Sort of like dueling engineers."

Tory blinked.

"Forgive him, he's young," Alvarez said, as they filed out and up the stairs, carrying the equipment. Alvarez was the first around the corner of the house, turning back to say something to Tory, when he saw the microphone out of the corner of his eye and heard the mechanical whir of a television camera.

"Ah, shit," said Faulkner.

"She said she'd be back," the ever-helpful Kurita reminded Alvarez. At least he hadn't said "Wow."

"So is this a repeat of the dynamic duo that cracked the stadium murder case?" the blond asked, right on cue.

"No comment," said Alvarez, turning to put his arm around Tory and shield her from a camera's bright light.

"This is Tory Travers, the engineer who was involved in the sensational discovery of a body in a stadium column." The blond didn't seem to need to breathe like normal people. There was no discernable break between sentences. "How do you feel about working with Detective Alvarez again, Ms. Travers?"

Tory, Alvarez, and Faulkner headed for Alvarez's car, while Kurita started shooing the reporters off the property. Jazz grabbed the blond's microphone and said distinctly, "You must not hear too good, lady. The man said no comment." Then he pulled the cord out of the bottom of the microphone.

Alvarez was feeling fonder of Jazz by the minute. He shoved Tory into the front seat of his car, shielding her from the camera with his body until the door was securely shut. Then he went around to climb in the driver's seat. Faulkner and Jazz piled into the back seat with a jubilant Cotton, while Kurita withdrew to his command post on the porch. The only problem with this arrangement was that the reporters had every right to wait on the street outside the car, and that's what they were doing.

"Did you get demoted?" Tory asked Alvarez as soon as he got in the car. She seemed to be taking the race to shelter in stride.

"No, why?" Did she know something he didn't?

"You used to drive a bronze Corvette."

"It's in the shop. This is a rental car, and I didn't pick the color," said Alvarez, trying to figure out what their next move should be.

Cotton had taken a liking to Alvarez, but she was absolutely wild about Jazz. "What the hell is this?" asked Jazz, pushing the dog away, trying to avoid being licked to death.

"It's a dog. A Hungarian dog." Alvarez had a sudden inspiration. He turned to Tory. "I got it for you, to say thanks for helping us out."

"Man, that's weak," said Jazz, as he unsuccessfully tried to remove Cotton from his lap.

"That's convenient," said Tory calmly. "Where did you get this Hungarian dog?"

"Well, it belonged to someone else," Alvarez admitted.

"Like who?"

"The woman who owned this house."

"You mean the one who was squashed by the column?" asked Jazz. "Man, that is *really* weak. And this is one friendly dog."

"I think it's one friendly dog that needs to p-p-pee," offered Scott.

"Hell, man, then you let it sit on your lap," said Jazz, trying to push Cotton over toward Scott.

"Oh, for heaven's sake," said Tory. "There's no need to make the poor animal suffer. I'll take it out."

"No," said Alvarez and Faulkner vehemently.

"What's it going to do, bite me?"

"No, but the press might," said Alvarez. He could see reality dawn on Tory. All he had to do was watch her face. Silence hung heavy in the car. The most audible sound was Cotton's heavy breathing.

"Shit," said Jazz after a moment. "I'll take the damn dog outside. I don't think they're going to mess with me." He did, and they didn't.

"I'll make the news again, right?" Tory asked, watching Cotton relieve herself not two feet from Alvarez's car.

"I didn't think this would happen," said Alvarez. "For what it's worth, I'm sorry." Tory went right on looking out the window.

Jazz and Cotton climbed back in the car. "Hey man, that worked good. What's the plan now, *jefe?*"

Alvarez realized that Jazz wasn't talking to him.

"We need to find whoever built that room," said Tory.

Alvarez picked his words carefully. "There's no 'we' to this, Tory. I really appreciate your help, but that's as far as it goes for your involvement in this case."

Tory kept looking out the window. "You don't know anything about local contractors. I do."

Alvarez always hated it when she said something overwhelmingly logical. "It's not that simple, Tory. There are a lot of other things involved here."

"Things you can't tell me about, right?"

Alvarez wondered what Tory could be looking at so intently, since the car windows were beginning to fog. Four people and one dog added up to a lot of exhaled breaths. The car was beginning to resemble a purple steam bath from Hell, complete with a distinct doggie odor. "That's right," he said carefully.

"Well, if it's simplicity you're after, let's try a simple scenario," Tory said to the window. "What if an insurance company wants me to track down the original builder, see if the builder has some type of insurance coverage?"

"Hey man, remember when you asked me if she was any good?" contributed Jazz gleefully. Pulling the cord from the reporter's microphone seemed to have inspired him. "She's got you there," he concluded triumphantly.

Tory looked at Alvarez then. "You call me up, beg me to come look at your goddamn crime scene, and you have the nerve to ask Jazz if I'm any good?" she asked.

"G-g-good help is hard t-to f-find," said Scott. Alvarez turned and looked at him. Scott spread his hands as if to say "I tried."

Alvarez looked back at Tory. "You don't know what you're getting into. You may be a great engineer, but believe me, crime doesn't have simple solutions." Then his beeper went off. He automatically checked the phone number shown on the display.

"Don't tell me, let me guess," said Tory. "Now that you've given me your speech about how all this is too complicated for me to understand, much less figure out, never mind the fact I've given you more information than you've gotten from anyone else so far, you suddenly have to go see a man about a dog. How convenient."

Alvarez noted that Tory could compete with the blond reporter for making long speeches without taking a breath, once you got her going. "Actually, I have to go see a woman about a baby," he said, "seeing as you're such a stickler for accuracy." Then he had an idea. It was almost as lame as trying to pay off Tory with the dog in his back seat, but at least it was an idea. "Okay," he said. "You have a point. I have to go check on something having to do with this case. I'll take you with me, see what you think."

It was rewarding to see Tory's mouth drop open. Alvarez turned to look at Scott. "I need to check on things at Mt. Franklin Hospital," he told his partner. "I'll take Tory in my car, so the TV people won't get another shot at her. You and Jazz follow me in Tory's car, Okay? Then they can drive home from there."

Scott looked at him like he had lost his mind. "Okay," he said dubiously. It was a good thing he didn't comment further, since Scott was responsible for the fact that Alvarez was not only driving around in a purple car, he was driving around in a purple car with a white fluffy dog in the back seat.

Tory fished her keys out of her jeans and handed them to Scott.

"Hey boss, why are you giving the keys to him?" asked Jazz.

"Because of the whiskey bottle under the passenger seat," said Tory.

"Man, she's got you there," intoned Alvarez. "And all this time I thought it was the dog's breath."

"If I'm no gonna drive, there's no reason for me to ride in the other car, man. I think you're trying to get rid of me," grumbled Jazz.

"I am," said Alvarez. "But consider what you left under the seat in the other car."

"That's a good point," Jazz conceded. "But we're not taking the damn dog with us in Tory's car, and that's final."

"You're sure she peed out there?"

"Shit yes, I'm sure. I wonder how you guys manage on your own."

"Are we ready?" asked Alvarez.

"What are you waiting for, for us to synchronize our watches?" replied Tory.

Alvarez sighed. "This sure ain't like no television show," muttered Jazz as he climbed out of the car, using one hand to open the car door and the other to restrain Cotton from following him. Alvarez refrained from pointing out that the TV crew waiting on the street had already made it exactly that.

It took ten minutes to get from Rim Road to Mt. Franklin General Hospital. Alvarez pulled into a space in the parking lot. The mustard-colored stucco building, set into the side of the mountain, was a dichotomy in an otherwise residential area.

"I never knew this was here," said Tory, breaking the silence that had dominated the ride.

"It's an old hospital, built in the nineteen twenties. There's no room to expand the facility and bring in a lot of fancy equipment, so there's no emergency room, and only routine procedures are performed here. This hospital serves a lot of poor people, a lot of Hispanics. This is where my sister and I were born," he added as an afterthought.

"Seeing where you were born is related to your investigation? This feels like a set up."

"I told you about the two dead women found in that room, but I didn't tell you everything. There's a child involved. She's here."

Tory's eyes widened. "A child was in that room when the ceiling came down?"

"Keep in mind that this information is confidential. The kid was found unharmed in an upstairs bedroom. But she probably lost her mother in that basement, and she may be in danger if your theory about the column is correct."

"What has she told you?"

"Nothing. Child Services thinks she's about six months old. Not the best kind of witness."

"What happens to her?"

"I had her admitted here anonymously, and put under plain clothes guard. It's going to be an administrative nightmare to try to keep Child Services from leaking her whereabouts while we try to figure out who she is, but I've got friends on staff here that will help."

Tory thought this over. "I'm no expert on six-month-old abandoned babies. So my guess is that I'm supposed to go look at this little girl and then I won't want to find out who built that room."

"That's the general idea."

"That's incredibly lame."

He was saved from having to answer by the arrival of Tory's RX, the radio blaring a Mexican music station. Alvarez looked over and saw Jazz take a long swig from a bottle in a paper bag.

"What if I'm not going to change my mind?" Tory continued. "What if I won't go look at this child? What then?"

"I take you in at gunpoint?" Alvarez suggested. "Get the handcuffs out of the glove compartment and handcuff you? You know, I kind of like that idea."

She gave him an exasperated look, but he could tell she was hooked. Anyone who was a sucker for kids and animals could be handled if you played your cards right. "Okay, let's do it," she said. "But don't drag Jazz up there, okay? I don't want to have to deal with both of you at the same time. He only drinks a few times a year, but if you say something to me that he thinks is insulting, he's probably at the point where he'll challenge you to a duel, using switchblades."

"Been a long time since I used a switchblade; might be kind of nostalgic, but you're right, I don't have time for that now. Roll down your window and tell them to stay put for ten, fifteen minutes."

She did, and then they walked from the parking lot to the hospital entrance. Alvarez held a quiet conference with someone at the front desk, and made a phone call. Then he motioned Tory to the elevators. "Room Three-fourteen."

"Aren't you afraid I might divulge that information?"

"I've got too much to hold over you, *cara*. Did you know it wasn't possible for me to get through your police record in one sitting?"

She glared at him. "You know that's not true. And don't call me *cara*."

They got off the elevator and started down the hall, passing a young black woman in a white coat who did a double-take when she saw Alvarez. She was stunningly tall, even towering over Alvarez. The difference in heights didn't keep her from giving him an enthusiastic kiss.

"David, *cómo está*?" After the kiss, she started thumping Alvarez on the back. "Your little one was admitted under the name of Agatha Sayers. What do you think? Kind of appropriate, huh? Since she's part of a mystery."

"You're brilliant, Karen. But then you already know that. What do you have for me?" Alvarez deliberately caught Karen's hand in his. Many more friendly blows to the back and he was going to have a coughing fit, something he didn't want to do around Karen.

"She appears to be a normal Caucasian female, approximately six months of age. Slightly dehydrated and hungry when she got here. From her state and the state of her diapers, I'd say she'd been left alone somewhere between twelve and twenty-four hours."

"I always knew you'd make a great diaper detective. Anything that would help identify her?"

Karen shook her head regretfully. "You're out of luck there. Standard baby clothes, standard baby blanket. No jewelry. No noticeable identifying marks. In fact, I'm glad I caught you before you went in to see her and got all excited. We kind of felt bad for her, David, nobody here with her and no toys or anything."

"So what did you do, call up an escort service?"

"No, *cabrón*. One of the nurses went through the lost and found, dug up some things for her to play with. We found a steel rattle with a 'C' on it and a couple of stuffed animals, things other patients left behind. So don't go thinking it's stuff that came in with her."

"Thanks for warning me. I might have gotten all excited and thought the 'C' stood for Clue, and that could have been a devastating career move. How's the guard?"

"Where do you find these people? He looks like a zombie on steroids. I keep checking to see if he has a pulse."

Alvarez laughed. "Excitable people don't work out real well in undercover work, Karen. I'll vouch for the fact he has a pulse, so don't go playing doctor with him. What did you do with him?"

"You'll like it. Aggie's in a room at the end of the hall, so if someone goes all the way down the hall, we'll know to take a look at them. There's a waiting area there. I put your man in an orderly's uniform. He's sitting in the waiting area, reading a newspaper and drinking coffee. It's so foolproof, I can't tell him from the rest of our orderlies." She laughed at her own joke.

"Karen, thanks. I owe you."

"*De nada*. It's the other way around. Got to run, patients to see and all of that." And she was gone, without once acknowledging Tory's presence.

"You could have at least introduced me," said Tory, looking after her. "That was really rude."

"Karen's learned not to ask about what I'm doing and who I'm doing it with. If there's something she needs to know, I tell her."

"Who is she?"

"A damned good pediatrician, and a walking miracle. Used to be a gang banger." Tory turned to look at him. "Don't tell me I need to explain that to you."

"No, those of us with lengthy rap sheets know about things like that." He waited to see if she could let it go. She couldn't. "What happened?"

"She met me."

"Oh," said Tory.

"Not like that. I saw her around, saw her on the basketball courts when she wasn't getting into trouble. I took her to the walk-on tryouts at UTEP. They told her they'd give her a scholarship the next year if she'd get her GED. The rest is history. One small victory for us, no big loss for the gangs. There were plenty others immediately lined up to take her place."

"Oh," said Tory again.

"Kind of a far reach from the things you deal with, right?" he couldn't resist adding.

"Don't run it into the ground."

They reached the end of the hall, and the stocky orderly lounging there came to his feet, shaking hands with Alvarez.

"Officer Lowell, this is Tory Travers. She's an engineer who's giving us some help with the crime scene, so I'm taking her in to see the kid."

If Officer Lowell thought this was strange, he gave no sign of it. Instead, he gave an impassive nod, shook hands with Tory, resumed his seat and picked up the newspaper again.

"That was really stupid," Tory muttered. "What's he going to think, that I'm so dense I think the baby is part of the crime scene?"

"Jesus Christ, Tory. Would you stop acting like a woman? I don't introduce you, you get pissed, I do introduce you, you get pissed. Make up your mind."

But Tory was already staring at the dark-haired little girl asleep in a hospital crib. "She's just darling," she whispered. "Do you think I could pick her up?"

This wasn't on his agenda. What was she going to do, get mushy on him? "I don't see why not," he said gruffly.

"Don't talk so loud," she admonished him. She bent over and picked up the child without waking her. "I always thought I'd have a daughter," she said, cuddling the sleeping baby. "But with Carl getting so sick after Cody was born, there just wasn't enough time."

This was really getting out of hand. The last thing Alvarez wanted to discuss with Tory Travers was her deceased husband. "Don't go mushy on me, Tory. That's not the point. This kid is part of what happened back at that house. She didn't have a choice. You do."

Tory didn't answer while she returned the sleeping child to her crib. Then she turned to him. "Okay," she said quietly. "Maybe you're right. But if an insurance company asks me to get involved as a consultant, I'll do it. If I said no, they'd just find another engineer."

"I'd rather they find another engineer," he said flatly.

"Sorry, Charlie. That's the best I can do for you today."

There was something bothering him. "Just how likely is it that an insurance company would want you to track down the original contractor?"

She smiled at him, a genuine smile, the first he'd seen that day. "Come on, detective. If someone is doing construction without pulling permits, do *you* think they're going to carry insurance?" The smile widened. "But it sounded good, didn't it?"

"Did Jazz know it was a scam?"

"Of course," said Tory. "He may be tipsy, but he's not stupid."

Alvarez groaned. "You know, Tory, if you weren't an engineer, you'd make a good career criminal. Tell me, was Delgado's office the first one you've broken into?"

"Temper, temper. Try being gracious, for a change. You got what you wanted."

"That's the problem, I always want more. How about coming to my house to look at my etchings after all?"

"Right," she said flatly. "Like I'll just park Jazz somewhere and tell him to wait. Why make empty offers? Do I threaten you, or something?"

"Or something," he agreed.

"Well, I'm busy tonight. Not to mention that by this time, Jazz is probably singing Christmas carols in Spanish to your partner."

"Christmas is over."

"I know." Tory looked at her watch. "My God, I didn't know it was this late. I left a passel of people at my house, and Cody's with that girl ..." She trailed off.

"Then how about dinner sometime?"

She looked at him carefully before she answered. "Dinner

sometime might be possible," she said slowly. Alvarez was hoping for a little more enthusiasm. "Especially if you'll tell me what's happening on this case," she added brightly.

Jazz was not singing Christmas carols when Tory finally headed her car toward the interstate, but he was in a jovially expansive mood. She wondered what he had to be so pleased about. As far as she was concerned, they'd ended up working on a holiday and been thrown off the job for good measure.

"I got a couple things to tell you, boss," he said, as Tory slid onto I-10 and headed north. "That Alvarez, man, he has the hots for you."

"That's interesting," said Tory, keeping her tone noncommittal. She'd had enough verbal sparring for one day.

"Well, boss, if you think that's interesting, you're gonna *love* the other thing I have to tell you."

"And what is that?" Tory asked evenly, keeping her eyes carefully on the road.

"I think I know how to find the people who built that room."

CHAPTER NINE:

TREMORS
Omaha, Nebraska:
Sunday, January 1, late evening

Derek Dowling's efficiency apartment was at the top of an upscale high-rise building, affording a panoramic view of downtown Omaha. Dowling personally didn't give a shit. In his opinion, the nicest thing about the efficiency was that everything, from the beer to the TV to the phone, was in easy reach.

Dowling sat in the dark, a beer in his hand, his feet up on the coffee table, looking out over the city. He had exhausted all his contacts, called in all his favors, racked his brain for any overlooked possibilities, and he *still* had no idea where his stool pigeon was.

Dowling was more fond of this particular pigeon than he wanted to admit. She had been desperate when he first met her, but that was a given. Desperation was an important prerequisite for stool pigeons. What had been surprising was the degree of intelligence and amount of sheer guts she had exhibited in the short time he had been running her.

Maybe someone else would have been more sentimental, wondering what had happened to her, and whether she was still alive. There was a time, earlier in his career, when he would have questioned whether he could somehow have prevented this colossal screw-up. But Dowling was older now and more cynical, and his thoughts were much more pragmatic. The fact of the matter was that until he knew whether or not she would resurface, he didn't know how to make his next run at Raymond Boyce. And there was no question that there would be another run.

So Dowling sipped his beer in the dark apartment and looked out over the holiday-lit city and wondered what his next action should be. When the phone rang, all he had to do was reach out with the hand that wasn't holding the beer. He answered it before the end of the first ring.

"Dowling here."

"We finally got some information about all the activity at Boyce's compound," said the voice at the other end.

"I don't give a shit," snarled Dowling. "You guys can do state-of-the-art surveillance until you can't pay the electricity bill. It doesn't matter if the President himself visits Boyce, I can't arrest him for the visitors he has. If you see Boyce carting bodies out of his damned mansion, then give me a call. Until then, don't fuck with me. I'm thinking."

Dowling was ready to slam down the receiver when he caught the words "something like that ..." coming out of the phone. He put the receiver back to his ear. "... left the compound while we were tailing Boyce on his trip."

"How the hell do you know anyone left, if you don't do surveillance on the compound while he's gone? And more to the point, why the fuck should I care?"

The voice on the other end of the line continued unruffled. This particular voice had conversed with Dowling through five political administrations, three marriages, sixteen states, and years now counted in decades. "The way we know is that Boyce just filed a missing person report with the Omaha police. The reason why you should-the-fuck care is that the missing persons are Boyce's wife and baby daughter. And by the way, Happy New Year, Derek."

CHAPTER TEN:

TELECOMMUNICATIONS
Las Cruces, New Mexico:
Sunday, January 1, late evening

The discussion following Jazz's announcement was anti-climactic. No matter how much Tory implored him, he refused to tell her anything else, saying he needed to think about it when he was sober. Then he practiced the ultimate avoidance strategy, falling asleep where he sat in the front seat. Tory switched off the radio and called home on her cell phone, finding out that Lonnie and Sylvia had already left.

"So are you alone in the house with that girl?" she immediately asked.

"Mom, be nice," replied Cody. "Remember, I'll probably be the one who picks out your nursing home." Tory snorted, for lack of a better response. When had her son elevated the art of being cool to Alpine heights? "Don't worry," he added. "Lonnie took her home. Sylvia offered, but I think Kohli was scared to get in the car with her."

"Maybe she's developed a crush on Lonnie."

Cody refused to rise to the bait. "He's going to be over here at nine tomorrow morning, which should give us plenty of time to get to El Paso for my eleven o'clock flight. I've got the kitchen all cleaned up, so when you get home, we can watch TV, just the two of us. I thought you'd like that, since I'm leaving tomorrow."

How could a mother be angry with a fifteen-year-old son who had cleaned up after a dinner party for six? Tory decided to switch topics. "I'm still not sure you should go," she said.

Cody sighed. "Mom, we've already been over this. It's just for a week. It's not like I'm joining a cult or something."

"My family *is* a cult."

"Then your dad is the only member left, Mom. I don't think it really counts as a cult if there's only one member."

"That's what you think," Tory muttered darkly.

"Mom, it's going to be okay. You know what they say about children and grandparents having a common enemy."

It galled her to think that Cody was probably right—maybe he *could* cope with her father better than she had ever been able to. Time to switch topics again. "We're going to have to talk about Kohli. You know that I thought she was a boy."

"What's to talk about? It was your mistake."

Did the child not know the meaning of the word defensive? Tory opened her mouth and then shut it again. Time for another topic. "What if the plane falls out of the sky?"

"Mom," said Cody, exasperation finally starting to creep into his voice, "Stop it. I'll give you something else to worry about."

"What?" she demanded. Thoughts of sexually-transmitted diseases, teenage pregnancies, structural collapses, and other potential disasters tumbled over each other in her mind.

"We're running up a really big phone bill, having this discussion now," said Cody matter-of-factly. "Why don't you wait until you're home to fuss and worry, and yes, before you ask, I'm already packed. Kohli helped."

"Does that mean she saw your underwear?"

"No, Mom. I had her close her eyes when I packed my underwear."

"Then why are you laughing?"

"Gotta go, Mom. There's a gang of Hell's Angels at the door, and they want to come in and party. But don't worry, I've got it under control. I'll feed them some of the leftover turkey." Cody hung up before Tory had time to tell him she was dropping Jazz off before she came home, but then it didn't sound like he was exactly waiting for her with bated breath. And she was pretty sure that he *had* been kidding about the gang of motorcyclists ...

There was a sudden noise so loud it made her jump, sure that something had gone horribly wrong with the car. When the noise repeated itself a few seconds later, she realized that Jazz's head had fallen back on the headrest and he was snoring. Tory poked him until he shifted his position and the snoring decreased. After that, it was less than ten minutes before she pulled up in front of Jazz's apartment.

Jazz's apartment was something of a historical landmark in Las Cruces, at least around the campus. Four apartments had once been attached to a building which housed Scrappy's Convenience Store, and were thus called The Scrappy Arms. Jazz and a bachelor civil engineering professor had occupied two of the four units as long as Tory could remember, enjoying $50/month rent for decades, and a location directly across from the campus. Not to mention convenient shopping, Jazz frequently pointed out.

When Scrappy Douglas, whose two business enterprises bore his name, finally expired, his offspring discovered that per the terms of Scrappy's will, they could never evict the two long-time residents. Undaunted, the heirs bull-dozed the site, constructing Scrappy's Beverages and Laundromat, complete with two one-bedroom apartments in the back. Jazz complained about the resulting increase in his rent, but Scrappy's will had addressed tenancy, not rent control. Tory figured the new amenities more than made up for any added expense. Sylvia referred to Jazz's home as the Suds and Duds Apartments, which for some reason never failed to infuriate him.

Tory woke Jazz and walked him to his door. "I don't feel so good," he said, fumbling for his key.

"I'm not surprised," said Tory. "You drank that whole bottle of whiskey by yourself."

"I think it was the turkey."

"Don't even start with that. I feel fine."

Jazz groaned. "You must not have had too much turkey then. I don't want to use up any of my sick days, so I'm calling in dead tomorrow."

"Not on your life," Tory said firmly. "We're going to discuss how to find the people who built that room, remember?"

"Your detective doesn't want you involved, remember?"

"There's nothing wrong with discussing it. And he's not my detective."

"*Mira*. Do I look *estúpido*?"

"You look hung over."

"That's why I'm calling in dead tomorrow."

"I'll see you at eight."

"You won't be in at eight. You'll hang around the house and mope until Lonnie takes Cody to El Paso, and then you probably won't be fit to be around 'til afternoon. I'll be in at noon."

"Nine thirty, or I'll have Sylvia come over and check on you." Jazz just groaned as he walked through the door.

When Tory got home ten minutes later, she found no Hell's Angels, but, as promised, a clean kitchen with leftover tamales in the refrigerator. However, there was no leftover turkey to be found, and Tango, the Transylvanian Hound, had an immensely satisfied look on his face.

Tango reminded Tory of Cotton. She hadn't asked Alvarez about the dog's fate. She told herself it was not her problem, and turned her attention to some last-minute hovering and fussing over her son.

When Tory had exhausted her hovering and fussing repertoire, she and Cody ended up comfortably installed on the

couch, watching the eleven o'clock news. There were seemingly endless results of various bowl games, and Tory had
almost convinced herself that she wouldn't be making an appearance on the news. Then there she was, her startled face on
the screen, quickly turned away as Alvarez put his arm around
her and hustled her out of sight.

Their images were replaced by a close-up of the blond
reporter in the red sweater. "Police are unwilling to comment
on reports that a collapse in this residence on Rim Road has
resulted in a loss of life. Earlier, we were told by Emmett
Delgado that the collapse was the result of construction unre-
ported to the El Paso Building Department. Mr. Delgado is
the head structural engineer for Webb Engineering, and is an
expert in structural collapses.

"Ms. Tory Travers and El Paso Police Detective David
Alvarez were both on the scene, but refused to comment. These
two individuals helped solve the sensational murder case involving the football stadium at New Mexico State University
last summer. Ms. Travers is the daughter of Tom Wheatley, a
former senator of Florida. Viewers may recall she left that
state after reporters broke a story about her under-age involvement with Jameson Barkley. Mr. Barkley, who was married at
the time, is now head of the powerful right-wing political
group, Christians in Government.

"Although Ms. Travers and Detective Alvarez refused to
talk to this reporter, Mr. Delgado had a statement to make
about his involvement." Here, the blond, who had not previ-
ously paused for breath, had to take a quick break to consult
some notes she held in her hand. "Mr. Delgado wanted our
viewers to know why he was out here on New Year's Day,
within hours of the discovery of the collapse." The reporter
gave up staring sincerely into the camera, and read from the
notes in her hand.

"Mr. Delgado says that no matter how muddy the waters become, no matter how acrimonious the relationship with administrative offices or law enforcement officials, no matter how insulated he is personally from the construction at this site, he, as an engineer, is here to protect human life and welfare. No other profession assumes such a heavy burden and is held responsible for upholding it."

The blond looked up at the camera and flashed a high-wattage smile. "All of us at *News Now TV* want to express our appreciation to Mr. Delgado for his dedication to his profession and his willingness to be open with the press. We'll have more on this story as it develops tomorrow. Happy New Year."

Tory put a pillow over her face and started groaning.

"Are you just going to make retching sounds, or is it more serious than that? Do you want a bowl to barf in?" asked Cody.

"I can't believe it. I just can't believe it," moaned Tory behind the pillow.

"It could have been worse," said Cody cheerfully. "They didn't say anything about you punching Delgado at that fundraiser last summer. If someone had gotten it on tape, that would have been background information worth showing."

Tory peeked out from behind her pillow with one eye. "Don't tell me all this doesn't bother you."

"Doesn't bother me a bit," said Cody. "I learned a great approach by the time I was in kindergarten."

"And what is that?" she inquired, half afraid to ask.

"Whatever anyone says, I just say 'That's my mom.'"

Tory was thinking that over when the phone rang. Cody got up to answer it. He put his hand over the receiver. "It's for you," he said. "It's Kohli's mom."

Tory put the pillow down and looked at her son in horror. "Oh, no," she whispered. "Now I've ruined everything for you."

"Yeah," said Cody calmly. "We'll probably have to call off the wedding."

Tory put the pillow back over her face again. "If you're not kidding, I don't want to know about it."

Cody stood with his hand over the receiver, calmly regarding his mother. "Of course I'm kidding. But it really is Kohli's mother, and she wants to talk to you."

"I don't think I want to talk to her. There cannot be another crisis today; my schedule is already full."

"Mom, did you ever stop to think, and then forget to start again? There's no way you can find out what she's calling about unless you talk to her."

"What could she possibly want to talk to me about, unless it's that horrible newscast?"

"Mom, stop it. Maybe she wants to discuss your recipe for roast turkey." Cody handed his mother the phone. "Just talk to her," he said. He always made things sound so simple.

Tory closed her eyes and spoke into the receiver. "This is Tory Travers."

The woman on the other end said, "This is Alexandria Hughes, Mrs. Travers. Please forgive me for calling so late, especially since we've never met. I understand that your son and my daughter are the best of friends."

"Yes," said Tory, because it seemed like Alexandria Hughes expected her to say something.

"I called because my husband and I just saw you on the eleven o'clock news, in the broadcast about the house on Rim Road."

"That has nothing to do with my son," said Tory firmly. "I was at that house at the request of the police and my past had no place in that story. As a matter of fact, I'm considering filing suit for slander," she said, before she realized the words were out of her mouth. Cody fell onto the other end of the couch like he'd been shot and put a pillow over *his* face.

"Really? Did the reporter fabricate information?"

Shit. Tory had forgotten the other woman was a lawyer. That question could take a couple of hours to answer. She wondered if Alexandria would like to hear the latest lawyer jokes floating around Travers Testing and Engineering Company. Probably not. She wondered when the day would ever be over and she could go to bed.

"Forgive me, that's not really any of my business." It seemed like Alexandria Hughes was ready to carry on the conversation without Tory's participation. "Are you a friend of Detective Alvarez, the police officer shown on TV?"

Now there was another question that could take a couple of hours to answer. Tory opted for simplicity. "Yes," she said.

"There was no mention of an infant involved."

"No," said Tory slowly. Maybe Alexandria would come to the point sooner if she continued to reply in monosyllables.

The woman on the other end sighed, obviously making up her mind about something. "Mrs. Travers," she said, "I have a favor to ask you, and I'd like you to hear me out before you give me an answer."

"Please, call me Tory." A request for a favor was infinitely better than discussing her relationship with Jameson Barkley.

"And you can call me Alexandria. After all, we're practically neighbors." Tory had an overwhelming sense of relief that Alexandria hadn't said they were practically family. "Caleb, that's my husband. Caleb and I know someone who may have some information about the case that your friend is investigating." It took Tory a moment to remember who her friend was, since she still had Emmett Delgado and Jameson Barkley on her mind.

"So why doesn't your friend contact the police?"

"Well, that's the problem. Our friend, our acquaintance, really, can't have any official participation in this case. She, uh, she sometimes operates slightly outside the law."

"She's involved in construction without getting building permits?" asked Tory, unable to keep the outrage out of her voice. "That's just great. That will put the female contractors in El Paso back about a hundred years. All two or three of them."

Alexandria cleared her throat. "Mrs. Travers—Tory. Please hear me out. Our acquaintance, let's call her Mrs. A. She doesn't have anything to do with construction. But sometimes she helps parents start a new life with their children."

"What's outside the law about that?"

Cody was becoming interested enough in the conversation that he took the pillow off his face. "What's she saying?" he lip-synched. When his mother ignored him, he pulled on the sleeve of her sweater. Tory was having enough trouble concentrating on this conversation without relaying it to a third party. She took her pillow and smacked her son in the head as hard as she could. He fell dramatically back on the couch, dead, which was a relief.

"She sometimes helps non-custodial parents start a new life with their children," said Alexandria Hughes in a tone totally devoid of any inflection.

Tory thought that over. "So what does this Mrs. A want?" she asked finally. Was Alexandria Hughes going to ask the whereabouts of the baby girl found in the Rim Road House? What kind of company was her son keeping?

"She wants us to help her set up an unofficial meeting with Detective Alvarez so she can give him some unofficial information."

Tory wondered if she had taken her dumb pill that morning, or if talking with lawyers late at night made everyone feel this way. She decided to go for it. "So ... why don't you call the police and set it up?" she asked.

"Well, that's the difficult part of this. Caleb and I, we're attorneys, so we're officers of the court, and all that. We don't feel comfortable being involved."

Tory wondered what that said about her. "Then why don't you tell Mrs. A to call the police herself?"

"Because it's better if there's a go-between. And Caleb and I, well, we do owe her a favor. I hope this will remain confidential, but I think you need some kind of explanation. Caleb and I weren't able to have children of our own, and we weren't able to adopt through conventional routes. I have muscular dystrophy, Mrs. Travers." Suddenly Alexandria didn't seem like such a terribly long name. "I'm not going to go into detail, and it's not important, but this woman helped us adopt Kohli," Alexandria Hughes continued. "Kohli needed parents, we wanted a child, and Mrs. A made it happen."

Maybe it was a good thing that Kohli wasn't biologically related to two attorneys, Tory thought. "And now Mrs. A is calling in her IOU." Tory didn't make it a question.

"Yes. Will you talk to her? Just talk to her, and if she can convince you, then call your friend and see if you can set up a meeting between the two of them."

Cody wasn't dead any more, and he was tired of waiting to find out what was happening. He pulled the sock off one of Tory's feet and started tickling her. She pulled her foot away and threw another pillow at him. What the hell, she thought. What a fitting end to a perfectly ducky day. It was kind of like making anonymous phone calls in reverse. "Okay. What's her name and number?"

"I can't tell you that. I'll have her call you."

Here she'd been involved for all of five minutes and she'd screwed up already. Tory refrained from apologizing. "If she's going to call tonight, it better be pretty soon. It's been a long day. In another half hour I'll probably be catatonic."

"She'll get back to you in just a few minutes. I really don't know how to say thank you."

"You already have."

"You have a wonderful son; he's quite a gentleman. You should be proud."

"Yes, well, thank you. 'Bye." Tory was busy trying to fend off her gentleman offspring with well-aimed kicks as he tried to remove her other sock. She hung up the phone.

Cody was leaning menacingly over her, holding the entire stock of couch pillows in his arms. "What'd she say? What'd she say?"

"Is there an echo in here? She said that you were quite a gentleman." The telephone rang. They fought over it, but Tory wrestled it out of his grasp.

"Tory Travers."

"Tory!" It was Sylvia. "I'm so glad you finally answered. I wish you would get call waiting. I thought maybe you had taken your phone off the hook. Did you see that terrible news story? That *puta*, the nerve of her. *Me cago en su madre*. But don't worry about it, it wasn't that bad."

Only Sylvia could pull off conflicting statements like that. But then only Sylvia would keep calling if she thought the phone was off the hook.

"I saw it, Sylvia, but I'm okay. Listen, I need to get off the phone. I'm expecting a call."

"You're expecting a call? From Dah-veed?" asked Sylvia joyfully. Tory had to hold the phone away from her ear. "So maybe this trip wasn't all business after all, *que sí*? I called Jazz, and all he would tell me is that he's calling in dead tomorrow."

"No, I'm not expecting a call from David Alvarez," said Tory immediately.

"Who then?"

Tory thought for a moment. "I mean yes." Tory crossed her fingers. It was almost the truth.

"You are, then? Expecting a call from Dah-veed?" asked Sylvia, momentarily confused.

"Yes," replied Tory, keeping her fingers crossed.

"Well, okay then." The line went dead. Sylvia was not one to waste time if a man was involved.

Cody pounced on his mother, and she had to tell him everything. He thought it was beyond cool, but then he was fifteen, and didn't need as much sleep as someone twenty years older. She had to agree to let him answer the next phone call, but drew the line at letting him say "Travers Undercover Investigations." They both jumped when the phone rang. He answered it on the first ring, and then handed it to Tory.

"Mrs. Travers," said a grandmotherly voice on the other end. "Thank you for letting me impose by calling you so late."

"You're welcome, Mrs.—" Tory drew the pause out, waiting for the other woman to supply her name. Cody had briefed her on this technique. The things one did for one's children.

"Mrs. A will do fine for now," said the woman without a pause, not falling for Cody's ploy. "I know this must all sound very strange. Alexandria must have had a hard time explaining what I want you to do, and why I want you to do it."

"It didn't sound so strange. I've often wished I had a non-custodial parent myself," Tory blurted out. She grimaced. She couldn't believe she had said that.

There was a pause while Mrs. A apparently decided not to pursue the subject. "Well, I'll get right to the point. Either the police found a little girl in that house where you were, or someone needs to go look for her. I don't know if anyone told you about her. If she wasn't there, they need to find her, and if she was there, she's in danger. That's why I want to talk to the detective who's handling the case. What do you think of him, this David Alvarez?"

"Is this a long distance phone call?" Tory was going to have to stop saying the first thing that came into her head.

"What a strange answer."

"Detective Alvarez is very good at what he does. He's intuitive, and he doesn't give up easily. But he's also very arrogant and overbearing."

"Most men are, don't you agree? And what does he think of you?"

"He thinks I should stay out of his case," Tory said flatly.

There was laughter on the other end. "And do you want to stay out of his case?"

"No, not if a child is in danger. And not if I think I can help."

"Perhaps you can, perhaps you can. Didn't Alexandria say you have a child yourself?"

Why did she feel okay about answering these questions from a stranger without a name? "Yes, I have a son. He's fifteen, and he's sitting here, dying to know what we're talking about."

"Then this is what I would like you to do: Tell your detective I'd like to meet with him. Tell him I have information about a little girl who was in that house. You live across the state line in New Mexico, and the house is in Texas, right? It would be a good thing, perhaps, to meet in New Mexico, where your detective would be out of his jurisdiction."

"Are you a fugitive?" asked Tory bluntly.

"No; let's just say that in my line of work, I know enough

fugitives that sometimes the police take an unhealthy interest in me. Unhealthy for my fugitive friends."

"Well, if you're not a fugitive, how about meeting at my house?"

There was laughter again. "I don't think your detective will like that idea." Tory wished that she would stop calling him "her" detective.

"Who do I tell him you are?"

"Just tell him Mrs. A. If he's any good, he'll figure it out."

"Okay. I'll call him and call you back."

"No dear, that's not a good idea. I'll call you."

Well, didn't Tory feel like a rank amateur now. "Okay. Give me half an hour. When do you want to meet?"

"I can be there by tomorrow night, any time after seven. And Mrs. Travers, one more thing."

"Yes?"

"Tell your Detective Alvarez that I want you to be at the meeting."

Of course Tory had to go over everything that had been said at least three times with Cody, who was inconsolable that they didn't have caller ID, and tell him that his scheduled trip to Florida couldn't be canceled. Now there was irony.

So by the time she dug out David Alvarez's home phone number, it was almost midnight. Soon the elusive Mrs. A was supposed to call back. If Tory hadn't been nervous already, she had her fifteen-year-old son as an enthusiastic audience. All she needed now was to call up Sylvia and ask her to come over and consult.

Alvarez picked up on the second ring. "Alvarez here."

Tory took a deep breath. "This is Tory."

"What's happened?" he asked immediately.

"I need to talk to you. Something has come up."

"Something you need to talk about *now?*"

It suddenly struck Tory how presumptuous her call was. "Is this not a good time?"

"No, goddamn it. It's not a good time. Is it a different time zone where you are?" She heard shuffling on his end, and then to her mortification, little moans interspersed with some heavy breathing.

"I really do need to talk to you," Tory said resolutely. "Can you please just excuse yourself and go to another phone? It's important, or believe me, I wouldn't be bothering you."

"It better be good, Tory. This damn dog you stuck me with has been whining and fussing all night, and you just woke her up."

"That's Cotton I hear?"

"Who'd you think it was, the damned *News Now TV* reporter? I hope to hell if it was her in bed with me, she wouldn't be whining."

"You let her sleep in bed with you?"

"The dog or the reporter?"

This conversation was hardly going as planned. Tory couldn't get the image of Alvarez in bed with a white fluffy dog out of her head. She squelched an uncharacteristic urge to giggle. "Maybe it's not a good idea to let her think she has the upper hand," she suggested.

"It's the only way she would shut up and go to sleep," he snapped. "Are you really calling to check who's in my bed?"

"No, of course not. I have some information about your case."

"What kind of information?"

"A woman who knows something about the baby wants to meet with you."

"Who is she?"

"I don't know."

"What do you mean you don't know?"

"She wouldn't tell me who she was."

"What do you have, a listing in the phone book that reads 1-800-TIP-TORY?"

"Just because there's a dog in your bed, you don't have to get testy."

"Testy does not begin to describe how I feel right now. The damn dog isn't who I wanted to end up with tonight," Alvarez said flatly.

"I have some neighbors who are custody attorneys," said Tory quickly. "They called me after they saw us on the newscast."

"Yeah. That was a piece of work. I got all teary when they read the part about Delgado's dedication to public safety. So what does this have to do with some woman knowing something about the kid?"

"My neighbors owe this woman a favor, but they don't really want to be involved. They're attorneys, and they feel it might compromise their position."

"And you and me, just being regular folk, it doesn't count?"

"Something like that. They said that this woman helps parents start over with their children." Alvarez didn't say anything. Tory took a deep breath. "Non-custodial parents," she added.

"No shit. Let's see. I got a collapse, but you think it was deliberate. I got two bodies, but because of you, I have to think maybe they were murdered. I got one kid, unidentified. Now I've got a potential kidnapping, and you want to set up a meeting with someone who doesn't have a name, who your neighbors don't want to touch with a ten-foot pole. If it gets any worse, Tory, I'm going to have to ask you to stop helping me."

"You already did," she reminded him.

"Yeah. Fat lot of good it did me."

"It seems to me it's doing you a lot of good," Tory retorted. "You wouldn't know half of what you know now if it wasn't for me. You just don't want to admit that I might be intelligent enough to come up with the answers."

"That was certainly the second thing I noticed about you."

"Do you want to hear the rest of this or not?"

"I'd be on the edge of my seat, if only I was sitting down."

"Do you want me to hang up? This is your job I'm doing, not mine."

"That's what bothers me. I'm trying to convince myself that I want to listen to the rest of what you have to say."

"Don't be so open-minded," Tory snapped. "Your brains might fall out." She was very close to hanging up the phone.

"Okay, okay, calm down. You already woke up Cotton, so I guess I might as well hear the rest of this."

"The attorneys asked if their friend could call me, and I said yes."

"Why does that not surprise me?"

Tory decided to ignore him. "The woman sounds very nice. All she wanted me to do was to try to arrange an informal meeting with you, preferably in New Mexico, since it would be out of your jurisdiction. So I told her I would ask you to meet her at my house. She said she could meet any time after seven tomorrow night."

Alvarez swore creatively and fluently. Tory held the phone away from her ear until he had calmed down some. "Are you crazy, or just stupid? What in God's name would prompt you to set up a meeting with someone you don't know in your own home? Does she know where you live?"

"Well, no," said Tory. "And she did say that you probably wouldn't like the idea."

"She may not have a name, but she has more sense than you do."

"Listen, do you want to know what she has to say or not? She's supposed to call back. I didn't plan on being on the phone this long."

There was a pause while he thought it over. "Tell her to meet me at eight o'clock at the Shady Lady Motel in Anthony tomorrow night. Room Ten. It's in the part of Anthony that's in New Mexico. Give her my phone number and tell her not to call you again. And go to bed and forget about all of this."

"No way. Mrs. A wants me to be at the meeting."

"Mrs. A? *Mrs.* A?" Tory held the phone away from her ear again. Alvarez had resumed yelling. "She told you her name was Mrs. A?"

"She said if you were a good detective, you could figure the rest of it out yourself. And she said she wanted me at the meeting."

"Do you have a death wish?"

"No. But I've had some time to think since we were at the hospital."

"It's too bad you didn't use it. I don't want you involved in this, Tory."

"Then I'll tell Mrs. A you don't want to meet with her." Tory held her breath and counted to ten while he swore at her, hoping he wouldn't call her bluff. Finally he wound down, and she listened to the silence on the other end of the line.

"Tell her the Shady Lady Motel in Anthony," Alvarez finally said. "Room Ten, eight o'clock. You be there at seven. Not seven oh five, not seven ten, but seven. Park in the back and don't bring a gun. Don't bring Sylvia. Don't bring Lonnie. Don't bring Jazz. For God's sake, don't bring Cody. And then you sit down and shut up and do every single thing I tell you, or I swear, I'll shoot you myself."

"You know, between the two of you, Mrs. A sounds safer to meet. I couldn't bring Cody even if I wanted to. He's ... flying to Florida tomorrow morning to spend a week with my father."

"I'll be damned. Good for him. Good for you." This news momentarily distracted Alvarez from his tirade. "I always knew you had a lot of guts. Not much sense, maybe, but a lot of guts. I'm almost afraid to ask, but is there anything else?"

"Can't we pick somewhere else to meet? I really hate to tell this person I've never met to go to room ten at the Shady Lady Motel. Where do you come up with these places? Don't tell me it's named after some business enterprise."

Tory could almost hear Alvarez grinding his teeth over the phone line. "If I recall, the last time you picked the place for a clandestine meeting, every relative and friend of Sylvia Maestes in Dona Ana County knew about it. That probably left about three people in the dark. For all you know, the Shady Lady is named after a madonna under a tree. Besides, we're not likely to get knifed there, unlike your favorite hangout. Okay? Now get off the phone and talk to your Mrs. A and set it up before I drive up there, put a tap on your phone, and throw you into protective custody."

"Is it really named after a madonna under a tree?"

"I thought you were already running late for your next cloak-and-dagger phone call."

"Tell Cotton good night for me," said Tory sweetly. She heard the phone bang down and the line went dead.

Tory barely had time to relate Alvarez's part of the conversation to an intent Cody before the phone rang again. Tory beat him to it. "Hello," she said breathlessly, a little amazed at her own success in setting up the requested meeting.

"What happened? What did you talk about?" It was Sylvia. How in God's name was Tory going to get her off the line this time?

"We talked about the case." Tory didn't even try to pretend that she didn't know what Sylvia was asking about.

"So did he ask you out?"

Telling Sylvia that she had just arranged to meet David Alvarez in room ten of the Shady Lady Motel in Anthony, New Mexico, was not something Tory planned to do. And she didn't think a lecture about the normal boundaries between an employer and employee would do any good. It never had. "When we have a real date, you'll be the first to know," she improvised, crossing her fingers again. Cody crossed his eyes at her. It took five more minutes to get Sylvia off the line. As soon as Tory hung up, the phone rang again.

Mrs. A was brief and business-like, repeating the meeting details once for verification and thanking Tory again. Then she hung up, and finally, the phone didn't ring. Tory looked at Cody in the ensuing silence.

"I don't suppose you'll change your mind and let me stay home and be your backup," Cody said, his eyes shining with excitement.

"Not a chance," she said flatly. Never had she imagined that sending Cody to visit her father would seem like a good thing. "This is not a situation that requires backup. I am simply doing a favor for the parents of your friend," Tory said primly. "Your friend *the girl*," she added for emphasis.

"So my mom arranged this meeting between the mysterious Mrs. A, who operates outside the law, and the super-sleuth David Alvarez."

"Looks like it. Pretty good for just a mom, huh?"

"And then my mom is venturing out to the Shady Lady Motel in Anthony, New Mexico, to be an integral part of this clandestine meeting."

"Yeah, that too." The reality of the situation, along with

exhaustion, was beginning to set in. With a twinge of a concern that she might be in over her head. Maybe somewhat.
Just a little bit.

"You know," said Cody, a big grin on his face, "it's too
bad you didn't tell Sylvia what's going on. She could give you
some help."

"What kind of help?"

"She could help you figure out what to wear."

CHAPTER ELEVEN:

RESEARCH
El Paso, Texas:
Monday, January 2, early morning

Alvarez had fed Cotton some raw hamburger during their first night together, but he didn't intend to make a practice of it, which meant a trip to the grocery store and a trip back home before going to work.

Exhibiting a lack of appreciation for his efforts, Cotton turned up her nose at the dog food he offered her. Seconds after he put her out in his small, fenced backyard, she was whining and scratching to get back in. He opened the door a crack and peered out at her.

"Did you go to the bathroom already?" he asked, feeling like a fool. It wasn't like he could look into her eyes to discern an answer.

Cotton nudged against the opening in the door until Alvarez widened the space to make sure nothing was wrong. Like a flash, she was back in the house.

"Oh, no, you don't," he said. "Last night was more than enough togetherness for me."

Cotton went straight to the pan of water he had put down on the kitchen floor. After drinking her fill, water ran down her muzzle and dripped on the floor. The dog walked over to him and nuzzled his pants leg. He looked in dismay at the water stains on his trousers.

Done with her brief display of affection, Cotton turned, ambled into the living room, bumped head-on into the couch, stopped, appeared to think a moment, and then jumped up and settled in like she belonged there.

"You think I'm going to let you stay there?" Alvarez asked incredulously. Since his intimidation technique depended a lot on looking into the subject's eyes, Cotton had the advantage. She continued to gaze at him inscrutably from her perch on the couch. At least, he assumed she was gazing at him. Tory was right, he thought. He'd let the damn dog get the upper hand last night, and now he was paying for it.

He looked at his watch. He was already running late. "Okay," he capitulated. After all, the dog was recently bereaved. "We'll give it a try, but just for today. If I find any unpleasant surprises when I get home, you're going to lock-up. And it's a short step from there to The Chamber," he admonished her.

Cotton gave a big sigh. Maybe she was already asleep; it was impossible to tell. Alvarez grabbed a paper towel, blotted his pants leg, and let himself out of the house. What good was a damn watch dog if she couldn't see anything? Scott Faulkner owed him big time for this one. And it wasn't over until it was over.

Alvarez didn't get into the office until nine-thirty, and Scott was already working the phones. "You're late," he said as he ended a call.

"I didn't sleep well last night," said Alvarez shortly. Scott raised one inquisitive eyebrow, conserving his verbal energy for what promised to be a long day. Alvarez noted the deep circles under his partner's eyes. "What's up with you, man? Did Donna make you sleep on the couch?"

"It was my choice. Scotty D-Don is teething," answered his partner. "It's a real bitch."

Alvarez thought Donna's naming of the baby after both parents was too cute by half, not to mention that both names were obstacles to someone who stuttered. But then no one had consulted him. "What have you got?" he asked.

"CSU's been on site s-since six this morning." It was Alvarez's turn to raise his eyebrows. "The head of the Building Department called the Chief last night, hot to salvage the b-basement. The Chief hit him with Tory's conclusions, and it's been d-d-dueling departments ever since. So far we're winning," said Scott with satisfaction. "But the Chief lit a fire under the CSU, just in c-case."

"They find anything good?"

"A small bloodstain on the floor by the hearth. Drug paraphernalia stuffed up the chimney, inside the flue."

"Bloodstain match either of the deceased?"

"They're working on it."

"Anything else?"

"An antique roll-top d-desk in the master bedroom, full of forgery supplies."

"No shit?"

"No sh-sh-sh-shit." Alvarez winced but Scott continued undaunted. "There were several baptismal certificates in what looks to be Lenora Hinson's handwriting."

"The skills of the rich and affluent are truly amazing. If we were talking some poor greaser *cholos*, we wouldn't be messing with baptismal certificates, man. We'd be dealing with the real thing, like counterfeit three dollar bills."

"K-keep talking like that and they'll send you to sensitivity training," said Scott uneasily. "With my luck, they'll send me with you."

"Hey, man, I'm cool. I've learned to say Hispanic instead of spic, even if it is three syllables instead of one. And if someone rates seven syllables, I use the term Mexican-American, *ese*."

"So what do you think?" asked Scott, doggedly returning to the original discussion.

"I think that one or both of the bodies were moved,

supporting Tory's conclusion that the collapse wasn't an accident. I'll bet my bright shiny shield that neither of those women expired from falling columns. And I think Lenora Hinson was involved up to her eyeballs in something illegal, like one of those groups that help non-custodial parents kidnap their own kids and disappear."

"Pretty g-g-good." Scott looked impressed.

"I had some help," Alvarez admitted. "You're not going to believe this, but Tory has some attorney neighbors who know someone with information about the kid. This woman wants an unofficial meeting with us. I set it up for eight tonight at the Shady Lady in Anthony. I want you in the room next door in case something unexpected goes down."

"Why the Shady Lady?"

"This woman wants to meet somewhere outside of our jurisdiction. I thought about Honolulu, but our travel vouchers would probably get bounced. If Honolulu is out, why not Anthony? The half that's in New Mexico, not Texas. Has kind of an exotic ring to it, doesn't it?"

"It d-d-doesn't have anything to do with the hidden cameras in the rooms at the Shady Lady?"

Alvarez gave his partner a shocked look. "Of course not. But if the owner owes us a favor and is willing to furnish us rooms for free upon occasion, why not make use of all the amenities? Especially the ones we don't officially know about."

"Why not indeed?" Scott grinned.

"What do you want to bet this woman is with this underground railroad organization?"

"I don't want to b-bet. I always end up losing. That's what they call it: The Underground Railroad for the 'Nineties. What's this woman's name?"

"That's what we're supposed to find out. Don't you just love a challenge?"

Scott shuffled through the mess on his desk, then handed his partner a file. Alvarez opened it to find several articles on the Underground Railroad. "I guess this is what happens when you get to work on time," he observed, flipping through the clippings. "Listen to this," he told Scott, and began to read from the file.

"'In cities and small towns alike, this secret coalition of otherwise law-abiding citizens work to shelter parents who believe their children have been sexually abused, and will do anything to keep it from happening again.'" Alvarez skipped over descriptions of fleeing parents and their abused children, looking for organizational information.

He found what he was looking for in an article from *People* magazine, of all places. "'Loosely organized, the Railroad has four independent, yet interlocking networks. Using clandestine techniques borrowed from the government's Federal Witness Protection Program, including aliases, disguises, doctored identification documents and falsely registered vehicles, the Underground wages a constant battle with the FBI, local police and private investigators out to hunt down the missing families." He looked up at Scott. "It doesn't say anything in here about secret rooms."

"You always say we're on the c-cutting edge," his partner replied.

Alvarez went back to reading. "'Anonymous, yet deeply committed, the railroad volunteers often come from feminist, children's rights and religious organizations. Also involved are hundreds of men and women who were themselves abused as children.'" He looked at Scott. "Any history of abuse in the Hinson family?"

"I'll get someone working on it."

Alvarez went back to skimming through the file. "Look at

this," he said, pointing to an article entitled "Midwest Mother Makes Millionaire Maniacal."

"You're not asking me to read that headline, are you?" asked Scott reproachfully.

Ignoring his partner, Alvarez read from the clipping. "'Annika Atkins, reputed leader of the Midwest arm of the Underground Railroad for non-custodial parents, appears to have no qualms about taking on one of Wall Street's own. Known as Mrs. A to friends and foes alike, this wealthy widow is a woman with a mission that extends far beyond the geographical boundaries of her native Nebraska.' That's her, Scott. That has to be her. She couldn't be here until after seven tonight, and she told Tory to call her Mrs. A. I want to know everything there is to know about Annika Atkins by eight o'clock tonight."

"You got it. But this might not have anything to d-d-do with the actual deaths," Scott cautioned him.

"I know. The mother and the kid could have been innocent bystanders when the old lady got whacked. That's why you'll follow the money trail and I'll talk to the boyfriend."

"About tonight. Think it might be an all-n-night stake out?"

"I don't see why," said Alvarez, then noted his partner's expression. "Pretty bad at home, huh?" Scott nodded. "Well, since the owner of the Shady Lady owes us a big favor, I don't see why it makes a difference whether we use the rooms for a few hours or for the whole night." He paused, then added, "Tory will be there."

"Why?" Scott looked worried. "Is there a st-structural problem with the Shady Lady?"

"Very funny. Supposedly Mrs. A wants Tory to be at the meeting."

"Why?" Scott still looked worried.

"Probably so the mothers in the room will outnumber the

police. My guess is that Tory can't resist sticking her nose in where it doesn't belong." He brightened. "Maybe I can convince her to stay over with us guys, like a slumber party."

Scott grinned. "Now there's something I'd be willing to bet on," he said, stutter-free.

Gary Cabrioni answered the phone at his office, and Alvarez identified himself as a police detective. "I'm surprised to find you in so early on a Monday morning," he told the doctor.

"I'm a general practitioner, so my responsibilities don't stop on weekends or holidays. I'm trying to get caught up with the paperwork for patients I saw over the weekend. But I'm sure you aren't calling to talk about my work schedule."

"No, I'm not. I'd like to come over and talk to you."

"In reference to what?"

"In reference to the discovery of Lenora Hinson's body yesterday."

There was a pause. "Mrs. Hinson isn't my patient," Cabrioni finally said. "She and her husband were my father's patients once, but that was years ago. Long before I took over my father's practice."

"So you know she's dead?"

"I watch the news and read the papers, just like anyone else."

"I'd really like to talk this over with you in person, Dr. Cabrioni."

"What for? Why are you interested in her death, anyhow? I thought she died as the result of some roof collapse."

"There are questions that we're trying to clear up."

"There's nothing I can tell you about Mrs. Hinson's death."

"Perhaps. But maybe you could tell me about her daughter."

There was another pause. "Who told you about me and Keaton?"

"Ryan Hinson." There was no answer from Dr. Cabrioni. "When would be a good time for me to come and talk to you?"

"You realize we'll be talking about a relationship that was years ago. A high school romance."

"When would be a good time?"

"I don't have a patient until ten-thirty, so you might as well come now, if you insist. But you'll be wasting your time."

"Let me be the judge of that." Alvarez looked at the address. "I'll be there in twenty minutes."

"I can hardly wait," said Cabrioni, and hung up the phone.

Dr. Cabrioni's office was in an older residential part of El Paso, close to the Ft. Bliss military post. The area had once been solidly middle class, but was now showing the unmistakable signs of a downward economic progression. The building that housed Cabrioni's practice was a modest, squat brick rectangle, unassuming, but well-maintained. Someone had obviously taken some time and effort to make sure the waiting area was decorated for the holiday season.

By the time Alvarez arrived at Cabrioni's office, a young Hispanic receptionist was at the front desk, answering the phone. She took three phone calls before she could talk to him.

"Monday's are always really busy, and after a holiday it's even worse," she told Alvarez in a no-nonsense tone that belied her youthful appearance. "I've already got two walk-ins coming in this morning, so he can't take more than fifteen minutes to talk to you."

"Yes ma'am," said Alvarez obediently, as he was led to a small, cluttered office. The receptionist looked pointedly at her watch, then left Alvarez to fend for himself.

The first thing he noticed about Gary Cabrioni was his resemblance to both Ryan Hinson and Dale Crandell in general build and coloring. It was enough to make Alvarez hope that Officer Kurita would turn up a witness who had seen a short, fat blond man entering the Hinson residence under suspicious circumstances.

"It's my mother," said Cabrioni flatly, in lieu of introductions.

"I beg your pardon?" asked Alvarez.

"You're staring at me. You're trying to put my last name together with my appearance." Now that Cabrioni mentioned it, Alvarez realized that the doctor was definitely a different ethnic mix than either Hinson or Crandell. It was a subtle difference, the combined effect of slightly thicker lips, somewhat darker skin tone, and wiry hair that defied a conventional style.

"I'm not staring at you any more than I stare at anyone else," said Alvarez. "I'm of mixed racial heritage myself," he said, opening his hands wide and shrugging to show that he meant no offense.

"My father was the son of an Italian immigrant." Cabrioni spoke as if he had recited the explanation many times. "The only way he could afford to go to medical school was to join the army. He was stationed in Germany and met my mother there, which was quite a feat."

"Why?"

"Because she was black, of Jamaican descent, but born in Germany. Not too many of those around. So I'm half black, even if it's not that apparent at first glance. It's not a heritage with a lot of advantages. I speak some Italian, not Spanish, and I missed out on any opportunities to be a brother. To this day, my mother speaks only broken English, and wouldn't know soul food if it bit her."

"Why are you telling me this, Dr. Cabrioni?"

"Because it's one of the reasons Lenora Hinson wanted to break up my relationship with her daughter. Ryan must have wanted company in the line-up of people who hated his mother, so he sent you to me."

"And did you hate his mother?"

"Yes."

"Why?"

"Lenora Hinson was a cruel, manipulative, evil woman. She couldn't see a person, a thing, a situation, without wanting to control it. She controlled every aspect of her two children's lives. There was no boundary between what was her life and what was theirs."

"And she was a patient of your father's?"

"She and her husband were both his patients, which was pretty unusual at the time. My father was an osteopath, like me, not an MD."

"I thought the two were pretty much the same."

"Now, maybe, but not so long ago, osteopathic doctors were considered quacks by lots of people. My father was the first osteopathic doctor allowed to practice in a hospital in El Paso. He worked hard for the acceptance of his chosen profession."

"And you took over his practice?"

"Yes. He and my mother are two of the happiest retired people I know."

"You were telling me that it was unusual for both the Hinsons to be your father's patients."

"Harold Hinson had an old back injury that my father treated successfully, so he and his wife both ended up using my father as their physician."

"And that's how you met Keaton?"

"No. Harold Hinson had been dead for two years before I ever laid eyes on Keaton. I met her in high school."

"The two of you went to high school together?"

Cabrioni gave a short, humorless laugh. "Not hardly. I'm a graduate of Stephen F. Austin High School. Keaton attended St. Michael's Episcopal School for Girls."

"You attended Austin? That's where I went to school." Alvarez was surprised. Austin was the second oldest high school in El Paso, an inner-city school that had more than earned its rough reputation. "I didn't think there were too many doctors' kids going to school at Austin."

"There weren't, but remember, my father wasn't the accepted type of doctor. He did okay, but we weren't wealthy by any means. And then there was the matter of my mother."

"Yes." Cabrioni didn't need to say anything else. The offspring of an Italian American married to a German of Jamaican descent wouldn't raise any eyebrows at Austin.

"Remember Lydia Patterson?" Cabrioni asked.

"No. But then I'm thirty-eight. How old are you?"

"Thirty, but I'm not talking about a student. Don't you remember? Lydia Patterson was the name of a big debate competition. Austin hosted it every year. All the high schools in the city sent debate teams."

"I wasn't very familiar with debate at Austin." Now there was an understatement. If Cabrioni had wanted to talk about rival gangs, the best way to get your switchblade in and out of your PE clothes, or putting baggies of catnip in your locker to confuse the drug-sniffing dogs, then Alvarez might have had something to contribute to the conversation.

"I was a senior the year Keaton came to Lydia Patterson. She was a sophomore." Cabrioni paused.

"I have a feeling you're not remembering her debating skills."

"Hardly." Cabrioni looked at Alvarez. "Have you talked to Keaton?"

"Yes."

"Then you know what she looks like. You should have seen her at fifteen. She was so wild, and absolutely gorgeous. I'd never met anyone like her."

"I can understand that. It's hard for me to even imagine a girl named Keaton walking the halls of Austin High School."

"It was her mother's maiden name."

"Certainly a change from all the Glorias, Sophias, and Irmas that I went to school with. I assume the attraction was mutual?"

"Yeah. You could say that."

"Did you have sex with her?"

Cabrioni's head jerked back. "You come right to the point, don't you?"

"Sorry. It's part of my job. Did you have sex with her?"

"Yes."

"When?"

Cabrioni looked out the window a moment before replying. "The third night after I met her."

Alvarez looked up, surprised in spite of himself. "Were you the first?"

"No, but for a while I thought I'd be the last."

"So what happened?"

"She grew up and married the man her mother intended for her to marry."

"I doubt it was as simple as that."

Cabrioni got up and walked over to his window. Alvarez wondered what he could find so interesting in the parking lot outside. "Remind me exactly why we're doing this, before I decide to end this conversation."

"Because Lenora Hinson's body was found in unusual circumstances, to say the least. This may well become a homicide investigation when we get the autopsy report. Regardless, there's a lot of other questions to be cleared up, and when we talked to Ryan Hinson, your name came up. So I'm here talking to you."

Cabrioni returned to his desk and sat down heavily, lacing his hands together in his lap and staring at them. "I've got patients to see. What else do you want to know?"

"So far I've got boy meets girl, boy gets girl. I'd like you to expand on what led up to boy loses girl."

"Keaton's mother barely tolerated me. I was allowed to date Keaton about twice a month."

"Doesn't sound like a lot of togetherness for two teenagers in love."

"It wasn't. Keaton snuck out every chance she got that summer."

"Then what happened?"

"I went off to college, to Trinity in San Antonio. I was going to get a degree in biology and be an osteopath just like my father. But Keaton had other ideas. She wanted to be a doctor, too, but she wanted to be an MD, and she wanted us to do everything together. Shit, I was nineteen and in love. If she'd have asked me to jump off a cliff, I would have jumped. So I told her sure, I'd be an MD with her."

"How did your parents take that?"

"It hurt my dad. My mother was worried about me, not about my career plans. She kept telling me that the Keaton Hinsons of the world don't marry boys who are half Jamaican. She was right."

"And when did you find that out?"

"My senior year in college. I'd applied to medical schools, but not a single osteopathic one. Keaton and I kept things together for almost four years, writing letters during the school year, and trying to make up for lost time on holidays and in the summers. She stayed here to go to college, because her mother didn't want to let her out of her sight. I think things got really bad after Ryan finally managed to move out. Keaton was all Lenora had left. She even chose the clothes Keaton wore. Each Sunday evening, she would go over the clothes she wanted Keaton to wear for the following week. Can you believe that?"

It had been a long time before Alvarez had even owned enough clothes to make it through an entire week, so he didn't feel qualified to comment. "So what happened?"

"I was home on spring break, and Keaton was finishing her sophomore year in college. She was always wound tight, but there was something different this time. She was like a violin string about to break. It scared me. She wanted to see me every day that I was home, and she didn't want to sneak out to do it. She and her mother had terrible fights about it. One night I picked Keaton up and I could see on her face where her mother had slapped her."

"So things were escalating between Keaton and her mother."

"Yeah. Keaton seemed desperate. She told me that she couldn't take living at home any more. Ryan was furious with his mother about the inheritance being tied up 'til he turned thirty-five, but at least he'd gotten out of the house. Like I said, the only thing left for Lenora to focus her attention on was Keaton."

"What was your response to all of this?"

"I asked Keaton to marry me."

"And?"

"She said yes. But the next day she called me and told me she never wanted to see me again, and that she was going to marry the son of her father's business partner. I went crazy. I drove over to her house, and her mother wouldn't let me see her. I started pounding on the door and throwing rocks at the windows. Mrs. Hinson called the police and they picked me up and took me downtown and called my parents. It was not my finest hour. The next day Mrs. Hinson called and asked to have all their medical records transferred to another doctor. An MD, of course. It was the crowning touch."

"All *their* medical records?"

"Yeah, for her *and* her husband, even though he had been dead for years. She was nothing if not thorough."

"Did you ever talk to Keaton again?"

"She called two nights later, at three in the morning. She said she couldn't stand knowing that I was still trying to see her. She told me to leave her alone and let her get on with her life and do what she needed to do. She told me that if I tried to see her again she'd kill herself."

"And what did you do?"

"I became a vegetable. I dropped out of school, wasting the hard-earned money my parents spent to send me to college. I sat in my room and refused to come out or speak to anyone. I didn't watch television and I didn't read the papers, so I missed the news about the society wedding that May, when Keaton Hinson married Dale Crandell."

"Well, obviously something happened between then and now."

"My hard-working father continued to provide room and board for the son who had belittled his chosen profession. He came into my room every evening and read me the sports section of the newspaper. I guess he thought there wouldn't be anything in there to upset me. My mother got me up every morning and nagged me until I got dressed. She bought records of every rock group she'd ever heard me listen to, and played them constantly."

"Most parents I know would pay good money *not* to have to listen to their children's music."

Cabrioni gave another one of his humorless laughs. "I think she thought I needed to listen to something besides my own thoughts. Or maybe she wanted me to realize that other people had been where I was. I remember she played the Stones song "Paint It Black" over and over, because she thought it would help. She cooked me strudels and sauerbrauten and pasta and made sure I ate. At the end of the summer I went back to school, finished my degree, went to medical school, became an osteopath and took over my father's practice."

"So you could say that both you and Keaton ended up doing what your parents wanted you to do."

Cabrioni looked up. "Yes, you could say that. The difference is that while my parents approved of my choices, they were *my* choices. I had parents who loved me, not parents who wanted to live my life for me."

"Sounds like you're pretty lucky."

"That's me, detective. A lucky guy."

"You said that you weren't Keaton's first sexual partner."

"That's right."

"Wasn't that a little unusual? For a girl of fifteen, coming from a sheltered upbringing?"

"I wouldn't know, never having been a girl of fifteen, coming from a sheltered upbringing."

Alvarez took a deep breath. He guessed he deserved that answer. "It sounds like Keaton was starting to rebel even before she met you, using sex as a way to get back at her mother's attempts to control her life."

"Like I said, I wouldn't know."

"Was she your first sexual partner?"

"You don't leave any stone unturned, do you? I'd love to be the one to give you your next physical exam. Yes, she was my first sexual partner."

"Given the fact that you weren't her first lover, and you were only together during the summers, didn't you worry that she had other sexual partners?"

"No," said Cabrioni flatly. There wasn't much arguing with the tone of his answer.

"What was your relationship with Ryan Hinson?"

"I barely knew him. He always struck me as the kind of guy who would suck up to anyone to get whatever he needed."

"What was Keaton's relationship with him?"

"She didn't like him very much, but she didn't have much of a relationship with him. Ryan is more than seven years older than Keaton."

"And you are an only child?"

"That's right." Cabrioni shook his head like he was shaking off thoughts of the past. "Now, since I think you've probed all the deep, dark recesses of my mind, I really do need to get to work."

"Oh, I doubt I've probed *all* the deep, dark recesses. Everyone I've ever talked to seems to keep some in reserve. What about your parents' relationship with Lenora Hinson?"

"My mother had no relationship with her. My father's relationship was strictly professional. I dated Keaton once or twice before I even realized her parents were my father's patients."

"How did Keaton's father die? Was your father involved?"

"Straight from my sex life to my father's professional reputation. That's pretty good, detective. You do pack a lot of jollies into one conversation, I'll say that for you. Did my father operate on Harold Hinson, forget to close him back up, and cause him to die? Did Keaton and her mother discover that the night I asked Keaton to marry me, and therefore decide that I would never see Keaton again? Hardly."

"So what did happen?"

"Harold Hinson dropped dead in his tracks at a relatively early age, struck down by a massive, fatal heart attack. He suffered from silent heart disease, virtually non-diagnosable a generation ago. He may have had angina, but he was probably the type who never said anything about it, and went to his grave without an inkling of what was wrong. And now, I really do have to get back to work."

"Are you married, Dr. Cabrioni?"

"No."

"Ever been married?"

"No."

"Do you ever see Keaton Crandell?"

"I've run into her maybe five or six times in the last eight years."

"And what happens when you see her?"

"I ask her how she's doing and she kisses me on the cheek and we make totally mundane conversation for about thirty seconds."

"You've already admitted you hated Lenora Hinson. Did you hate her enough to kill her?"

"What am I supposed to say to that? You already told me her death looks suspicious. No one in their right mind would say that they hated her enough to kill her."

"The truth is an amazing weapon."

"Yeah, I bet all the innocent bastards in jail would agree with that. Yes, I hated her. Enough to kill her? Obviously not." He thought for a moment. "Did she die quickly?"

"Probably."

"Then that rules me out."

"See what I mean about the truth being an amazing weapon? How did your parents feel about Lenora Hinson?"

"I have no idea. I doubt they thought about her much."

"Two loving parents with an only child who was terribly hurt? You don't think your mother hated Mrs. Hinson?"

For the first time, Cabrioni's laugh sounded genuine. "If my mother wanted someone dead, Detective Alvarez, she'd make a very life-like doll of that person, stick a pin through the heart, and that person would fall down dead. She wouldn't need to drop a roof on someone's head to get the deed done."

"You don't believe that."

"You don't know my mother."

Alvarez laughed. "Fair enough. I've always believed my grandmother could strike someone dead with a glance." Alvarez made a show of consulting his notes. "You said that when you were nineteen, you would have done anything for Keaton, even jump off a cliff. So would you do anything for Keaton now?"

Cabrioni looked long and hard at Alvarez without answering. "I have the feeling I shouldn't have had this conversation with you. But it's too late for that, so I guess you'll just have to decide whether you believe me when I tell you I don't know the answer to that question. But I don't foresee it being a question I have to answer for myself."

"Where were you on New Year's Eve?"

"With my parents."

"And they'll substantiate that?" Cabrioni looked steadily at Alvarez and didn't bother to answer. "One last question," said Alvarez. "Do you have a fiancée?"

"No."

"A girl friend?"

"Detective, I have a dog. And that suits me just fine."

Now there was a scary thought.

CHAPTER TWELVE:

VAGUE RECOLLECTIONS
Las Cruces, New Mexico:
Monday, January 2, early morning

One of the unexpected results of the phone calls from the mysterious Mrs. A was Cody's newfound reluctance to leave for Florida. He wanted to work out all sorts of complicated systems for Tory to report back to him. When she pointed out that he didn't know his grandfather's plans for the evening, and she had no idea what time she would get back from Anthony, he reluctantly agreed to wait for a phone call the morning after the arranged meeting.

Tory conceded that if Cody hadn't heard from her by noon on Tuesday, he could call all her male acquaintances with her blessing. He informed her that he would start with Lonnie, move on to Jazz, and then call "that detective guy in El Paso."

Lonnie arrived promptly at nine, as expected, and Tory managed to answer his questions about the Rim Road house inspection and tell Cody goodbye with equanimity. Then she cried on the drive to work, ending up sitting in the parking lot and trying to repair the damage by dabbing at her face with a tissue and breathing deeply for a few minutes.

Cody was flying from El Paso to Dallas, Dallas to Atlanta, and Atlanta to Jacksonville. He would be met in Jacksonville by her father's private pilot, who would fly her son to the Wheatley estate on the outskirts of Ocala, Florida. Four take-offs and four landings, with her father at the end of it all. It was almost more than Tory could bear.

Sylvia Maestes did not believe in differentiating between the personal and the workplace. A vision in a purple jumpsuit with silver trimming, she jumped up when Tory walked in the door, leaned over and clasped Tory to her bosom in an awkward embrace with a desk between them. *"Pobrecita Torita,"* she cooed. "Did you send the little one off? He'll be okay, *es verdad*. It's time he gets to meet your family, *que no*? Just because they don't like you doesn't mean they'll feel the same way about him. And now there's Kohli, so he has something to come home to."

"I was rather hoping he would come home to me," Tory muttered as she fought her way up for air. It was like trying to get free from a Tar Baby. A piece of silver trim at the neckline of Sylvia's jump suit caught in Tory's wristwatch as she tried to disentangle herself from her secretary. "And he's not meeting my family, he's just meeting my father. And my father's staff. His staff doesn't feel one way or another about me, I don't think. Unless ..." Tory stopped herself before launching into a full-blown defense of her former life. Fortunately the phone rang, and Sylvia reached over and grabbed it while she simultaneously wriggled her neckline free of Tory's wrist.

"Travers Testing and Engineering," Sylvia cooed into the phone. "Happy first Monday of the New Year." Her expression darkened as she listened to the voice on the other end. "No. No. I already told you no. *Claro que no*. Me? You want to talk to me? *Y voy a recibir un premio por las respuestas correctas? Creo que no, pendejo*. And don't call here again."

Tory took advantage of Sylvia's involvement with the phone call to take off her coat and hang it in the coat closet. "One of our better clients?" she asked mildly. "Offering to give you a prize for the right answers?" At least it was hard to continue thinking about plane crashes.

"No. That was the third call from the newspaper. The local television station already called twice. Now they're asking to interview me."

"I vote you hold out for the television station. That outfit would be wasted on the newspaper."

"You think so?" Sylvia looked down at herself and made a minute adjustment to the neckline of her jumpsuit. It started out as a slight wiggle of her chest area and progressed all the way down to her hips. "There," she said, satisfied that she was now optimally encased in the stretchy purple material. "There's a shit load of work, so you might as well stop moping around and get to it." Obviously the tea and sympathy time was over. "Hey," she said, suddenly, turning back to Tory. "What's the story with you and Dah-veed? I got the feeling you wanted to get rid of me every time I called you last night."

And Jazz was always saying you had to hit Sylvia over the head with something to get her attention. "There's no 'me and David,'" Tory said. "It's business, and unfortunately, it's business that got leaked to the press. I'm just helping the police figure out what caused the collapse at the house on Rim Road."

Sylvia gave Tory a sharp look. "You're not going to be discovering any more bodies, are you?"

"No more bodies," Tory reassured her.

"Well, okay then. Jazz has been looking for you. I think he has a hangover, but don't let him know I told you."

"*No se preocupe.* Is he at his desk?"

"Either it's him or his evil twin. He told me the only thing worse than seeing me first thing in the morning in my new outfit was seeing two of me first thing in the morning in my new outfit. Take him some coffee. Maybe that way he won't bite your head off."

Tory followed Sylvia's advice, but when she approached Jazz at his desk, he looked more contemplative than adversarial. Tory placed the coffee on his desk and sat down in a chair beside him. "Sylvia said you noticed her new outfit," she remarked cautiously, in order to test the waters.

"Maybe her sole purpose in life is to serve as a warning to others," said Jazz darkly. "You're late."

"I had to see Cody off, and besides, I thought you were calling in dead."

"I changed my mind. I've been thinking."

"Want to tell me about it?"

"That's what I've been thinking about."

"You were a little more emphatic last night, in case you don't remember. You told me that you thought you could find the people who built the room in that house on Rim Road."

"I remember what I said just fine, boss. *Nada es mal fácil.* What I've been thinking about is if I should tell you. You have a habit of ending up in trouble, where maybe someone else would have the sense to walk away."

"I'm really glad you feel you can talk frankly, me being your boss and all."

"You know what I mean. And the last time it happened, I was in the hospital and I wasn't able to help you. You didn't tell Lonnie what was going on, and even that hot-shot detective wasn't there when you needed him."

"I seem to recall that I managed to take care of myself."

"Yeah. That time. But I've been thinking. That Alvarez told you to stay out of this, and I think he's right. Let somebody else find out who brought the column down on those rich *gringa* women."

"I talked to Alvarez last night and he's changed his mind."

"You're shitting me. Drinking don't impair my hearing, boss. I heard what he told you."

"Well, I think he felt bad about some of the things he said. He just needed some time for his conscience to eat at him."

"I would never guess his conscience was hungry."

"Look, nothing bad is going to happen."

"I hate it when you tell me that, boss. Almost as much as I hate it when the *Chicana Madonna* out there says 'I have a plan.'"

"Want me to get Sylvia to worm it out of you?"

"Hell, no. Anything but that. She's already asked me to repeat everything Alvarez said to you about twenty times. Next time, take her along instead of me."

"She wasn't appropriately dressed."

"You've got a point there. But when is she?"

"Are you going to tell me what you know or not?"

"Yeah, I'm gonna tell you what I know. The question is, are you gonna tell Alvarez?"

"Of course I am."

"Before or after?"

"Before or after what?"

"Before or after he needs to know."

Tory glared at him. "I don't think you do know how to find the people who built that room. I've thought and thought about it, and I don't know. If I can't figure it out, I don't see how you can."

Jesus Rodriguez could never resist a challenge. "It's the wood."

"What wood?"

"The wood in the column."

Tory closed her eyes and visualized the column. "Dark wood. Hard wood. Highly varnished. Very glossy." She opened her eyes. "Shit, I don't know. What about the wood?"

"It's Brazilian cherry wood. Imported. Very rare, very expensive. Definitely not common in this area."

"How do you know?"

"Because we did the construction inspection for the new

All Souls Episcopal Church in El Paso. Remember, after the arsonist burned the old church down?"

Tory did remember that. A schizophrenic vagrant had wandered from town to town in the southwest for months, setting fires in churches for reasons understood only by him. Many hadn't caught, and most of the ones that did caused only minor damage. But five years ago the fire set in the Episcopal church in downtown El Paso burned most of the sanctuary to the ground. Ironically, that was how the arsonist had finally been apprehended, since he couldn't resist hanging around to survey his handiwork.

"I remember that the sanctuary had to be rebuilt, but they were able to save the parish hall and the administrative offices. We did inspections for the new construction. They built some modern structure to replace the old sanctuary."

"They built one hell of an ugly church," said Jazz flatly. "A doctor can bury his mistakes, but all those poor Episcopalians can hope to do is plant a lot of trees."

"What does that have to do with a Brazilian cherry wood column?"

"That column came from All Souls."

"Are you sure?"

"I'm sure. It took me a while to remember why. Scav Herrero offered me that column if I would look the other way when they were supposed to fix some formwork."

"Scav Herrero. I haven't seen him on a site for ages." Tory and Jazz sat in silence while she thought this over. "It's kind of a leap to go from there to conclude that Scav Herrero built the room in the Rim Road house," she finally said, trying to keep the excitement out of her voice.

"Maybe, but I don't think so. Scav's a damn good carpenter, but he's always hustling for the next dollar, dirty or not.

There's no construction site where he couldn't find something to scavenge. He mainly used the stuff on other jobs, since there's not much resale value in scavenged materials."

"So you think building a concealed room would be the type of job he would do?"

"For the Scav Herrero I know, it would be right up his alley."

"Do you think he would tell you about it?"

"If there was something in it for him. But I'd have to find him first."

"And how would you do that?"

"I've got some ideas. But I need to do it by myself. I don't need a tall, blue-eyed *gringa* following me around, making everyone nervous."

"So when could you start looking for him?"

"The same time you want me to do everything else. Yesterday, right?"

"Sounds like a good schedule to me."

"How you gonna pay for this, boss?"

"What we need is a fat project in El Paso. Something requiring lots of research. Too bad nothing comes to mind."

"Tor-eeeeeeee." It was Sylvia, calling from the reception area. Tory wondered why they bothered with a phone system that included an intercom. "I've got a Sidney Dallas on the phone for you. He's with National Reliance Insurance Company and he wants someone to investigate a structural collapse in a house on Rim Road, *muy pronto*."

"Wonder how we'll work it into our busy schedule," said Jazz. He stood up to finish his coffee.

CHAPTER THIRTEEN:

MAKING CONNECTIONS
El Paso, Texas:
Monday, January 2, mid-afternoon

After talking to Gary Cabrioni, Alvarez figured he'd stick to a medical theme and check with the ME. A personal visit might reap more results than a phone call, he reasoned, since Pat Cornell dealt with disembodied individuals as a matter of course.

He was walking down the tiled corridor of the morgue trying to think whether he knew any new corpse jokes when he literally ran down the little ME. He grabbed her by her shoulders to steady her. Without a hard hat on, she was even smaller and more insubstantial than he remembered.

"Alvarez."

"You remember me."

"I'm not likely to forget. Your case just screwed up my whole day."

"Hey, I haven't tried to put any pressure on you. Yet," he protested.

"You, I wouldn't worry about. I got a directive from the Chief of Police *and* the mayor's office to schedule your stiffs ASAP."

"That must be the good news. Why do I sense that bad news is going to follow?"

"Because your so-called detecting skills are enabling you to figure out a no-brainer. There's been a leak to the press. Someone talked about the baby and the fact that the room in the basement was a concealed room—"

"Good help is so hard to find these days," he commiserated, remembering Scott's comment in th back seat of the rental car.

"So the press has been crawling all over any available city official for a statement," she continued without acknowledging his input. "They want something to say, and I'm supposed to give it to them. Then it'll be your turn to be on the hot seat."

"It's always nice to have something to look forward to. So when do you do the autopsies?"

"I'm on my way to my office to eat lunch. That's allowed, you know. It's in my employment contract. I'll have to do them first thing after lunch, which really screws my schedule for today."

"What's for lunch?"

"Old El Paso burritos," she said after a suspicious pause. "I heat them in a microwave in my office."

"It's good to support local business. Got enough to share?"

"Not a chance."

"But you'll call me?"

"I'll call you, don't call me." Pat Cornell continued down the corridor without a backwards glance. Alvarez was left with the unbidden thought that Cotton was one female who would probably be happy to see him for lunch, and she would like burritos, whether they were a local product or not.

Back at the office, Scott was nowhere to be found, so Alvarez put in a call to the hospital. Karen's voice, when she came on the line, was vibrant and energetic as usual.

"*Qué pasa?*" she asked.

"The stuff with the kid may get sticky," he said.

"You mean Aggie?" It took Alvarez a moment to remember that the kid had a name, even if it was a temporary one. "I assumed it was going to get sticky," continued Karen calmly, "or you would never have sent her to me."

"The kid may have been kidnapped by a non-custodial parent. Are you sure you didn't see any signs of abuse?"

"None."

"Two things. First, the information about the kid has been leaked to the press, so I really need you to keep a lid on things over there."

"The only ones who know about Aggie are me and your guys. You worry about your guys, and I'll take care of myself. What's the other thing?"

"What could you do for me if I needed you to hold the kid for a few days?"

There was a pause while Karen thought this over. "You mean if someone shows up to claim Aggie and you want to buy more time to figure things out?"

"I always knew you were bright."

"I have other outstanding qualities, too. You don't ask for much, do you?" There was another pause. "Well, I could claim she was coughing from dust inhalation. No, we wouldn't really hold a kid for that. How about an ear infection? It could be complicated by the fact that she was dehydrated when she was brought in."

"I thought you said she was in good shape."

"Listen, I'm trying to work with you. I can't withhold a healthy child from a parent, so if we play this game, Aggie came in with an ear infection, and she was significantly dehydrated."

"How much time would that give us?"

"Maybe two, three days, while we waited to make sure the antibiotics were taking effect. If we were really being conservative."

"Can you do that for me?"

"I can, but I don't like it. I'll be falsifying a diagnosis, and giving Aggie antibiotics she doesn't need."

"It's for a good cause, *cara*. I knew I could count on you. You're the best."

"I bet you say that to all the women you exploit."

"*Que no, chica*. I only say it to the good-looking women I exploit." Alvarez hung up the phone as Scott eased himself into the chair behind his desk and gave his partner a wary look.

"So while I've b-been out working, you're here in the office exploiting women?"

"It's for a good cause," Alvarez reassured him. "What have you got?"

"Pinnacle's in bad shape, like my dad thought, but not much worse than some other d-development firms. One guy said he didn't think Ryan Hinson could afford a d-d-divorce right now."

"So where does the money go?"

"That's an interesting question."

"I hate it when you say that: it means you don't know the answer."

Scott ignored him. "Ken Herneese is the s-son of Joshua Herneese. Joshua Herneese is the attorney who set up Harold Hinson's original will, and probably finagled the t-trust fund conditions."

"'Finagled,' now that's a good technical term," commented Alvarez. "And did I hear a 'probably' in that sentence?"

"You did," said Scott, unperturbed. "Joshua Herneese had a stroke t-two years ago, and is practically a vegetable, according to his s-s-son. Junior admits that dad may have set up c-conditions that weren't exactly dictated by the will, but he says we'll never prove it. I believe him."

"So where does the money go?"

"He can't tell me until he informs the heirs, or he'd be violating client c-c-confidentiality."

"Did you use the technical term 'warrant' in your conversation with him?"

"No, he says he wants to cooperate. The money goes to s-s-some charities and a few individuals, all local. Herneese is going to get them together in his office tomorrow at t-ten and read the will. We're invited."

"Just when I was running out of interesting engagements on my social calendar."

"A couple strange things," continued Scott. "Herneese wanted to know what happened to the dog."

"Cotton?" asked Alvarez intently. "He wanted to know about Cotton? Maybe Lenora Hinson bequeathed Cotton to someone." The more he thought about this theory, the more he liked it.

"I don't know," mused Scott. "He asked if anyone inquired about the d-d-dog or expressed an interest in taking her. He seemed pretty amused by the whole thing."

"Not half as amused as I am. What else was strange?"

"Herneese seems to despise Lenora Hinson. Not just dislike her, but d-d-despise her."

"Maybe he holds her responsible for manipulating his father."

"Probably so. Did you realize we haven't c-c-come across one person who liked her?"

Alvarez had to agree with that. "Here she is a wealthy woman, involved in all kinds of charity work. You'd think there would be at least one person out there who felt grateful."

"'We do not quite forgive a giver. The hand that feeds us is in danger of being bitten.'" It never failed to fascinate Alvarez that Scott never stuttered when he threw out his obscure quotes. "Emerson," Scott added for Alvarez's benefit.

"Yeah, well, her hand didn't get bit, it got dead," countered Alvarez. "How could Lenora Hinson be so rotten to everyone she knew, including her own children, and do all this charity stuff?"

"'One can always be kind to people about whom one cares nothing.'"

"Who said that?" asked Alvarez, curious in spite of himself. "Ann Landers?"

"Oscar Wilde."

"How about a quote to shed some light on a concealed room? And don't give me that 'now you see it, now you don't' shit."

Scott thought for a moment. "'We dance around in a circle and suppose. The secret sits in the middle and knows.'" He smiled, looking very pleased with himself. "Robert Frost."

"*Si el frío es el infierno de la montaña, entonces el viento es el consorte del demonio*," said Alvarez.

Scott looked puzzled. "If c-c-cold is the hell for a mountain, then wind is the d-devil's companion?" he translated haltingly.

"Consort. Devil's consort," corrected Alvarez.

"What the hell does that have to d-do with anything?"

"Nothing. It was something my grandmother used to say, and I was tired of sitting here listening to you and feeling like a *poco culto*."

Scott's reply was interrupted by the phone on his desk. He answered it, carried on a conversation in monosyllables, took some notes, then hung up and looked at Alvarez. "Missing p-persons has a match," he said. "One Raymond Boyce is flying in from Omaha, Nebraska. He'll b-b-be at the morgue at one tomorrow."

"Thus the plot thickens," contributed Alvarez, still trying to catch up.

"Funny thing from records in Omaha," Scott continued.

"What?" asked Alvarez. He couldn't think of a single quote having to do with either missing persons or the state of Nebraska.

"They say Boyce's wife and d-daughter went missing four days ago. But he waited 'til yesterday morning t-t-to file with missing persons."

Scott's phone rang again, and he carried on another minimalist conversation. He hung up, and the phone immediately rang again. Listening to Scott's part in the conversations was less than enlightening, so Alvarez spent the time trying to think of a quote to rival his partner's about the concealed room. Nothing came to mind.

Scott hung up again. "It's official," he said.

"What's official? Someone else cleared the case while we've been sitting here contemplating *Bartlett's Quotations* and high school literature classes?"

"I don't use *Bartlett's Quotations*," said Scott indignantly. "You d-don't use *Bartlett's Quotations* where I went to school."

"We didn't use it at my high school, either," said Alvarez truthfully. "*Qué pasa?*"

"That was CSU, then Pat Cornell."

"*No me digas*! The love of my life, and you didn't let me speak to her? I could've hummed the Mickey Mouse theme song."

"It's officially maybe a homicide."

"*Mierdadotas*. The only word worse than 'probably' coming out of your mouth is 'maybe.' What the hell do you mean, officially *maybe* a homicide?"

"The Jane Doe is a heroin overdose. Lenora Hinson is more c-c-complicated. She died from a blow to the head. The brain stem was severed, and she d-d-died instantly. The blood found near the fireplace is hers."

"So what does mouse woman have to say about this? Do we have a homicide or not?"

"They're not quite sure."

"What do you mean, they're not quite sure?"

Scott took a deep breath. "Maybe she was hit or m-maybe she fell. If she fell, maybe she was pushed, or maybe it was an accident. They put both deaths between f-five and ten p.m. Saturday."

"Between five and ten p.m.?" asked Alvarez in disbelief. "That's the best she can do?"

"She's cautious," said Scott.

"She's a rodent," said Alvarez.

Scott didn't argue the point, but continued to use the blameless pronoun "they" in talking about the autopsy findings. "They think the Jane Doe d-d-died before Mrs. Hinson, but they don't know if it would stand up in court." Scott shrugged to indicate his opinion of the information.

"Well, I'm sure glad things are consistent. It'd be hell to get something clear-cut about this case. I don't know if I could cope." As if on cue, Alvarez's phone rang. "Finally, someone wants to talk to me."

"What the fuck is the Special Case Force?"

Alvarez took the receiver away from his ear and looked at it for a moment before answering. "We're an elite group open only to owners of Sugar Smacks secret decoder rings," he answered. "And who the fuck wants to know?"

"Derek Dowling, DEA. What are you, a bunch of prima donnas who sit in the office all day?"

"We're special detectives assigned to special cases, hence the catchy name, Special Case Force. I must admit it's not as catchy as Derek Dowling, DEA. Were you born with that name, or was it created for special effect?"

"You sound like as big an asshole as I heard you were."

"*El prudente siempre plancha nalgas,*" said Alvarez calmly. This conversation was beginning to get interesting. Maybe if he talked to this guy long enough, he would even find out why Ken Herneese was interested in Cotton. Stranger things had happened.

"I don't know what the hell you just said, but I don't give a fuck. You listen to me. You've got one Raymond Boyce coming down there to view two Jane Does in your morgue."

"*Uno,*" said Alvarez mildly.

"What the hell do you mean, '*uno*'?"

"We may be low-lifes compared to the DEA, but we can count. We've only got one Jane Doe in the morgue for Raymond Boyce to identify."

"What about the kid?"

"The kid's alive."

There was a great deal of creative swearing on the other end, with some terms that Alvarez thought might be Scandinavian. It was amazing how there was always a chance to grow and learn on this job. Finally Dowling wound down. "These guys never get things right," he snarled. "How the hell do they expect us to bring down Raymond Boyce if they can't tell a live body from a dead one?"

Alvarez didn't feel qualified to comment on that. As he had said earlier, good help was hard to find. "Why are you interested in Boyce?"

"He finances drug deals. He's into information technology, mainly credit card theft. A few thousand here, a few thousand there, by the time the sucker figures out what's going on, the credit card company has to foot the bill, and Boyce has added to his purchasing power. We figure he's one of the three largest importers in the country."

"So if you know he's such a bad guy, what's the problem?"

"He runs a tight operation. Things happen to people who cross him, things he can't be tied to. He's got lots of people in his pocket, including cops and judges. We had a sting operation all set up, a sweet deal put together by a real insider, and then yesterday, bingo, the whole thing gets declared illegal on a technicality."

"Why should we give a shit?" asked Alvarez conversationally.

"Maybe I can get him for something else. Something simple. Maybe he offed his wife. We think he did his first one, but we couldn't prove it. Maybe he got sloppy this time."

"I hate to rain on your New Year's parade, but I think you're barking up the wrong tree. There's more weird shit to this case than a three-dollar bill, but I don't think your guy did his wife."

There was a pause. "Do you always talk like that?"

"Only when I speak English. My partner taught me all the clichés I know."

"How do you know Boyce didn't off his wife?"

"I don't. But it doesn't feel right. First, she was found in a concealed room, one that nobody knew about."

"Well, obviously someone found out about it."

"We had one of those famous anonymous phone calls. If it was a hit, why would we get called? The roof collapsed on top of two bodies. One was the owner of the house, the second one was our Jane Doe, the one you think is Boyce's wife. The kid was found in an upstairs bedroom."

"So what's to say that Boyce didn't track his wife to your concealed room and put out a hit on her?"

"That's possible, but death by a drug overdose seems like a strange way to execute a hit. Maybe things are different in the midwest, more wholesome like. Here we usually go for the straightforward method, three shots in the back of the head, or a switchblade in the jugular, something like that."

"She died of a drug overdose?"

"Heroin."

"Goddamn, if I'd only known she had a habit. It would have made things so much easier."

"Yeah, well, I wouldn't know about that. Wish we could make it work, though. The old woman may be a homicide and it would be real convenient if we could pin it on your guy. The only problem is that she left a shitload of money and a shitload of people who couldn't stand her."

"Don't be such a pessimist. Boyce has a reach like you wouldn't believe. I hope you're not one of these guys with territorial problems, because I'm coming out there."

"Hey, some of my best friends work for federal agencies."

"Name one."

"The Fish and Wildlife Service."

"I meant the agent, you asshole, not the agency. What's the big deal that you know someone who works for the Fish and Wildlife Service?"

"It's Louie Peron."

"No shit? You know Louie Peron?"

"No shit. We went to school together."

"Peron's a classic. He's set the standard in undercover work for the next century. Who else would have had the balls to put on a gorilla suit and let rare animal smugglers buy him?"

"It was dicier than you know, man. He was being bought to mate with a female gorilla. If they hadn't made the bust when they did, he would have had to stay in disguise and come through. Now that's what I call deep undercover work."

"I get the feeling you're pulling my leg."

"It's been known to happen. So will you be flying in on the same plane with Boyce?"

There was a humorless laugh on the other end. "Hardly. You think DEA pays for private planes? Boyce won't be coming in flying coach, that'll be me. He'll be traveling with at least three or four guys, real nasty types, but all the paperwork for them to carry concealed will be in order. You can count on it. That's the thing about these computer thugs. They're experts at the paperwork."

"You have to remember something about computers."

"Yeah, what's that?"

"They make very fast, accurate mistakes."

"I heard you were a wise-ass. I'll be there tomorrow. Where can I catch up with you?"

"How about one p.m. at the morgue? That's where we'll be meeting Boyce. The more the merrier."

"Yeah, he'll be tickled pink to see me."

"So how do we tell you from him?"

"I'll be the one without the bodyguards."

"Good point."

"Yeah, being on this Special Case Force, I would have thought you could have figured that out."

"Well, you're catching us at the end of siesta time, and we need all the help we can get from you federal guys. Why don't you give us a head start and send us some information on this Raymond Boyce?"

"How long do you want your fax machine tied up?"

CHAPTER FOURTEEN:

SETTING UP
Anthony, New Mexico:
Monday, January 2, early evening

Alvarez settled into Room 10 at the Shady Lady about six PM. It wouldn't be called checking in, because his name would never appear on the register. Scott arrived a few minutes later. "I want to check out the video system," Alvarez told his partner in way of greeting.

"It's supposed to be idiot p-proof."

"So stand there and smile."

"The activation button is behind the n-night stand."

"How original."

"What's the plan for backup?"

"I'll knock three times on the ceiling if I want you." Scott gave Alvarez a disgusted look. "Okay, I'll knock on the adjoining door if I need help. If it's just a chatty meeting with Annika Atkins and Tory Travers, I think I can handle it."

"You never can tell," said Scott philosophically.

"That's why I want you next door, waiting and ready, in case I decide to throttle one of them. Looks like this system works fine. Let's adjourn to your room. We can review our numerous theories so we'll feel justified when we fill out our time sheets. Then we can eat junk food and watch TV."

"I d-didn't know we had any theories."

Faulkner and Alvarez decamped to Room 9. Alvarez settled into one of two gray armchairs that were standard issue at the Shady Lady, while Scott reached into a large box and started laying files on the bed. Files on people, files on organizations, autopsy files, evidence files, for all Alvarez knew, files on files.

"I've come up with four m-major questions, and three major issues," said Scott, sitting in the second armchair after he finished dealing out the files. Scott had a penchant for counting and prioritizing things. Alvarez bet there was even some secret order to the way the files had been laid out on the bed.

"That's all? Just four questions?"

"M-major ones," clarified Scott.

"Okay, said Alvarez. "What are they? Maybe if we can answer your four major questions, we won't have to deal with your three major issues. I'm always intimidated by issues."

"What happened to Mrs. Hinson? Why a c-concealed room? Who is the second woman? What happens to the b-b-baby?"

"You missed one."

"What?"

"Who ends up with Cotton?"

Scott was silent for a moment, but Alvarez was pretty sure he wasn't thinking about Cotton. "Because of the d-defense wounds on Mrs. Hinson's arms, we assume a third person was involved," Scott said finally.

"Okay, I'll give you that." Alvarez picked up the file from the CSU and skimmed through it, like he might discover something new. "Forensics won't help us there, because there are latent prints all over the house. Not to mention stuff may have been wiped clean."

"Which might indicate premeditation."

"Or a cover-up after an accident. Anyone who reads a book or watches TV knows about getting rid of fingerprints. That's what popular entertainment is for."

"Wait 'til it's p-popular knowledge that blood leaves a chemical residue, and everyone starts using Lysol," said Scott glumly.

"Or a generic equivalent. I think there's a study out that shows a low correlation between criminal activity and brand loyalty. Where were we?"

"T-trying to avoid the issues."

"Right. Let's assume the concealed room was built as part of the Underground Railroad, and that Jane Doe and the kid belong to Raymond Boyce. We're still no closer to knowing what happened to Lenora Hinson. So what are your three issues?"

Scott counted them off on his fingers. "Lenora Hinson's money. The Underground Railroad. Boyce's c-c-criminal activity."

"And you thought I needed sensitivity training. You mean Boyce's *alleged* criminal activity. Lucky no one but me heard you say that, *ese*. I have another question for you."

"Is it about the d-d-dog?"

"No, it's not about the dog. I'd actually forgotten about the dog there for a moment. My question is why we're asking these questions."

Scott looked at him unblinkingly for a few minutes. "That's a good question," he finally said.

"It's about time I got some recognition for my contributions on this case. Exactly why do we care what happened to Lenora Hinson? The best we could prove would probably be manslaughter, unless we can show premeditation. It would be nice to tie the DEA's guy to these deaths, but I can't see a professional hitman staging an overdose and then hitting an old lady in the head. That would mean the standards of professionalism are really slipping out there."

"Not to mention that someone working for Boyce wouldn't leave the b-b-baby."

"Yeah," said Alvarez.

"We'd n-need a strong motive to show premeditation," Scott continued with his current line of logic.

"Every single person we've talked to disliked Lenora Hinson."

"Not that Rodney Kiepper guy."

Alvarez had to think a moment to place the person Scott was referring to. "Nah, he didn't like her, either. I'd bet ten bucks on it. He was just being polite, and we didn't talk to him long enough. But smacking the old lady in the head could be a spontaneous act, as well as a premeditated one."

Scott nodded his agreement. "And why do we care about the c-c-concealed room?" he mused. "Assuming the other woman was the baby's mother, she's d-d-dead now, and any potential kidnapping is over."

"And why do we care about Boyce's criminal activity?" Alvarez felt like they were on a roll, eliminating questions and issues left and right. "That's DEA's problem."

Scott grimaced and looked glumly at his partner. "That still leaves us with the last question. What happens to the b-baby?"

"Right," said Alvarez after a pause. "Which, unfortunately, leads us back to Boyce's criminal activity and the Underground Railroad."

"Alleged criminal activity."

"I was just testing you."

There was a long period of silence. "I still like the money angle," said Scott finally.

"You always do. There must be some appropriate quote about being captive to your upbringing." Since Scott looked like he was considering this as a challenge, Alvarez quickly continued. "So Jane Doe kidnaps the kid and comes to stay with Lenora Hinson, the congenial El Paso Underground Railroad hostess."

"Not congenial."

"Okay, but even if Lenora Hinson resembles the Wicked Witch of the West, she can offer some advantages you don't find at a Motel Six, like a real, honest-to-God concealed room and multiple IDs."

"Okay."

"But Jane Doe has a heroin habit, something she hasn't revealed to the friendly Underground Railroad workers."

"They're supposed to do really d-detailed background checks."

"So they screwed up. Jane succumbs to the pressures of being on the run, shoots up and ODs. Somebody who stands to inherit Lenora Hinson's money comes calling, and finds her in the basement room with the newly deceased Jane and her baby. This person is appalled that the old lady is funding an illegal activity. There's a fight, and then suddenly there's two dead bodies to contend with instead of one."

"So this person takes the b-baby upstairs and waits twenty hours or so, makes the call."

"Yeah. Whoever made the call had to know what went down."

"And this p-person, who isn't with the Underground Railroad, just happens to know that p-pulling down the column will cause a c-c-collapse?"

"You're the one who wanted a money angle."

"Tory thinks the p-person who p-pulled out the column was involved in constructing the room."

"*Tremenda cagada.* Don't tell me my own partner is going to start sentences with 'Tory thinks ...'"

"She's got a point."

"Yeah. Sometimes I think it's on the top of her head. So you think it has to be someone who knew about the Underground Railroad." Scott didn't contradict his statement. "Shit. That screws the money angle, as far as I'm concerned."

"Maybe not."

"How so?"

"Why would someone with the Underground Railroad attack Mrs. Hinson?"

Alvarez thought this over. "Because our mysterious third person discovered that Lenora Hinson altered her will to leave all her money to Jane Doe and the kid?"

"How c-could she will money to someone who was adopting a new identity?" asked Scott logically.

Alvarez thought some more. "Because she threatened to stop funding the Underground Railroad?" Scott nodded. "But then what would Lenora Hinson use a perfectly good concealed basement room for?" Scott didn't seem to have an immediate answer. "I've got it," said Alvarez, inspired. "Jane Doe didn't like the accommodations. There was a fireplace, but no jacuzzi. So she knocked Mrs. Hinson over the head with something, let's say a brass candlestick, to be in keeping with the general decor. Then she felt so much remorse she OD'd."

Scott shook his head. "That leaves out the phone call, the collapse, and the ME thinks Jane Doe died first."

"Picky, picky. Do we think it's significant that they both died on New Year's Eve?" asked Alvarez, trying a different approach.

Scott shook his head. "Neither K-K-Keaton or Ryan knew their mother's plans for New Year's Eve. It wasn't a holiday they usually spent t-t-together."

"Yeah," said Alvarez. "I bet harboring fugitives in your house puts a real crimp in your holiday party schedule. And I'll bet the Crandells and the junior Hinsons all attended New Year's parties, right?" Scott nodded. "The kind where there's so many people coming and going it's hard to say who was there and who wasn't, right?" Scott nodded again. "And before that, they were all at home getting ready." He didn't need to look at Scott for another affirmation. "Shit," he concluded.

"So where does that leave us?" asked Scott.

"I thought you'd never ask. With the sex angle."

"What sex angle?"

"Gary Cabrioni is still madly in love with Keaton Crandell, but she refuses to leave her husband because she doesn't want to give up her daughter."

"Does the column c-come in here somewhere?"

"Why, you think they used it as a trapeze or something? Be patient. Cabrioni becomes involved with the Underground Railroad through treating abused children. He still hates Lenora Hinson, but he has to work with her because there just aren't that many local women who decide to break the law and have lots of money to spend doing it. So somehow he's involved in the construction of the damned room."

"Maybe he worked his way through med school as a c-carpenter?"

"I don't think so, but it would make a good touch. Anyhow, he meets Jane Doe and falls in love with her baby. The baby represents everything that he and Keaton could have had together, except for Keaton's interfering mother." Alvarez stopped.

"What?"

"Something. On the edge of my mind, having to do with kids. But it's gone now. Where was I?"

"Cabrioni likes the b-baby."

"Right. In addition to helping Lenora kidnap kids, he's also treating the mother for her drug addiction."

"A handy guy."

"No shit. But everyone has their breaking point, and Cabrioni has his. He gives Jane a fatal injection, and smacks good old Lenora over the head with the aforementioned brass candlestick. Then he calls up Keaton and tells her that if she'll run off with him, they've got a ready-made daughter to replace the old one."

"There's a big problem."

"What? No brass candlestick? He took it with him, man."

"K-kids aren't interchangeable like that. And you don't just show up one day with a b-baby."

"There's that class thing again. Girls did it at my high school all the time." Alvarez cocked his head. "Is that knocking I hear?"

Scott listened. "I think so."

Alvarez grinned. "One guest here, one to go. And I think it's the good-looking one knocking on my motel door."

"Enjoy it while you c-can. I don't think there'll be a repeat p-p-performance."

"I've got a quote for you on that one."

"Yeah?"

"'O ye of little faith.'"

Tory was nervous already, having parked behind the Shady Lady and walked back around to the front. Alvarez's purple wagon was the only car sitting in the parking lot, but six other cars were parked behind the one-story building. Tory took a deep breath, checked once more to make sure the faded number on the door was a ten, and knocked sharply. Nothing happened. She waited, and then knocked louder. The door adjacent to Room 10 opened, and Tory jumped.

"Hi, pretty lady," said Alvarez congenially. "Right on time, as usual. Come in and join the party."

"You said Room Ten." It sounded petulant even to her, but she was trying not to show how much he had startled her.

"Room Ten is for the meeting. The party is in Room Nine," said Alvarez, leaning out, grabbing her wrist and pulling her inside. "You remember Scott," he said, gesturing at his partner. Alvarez removed Tory's down jacket and hung it on the back of the desk chair while she stood staring open-mouthed at Scott.

"You were supposed to come alone," she said accusingly, turning to Alvarez.

"We're the good guys," said Alvarez conversationally. "That means we're allowed to cheat." He stretched out on the bed, careful not to dislodge any of the files Scott had arranged there. He clasped his hands behind his head and openly studied Tory. She tried to keep herself from wondering if her black jeans and cropped black sweater were inappropriate for the situation.

Scott, a captive to his upbringing, stood and gestured at the armchair Alvarez had vacated. "Please have a seat, Mrs. Travers," he said politely. Tory abruptly sat down.

"Did you come alone?" asked Alvarez.

"Yes."

"Are you carrying?"

Tory looked at him. "Are you?"

Alvarez shook his head. "I don't know, Scott. We may have to search Mrs. Travers and disarm her."

Scott resumed his seat and leaned forward to talk to Tory, his elbows resting on his knees. "He's t-t-testy because he doesn't want you here," Scott said earnestly. "But you've been a lot of help, and we're grateful."

"Thank you," said Tory primly.

"I have to ask if you have a g-gun on you, because we need to c-c-control as many things about this meeting as we can," said Scott.

"Since you asked so nicely, Detective Faulkner, no, I don't have a gun on me. Are all those parked cars in the back of the building part of controlling the situation? What do we have here? A full-blown SWAT team for one woman?"

Scott cleared his throat. "Some of the c-c-customers, I mean c-c-clients ..." He started over. "Some p-p-people who rent rooms here, they don't want their car visible from the road." He looked dubiously at Tory to see if he'd made his point clear, as if he hoped he wouldn't have to stutter through any more of an explanation about the parking arrangements at the Shady Lady.

"Okay," she said evenly. "Then I have another question. What are you doing here, Detective Faulkner?"

"I'll field that one," said Alvarez. "You know all those shows and movies where the cop figures out who the bad guy is and then takes off to apprehend him alone? It doesn't happen. You want to know why? Because at the police academy, every day you have to write five hundred times 'I will not go looking for criminals without backup.'"

"So exactly who is the criminal you're looking for here?" Tory shot back.

"Does that mean you're speaking to me again, *querida*?"

"Listen," said Scott. "You t-two need to declare a t-truce, or I'll have to do all the t-t-talking. And n-n-nobody wants that."

Alvarez cocked an eyebrow at Tory. "He does have a point," he conceded. "Want to come cuddle with me, and we'll try to bury our differences?"

"I don't think we have time to dig a hole deep enough," she said, matching his tone, "so I'll just stay put."

"Well, let me continue my peace-making efforts by pointing out that you look lovely tonight. I really like the theme of dressing in black. Planning any other clandestine meetings later on?"

"I thought about consulting Sylvia concerning appropriate attire, but you told me not to discuss this meeting with anyone, so this is the best I could do on my own. It's not like I've ever done this kind of thing before."

"More's the pity," muttered Alvarez. "By the way, Sylvia told me something about sex change operations. She's working without a license, I assume. So many things to investigate, so little time."

Tory didn't see much way of avoiding some basic explanation of Sylvia's last conversation with Alvarez. "My son has a friend who turned out to be a girl," she said, choosing her words with care.

"It happens to the best of us," said Alvarez. "I hope it wasn't too much of a shock to him."

Tory flushed. "Cody knew she was a girl, it was the rest of us who didn't."

"What does that have to do with Sylvia?"

"This girl looked like a boy until Sylvia got her hands on her. Then she turned out to be gorgeous."

"I see," said Alvarez, looking anything but enlightened. "So your son is visiting your father?" he asked after a pause.

Tory was relieved to change subjects. "Yes. He left this morning, and he wasn't thrilled about leaving me to cope with all this excitement on my own. If I don't report in by noon tomorrow, he plans to call all my male acquaintances to come to my aid. I think you're number three on the list."

"I hope he'll have the good sense to call Sylvia before he calls anyone else. As I recall, she had a pretty good system for keeping tabs on everyone in Dona Ana County."

Tory took a deep breath. "So, have we made small talk long enough?" she asked.

"Long enough for what?"

"Long enough to start talking about the case."

Alvarez sighed. "I was afraid that was what you meant. I don't suppose you'd believe that we've decided you're a suspect."

"That's not even remotely humorous."

"Because if you were a suspect," Alvarez continued as if she hadn't spoken, "we couldn't possibly discuss this case with you."

"I want to know everything you've found out."

"You don't ask for much, do you? Every time I give you information, amazing things happen, things I never imagined."

"Not every time," Tory protested.

Alvarez continued as if she hadn't spoken. "Not to mention your dubious track record for being forthcoming yourself."

"Okay," said Tory resolutely, "I'm willing to trade information."

"Shit," said Alvarez. "I should have known. Exactly what information do you think you have to trade?"

"If I told you, it wouldn't be trading."

"She's pretty good," said Scott, without looking up from the file he was studying.

"You don't even begin to know," said Alvarez grimly. "She does breaking and entering, too."

"Really?" asked Scott, looking up, all attention now.

"There were extenuating circumstances," protested Tory. "Who was in my body when I agreed to come to this meeting?"

"It certainly wasn't me," said Alvarez, "assuming that wasn't a rhetorical question. And you didn't agree to come, you demanded to."

"Enough," said Scott. "You're already involved, Mrs. Travers, so we'll t-tell you what you want to know. But you have to k-keep it to yourself, and you can't go off investigating on your own."

"Okay," said Tory immediately.

"It makes me nervous when you're so easy," said Alvarez. "So what information do you have?" he asked again.

"I know who Mrs. A is," said Tory. Scott and Alvarez looked at each other.

"How do you know that?" asked Alvarez in measured tones.

"I did some research on the internet. There's an organization called the Underground Railroad that helps parents kidnap their children, if they think they're being abused, and disappear with them. Annika Atkins is in charge in the midwest, and she's known as Mrs. A."

"That's pretty good," Alvarez said. "We came to the same conclusion. Our Jane Doe was probably on the run with the baby, and the room in the basement was probably built to harbor fugitives in this Underground Railroad. Which means Lenora Hinson was involved."

"So Mrs. Atkins knows who Aggie really is, and doesn't want her to go back to her father," said Tory, as if that was obvious to anyone who thought about it for more than two seconds.

Alvarez looked at her for a long moment. "Annika Atkins is going to be on thin ice," he said finally, "giving us information without implicating herself or others. No matter how you cut it, if these people with the Underground Railroad are aiding kidnappers, they're breaking the law."

"Maybe some laws need to be broken."

Alvarez groaned. "Operating outside the law is *never* an answer," he said. "We have to believe that. *You* have to believe that, or all the things that separate us from the rest of the animal kingdom cease to function. But this is a useless discussion to have with you. I've seen your rap sheet, remember?"

"We're not talking about me, we're talking about Annika Atkins. And you have to admit she's done some good."

"Why, because a magazine story says so? How do you know these kids end up any better off in the long run? Who follows up on it? Who's out there impartially evaluating the data, something you're so fond of doing? Annika Atkins is a dangerous person," said Alvarez flatly. "Any other conclusion, and you're kidding yourself."

"Why is she dangerous? Because you say so?"

"No, because she's got a c-c-cause, and nothing to lose," contributed Scott, who was willing to let Alvarez fend for himself in some conversations, but not this one.

"She's made sure the press has a lot of information about her," said Alvarez. "She married young, had a daughter by the time she was twenty."

"That's not exactly a crime," bristled Tory.

"No one said it was, and like you said, we're talking about her, not you. When the child was five, Annika Evanston, as she was known then, divorced her husband and accused him of incest. The courts didn't see it that way. They thought the mother had emotional problems and no means of supporting the child. She fixed the economic part by marrying a rich man, and spent the next ten years petitioning the courts to change their ruling, to no avail. Then her daughter committed suicide at age fifteen."

"Doesn't that prove something?"

"Not a thing. Who's to say the suicide wasn't the result of a turbulent, highly publicized upbringing? Sorry to tell you this, but other fifteen-year-olds commit suicide all the time. In any case, Annika Atkins didn't have any more children, and she committed her life to helping other parents who can't prove incest or abuse. Since her husband died six years ago, leaving her as his sole heir, she has significant financial resources at her disposal. A fanatic with money, a recipe for trouble."

"I still don't think you can discount everything she's done," argued Tory. "Sometimes the courts make mistakes. All systems fail sometimes. Maybe we need someone like Annika Atkins for situations like that."

"You're forgetting there were two bodies in the basement," said Alvarez bluntly. "The one we assume is the kid's mother died of a heroin overdose."

"Oh," said Tory. It was the same "oh" she uttered when Alvarez told her that the stunning black pediatrician had been a gang whore. She took a deep breath, thinking over the new information. "Okay, you must assume the mother had a drug habit, or you'd be looking at her death as a homicide, right?"

"Right. Believe me, this woman was a junkie."

"But what do we know about Aggie's father? I doubt he's Mr. Household America."

"Why are you automatically championing Annika Atkins?" asked Alvarez, irritation plain in his tone. "Because she was nice to talk to on the phone?"

"I'm not her champion. If there's someone who needs a champion in all of this, it's Aggie," said Tory. "And besides, you didn't answer my question. What do you know about Aggie's father?"

"Someone named Raymond Boyce filed a missing persons report on his wife and infant daughter a few days ago. He's flying in from Omaha tomorrow to identify Jane Doe's body, and we think it's a match. Geographically, if it was his wife on the run, Annika Atkins is the person she would contact for help. It all fits."

"But what do you know about this Raymond Boyce?" persisted Tory.

"This much," said Scott, holding up a two-inch file.

"DEA says he's a major drug importer," said Alvarez. "They've been after him for years, but they can't make anything stick. He deals in information technology, and finances his drug deals through credit card fraud. Supposedly he has all kinds of people in his pocket and on his payroll, including cops and judges."

"But what kind of father is he?"

"Hell, Tory, that's not something the DEA prioritizes in

its investigations," said Alvarez in exasperation. "For all we know, between drug deals and blackmailing people, Boyce comes home and acts out episodes of Life With Father."

"Maybe he tracked his wife down and killed her."

"Okay, say he did. Then why didn't he just take his daughter home with him, instead of flying back to Nebraska and filing a missing persons report?"

Tory didn't have an answer to that question. "Does he have other children?" she asked finally.

"One grown daughter, a jet-setter who models for fashion magazines. And no, she's never filed any kind of complaint about him. From what these files say, the two of them are close. She stays with him when she's in the area."

"What about her mother?"

"She died in a sailing accident when the girl was ten. There was an inquest, and the death was ruled accidental."

Tory thought about that but couldn't come up with anywhere to go with it. "What about the other woman you found in the room, the one who owned the house?"

"I was wondering when you'd get around to that. She died from a blow to the head."

"So neither woman died as a result of the collapse?"

"It doesn't look like it." Alvarez picked up a file labeled "Forensics, Column" and held it out to her. "The lab found rope fibers at the base of the column, just like you theorized. It's somewhat circumstantial, but if you combine that with your structural analysis, it looks like someone pulled that column down."

"Well, it's certainly nice to know that the police concur with my analysis," said Tory, "since I got a call from the carrier who provided the homeowners insurance and I'll be writing up my notes and conclusions in a report for them."

"That will thrill Ryan Hinson," said Alvarez. "Maybe you can cite us as expert consultants. Be nice for a change."

"The conclusion that someone pulled that column down p-plays hell with all our theories," said Scott.

"Which is not something we think Raymond Boyce would know to do," said Tory, holding the file that Alvarez had handed her without opening it.

Alvarez frowned. "There's that 'we' again. I don't know about Scott, but it strikes terror in my heart."

The phone rang before Tory could reply. Alvarez answered with "Room Nine," listened, then replaced the receiver. "Slam says someone called for Room Ten, and he took a message like we asked him to. She said her plane had been delayed, and she'll try to be here by eleven."

"His name is really Slam?" asked Tory, curious in spite of herself.

"It's short for s-s-slammer," contributed the ever-factual Scott.

"As in time spent there," Alvarez expanded on the theme, in case she hadn't grasped the central idea.

"You're kidding," said Tory flatly.

"How else do you think we rate ritzy rooms like this for free?" asked Alvarez. "We asked the Las Cruces Hilton to give us a couple of rooms gratis, and they turned us down flat."

Tory looked at Alvarez and decided not to pursue the subject of Slam and his business enterprises. Or why he owed the two detectives a favor. She looked at her watch. "You mean we have to wait three and a half more hours?" she said instead.

"Why, *chica*, you have somewhere to go?" asked Alvarez.

"We're prepared," Scott reassured her. He opened the large cooler on the floor, displaying a wide assortment of soft drinks, chips, and Twinkies.

"Twinkies?" she asked. "My tax dollars go to support police officers who eat Twinkies on the job?"

"You're from New Mexico, so your tax dollars don't do us diddly," responded Alvarez, reaching for a package of Twinkies. "Civilians don't realize that the majority of police work is boring. That's BORING, in capital letters. The time that we don't spend asking the same questions over and over, or filling out paperwork in triplicate, we spend waiting. We've gotten really good at it. Wait 'til you find out how we spend our time, after we've exhausted all our investigative theories."

"How?" she asked cautiously, not sure she really wanted to know.

"We play truth or dare," said Alvarez with a big grin.

CHAPTER FIFTEEN:

DOING TIME
Anthony, New Mexico:
Monday, January 2, evening

Tory looked at her watch again. Exactly one minute had passed since she'd looked at it the last time. She resisted Alvarez's last conversational gambit for about twenty seconds more before she came up with an unoriginal response. "You're kidding," she said.

Alvarez answered, "Ask Scott if you don't believe me."

Scott leaned over and selected a bag of chips out of the cooler, ripped it open and offered some to Tory, who shook her head. "No, he's not kidding," said Scott. He started munching on the chips.

"It's an activity sanctioned and encouraged by our department," said Alvarez.

"*Now* he's kidding, right?" Tory asked Scott. Scott shook his head and continued eating chips.

"Two years ago we had to go to this partnership bonding seminar," said Alvarez.

"And we weren't even b-being disciplined," added Scott.

"It was kind of a Sigmund Freud meets Outward Bound expanded into the Fifteen Minute Manager, the brain child of some touchie-feelie asshole trainers who flit around the country inflicting themselves on innocent, hardworking cops like us."

"Innocent and hardworking," repeated Tory slowly.

Alvarez ignored her. "We had to go through eight hours of this shit, like we don't get enough togetherness on this job already. We got a list of topics, and we had to spend fifteen minutes telling our partner how we thought he felt about each topic. Try talking for fifteen minutes if your heartfelt opinion is that your partner doesn't give *mierda* about the benefits of teaching ebonics in public schools. Ebonics in El Paso, that's rich."

"D-do you know how hard it is for me to t-t-talk for f-fifteen minutes about *anything*?" asked Scott. "Eight hours minus one hour of evaluation and one hour of breaks, divided by two, is twelve fifteen-minute sessions per person," he said in disgust, stutter-free.

"It's not too great being stuttered *at* for twelve fifteen-minute sessions, either," added Alvarez. "And the real pisser was that you never got to say how *you* felt about any of the stupid topics. It was supposed to be an exercise in putting yourself in your partner's place, and then developing tolerance for his perceptions about you."

"Anyhow, we came up with our own version," said Scott.

"And what is that?" asked Tory, fascinated in spite of herself. "You line people up against a wall and shoot at them until they give you an answer you like?"

"No, *cara*," said Alvarez. "It's obvious you're a rookie. That's an interrogation technique you just described, not something you do with your own partner."

"That would lead to a lot of t-turnover," said Scott thoughtfully, still munching.

"One person comes up with a question," continued Alvarez. "If your partner bails out, no one has to answer, but if he answers, then you have to answer, too."

"Like, if he asks me s-something about my sex l-life with Donna, I don't answer," said Scott cheerfully. "Then he gets to choose another topic."

"The answers have to be the truth," said Alvarez.

"I can't believe this," said Tory. "What's the point?"

"It passes the time," said Scott.

"Then the team-building aspect comes in," added Alvarez. "You decide together who told the best story."

"You said it had to be true."

"Figuratively speaking," clarified Alvarez.

"Figuring out who had the b-best story isn't easy, either," said Scott, frowning. It looked like the memory of past grievances was coming to mind.

"It gives it a certain edge that we're usually armed when we play," explained Alvarez.

"This is crazy," said Tory.

"Now, if you played with us, we could have a majority vote," said Alvarez, popping the second Twinkie into his mouth.

"Unless we each voted for our own story," said Tory immediately.

"Yes, there is that. But there's another problem."

"What?"

"You have to tell the truth. It's a non-negotiable rule. So you might have to disqualify yourself, *cara*."

"That's not true."

"Good. Since you're the rookie here, we'll let you choose the question."

Tory opened her mouth to object, and then closed it again. She looked at her watch, surprised at how much time had passed.

"See what we mean," said Scott.

Tory took a deep breath. "Okay," she said.

"What?" asked Alvarez.

"I'm thinking."

"As long as you don't take longer to think than Scott does to answer, I guess that's okay," said Alvarez affably.

"You already know that I'm not armed," Tory hedged.

"So?" asked Alvarez, his eyes narrowing. It was obvious to Tory that the two detectives took their pastime seriously.

"So I think I should get two votes," she said.

Alvarez and Scott looked at each other, and Scott shrugged. "Scott says okay," said Alvarez. "He's conserving his energy for the contest. He's trying to think of something to say in case you ask about his sex life with Donna."

"It can't have to do with sex," said Tory immediately.

Alvarez groaned. Scott turned his chip bag upside down to see if he'd missed any. "If it has to do with ebonics, I quit," said Alvarez flatly.

"You always did strike me as a 'take my marbles and go home' kind of guy," quipped Tory, getting into the spirit of things in spite of herself. It was seductive, this sensation of camaraderie, feeling that by spending time together in this shoddy room, the three of them could somehow figure out what had happened in the basement of the Hinson house. She needed to remember she was an outsider, a civilian, or pretty soon she would be overcome with an urge to eat a Twinkie.

"Don't be a tease, *cara*," said Alvarez, popping the top on a can of soda. "It's time to come through."

The extraneous thought came to mind that when she related the evening's events to Cody, she wanted him to be proud of her. She reached back into her past and was struck by inspiration. "I want to know," she said slowly, "the most outrageous thing you ever did as a teenager, and what effect it had on your life. Not the stupidest, not the most reckless, but the most outrageous. And it can't have to do with sex," she repeated emphatically.

"Hmm," said Scott contemplatively, eyeing a package of Twinkies.

"Shit," said Alvarez after a moment. "Maybe ebonics isn't such a bad topic."

"I think that means you go first," said Tory.

"I got caught shoplifting tampons," said Alvarez shortly.

"See how this works?" asked Scott, tearing open a package of Twinkies. "All the years I've worked with this g-g-g-guy, and I never knew he shoplifted tampons."

"Why?" asked Tory, fascinated.

"My younger sister, Anna, is retarded. There are trendy terms for it, but that's what she is, retarded. My mother couldn't send her out with money to do any shopping, so if we needed something in the middle of the week, I was supposed to go buy it. When I was fifteen, my mother sent me out to buy tampons. I was so embarrassed that I shoplifted them. I got caught."

"Then what happened?" asked Tory.

"They called the police, *por cierto*. Second chances are for rich white kids, not some skinny Mexican *cholo*. A cop named Howie Quintana fielded the call, and he gave me a choice. He could call my mother, or I could pull a two-hour shift in a squad car every day after school for a week."

"So Howie Quintana became your mentor because you shoplifted tampons?" asked Tory. This sounded like the plot outline of a made-for-TV movie.

"Hardly. I wouldn't have survived riding in a cop car on his beat, which was my home territory, so he paired me up with a cop out in Ascarate. We fixed it so that after school, I walked about a mile to a convenience store, which was a real pain in the ass. The Ascarate guy picked me up there, so none of my good buddies would see me hanging with a cop."

"And what became of Howie Quintana?" asked Tory, envisioning the closing credits rolling on a TV screen.

"A couple years after I got out of the Police Academy, he was hauled up on graft and bribery charges. I've always thought he went real easy on me because compared to what he was bringing down, one box of tampons was no big deal."

"Oh," said Tory. She seemed to be saying that a lot lately.

Alvarez took a long swig from his soda can. "I'm done," he said.

"My mother c-c-caught me hiding in the women's restroom at the b-beach when I was sixteen, and made me go to a therapist for a year," said Scott without preamble.

"Why were you hiding in the women's restroom?" asked Tory. This was not turning out the way she had envisioned.

"Because of the ice cream g-guy."

"See what we mean?" interjected Alvarez. "All the years I've worked with Scott, and I never knew about the ice cream guy."

"He was a really big guy, a b-b-body builder with t-tattoos all over his arms," continued Scott. "I got up to the counter and he said 'V-v-v-v-v-v-v-vanilla or ch-ch-ch-ch-ch-chocolate.' That's how he said it, he stuttered worse than me."

"So why did you end up in the women's restroom?" asked Tory. It was interesting to note that detectives were as bad as anyone else about not answering questions.

"I had to tell him which flavor I wanted," said Scott.

"What was the problem with that?" asked Tory.

"Because you had to say either 'v-v-v-vanilla' or ch-ch-ch-chocolate,' right?" interjected Alvarez.

"That's not fair," said Tory. "You already know this story."

"Not true," he retorted. "Let me remind you that I'm a trained detective."

"I can't even remember which one I t-tried to say. I was so nervous I stuttered more than usual," continued Scott. "He was sure I was making fun of him, so he c-came over the counter at me. I ducked around the corner of the b-b-building and there was the women's restroom. I hid in a stall, but then my mother and my s-s-s-sister Cassidy came in."

"Cassidy?" asked Alvarez. "You have a sister named Cassidy?"

"It was my mother's maiden name."

Alvarez looked at Tory. "This must be a class thing. Your mother's maiden name wasn't Victoria, by any chance, was it?"

"No," said Tory. "But then my mother's first name was LaBelle, and that's bad enough all by itself."

"No argument there," said Alvarez. "No girl in my high school had a name like Cassidy or Keaton, but there was a Neewollah. Get it?" Both Tory and Scott shook their heads. "It's Halloween spelled backwards," he explained. "Her birthday was October thirty-first."

"That may actually be worse than LaBelle," admitted Tory.

"Maybe it's good that this name thing wasn't part of my heritage," mused Alvarez. "Otherwise, my sister Anna would be named Hobarten. She may be retarded, but believe me, she isn't that retarded."

"I can't believe you said that," said Tory.

"Why?" asked Alvarez. "It's true."

"D-do you want to hear this, or not?" asked Scott.

"So you're hiding in a stall in the women's restroom at the beach," said Alvarez. "This has some interesting possibilities. Go on."

"It can't have to do with sex," Tory reminded Scott.

"My mother recognized my t-t-tennis shoes and hauled me out of the stall. I was t-too embarrassed to t-tell her what had happened, especially in front of my sister, so she made m-me go to therapy for a year. To explore my sexual identity issues."

"He's disqualified. He mentioned sex," said Alvarez triumphantly.

Tory ignored him. "What did you do?" she asked Scott.

"I didn't have any issues to t-talk about, and a year is a long time. So we ended up talking about c-careers. I took a

Myers-Briggs test, and decided that I wanted to b-b-be a police-man. When my parents found out, they tried to g-g-get their money back from the therapist."

"The search for blame is always successful," said Alvarez reflectively.

"How about you, Mrs. Travers?" asked Scott politely.

"For heaven's sake, call me Tory," said Tory, thinking how best to start her story for dramatic effect. She found herself feeling amazingly competitive. "I died on network TV news," she said.

"Pretty c-c-cool," said Scott, impressed.

"How?" asked Alvarez. "Did someone wring your neck?"

"I grew up in central Florida, where my father was a state senator. My brother and I went to private schools, so most of the kids I knew were from wealthy families."

"Now there's a surprise," said Alvarez.

"You're just jealous that your story isn't as good as mine," said Tory.

"We haven't heard it yet," Alvarez reminded her.

"When I was fourteen, my girlfriend had a boyfriend at the University in Gainesville."

"Precocious, was she?" asked Alvarez pleasantly.

"She was sixteen," said Tory defensively. "Anyhow, I used to go with her to see this guy in Gainesville, which was about an hour away. It was the first time I was around people who cared about something besides the next political opinion poll, or what model car their parents were going to buy them for their birthday. Her boyfriend was involved in a peace move-ment group."

"Why do I sense an episode of breaking the law coming up?" asked Alvarez.

"I didn't break the law," retorted Tory. "And besides, what do you call shoplifting?"

"So how did you die on the network news?" asked Scott.

"Every year there's a homecoming parade at the university. It's a big deal in Florida. They televise it and bring in all the local dignitaries. Some of the students had infiltrated an ROTC drill team that was going to march in the parade."

"People infiltrated a college ROTC group?" asked Alvarez. "They must have had a lot of spare time on their hands."

Tory glared at him. "Do you want to hear this or not? The guys who had infiltrated the ROTC drill team were going to shoot blanks into the crowd, to show what real warfare was really like. They needed volunteers to die."

"I bet you were the first one to raise your hand," said Alvarez.

Tory ignored him. "It was really neat. There were about fifteen of us, all different kinds of people. One was this little Quaker lady who was seventy-six years old. We put fake blood packets under our clothes and went to watch the parade. When the guys in the drill team started firing on the crowd, we burst the blood packets and fell down like we'd been shot."

Scott and Alvarez were staring at her. "Were there cops there doing crowd control?" Alvarez asked slowly.

"Yeah, they went wild," said Tory. She hadn't thought about the excitement of that day in years. "Everyone started running away, and the cops pulled out their guns and disarmed the ROTC group. One of the TV cameras did a close up of me where I'd fallen, covered with all this red stuff that looked like blood."

"I'm not surprised," muttered Alvarez. "Then what happened?"

"They called in the ambulances, but by the time they got there, some of the guys had told the cops that the shots were only blanks. So we didn't end up actually going to the hospital, or anything like that. But the story had already been broadcast. Then it made the national news again when everyone found out it was just a demonstration."

"Tory," said Alvarez slowly, "did any of you realize that a policeman could have shot someone, believing he was preventing other people from being killed?"

"We thought of that," said Tory. "We knew there were only two policemen for every quarter mile of the parade route, and the guys who shot the blanks were in the middle of a group of guys who all looked the same." Alvarez just raised his eyebrows. "And they wore bullet-proof vests under their uniforms. And besides, we were younger then, and things just didn't seem so dangerous," she concluded lamely.

"You say you were fourteen?" asked Alvarez.

"Yes," said Tory.

"And your son is how old now, fifteen?" Tory nodded. "Maybe being privy to a sex change operation isn't such a bad thing," Alvarez said.

"What about your p-parents?" asked Scott.

"My mother had hysterics," said Tory.

"Well, at least that showed she cared," said Alvarez.

"She had hysterics the day after it all happened," said Tory flatly. "When my parents realized that my name would be released to the press as a participant in the demonstration."

"It probably bought your father a lot of sympathy votes from other parents who wished they could shoot their own teenagers," said Alvarez. He looked at Scott and Scott nodded. "It's unanimous," he said. "We think you win."

Tory felt inordinately pleased with herself. "What do I win?" she asked proudly.

"Ah, *cara*," said Alvarez with a smile. "You should always ask these things before you enter the contest. The prize is dinner with me."

Tory looked at Scott. "Is he telling the truth?"

"Are we still p-playing?" asked Scott.

"No," said Alvarez quickly.

"Then he's t-telling the truth."

"And the second part of the lesson," said Alvarez, "is that sometimes there are games you *want* to lose."

CHAPTER SIXTEEN:

SEX, LIES, AND VIDEO TAPE
Anthony, New Mexico:
Monday, January 2, late evening

"Don't tell me you're a 'take my marbles and go home' kind of girl," said Alvarez, "especially since you won. It wouldn't be sporting."

"I assume I get to pick the place," said Tory crisply.

"If I get to pick what you wear."

"What about the State Line?"

"Don't tell me I'm such a threat that you won't have dinner with me unless it's out of my jurisdiction."

"No, you idiot. I mean the State Line Steaks and Barbecue. On Sunland Park Drive."

"Seven-thirty, tomorrow night. Something red and slinky."

"Yes, yes, maybe and in your dreams."

"Let's not argue over trifles. I've got a new game I want to play."

"I can hardly wait. If there are any more delays, I'm going to get my own room."

"That wouldn't be a good idea," said Scott and Alvarez in unison. "Slam is kind of particular about the people he rents rooms to," explained Alvarez. "Besides, you might like this game."

"What is it?" asked Tory dubiously.

"It's called 'You Play the Dead Person,'" said Alvarez. "After all, you've got the best credentials for the role."

Scott stifled a yawn. "What are you up to now?" he asked Alvarez. "I can't referee much longer, I'm b-b-beat. Teething baby," he said to Tory in way of explanation.

Alvarez picked up Lenora Hinson's autopsy file and slid

out a packet of pictures, looking for the ones he wanted. He spread them out on the end of the bed. Scott took a look and said, "Mrs. Hinson's d-defense wounds. What about them?"

"Are we making a mistake by assuming these are defense wounds?" asked Alvarez.

Tory moved closer to look. "What are these?" she asked.

"Pictures of Lenora Hinson's forearms. She has two wounds, each in the middle of a forearm, almost exactly alike."

"It looks like the skin was torn," said Tory.

"You're right. As you get older, your skin gets thinner and more fragile. Lenora Hinson took blood-thinning medication, which aggravates the condition. So when someone grabbed her, the skin tore, in addition to the bruising you see in the pictures."

"How do you know it wasn't an accident?"

"Because we can distinguish his finger and thumb marks. See?" Alvarez pointed out what he was talking about. "The thumb marks are pointing up, identical on each arm. And that's what bothers me."

"How do you know it was a man?" Tory persisted.

"Think we're being sexist?" asked Alvarez. "Mrs. Hinson wasn't a small woman. It says here she was five-seven and weighed one-fifty." He looked at Tory. "I know you're five-ten. How much do you weigh?"

"I can't believe you're asking me this," said Tory.

"Okay, be a wuss. We're close enough for government work. Hinson had on a sweater when she died, the same as you, so that works."

"Works for what?"

"Here, put your hand up like this." Alvarez raised his hand like he was going to arm wrestle. "Now, grasp your forearm with your other hand, with the grasping thumb pointing up."

Tory complied. "Look, your fingers barely meet your thumb. On Hinson's body, the fingers overlap the thumb print."

"You've wanted to clear K-K-Keaton ever since she said you were g-g-good looking," commented Scott.

"Who is Keaton?" asked Tory.

"It's not important," said Alvarez. "Put your hand up against mine." Tory hesitated. "Scott's here to chaperone, so nothing's going to happen," Alvarez told her. Goaded into action, Tory leaned over and pressed the palm of her hand against his. "Look," he said. "My fingers are about three-quarters of an inch longer than yours. So when I grab you"—he grasped Tory's forearm to demonstrate—"my grip overlaps with my thumb." Tory sat still just long enough for him to prove his point before she pulled her arm away.

"So we assume the d-defense wounds were inflicted by an adult male," said Scott, "or a very l-large woman. Larger than either Marshay or K-K-Keaton. That still doesn't prove they weren't involved in whatever happened," he reminded his partner.

"It's the defense part that bothers me," said Alvarez. "Get up," he said to Tory, as he came off the bed in one fluid motion. She reluctantly stood up, facing him. "Now," said Alvarez to Scott, "if I wanted to grab her, overpower her, how would I do it so that I grabbed both her arms the same way, with my thumbs pointing up?"

He reached out, grabbed one of Tory's arms, spun her around, jerked the arm up behind her back and brought his other arm around her throat. It all happened before Tory had a chance to realize what he was doing. "Note," he said, not even breathing hard, "once I grab her, I can't afford to change my grip, or I may lose control of her. And my thumb is pointing away from her hand."

Tory felt like a fool, facing Scott, who calmly regarded her as she stood there with Alvarez's arm around her throat. She suddenly wished she'd told Scott that his story should have won second place. "I think you've made your point," she said instead.

"This is a fun game," said Alvarez into her ear, "but only with trained professionals. Don't try this at home." Then he let go and spun her back around to face him again.

"Next time," Tory hissed, "you play the dead person."

"Her arms need to be up," said Scott. Tory immediately raised both hands in the air before someone did it for her.

"The universal sign of surrender," Alvarez laughed. "And I'm not even holding a gun on you. I like this."

"Lower," said Scott.

Tory lowered her arms until her elbows were parallel with her shoulders. "This is ridiculous," she said. "I feel like a goal post."

"Too far apart," said Alvarez. "The way you're standing now, I'd try to grab one arm or the other, but not both at the same time."

Tory clasped her hands slightly above her head, her elbows now level with her chin. "What are you doing?" asked Alvarez. "Praying for mercy?"

"Hardly," said Tory, struck by inspiration. She dashed over to the nightstand by the bed, grabbed the phone book, and brandished it above her head at Alvarez.

"What have you got?" asked Alvarez.

"A phone book. What does it look like?"

"Not you," he said impatiently. "You're Lenora Hinson. What do you have in your hands?"

"A lamp?"

"Too awkward."

"A candlestick?"

"I tried working it into a story already, but we didn't find one."

"A rolling pin?"

Alvarez shook his head in exasperation. "Don't be ridiculous."

"Well, help me out here," said Tory in frustration. "I feel like I'm playing some insane game of charades and I've only got half the rule book."

"You just recited our job description," said Alvarez. "What we didn't tell you is that you have to stand just like that until we come up with the right answer."

"Fireplace t-tools," said Scott suddenly. "A poker."

"Yes," said Alvarez slowly. "I like it. Let's see if forensics picked up Lenora Hinson's prints on the fireplace tools. Maybe in a pattern consistent with holding a poker with both hands like a weapon, if we should be so lucky."

"Did we figure out something?" asked Tory, replacing the phone book and dropping back in her chair.

"We figured out something that *might* have happened," said Alvarez carefully. "It could also be argued that she was pulled up from a kneeling, supplicant position."

"Oh," said Tory, disappointed.

"But nothing we've learned about Lenora Hinson indicates that she was a kneeling, supplicant type of person."

"That was kind of exciting," said Tory. "The part where we figured out what might have happened," she added for clarification.

"Well, that was fun," said Alvarez. "The bad news is that I'm fresh out of games, boys and girls."

Tory looked at her watch. "It's ten p.m.," she said.

"See how time flies when we're having fun?" asked Alvarez.

"But game time is over. It's back to the drawing board, no TV for us tonight."

"Which is just as well," said Scott, "seeing as we're in mixed company."

"What does that mean?" asked Tory.

"The TV selections here are a little different than those at home," said Alvarez, "so it's back to story-telling. One concealed room, two bodies, one live baby. Who wants to go first?"

They reviewed the information about the case, breaking it into pieces and trying to reassemble various parts into a theory that answered all the questions. Tory even broke down and ate some chips, but she drew the line at Twinkies.

No matter how they cut it, which pieces of information they used, whether Mrs. Hinson was attacking or pleading with someone, they came up with the same problem. The people with motives for wanting Lenora Hinson dead all claimed they had no knowledge of the concealed room and Underground Railroad. The stories with someone from the Underground Railroad involved in the deaths and cover-up lacked credible motives.

At ten forty-five, Alvarez suggested he and Tory adjourn to the next room. Scott took Alvarez's place on the bed, stretched out and closed his eyes.

"It's nice to know you'll be here continuing our intensive investigative work," said Alvarez.

"Make sure you knock real loud if you need me," said Scott, without opening his eyes. "I hope I don't see you 'til morning."

"He's staying here all night?" asked Tory in surprise, gathering up her down jacket as she followed Alvarez into an identical adjoining room.

"We both are," said Alvarez. She sat in another gray armchair while he stretched out on the bed again. "Detectives cherish any opportunity to sleep," he told her, reaching behind the night stand. "Slam doesn't care if we use the rooms for a few hours or the whole night. Or if he does, he won't say so."

"What are you doing?"

"Making sure the phone is connected. Never assume anything. I'd hate for Slam to try to call and have it be unplugged."

"So you'll both stay here all night?"

"Sure. Scott's baby is teething, so it's easier for him if we just crash here tonight, and it would look weird if only one of us was on an all-night stake-out. Or whatever we call this meeting that really isn't a meeting."

"What about Cotton?" Tory asked.

"Boy, you don't miss a thing," said Alvarez. "I went home at lunch and installed one of those damn dog doors. Pretty ironic. Sometimes we have to give lectures on home security to citizen groups, and here I am, sawing a hole in my back door."

"Good," she said, approvingly. "That was a responsible thing to do."

"Let's talk about your responsibilities. I've got some ground rules for this upcoming meeting. First, you sit right there in that chair, you don't get up, you don't move around, you don't go anywhere unless I tell you to. Got it?"

"Got it."

"This Mrs. Atkins obviously feels good about you, or she wouldn't have asked you to be here, so it seems pointless to tell you not to say anything."

"Good thinking."

"Don't get carried away, Tory. In every investigation, we have to make split-second decisions about what we tell people and what we don't tell people. We're professionals, and we still screw this up on a regular basis. We look back later and realize that we made the wrong decision. Do you understand what I'm telling you?"

"I think so."

"Case in point," Alvarez continued, "we kept the kid under wraps. Still, the information got out. Mrs. Atkins knows about her, so she probably knows how the kid and her mother got here. But we haven't told her anything about how the two women died, or a bunch of other things we've discussed with you. So every time you get ready to say something, I want you to consider what information you'll be giving to Annika Atkins before you say it."

Tory thought this over. "So when you talk to people, they might not tell you what you want to know unless you ask a specific question that gives away information," she said, thinking it out as she went along. "But if you ask them about everything, then maybe you've given them information that they shouldn't have."

"Because if someone blurts out something you haven't told them, that tells you something," Alvarez finished for her. A flash of light crossed Tory's face as a car pulled up in front of Room 10. "It's show time," said Alvarez. A few moments later there was a knock at the door. Tory started to get up, but Alvarez dramatically drew his finger across his throat, so she stayed put and let him open the door.

"Mrs. Atkins?" asked Alvarez.

"That's me," said a cheerful grandmotherly voice, and a small woman in a black coat entered the room along with a blast of chilly winter night air. Alvarez wordlessly removed Mrs. Atkins' coat as he had done for Tory, and hung it on a desk chair identical to the one in the next room.

Mrs. Atkins looked like someone's retired gym teacher. She was a small, compact woman with short gray hair and a brisk no-nonsense manner. She wore black slacks and a gray turtleneck sweater. She offered her hand to Tory and said, "Mrs. Travers? I'm Annika Atkins. Please call me Annika."

"And you can call me Tory," said Tory, after scanning her reply for any hidden informational content.

Alvarez was back lounging on the bed, watching the two women. "Have a seat," he said, and Annika Atkins sat in the vacant armchair across from Tory. "I like the color scheme," he said. "Did the two of you coordinate your outfits?"

"You must be David Alvarez," said Annika Atkins cheerfully, as if she fielded such questions at eleven PM in shoddy motel rooms as a matter of course.

"You can call me Detective," said Alvarez conversationally.

"But of course. You must be testy at me dragging you out of your jurisdiction, and asking Mrs. Travers to come along. And then being late on top of it."

"You could say that," said Alvarez. "Exactly why are we here, Mrs. Atkins?"

"Call me Annika."

"I wasn't raised to address my elders by their first names."

Annika Atkins' laughter sounded genuine. "Oh, Detective Alvarez, let's not start fencing over something as simple as names. I'm sure you have no problem calling someone by their first name if that unsettles them. But since I've invited you to call me Annika, you think it will be to your advantage to call me Mrs. Atkins and keep a certain distance between us."

"That's one way of looking at it," said Alvarez.

"My dear, when you've talked to as many detectives as I have over the years, you get pretty good at these things. You call me what you want, and for my part, I'll do my best not to call you 'son.'" In spite of Alvarez's warnings and precautions, Tory found herself relaxing, charmed by the woman.

"Sounds like a plan to me," said Alvarez evenly. "So why are we here? And why," he nodded at Tory, "is she here?"

"We're here to talk about Hannah. And Mrs. Travers is here to appeal to your better nature. I thought you just might behave better, and be more willing to listen, if she was around."

Alvarez chose to address only the first statement. "Are we talking about Hannah Boyce?" he asked.

"Oh dear," said Mrs. Atkins. "I was so afraid of that. So has Raymond Boyce contacted you?"

"He's flying in tomorrow to identify his wife's body. If that's a positive ID, we assume his next step will be to claim his daughter."

"Hannah. Her name is Hannah. Well, at least that gives us some time."

"Time for what?"

"To figure out how to keep Raymond Boyce from getting his hands on Hannah."

Alvarez calmly surveyed Mrs. Atkins from where he sat on the bed. Tory hoped that he was giving her credit for having spoken only six words since the interview began. "Why would I want to keep Raymond Boyce from claiming his daughter?" he asked.

"Her name is Hannah. It's so much harder to depersonalize someone if you use their name. Can you say Hannah, detective?"

"Why would I want to keep Raymond Boyce from claiming his daughter, Hannah Boyce?" Alvarez's tone was even, but Tory could see a muscle clench in his jaw. In spite of Mrs. Atkins' cheerful demeanor, an undercurrent of tension was starting to fill the room.

"What do you know about Raymond Boyce?"

"I know the DEA wants him for fraud, money-laundering, and drug distribution," said Alvarez. "And that's just a start."

"Does that sound like the kind of person who would make a good parent for Hannah?"

"I don't know," said Alvarez shortly. "That's not part of my job."

"And that's a big part of the problem," said the gray-haired woman who looked like someone's benevolent grandmother. "Why do you think the DEA can't send Raymond Boyce to prison, where he belongs?"

"I don't know that, either. It's not my case."

"But you have a pretty good idea, don't you?"

"Because he has too many contacts."

"So if he has too many contacts for the DEA to be able to touch him, how do you think one lone woman would fare, if she wanted to leave him to protect her child?"

"So we're talking about Boyce's wife now."

"Alicia Boyce. She has a name, too." Annika Atkins turned to Tory. "If you realized that you were married to an evil man, too powerful for even the federal law enforcement agencies to bring down, and you wanted to protect your child, what would you do?"

Tory gave the question her full attention, turning over the possibilities in her mind. "If I really thought he would hurt my child," she said slowly, "I'd probably run." Mrs. A turned to Alvarez as if she'd proven a point. "But I'd probably shoot him before I left," Tory added truthfully. "It would be cleaner that way."

Alvarez laughed. "You just never know what you've bargained for when Tory Travers comes to the party," he said. "Ask Emmett Delgado."

"I don't understand," said Annika Atkins.

"An in-joke," Alvarez said shortly. "So are you telling me that you helped Mrs. Boyce kidnap her own child? It's not even a custody issue. She and her husband weren't divorced."

"I'm not telling you anything right now. I'm here to talk over some theoretical situations with you. What chance do you think a wife of Raymond Boyce would stand in a divorce court?"

"Not good," admitted Alvarez.

"Not good at all. The results would probably be fatal. Anyone married to Raymond Boyce ends up knowing more than is good for them. That's why his first wife died."

"Nothing was ever proven."

"Don't be naive, detective. Alicia Boyce wanted out of her marriage and she wanted to protect her child. Coming to us was the only way she could do that."

"Theoretically, of course."

"Theoretically, she was really scared. So scared that she called and put all the plans into action a day early."

Alvarez leaned forward, intent. Tory realized that this was the first bit of hard information that Annika Atkins had conveyed. "So is that why something went wrong?" he asked.

Mrs. Atkins returned his look with the same intensity. She started to say something and then changed her mind. "I don't know," she said simply.

"Theoretically, do you know anyone who wanted to harm Boyce's wife and daughter?"

"You mean Alicia and Hannah. No one other than Raymond Boyce."

"What about Lenora Hinson? What do you know about her?"

"Theoretically," sighed Annika Atkins, "not very much. You probably know quite a bit about our operation by now, Detective Alvarez."

"Not as much as you could tell me."

"So you know that we operate on a need-to-know basis," continued Mrs. Atkins calmly. "People involved in our operation know the contact before them, and the contact after, but nothing else."

"Except for the leaders."

"No, that's not true. Especially for us. It's safer that way."

"And would you tell me if it wasn't true?"

"No," Annika Atkins smiled regretfully. "I wouldn't."

"So what do you know about Lenora Hinson, theoretically?"

"Why should I risk telling you anything?"

"Because you want something from me. Maybe if you help me, I'll help you."

"And if you'd already made up your mind not to help me, would you tell me?"

"No," said Alvarez, as simply as she had a few moments earlier.

"Ah," said Mrs. Atkins, looking at Tory. "I can see why you're fond of him, in spite of his shortcomings."

"I never said I was fond of him," Tory said immediately.

Alvarez hadn't taken his eyes off Annika Atkins since she'd told him that Alicia Boyce entered the Underground Railroad a day early. "Mrs. Atkins is using her abilities as a great judge of character," he said.

"Ah," said Mrs. Atkins again. "So that's the way the wind blows."

"Sooner or later," agreed Alvarez. Tory was beginning to wonder why he had warned her about participating in this conversation. The gray-haired woman in the armchair and the intent detective supposedly lounging on the bed seemed to be doing an intricate conversational dance known only to themselves.

"Lenora Hinson, then," said Annika Atkins. "Theoretically."

"Yes," said Alvarez. "Lenora Hinson, theoretically."

"She became very active in our group about five years ago.

She was recruited by someone who was seeking cash contributions for some of our efforts. She had the room constructed in her basement without consulting me or any of my counterparts." Mrs. Atkins spread her hands helplessly. "It's not possible to tell someone what to do with their own house. After the room was constructed, she became the major contact for moving people through this area of the country."

"So she kind of came in and took over without anyone's permission, or invitation?" asked Alvarez.

"Yes," said Mrs. Atkins. "You could say that. It didn't bother me personally, but it was a risk."

"What was a risk?"

"Always moving people to the same place."

"Yes," said Alvarez, "I can see that. Did that cause problems with your other people in this area?"

"I wouldn't know. I try to know as little as possible about the other regional organizations. I knew that we, theoretically, could take Alicia Boyce into our system in Omaha, and that she would be given safe passage to El Paso."

"Did Mrs. Boyce know she was coming to El Paso?"

"We tell the parents where they're headed, so they know what to pack and so they can talk to their children about where they're going." Annika Atkins seemed to stop herself from warming to the subject. "That helps with older children. All theoretically, of course."

"Did Mrs. Boyce know that Lenora Hinson was her contact here?"

Annika Atkins thought the question over. "Theoretically, yes," she said finally.

"And who was the contact after Lenora Hinson?"

"That knowledge died with Mrs. Hinson."

"I doubt that," said Alvarez. "Are you telling me you don't

know one other single contact for the Underground Railroad in this area?"

"That's what I'm telling you."

"Then this meeting is over," said Alvarez, and started to stand up.

Annika Atkins looked nonplussed for the first time. "Don't you want to know what prompted Alicia Boyce to go on the run?"

"Not unless it's directly related to my investigation. My investigation involves the deaths of two women and the collapse of a basement room in a private residence. It doesn't involve credit card fraud, it doesn't involve marital discord, and it doesn't involve custody issues."

"I want to hear why Alicia Boyce went on the run," said Tory.

"Good job," said Alvarez. "Right on cue. You just played right into her hands, Tory."

"Nonsense," said Annika Atkins, dropping some of her cheerful demeanor. "You're playing right into *his* hands, Mrs. Travers. He wants to know what I have to say, but he doesn't want to have to ask. If he asked, then he might feel responsible for doing something with the information."

"Bullshit," said Tory bluntly. "I'm not playing into anybody's hands. It took thirty minutes to drive down here, and then I waited four hours for you to arrive. I want to hear what you have to say because I want to hear it. It's as simple as that."

"She doesn't tend to mince words," commented Alvarez.

"You say Alicia Boyce wanted to leave her husband," continued Tory. "You say she was scared to leave him, that he might have her killed, or at a minimum, she would never be able to leave with her child. But why didn't this Alicia Boyce leave her husband before she ever had the child?"

"That's a good question," said Alvarez.

"Because she didn't have the nerve to leave," said Annika Atkins.

"What changed?" asked Tory.

"She found this." Annika Atkins reached into her purse and pulled out a video tape. "She found this tape of her husband and Patty having sex. Lots of sex. Lots of different ways, lots of different times. There are probably more where this came from. On this one, Patty looks about twelve. And there's no question that it's Patty, Detective Alvarez, before you even ask. She identifies herself on the tape."

"Who is Patty?" asked Tory.

"Ask your detective," said Mrs. Atkins. "He knows."

"Patty is Raymond Boyce's adult daughter by his first wife," said Alvarez wearily. "She's only a few years younger than Alicia Boyce."

"Here," said Mrs. Atkins, holding the tape out to Alvarez. "If you don't believe me, look at it yourself, and then decide."

Forgetting everything she'd been told, Tory stood up. "I'm out of here," she said. "You two do what you want, but I'm going home."

"Don't even think about stepping outside," said Alvarez instantly. "If you have to leave, go next door to Scott's room." Tory abruptly sat back down to review her options.

"Scott?" Mrs. Atkins looked regretfully at Alvarez. "I'm disappointed in you. Next you're going to tell me that you're wearing a wire."

"No wire," said Alvarez. "I have an excellent memory."

"But you brought another police officer. Do you really think I'm such a dangerous person?"

"Without a doubt. The most dangerous kind." Alvarez echoed Scott's words from earlier in the evening. "Someone with a cause and nothing to lose."

"And lots of money," Mrs. Atkins reminded him. "You might want to think about that."

Alvarez stood up. "That too," he said. "But I still won't watch your tape. You know as well as I do that it's inadmissible in a court of law." He walked over to the desk chair and picked up her coat.

"If things like this weren't inadmissible, then people like Alicia Boyce wouldn't have to go to people like me," said Annika Atkins, standing up herself. "I'm not going to just disappear into the night," she said as Alvarez helped her into her coat.

"No," he replied. "I doubt you will."

"You might be surprised where this tape shows up."

"I might be. Then again, I might not."

"Are you telling me that while you won't lift a finger to help me, you won't lift a finger to stop me, either?" Mrs. Atkins asked, turning to face him.

"As far as I'm concerned, you haven't broken any laws in my jurisdiction," he answered. "Yet."

"Will you answer one question for me?"

"You can ask and see."

"What time is Raymond Boyce supposed to identify Alicia's body? I can probably find out on my own, but it's been a long day for me, and I'd really appreciate it if you would tell me."

"One p.m., city morgue."

"Thank you," said Mrs. Atkins, recovering some of her earlier cheerfulness. She shook hands with both Alvarez and Tory. "Thank you for coming," she said to Tory. "I'm sure I'll see you again," she told Alvarez.

"That's up to you," he answered, and opened the door for her. As soon as he closed it behind her, he dropped into the chair opposite Tory, reached out, took both her hands and began to rub them in his. Tory was surprised to realize that her hands were freezing cold. She must have had sweaty palms and not known it.

"How are you doing?" he asked.

"I'm okay," she said slowly.

"Are you sure?"

"Are you going to get all solicitous now? Just to keep me off balance?"

"I might do that," he said. "As long as we don't have to discuss any of what just went down."

Tory felt drained. "That's okay by me," she said.

Alvarez looked surprised. "You mean for once you're not going to tell me what to do?"

"No," she said simply. "I don't know what you should do. You didn't tell her the baby's mother was a drug addict."

"There wasn't any point," he said. "If she knows something she's not telling us, maybe she'll slip up. If she doesn't know, she's going to find out sooner or later, and why not later? I don't imagine making this trip was easy for her."

"I don't know how to act when you're being this nice," said Tory truthfully.

"Okay," said Alvarez. "I'll revert to my normal self, so you'll feel more at home. How would you like to stay here with me tonight?"

"Here?" asked Tory. "You mean at the Shady Lady?" It was a stupid question, but he'd caught her off-guard.

"Yes, I mean here, not in the next room with Scott, that's for sure." He hadn't let go of her hands, but now he stopped rubbing them. "Your son is gone, no one is waiting for you, and we could just lie down and be together. Nothing more than that. How long has it been since you slept with someone, Tory?"

She recoiled at the shocking intimacy of his question and pulled her hands away. "Well, I really feel more at ease now. This is the David Alvarez I know so well."

"Not that well. I'd be a perfect gentleman."

"How do I know you mean that?"

"Well, for one thing, I'm videotaping everything that's going on in this room," he said truthfully.

Tory stood up, but not quite as emphatically as she had intended. "Thanks for the invitation, I think, but dinner is really all I can cope with right now."

He shrugged and smiled and stood up with her, watching her while she put on her coat. "At least let me walk you to your car," he said.

"I think I can manage that," she replied.

He walked her around the building to the cars parked in the back. She noticed with one part of her mind that there were different cars parked behind the building now. Alvarez waited patiently while she fumbled with unlocking the car door. Tory turned around to face him, but she couldn't quite raise her eyes to meet his. "Thanks, I think," she said, looking at his collar. "It sure has been a different kind of evening."

Alvarez put his hands on the roof of her car on either side of her, and leaned looking down at her. "You're a real pain in the ass sometimes," he said.

"Yes, well, goodnight," she replied, looking steadily at his chin.

"In a moment," he said, "I'm going to have to kiss you. You could probably still stop me."

Tory raised her eyes as far as his mouth, and said the first thing that popped into her mind. "You have really straight teeth," she said. "Did you have braces as a child?"

Alvarez took his hands away and put them on top of his head like someone was holding a gun on him, but he was laughing. "This isn't the time, or the place," he said. "But someday I'm going to ask how your husband got you to lighten up long enough to make love to you."

Before she could reply, he opened the car door and guided her in, then squatted down next to where she sat in the driver's seat. "Lock your doors and drive straight home," he told her seriously. "Tomorrow night, seven-thirty, the State Line. Be there, or I'll put out an APB." Then he kissed his index finger and touched it briefly to her lips, shut her car door, turned around, and was gone in the darkness.

Tory drove home in a disgustingly adolescent dream-like state, singing along with the radio, something she hadn't done in years. Then she remembered.

"Shit," she said out loud, braking. "I forgot to tell him about Jazz and the Brazilian cherry wood," she continued to talk out loud to make the words more real. "We started playing those stupid games and I forgot. But he'll never believe I forgot."

She thought about driving back to the Shady Lady. She thought about knocking on the door to Room 10, and Alvarez opening it, and how his eyes would narrow the way they always did when he smiled. And he would draw her inside, saying, "So you changed your mind, *cara?*"

No, she told herself, accelerating again and continuing to head for home. Been there, done that. "You could call him at the Shady Lady," the sensible part of her brain told her. "But he would ask if I was sorry I hadn't decided to stay," she told herself right back. "That's not a conversation I'm up to having right now. And besides, if I forgot about it for a few hours, why not a few hours more? Nothing may ever come of it, anyway."

She simply decided to think about it tomorrow.

CHAPTER SEVENTEEN:

LEGACIES
El Paso, Texas:
Tuesday, January 3, mid-morning

Alvarez was grateful that the meeting with Ken Herneese and Lenora Hinson's heirs wasn't until ten AM. It allowed him and Scott to sleep until eight, drive home to shower and change, and still arrive promptly.

Cotton was thrilled to see Alvarez when he returned home. She made embarrassing little mewing noises that didn't seem to be appropriate coming from a dog. Alvarez broke down and dug up an old tennis ball from the back of a closet, and spent some time in the back yard throwing it for her before he cleaned up for the coming day. After he fed her, there was still time to call forensics and ask them to go back through their files regarding latent fingerprints.

A technician told him that Lenora Hinson's prints were on the fireplace tools, in addition to other unidentified partials, and nothing in the print patterns particularly indicated that any of the fireplace tools had or hadn't been used in the way that he and Tory and Scott hypothesized. Sometimes you win, sometimes you lose, and more often than not, the answer is maybe, thought Alvarez.

He dressed carefully in a suit and tie, the uniform so near and dear to those of the legal profession, and because anything less could imply a lack of respect for the dead. He arrived at the offices of Hamilton, Hamilton, Herneese and Inungary early enough to have time to wonder about the suitability of those names for female offspring. He had just come to the conclusion that Inungary was worse than Hobarten when Scott arrived, looking more animated than usual.

Scott motioned him over to the drinking fountain. "I f-feel like I finally got some sleep last night," Scott told him. "I thought of something this morning."

"Does this mean we're going to have to start sleeping at the Shady Lady to solve all our cases?" asked Alvarez. "I'm not sure I'm that ambitious. What have you got?"

"The house," said Scott triumphantly.

"What about the house?"

"Whoever gets the house probably knows about the room in the basement," said Scott, stutter-free. "I think she'd l-l-leave it to someone who could carry on her work."

"Pretty good," said Alvarez admiringly. "Why didn't I think of that?"

"Because we're all c-captive to our upbringing," Scott answered. "When d-did you ever have to worry about an inheritance?"

"I think I like you better when you're sleep deprived," said Alvarez.

A young woman who looked like a walking fashion plate approached them. "Mr. Herneese is ready to convene the meeting now," she said in hushed tones. "I'm here to show you to Conference Room C."

Alvarez and Scott followed her down the hall. "What do you think?" Alvarez asked his partner.

"The reporter, but not by much," Scott said. Alvarez nodded his agreement as they were escorted into a cavernous conference room, decorated in muted beiges which complimented the dark wood furniture. Alvarez knew without touching a single surface that nothing in the room was veneer.

Scott introduced him to Ken Herneese, who looked much too young to hold a partnership position. Herneese was a slight young man in a stylish linen suit, with black, wire-frame glasses and a long, straight ponytail that reached half-way down his back.

After the cursory introductions, Herneese invited Scott and Alvarez to join the others already seated at the large oval table. Alvarez counted ten people all attired in somber clothing, except for Keaton. She wore a fire engine red sheath that was very tight and very short. Alvarez wondered if she would consider lending it to Tory for their dinner date.

Next to Keaton sat Dale Crandell, looking solemn and attorney-like in a black suit. Ryan Hinson was similarly dressed, and his wife wore a modest black dress that would be suitable for a funeral. Marshay was sitting very close to her husband and appeared to have his arm in a death grip. Alvarez wondered if the possibility of a windfall for Ryan had breathed new life into their marriage.

Across the table from the family group, almost as if he wanted to get as far away from them as possible, sat the head master for St. Michael's Episcopal School for Girls, Rodney Kiepper. He did not look happy. Next to him sat a small Hispanic man in clerical dress, who Alvarez guessed to be in his sixties. Scattered around the table sat four other people Alvarez did not recognize, two men and two women, all middle-aged, all white, all dressed in various shades of brown, blue or gray. As Alvarez finished his assessment of the attendees, Keaton winked at him from across the table.

Ken Herneese seated himself at the top of the oval and cleared his throat to let everyone know that he was ready to begin, which Alvarez figured was more couth than pounding on the table. He was fascinated by the concept of the oval table, round enough to give lip service to King Arthur's attempt at egalitarianism, but subtly shaped to convey that the person who sat at the top of the oval was in charge. Alvarez stretched out his legs and waited for the show to start.

"We're ready to begin now," said Herneese in a tone that would have been suitable for a seance. "Before we start with these proceedings, we at Hamilton, Hamilton, Herneese and Inungary would like to convey our sincerest condolences to Lenora Hinson's family and friends. The community has truly lost a valuable benefactor with her passing." The young man then commenced to make deliberate eye contact with each person sitting around the table. Alvarez resisted an overwhelming urge to look at his watch.

"I have asked you here today so that Lenora Hinson's last will and testament can be conveyed to her heirs," Herneese finally continued. "Unfortunately, because of the unusual circumstances surrounding Mrs. Hinson's demise, Detectives Faulkner and Alvarez are here with us today, and for their benefit, I am sending around a sign-in sheet. If you would please sign your name, address, place of work, and phone number, it will make it easier for them to contact you should they need additional information."

Alvarez was further fascinated to observe that the sheet of paper Herneese passed to the person sitting next to him was not white bond, but an understated gray. He wondered if they purchased it in quantity for occasions just like this.

Herneese took a deep breath through his nose and exhaled through his mouth, rather like a singer preparing for a recital. "Let me clarify two points before we proceed. One: Lenora Hinson bequeathed her earthly goods to both individuals and organizations. All of the adult individuals named in her will are present here today. However, I was able to contact only four representatives of the organizations named in her will, since I was working on such short notice."

Herneese paused to look meaningfully at Scott and Alvarez. Alvarez nodded his acknowledgement of the pressures under which Herneese, Jr., was functioning. He did his best to make it a regal nod. After nodding back at Alvarez, the attorney continued. "However, since these organizations are all charities, I feel those not represented today will not find fault with the way we have chosen to disseminate information to the rest of you. Does anyone have any objection?"

No one said anything. Alvarez wondered how many people sitting around the table understood the question. He wondered if he did.

"Good." Herneese took another deep breath in through his nose and exhaled though his mouth. "The second point. Lenora Hinson chose not to bequeath her earthly goods in the form of individual gifts, but instead, to have her estate liquidated and the proceeds dispersed."

"Bummer," Alvarez said under his breath to Scott.

"Her choice was unusual," continued Herneese, "but she was quite clear on this point: Two items are to be subtracted from the estate net worth before dispersion in accordance with the terms of her will. One is the fee to Hamilton, Hamilton, Herneese and Inungary." Alvarez noticed that there was no gasp of surprise from anyone sitting around the table. "The second item is the funding of a trust, to be endowed by our firm at an appropriate level to yield an allowance for the person providing care and shelter to Lenora Hinson's Puli, Carumba Cotton Candy, otherwise known as Cotton, for the remainder of the animal's life. The trust will initially yield a monthly allowance of the following amount." At this point Herneese named a figure that was roughly half of Alvarez's monthly take home pay. "It will be adjusted for cost of living increases annually," the attorney added.

"Hot damn," said Alvarez.

"You mean hot d-d-dog," muttered Scott.

Herneese looked at the group over his glasses. "We at Hamilton, Hamilton, Herneese, and Inungary, ever mindful of our fiduciary responsibilities, have looked into the matter of the welfare and ownership of the animal in question. We have ascertained that previous to the reading of this will, no family member or friend of Lenora Hinson inquired about, or offered shelter to the aforenamed animal. Because of the sole action of Detective David Alvarez, the aforementioned animal was not euthanized, therefore we declare Detective David Alvarez to be the owner of Carumba Cotton Candy and the beneficiary of the trust, and we will defend any and all claims against this decision with legal representation, at no charge to Detective David Alvarez." Herneese paused to favor the group with a smile.

Even through the shock of hearing what Herneese had to say, Alvarez could recognize someone with an ax to grind. An attorney offering to provide legal services for free? Ken Herneese must have nursed a grudge for years about Lenora Hinson manipulating his father. In spite of all the deep breathing and somber pronouncements, Alvarez guessed he was having a rip-roaring time. Herneese probably wished he'd had the nerve to wear red like Keaton.

Keaton started laughing. "That's inspired," she said. "I bet she's laughing her head off, wherever she's burning in hell."

Her husband glared disapprovingly at her. "If you're not feeling well enough for this," he said sternly, "we can leave."

"I'm feeling just fine," Keaton retorted. "I haven't had so much fun in years."

"Shit," said Ryan Hinson succinctly. "A real bitch to the end." Marshay gave him a business-like jab in the ribs. Alvarez hoped it was either Lenora Hinson or Keaton that Ryan was talking about, and not Cotton, or he just might have to take the remark personally.

"I think I should get part of the c-credit," whispered Scott. "I'm the one who convinced you to t-t-take the dog."

"You don't need a dog," Alvarez whispered back. "You have Donna."

Scott froze in place. Then he turned slowly sideways to look at Alvarez, who had the distinct feeling that for once he had gone too far. "I'm sorry," he whispered quickly. "I didn't mean that the way it sounded. Give me a break; I'm still in shock."

"This might make you a suspect," replied Scott in frosty tones.

Ken Herneese did another one of his inhale-exhale routines. "If we can continue," he said, not making it a question. "The following ten organizations each have been bequeathed monetary amounts, so these will come from the proceeds of the estate after the legal fees and trust fund costs have been deducted." He went on to name an amount that was roughly five times what Alvarez had paid for his house, and then named ten charities as beneficiaries, ranging from the City Humane Society to something called the El Paso Society for Socially Correct Historical Preservation.

Alvarez wondered fleetingly what type of historical preservation might be deemed as socially *incorrect*. He figured he would match the four people present with the organizations they represented when he got his hands on the sign-in sheet.

"The following bequests are also monetary amounts, which will be subtracted from the net worth of the estate." Herneese cleared his throat again. "It was Lenora Hinson's express wish that the following be read in the presence of her heirs: 'To Marshay Harding Hinson, as her value is significantly less than my son's, I leave the amount of one dollar. To my son, Ryan Harold Hinson, and to my daughter, Keaton Hinson Crandell, having been sorely disappointed in both, I leave the following amount: ten dollars to each.'"

Herneese looked up to take another break from his arduous duties. Alvarez would bet his bottom dollar, which had just recently been significantly enhanced, that Herneese was savoring every minute of this.

"Bitch," said Ryan Hinson again, and this time Marshay did nothing to discourage him. Keaton put a hand over her mouth to stifle a giggle. The look that Dale Crandell was giving Ken Herneese would have been sufficient to turn a Medusa to stone.

"The following three bequests are percentages of the net worth of the estate, after the legal fees, trust endowment, and previous bequests have been subtracted: As before, it was Lenora Hinson's wish that the following be read to her heirs: To Father Stephen Sanchez,'" continued Herneese solemnly, "'hoping that his wisdom will outweigh the character defects of my children, I leave twenty-five percent of my remaining estate. In return, I ask him to administer my children's trust funds, and hope that he will have the wisdom and the backbone to act as I would in this capacity.'"

Herneese paused to look at the Hispanic man in clerical garb, who was sitting calmly with his hands folded in front of him. "May God have mercy on her soul," he said simply.

Herneese did some more deep breathing. "'To Rodney Kiepper, I bequest twenty-five percent of my remaining estate. I trust that in return, he will continue on with our work as I would have wished.'"

Unlike Father Sanchez, Rodney Kiepper did not look up to meet Herneese's dramatically timed gaze; his face was buried in his hands. Alvarez saw Father Sanchez reach out and squeeze the man's shoulder encouragingly.

Herneese omitted the inhale-exhale exercise. Alvarez wondered if he was saving the best for last. "'The remaining fifty percent of my estate, I leave in trust to my only granddaughter, Hero Dominique Crandell, in spite of the ridiculous name that her mother saddled her with. The funds are to be held in trust until she reaches the age of thirty-five, with the appointed trustee making all such disbursements as are deemed to be appropriate and beneficial to her well-being.'"

Even Alvarez, with his limited knowledge of trust funds, realized that this gave the named individual a wide berth in deciding what money could be spent, and for what. "'To emphasize my belief in the nuclear family structure,'" Herneese continued, "'and in order to encourage my daughter to remain in her marriage and give it the attention and effort it deserves, I name the biological father of Hero Dominique Crandell to be trustee of this fund.'" Alvarez looked across the table at Keaton and saw the blood drain from her face.

Ken Herneese looked over his glasses at the group one last time. "Since, in the past, there have been questions about the discharge of the executive duties of Hamilton, Hamilton, Herneese and Inungary in relationship to the estate of Harold Hinson, and since these questions have been raised by the offspring of Harold Hinson, and since we wish to avoid all perceptions of impropriety in the future, we will require blood test proof of paternity before formally naming the trustee of Hero Dominique Crandell's trust fund. Just as a formality. Of course." Herneese said his final words as Keaton fainted and fell from her chair.

Alvarez flashed on what he had been trying to remember earlier. One of the first things Alvarez noticed when Gary Cabrioni explained his ethnic background was his dark kinky hair that defied a conventional style. What had registered in his subconscious was the fact that Dr. Cabrioni's hair was identical to the dark, kinky hair that had floated around the elfin face of Hero Crandell when she opened the door to her house.

While this was an interesting connection, Alvarez figured that Keaton wasn't going anywhere right now. Ryan, Dale and Marshay were all crowded around her. Rodney Kiepper stood up and made a move to join them, but Father Sanchez laid a restraining hand on his arm. "Don't, Rodney," he said. "The poor child has enough people gathered around her already."

Scott made a bee line for the four people Alvarez didn't know. "Excuse me," said Alvarez to the two men beside him. "I know that this may be a difficult time for you, but we're investigating the circumstances of Lenora Hinson's death, and time is of the essence. Could I talk to both of you later this afternoon?"

"I'm the rector for All Souls Episcopal Church, downtown," said Father Sanchez. "If you come before five, I'll be in my office, or somewhere around the church. I have a secretary who is very good at tracking me down." He smiled warmly at Alvarez. "If you don't come before five, I live in the parsonage behind the church, and you would be welcome any time, my son."

"School is out right now," said Rodney Kiepper shortly, "so you won't find me in my office. If you really think you need to talk to me, you can try to catch me at home. You'll find my address and phone number on the sign-in sheet." He turned abruptly and walked out of the room.

"You'll have to forgive him," said Father Sanchez. "He's upset. He had a difficult relationship with Lenora. She could be a trying person."

"And did you have a difficult relationship with her, Father?" asked Alvarez.

Father Sanchez smiled. "I think, Detective," he said, "where Lenora Hinson was concerned, I would be suspicious of anyone who said they *didn't* have a difficult time with her. And now, if you'll excuse me, I'm going to go see to my friend. I think the family needs some time alone to sort things out."

The family had sorted things out sufficiently to get Keaton back in her chair, looking pale and shaky but tight-lipped with determination. She seemed to have recovered enough to be in a heated argument with her brother and husband. "I don't give a fuck what you want," she said clearly. "I'm not a child, and I'm not an invalid, so get your fucking hands off me and give me some room. I'll talk to anyone I want to talk to, and I want to talk to the detective who has Cotton."

"That would be me," said Alvarez, walking over and extending his hand to help her up out of the chair.

"She doesn't know what she's saying," said Dale Crandell, glaring at Alvarez.

"She seems to be speaking perfectly plain English to me," he replied. "Is there something you want me to translate for you?"

"There's a small room adjoining this one," said Ken Herneese, appearing at Alvarez's shoulder like a stealthy ghoul. He was practically rubbing his hands in delight at the general mayhem and discord his performance had produced.

"Thank you," said Keaton, standing up with an amazing amount of dignity, simultaneously showing an amazing amount of shapely thigh.

Alvarez gestured to the door that Herneese had indicated. "After you," he said.

The room had a small, round table and four chairs. Alvarez figured it must be for warm-up contests to determine who would sit at the head of the oval table. Keaton walked right past the table and chairs and headed to the corner of the room, where she picked up a wastebasket and threw up into it. From what Alvarez could tell, she didn't get a speck on her. It was an impressive demonstration, and when she was done, he offered her his handkerchief and told her so.

"Anyone who ingests as many chemical substances as I do gets good at throwing up," she said shortly.

"Would you like some water?" he asked. He felt sure that was what Scott would do under the circumstances.

"Please," Keaton said, and Alvarez went out through the conference room to the drinking fountain in the hall. Scott was in one corner, talking intently to Ken Herneese. Dale Crandell, and Ryan and Marshay were all sitting at the conference table, watching Alvarez's every move. Alvarez noticed that Dale Crandell had taken Ken Herneese's former place at the top of the oval.

When Alvarez returned with the requested water, Keaton was sitting in one of the chairs, her chin resting in one elegantly manicured hand, appearing to be deep in thought. He handed her the paper cup and kicked the door closed behind him, shutting out the baleful faces of her waiting family. He could think of several opening questions, but he decided he would let her speak first. After all, she was the one who had requested this interview.

"Have you ever heard of the Law of Unequal Dispersion?" she asked suddenly.

"No," he said.

"It states that whatever it is that hits the fan will not be evenly distributed," she said pensively.

"I think you have bigger problems than that," he replied.

"I know. Do you have a cigarette on you?" she asked suddenly. He shook his head. "What kind of detective are you?"

"A non-smoking one. What's on your mind?"

"Like you said, I've got big problems. I don't want you to be one of them."

"Look, it's pretty obvious to me that Hero is Gary Cabrioni's daughter," Alvarez said, tired of dancing around the subject. "If the three people sitting out there waiting for you haven't figured it out yet, believe me, they're going to. And if they don't, that ghoul of an attorney will be happy to make sure they find out."

"He's getting even with us."

"For what?"

"For what my mother did to his father, and then for all the hell Ryan raised about it."

"What did your mother do to his father?"

"She blackmailed him into changing the conditions of the trust funds that my father's will had set up."

"How do you know that?"

"I was thirteen when my father died. Ryan was twenty, and he was already off at school. Lucky bastard, he pulled that off while my father was still alive. By the time I was old enough to go to college, there was no way my mother was letting me out of her sight."

"So how did she blackmail Herneese's father?" Alvarez asked, to get her back on track.

"I heard her one night, after the funeral, after Ryan had gone back to school. She was talking on the phone to Daddy's attorney, and she told him that if he didn't do what she wanted, she would make sure that Pinnacle never sent any more work to his law firm. Then she told him she would make sure everyone knew he'd had an affair with the wife of one of his partners."

"How did she know about something like that?"

"I don't know. My mother made it a habit to find out about things that she could use against people."

"I talked to Gary Cabrioni," Alvarez said carefully. Keaton didn't look at him. "He still doesn't know why you called it off between the two of you."

"And you want me to tell you."

"Right. It's something I need to know, now that your old boyfriend seems to be the big winner in the inheritance game."

"You won't understand it."

"Try me."

"Sometimes I don't understand it. I wonder what I could have done differently." Keaton took a deep breath. "The night Gary asked me to marry him, I told my mother that's what I was going to do. She went insane, yelling hysterically and chasing me around the house with a broom. Can you imagine?" she asked rhetorically. "As Ryan likes to say, she was a woman with more money than God, and she's chasing me around the house with a broom to get me to do what she wants."

Alvarez thought back to Tory brandishing the phone book at him. "So how did she make you do what she wanted?" he asked. "I figure it took more than a broom to bring you to heel."

This time Keaton did look at him. "She told me she would ruin Gary's family. She would get another doctor to testify that my father had signs of heart disease, signs Gary's father missed, and she would sue him for malpractice. Did Gary tell you about him and his father being osteopaths?" Alvarez nodded. "Gary was so proud of everything his father had done. All my life I had seen my mother do horrible, cruel things to get what she wanted. I was young, I had never lived away from home, and I believed her. So I told Gary it was over. A few weeks later I realized I was pregnant. My mother wanted me to marry Dale, so there was a wedding and a supposedly premature baby followed. End of story. Damn, I wish you had a cigarette."

Alvarez tried factoring this information into what they already knew about the death of Lenora Hinson. "You realize," he said slowly, "that this will makes Gary Cabrioni benefit from your mother's death."

Keaton was looking at him intently now. "You can't think he had anything to do with it," she said urgently. "He never knew. I did everything in my power to make sure he never knew."

"Well, if it makes you feel better, I believe you," said Alvarez. "If you're lying, it's a damn good performance."

"What am I going to do now?" asked Keaton.

"I don't know," said Alvarez. "We'll have to talk to Cabrioni, see how he reacts to this information. So if you want to be the one to tell him, you better do it quick."

"Where will I go? What am I going to do?" asked Keaton again.

"I don't know," he answered her honestly. "If you were poor, or a battered wife, I could recommend a shelter. But our systems don't work too well for exceptions to the rule. You don't fit into the framework of problems that social institutions try to address." Unbidden, Alvarez remembered Annika Atkins saying much the same thing to him the evening before.

"You know," said Keaton, "I'm twenty-eight years old and I've never had a job. I can't believe that my goddamned mother can reach out even from her grave and ruin my life more than she has already."

The phrase "poor little rich girl" ran through Alvarez's mind, but he couldn't say it. He found he felt genuine pity for the woman sitting in front of him. "I don't like to give advice," he said, "but I had a grandmother who was tough as nails. She helped raise me and my sister, and she told me over and over that no one can ruin your life but you. Besides, look on the bright side, in a few years you'll inherit a bunch of money, and you won't have to worry about a job."

"That's not going to solve this mess," Keaton said somberly. "I never loved Dale, but he's been a decent father to Hero. What am I going to tell her?"

Alvarez didn't have an answer to that. "Hero Dominique," he said instead. "That's quite a name for a little girl."

"Dominique means 'belonging to God.' I thought if I gave her a brave name and a spiritual one, it would keep her safe."

"I don't have kids," said Alvarez, "so I'm no expert. But every parent I've ever talked to, including my old grandmother, has told me that there is nothing anyone can do to keep a child safe."

"Would you sit with me a few more minutes before I have to go out there?" Keaton asked.

"Yes," he said. And he did.

Keaton's family ushered her out the minute she exited the small room. Scott was the only one left sitting at the oval conference table. "Thanks for hanging around," Alvarez said.

"I wanted to m-make sure you didn't get in over your head," said Scott.

"I can handle Hinson and Crandell."

"It was you alone in a room with K-Keaton I was concerned about. How d-does it feel to be an heir?"

"I don't know. I haven't thought about it. I'll tell you one thing, though."

"What's that?"

"Carumba Cotton Candy is dining on sirloin tonight."

Alvarez told Scott what Keaton had told him. They decided it warranted asking Ken Herneese and Gary Cabrioni a few more questions, but not much more at the moment. There were other more interesting leads to investigate now.

"According to Herneese," said Scott, "the will t-today was one of many. She drew up a n-new one every few months."

"It would be interesting to know who won the grand prize in some of the earlier versions. I'd be really interested to know how Ryan Hinson fared in some of those other wills."

"I'm on it. It'd be a real p-pity if he offed his mother and then found out he chose the wrong time p-p-period to do it."

"No kidding. And I really liked the phrasing in the bequest to Rodney Kiepper—something about him continuing on with their work in the way that she would have wanted him to. There's something bothering him; I want to know what it is."

"We may be letting ourselves be distracted by the b-big winners."

"You're right. The money she left each of those charities would buy five houses like mine."

"Sometimes one individual c-c-controls a charity, whether it's incorporated or not," said Scott. "If that's the c-case, money can be funneled to causes that may not be listed in the charter."

"You are an endless source of useful information, *ese*. So you're going to check out the ten third-place winners?"

"Unless you think I need to place you on my list."

"Very funny. Since you're so generously taking on ten leads, I'll cover the two second-place winners. Both Sanchez and Kiepper said they could talk to me later this afternoon."

"M-my stuff is going to take a while. Can you handle the meeting at the m-morgue without me? And can you try not to piss anyone off?"

"Piece of cake, man. At the morgue, I can always count on at least one person not to give me any grief."

CHAPTER EIGHTEEN:

MULTIPLE VIEWPOINTS
El Paso, Texas:
Tuesday, January 3, early afternoon

Things were looking up. After assuring Ken Herneese that he would get back to him regarding Cotton's monthly trust payments, Alvarez had time to turn in the odious purple rental car and pick up his treasured bronze Corvette. The cashier was surprised when he signed the charge slip without complaint and even wished her a good day.

It was good to have his car back, but it meant he was the last one to arrive at the morgue. Four men, two Hispanics and two Anglos, were waiting in the lobby when he arrived.

Alvarez pegged the tan, fit-looking man in a tailored gray suit as Raymond Boyce, because of the clothes and the two body-guard types hovering around him. Boyce stood up when Alvarez walked in. In addition to the tabloid-worthy good looks, ready smile, and straight white teeth of a politician, Alvarez was irritated to note that Boyce had a couple of inches of height advantage on him.

"You must be Detective Alvarez," said Boyce, offering his hand. "I'm Raymond Boyce, and these are my associates." He waved the two Hispanic men, who looked like a South American version of Mutt and Jeff, dismissively aside. Alvarez would bet one month of Carumba Cotton Candy's maintenance allowance that the two associates were carrying, and that whatever was concealed underneath their jackets was newer and jazzier than any firearm he owned.

The fourth man in the lobby, a lanky figure as tall as Boyce, pushed himself off the wall where he was leaning and stopped chewing gum long enough to offer his hand and mutter, "Derek Dowling, DEA." His suit was also gray, but unlike Boyce's, it looked like he had slept in it.

Boyce immediately said, "He has absolutely no business being here. This man has an obsession with me and my family. It's bad enough to be hounded by him, but to have him intrude in a personal tragedy like this is obscene."

"Hey, Mr. Boyce," said Dowling, resuming his rapid gum chewing, "we've been through a lot together in the last few years. I just want to pay my respects to Alicia, and if there's any way I can tie you to her death, I'm here to nail you to the wall with it."

Boyce opened his arms wide in his appeal to Alvarez as a reasonable man. Mutt and Jeff remained where they had been bidden, a good three steps behind Boyce, but balanced on the balls of their feet, ready for action.

With Boyce gesticulating, Derek chomping gum, and the two Frito Banditos ready to roll, all Alvarez needed was an appearance of the morgue mouse-woman, hissing, but it seemed she had decided to skip this meeting. He could only imagine what alternative activities she was pursuing at that very moment.

"I'm sorry for your loss, Mr. Boyce," Alvarez said automatically. "Mr. Dowling is a fellow law enforcement officer. He'll be present during the identification of our Jane Doe, but he'll certainly limit his comments during that time, won't you, Mr. Dowling?"

Dowling was back to leaning against the wall, chomping gum, looking like he found some hidden source of amusement in the current situation. "Whatever you say, Detective. Who am I to disagree with a member of the Special Case Force?"

Alvarez chose to ignore him. "There's two ways we can do

this, Mr. Boyce. We can view the body directly, or you can view a video image in a special room with a screen for that purpose."

"I'm an old-fashioned kind of guy," said Boyce. "If the body is Alicia's, I want to be able to say that I looked at her one last time, as difficult as that may be."

Dowling had a coughing fit. Alvarez hoped he'd swallowed his gum. He stepped up to the reception counter, flashed his badge, and explained what he wanted. A white-suited technician appeared and led them down a corridor to the cadaver storage room. When Mutt and Jeff started to follow, Alvarez told them to wait in the lobby. He was tempted to say "stay," but he figured one wise ass in their temperamental group was enough.

The technician matched an identification number on his clipboard with one on a stainless steel drawer, then looked to Alvarez for direction. "Are you ready, Mr. Boyce?" asked Alvarez.

"I'm ready," said Boyce. The technician pulled the drawer out and then drew the white sheet down to reveal the face of the corpse. She looked exactly like Alvarez remembered her, no surprise there, but he couldn't say the same for the two other men.

"My god," said Boyce, true anguish in his voice. "It's Patty—it's my daughter Patty—"

"What the fucking hell—" said Dowling, pushing Boyce aside to take a look.

"What kind of set-up is this? What happened to my daughter? Who the hell killed my daughter?" Boyce grabbed Alvarez by the front of his shirt and shoved him up against the wall of steel drawers. The technician, wide-eyed, stood frozen in place, as if undecided whether it would be more prudent to push the drawer closed again, or to remain motionless and hope to escape any further notice.

Then Dowling pulled Boyce off Alvarez, spun him around, and pushed *him* up against the wall of steel drawers. If this was going to turn into a free-for-all, Alvarez sure as hell wished the technician were taller.

"Dowling, get your hands off him," Alvarez said quietly. Dowling complied, but he didn't step back, and that left him and Boyce staring at each other with less than six inches between them. "Okay," said Alvarez, while the technician continued to hover over the body, watching them all like a nervous rabbit, "that's a good start. Now, the two of you step apart, real easy. It seems like everyone has had a shock here, and we need some time to sort it out."

The technician took this as a cue to abruptly push in the drawer bearing the earthly remains of Patty Boyce. "Do you need me anymore?" he asked in a squeaky voice. Alvarez shook his head, and the man scurried out the door, probably to report back to his mouse master. Boyce and Dowling had sorted themselves out into opposite corners of the room. Dowling was back to chewing his gum furiously, but he no longer looked amused.

"That's my daughter," said Boyce again, slowly, as if he was still trying to comprehend the fact.

"He's right about that," said Dowling shortly. "That's Patty Boyce on the slab there, not Alicia."

"What's the meaning of this?" asked Boyce, outrage in his voice again. "What happened? How did she die? Who's responsible for this?"

"When was the last time you saw your daughter?" asked Alvarez.

"I don't know. Sometime after Christmas. She came and went as she pleased, she had her own place."

"Did she know your wife and her half sister were both missing?"

"No. I didn't know where to contact her. She left a note that she was off to Europe for a fashion shoot. She did that a lot, weeks might go by before I heard from her. If you had any part in this—" he took a menacing step toward the DEA agent, who didn't miss a beat chewing his gum.

"Hey, Boyce," said Dowling. "Don't look at me. I can't help it if large numbers of your family go missing. Kind of makes you wonder where Alicia is, doesn't it? And what kind of holiday stories she might have to tell."

Alvarez watched Boyce's eyes narrow as the impact of Dowling's words hit him. "We're not going to do this here," he said. "It's a short walk over to my office. I want to talk to both of you. Separately."

Boyce was no longer trying to appear reasonable. "You think you want to talk to me? You got that wrong. I want answers, and I want them now. What happened to my daughter?"

"She died of a heroin overdose," said Alvarez flatly.

That stopped Boyce cold for a moment. Either the news was a surprise to him, or he was a damn good actor. "Then why the hell couldn't a detective in this shit hole of a town tell the difference between my wife and my daughter?" he demanded.

"I don't know," said Alvarez deliberately, making a split-second decision. "Someone offered to show me a video of your daughter last night, but I declined to watch it. Maybe if I had, I would have known the Jane Doe was your daughter."

Boyce had the look of an angry man trying desperately to digest too many pieces of information at once. "What tape? What are you talking about?" he asked, his tone elevating to a yell.

"Yeah, what the fuck are you talking about, Alvarez?" echoed the DEA agent. "Someone offered you a video of Patty?"

"My understanding was that it was a private issue video,"

said Alvarez, watching Boyce while he said it. Boyce narrowed his eyes again, like he was thinking over but discarding various responses. "My office, gentlemen," said Alvarez, and walked out of the room.

All hopes of getting everyone out of the morgue without further uproar vanished when Alvarez entered the lobby and found Annika Atkins waiting for them. He was beginning to think that the appearance of the mouse-woman would be a good thing, but no one materialized to come to his aid. The technician was long gone, and the woman at the reception counter took one look at the group in the lobby and decided she was needed elsewhere.

"Mr. Boyce?" said Annika Atkins, standing. The fact that all three men towered over her, and that Mutt and Jeff were watching uneasily from the other side of the room, did nothing to daunt her.

"Do I know you?" asked Boyce shortly.

"No, you don't know me, but you will. I'm here to see that you get what you deserve."

Boyce looked like someone on sensory overload. Dowling came to point like a bird dog catching a scent. "Who is this, Alvarez? A senior-senior detective? You sure run an unusual operation down here."

Annika Atkins acted as if she and Raymond Boyce were the only two people in the room. "You came down here thinking no one would stand in your way. All you had to do was identify Alicia's body, give some lip service to the unfortunate and mystifying circumstances of her death, pick up Hannah and go home."

"If she were mine, Alvarez," drawled Dowling, "I'd make sure she got briefed. But maybe she's too far past retirement age for it to matter."

"I don't know who you are, lady, but you obviously don't know me, or you wouldn't be talking to me like this," said Boyce. "I've just suffered an enormous personal loss. So shut up and get out of my way, before I have one of my men take care of you."

Annika Atkins reached into her purse and pulled out a video tape. She had to stand on her toes to wave it in front of Boyce's face. "I'll be happy to shut up and get out of your way, Mr. Boyce, just as soon as you relinquish all claims to Hannah. I'm going to see to it that she doesn't end up like your other daughter."

"Don't even mention Patty to me," said Boyce, anguish in his voice again. "She's lying dead in there, so put up whatever you think it is you're threatening me with and get out of my way."

For the first time, Annika Atkins acknowledged the presence of other people in the lobby. "Is it true?" she asked Alvarez. "The body isn't Alicia's?"

"Doesn't appear to be. Both these gentlemen have identified our Jane Doe as Patty Boyce."

Annika Atkins blinked. "Then where is Alicia?"

"That's exactly what I want to know, old woman, and it's what I plan to find out. So get out of my way," said Boyce.

Mrs. Atkins stood her ground, Alvarez had to give her that. She resumed waving the video tape in front of Boyce's face. "Do you have any idea what this is?" she asked Boyce.

"Do you have any idea who I am?" roared Boyce, back to yelling.

"Do you have any idea who I am?" Annika Atkins yelled back. "You see these two men here, this detective and the other one? They have to work inside the law. They have to follow rules and procedures. Detective Alvarez tells me I'm dangerous,

Mr. Boyce, and you better keep that in mind. I have one purpose in life right now, and that's to make sure you don't get your hands on Hannah, whether Alicia is alive or not."

"No one threatens me," said Boyce ominously. Mutt and Jeff started to move forward in tandem.

"Back off," said Alvarez. The woman from the reception desk peeked around the corner, a phone in her hand. "All of you, back off. I want each of you, especially you," he pointed at Boyce, "without your goons, in my office. We're going to walk over there now, and then I'm going to talk to each of you one at a time. Got it?" He was looking straight at Boyce, and Boyce narrowed his eyes, but then nodded.

"Got it," Boyce said. "Not because you're in charge, but because I want some answers, and you better have them."

Alvarez opted for maintaining momentum instead of discussion. "Let's go," he said. "Out the front door and to your left."

Boyce held his glare a moment more before looking over at the two Hispanic men across the room. "Wait for me outside the police department," he said, then turned and shoved the lobby door open so hard that it banged back against the outside wall. He turned left and walked like he knew where he was going. Alvarez followed close on his heels, Dowling and Annika Atkins behind him, with Mutt and Jeff trailing a ways back like Mary's little lamb. Alvarez decided that no matter how many leads Scott was checking out right now, he'd gotten the easy part.

"Ma'am," he heard Dowling say behind him, in a respectful tone he'd never heard before, "my name is Derek Dowling. I'm with the DEA, and you look like someone I want to get to know."

***

When Alvarez ushered his group, *sans* Mutt and Jeff, up to the second floor area that the Special Case Force called home, one of the three division secretaries waylaid him. She was his favorite one, a young Hispanic single mother with an engaging sense of humor, so he took the time to listen patiently to what she was saying.

"You've got several calls," she told him without preamble.

"Any from Scott?" She shook her head, and he waved off the handful of messages that she was offering. "They'll have to wait. I need to talk to these people and get them out of here before a fight breaks out. The little gray-haired woman, she looks harmless, but you keep an eye on her for me, okay? I'm going to use an interview room for this one, then I'll be back for the other two."

He left Dowling and Annika Atkins in the secretary's capable hands while he ushered Raymond Boyce into a vacant room. Boyce appeared to have gotten his grief in hand during the walk to the police station. He sat down and regarded Alvarez with the look of a man used to getting what he wanted.

"What tape were you referring to earlier?" he asked as soon as Alvarez shut the door.

"I'm can't recall right now, but maybe it will come to me later," said Alvarez evenly. "I'm investigating two women found dead under suspicious circumstances, so I'm sure you'll understand why I want to be the one to ask the questions."

"And I'm sure you'll understand that I have a vested interest in your investigation. I came down here thinking that I would identify the body of my wife and claim my daughter and go home. I find my older daughter is dead, my wife is nowhere to be found, and I have yet to be told the whereabouts of my other daughter. So why don't you sit back like the good bureaucrat that you are, answer my questions, let me take care of my business, and I'll get the fuck out of this godforsaken place."

"It doesn't work that way," said Alvarez pleasantly.

Boyce leaned forward. "I'll tell you how it's going to work. I want to find my wife, I want my daughter Hannah back, and I want to find out who's responsible for Patty's death."

"I would imagine the person responsible for Patty's death is the one who sold her the drugs, unless we want to get philosophical and hypothesize about what drove her to use them," said Alvarez reasonably.

"What do you know about Patty's death?"

"What do you know about it?"

"I've already told you everything I know."

"Then there's no point in continuing this conversation."

"Who the fuck is that woman out there?"

"You'll have to discuss that with her."

"I'm not sure you'll like the results."

"Are you threatening her?"

Boyce knew enough to back off from that. "I'm not threatening anyone. I want to know what you know. I can help with your investigation; I have resources at my disposal that you don't have."

"I don't want your resources. I want your cooperation."

"Let's discuss who has information about this case," said Boyce. "I know that you and Scott Faulker are the detectives assigned to it. I already talked to Emmett Delgado. Where do I find the other engineer?"

"You already talked to Delgado? It doesn't sound like you were exactly overcome with grief, working in a meeting before coming to the morgue."

"You didn't answer my question. Where can I find the other engineer?"

"I'm not going to answer that."

Boyce gave him a long look. "That tells me something. Wasn't she the one you so tenderly put your arm around on TV?"

Alvarez fantasized slugging Raymond Boyce. "I knew Omaha sounded boring, but I'm surprised a busy man like you has time to watch the El Paso news."

"Information is my specialty. I didn't get where I am today by going into situations unprepared. I know who you are, where you live, what cases you've solved, and yes, I know about the case last summer that involved Mrs. Travers. I know the name of Scott Faulkner's wife and the birth date of his son."

"For someone who knows so much, how come you don't know about little old ladies who come out of the blue to threaten you?"

"By this afternoon, I'll know more about her than you would after a week of research."

"Do you know any reason why your daughter Patty would take her half sister and come to El Paso?"

"No."

"Do you have any idea of the whereabouts of your wife?"

"No."

"For someone who has so much information at his fingertips, it sounds like you don't do such a good job of keeping track of your family members, Mr. Boyce. Maybe that's a good reason for leaving the investigating to us."

"Where is Hannah?"

"She's at a hospital where she's being treated for dehydration and an ear infection."

"I want her discharged to me immediately."

"That's not possible. The doctor in charge said she had to be held for two to three days observation, minimum."

"You give me the doctor's name and number, and we'll see about that."

We sure will, thought Alvarez, as he wrote down Karen's phone number, hoping this was one of the days that a hectic schedule would keep her from returning calls promptly.

"I plan to stay abreast of the developments in this investigation, Detective Alvarez, with or without your cooperation. It would be easier for all of us if you'd do it my way."

"Well, Mr. Boyce, I already answer to one boss, and that's plenty for me."

"I could make it worth your while."

"Save your breath. You're talking to a man of independent means."

Boyce narrowed his eyes again. He seemed to do that whenever someone said something that surprised him. "If you are, detective, you've sure hidden it well."

Alvarez had a momentary vision of someone taking out a hit on Carumba Cotton Candy, and hoped it wouldn't come to the point where he would have to seek protective custody for her. Maybe a hair cut and a dye job would suffice, but then would Ken Herneese recognize her as the recipient of Lenora Hinson's largesse? He shook the thought away. Hostages to fate, even if they were canine ones, always ended up complicating the hell out of everything.

"I hope your associates have all the paperwork in order for carrying concealed," he said. "As far as I'm concerned, you haven't broken any laws in my jurisdiction, and I'd hate to see that change."

"My associates have everything in hand, Detective. You can count on it. Enrique, Hector, and Alfonso are the best. They're Cuban, so much more suited for their line of work than some other nationalities. So many Mexicans that I've come across tend to be lazy and stupid, wouldn't you agree, Detective Alvarez?"

"Well, I'm half Mexicano myself, Mr. Boyce, which I'm sure comes as a surprise to you. But by the time I finished college, I learned how to count reasonably well, and I only counted two goons out there with you earlier, not three. Do we have one running around unsupervised?"

Boyce stood up. "I'm sure I'll be in touch."

Alvarez let him go, thinking over their conversation for a moment before going out to where Annika Atkins and Dowling were waiting. They were deep in conversation with each other, almost like old friends, which was not exactly what Alvarez had had in mind. Maybe he should have put them in separate holding cells while he talked to Boyce.

"You," he pointed at Dowling. "I want to talk to you."

Dowling pulled out a fresh stick of gum and inserted it into his mouth. "So, I'll see you for dinner then?" he asked Annika Atkins as he stood up to follow Alvarez into the interview room.

"I wouldn't miss it for anything," she said.

"Do you happen to know what the fuck is going on?" asked Alvarez pleasantly. "I feel like I'm playing Blind Man's Bluff with one hand tied behind me."

"Well, this hasn't been such a great day for me, either, hot shot. Here I thought maybe I could tie Boyce to his wife's death, and his daughter turns up dead instead. I hate to admit it, but I think he was as surprised as I was."

"So I'm going to ask again. Do you know what the fuck is going on?"

"I had a chance to think about it while I was out there talking to Mrs. Atkins, and yeah, I think I've got a pretty good idea what happened."

"Want to enlighten me?"

"Does this mean you'll keep me posted on your investigation?"

"We'll see. So far, you haven't done shit for me."

"Patty Boyce was our stool pigeon in a sting operation to indict Boyce."

"How did that come about?"

"She was a junkie, man. And you know how anyone who works with drugs feels about junkies. They're bad for business. One of the local cops in Nebraska realized who she was when she was remanded to a treatment center for check-kiting charges. He brought it to our attention, and we used it to recruit her."

"Work for us, or we'll tell Daddy that you're sampling the family wares?"

"Something like that."

"What did you need her for?"

"We had a wire tap authorized, but we needed someone inside to place the bugs and then pull them, because Boyce has his place swept regularly. Patty was ideal. She knew who everyone was, and she could come and go without notice. Her father adored her."

"So I've been told," said Alvarez drily. "What went wrong?"

"Someone blew the wire tap. All of a sudden, the authorizations we had were no longer legal."

"How the hell do you fuck up something like that?"

"You don't want to know. Just take my word for it. Whoever did the fix must have told Boyce, and Patty must have known that it was just a matter of time before he went looking for the person on the inside. At the same time, if she was listening in on conversations, she would have known that Alicia was getting ready to run with the kid."

"So she took the kid and used Alicia's escape plan? That's pretty cold-blooded."

"I don't blame her for not wanting to wait around for us to pull her out and give her a cover. She had a lot of guts for a stool pigeon. Taking things into her own hands sounds just like something Patty would do, and she wasn't overly fond of her stepmother, either."

"It sounds like you knew her pretty damn well."

Dowling chose to ignore the comment. "You've got to admit, it was quite a set up. A ready-made escape plan, a road to a brand new life, all set and ready for someone who looks a lot like you."

"Not to mention it got her out from working for you."

Dowling pulled out a fresh stick of gum, unwrapped it, spit the spent wad out into the foil, and popped a new stick into his mouth. "Yeah, there is that," he admitted. "But there's no point sitting here crying over spilt milk, while Boyce is out there making hay. See, I've been working on some midwestern clichés for you."

"Before we move on to greener pastures, so to speak, one last thing about Patty. I assume you think her death was a bona fide overdose?"

Dowling didn't have to stop chewing his gum to think that over. "I'd say so. She was clean when she was working for us, but once a junkie, always a junkie. Let's move on to your greener pastures, home boy. If you were Alicia Boyce, where would you be?"

"Trying to stay away from Boyce and look for my kid at the same time."

"Bingo. I want to find Alicia Boyce before her husband does."

"Because you want to reunite her with her daughter?"

Dowling gave Alvarez a hard look. "Yeah, right. Because I never thought about trying to turn her. Imagine the stories

Alicia Boyce could tell—drugs, fraud, *and* incest. She could do in one interview what we've been trying to do for years."

"*If* she's alive."

"She's alive all right. Otherwise Boyce wouldn't be hanging around, he'd be laughing in our face. So where the hell is she?"

It was an intriguing question. "You discover your kid and your stepdaughter are gone," said Alvarez slowly. "So you call up your friendly contact at the Underground Railroad."

"Who doesn't want to fucking talk to you," continued Dowling, "because you're supposedly already gone, so who the hell is it on the telephone asking about their secret stuff?"

"Either they let it slip, or you figure it out," said Alvarez. "Your stepdaughter entered the Underground Railroad with your kid."

"And who can you trust?" asked Dowling. "If your husband can buy off cops and judges, maybe he's bought off someone in this Railroad outfit. Maybe he knew about your plans all along, and the whole thing was a setup. But you can't stay put, because how will you explain the kid being gone? And besides, maybe he already knows."

"Alicia Boyce knew she was coming to El Paso, and she probably knew the name of her contact here," said Alvarez. "This is where she'd come. She hears about the collapse and the two bodies on the news, but nothing about the kid 'til the next day."

"No one to turn to, no one she can trust, no way to even know for sure if Patty and her kid are the ones in the news," mused Dowling. "Major bummer." He chewed his gum and thought some more. "I'd be looking for some way to verify my theories about what happened, maybe hook up with some sterling, squeaky clean detective who could help me out. I think I'd head to—"

"—the morgue," Alvarez finished for him. "I'd head to the

morgue, try to come up with some excuse to see the Jane Doe from the collapse."

"You run security tapes of the lobby there?"

"We do now," said Alvarez, reaching for the phone.

"Tell them that the woman we're looking for looks just like the one on the slab," said Dowling helpfully. Alvarez gave him a look of such utter distaste that the DEA agent kept silent for the rest of the one-sided phone conversation.

When Alvarez hung up, he told Dowling that there had been no other parties asking to see the last remains of Patty Boyce. "So maybe this will work," said Dowling brightly.

"If Boyce doesn't find her first."

"That will probably depend on dumb luck and how much cash she had lying around," said Dowling philosophically. "She uses a credit card and she's dead. Figuratively speaking, we hope."

"How much cash would you leave lying around if you had a wife you wanted to keep under your thumb?" asked Alvarez.

"Yeah, there's that. On the other hand, if Boyce finds her first and kills her and we can pin it on him, that would do the job just as well."

Alvarez sighed. "It's always comforting to know that there's more than one way to skin a cat. Is that why you've decided to get cozy with Annika Atkins?"

"Hey, man, she has access to information I never even knew existed. That woman is a dream come true. If anyone can push Boyce into making a wrong move, I'd put my money on her."

"If he doesn't take steps to eliminate her first."

"It turns out we're staying at the same motel. Small world, huh? We're having dinner tonight, trading information. Want to join us? It has to be early; she says she's all tuckered out."

"Sorry, I've got other plans. Maybe I can count on you to keep Mrs. Atkins out of Boyce's face for the time being."

"I'll try, but my mother always told me to respect my

elders, so if Mrs. A gets a wild hair up her butt to go broadcast that tape on closed-circuit television wherever Boyce is holed up, what can I do?" Dowling spread his hands to illustrate his powerlessness over the small grandmotherly woman who waited outside the interview room.

"Yeah," said Alvarez. "If you thought she could bring down Boyce by doing that, you'd drive her over there yourself."

"Hey, man," said Dowling. "It's a living."

"No," said Alvarez. "For the two of you, it's a religion. I just don't want any burnt sacrifices in my town."

"You concentrate on finding Alicia Boyce before her husband does. That's the best way to prevent any burnt sacrifices."

"As long as I offer her up to you."

"You got a problem with that, detective?"

"I've got a problem with all of it. Every single thing about this fucking case smells to high heaven. So send in your newfound friend out there and get out of my face."

Instead of Boyce's antipathy and threats, or Dowling's cynical manipulations, Annika Atkins seemed in a reflective mood when Alvarez escorted her into the interview room.

"I've been thinking, Detective Alvarez," she said.

"I hope that's a good thing," he replied.

"Last night, you thought Alicia Boyce was the one who died in that basement of a drug overdose."

"That's right."

"But you didn't accuse me of making a fatal mistake and helping a woman who was a drug addict take her child and go on the run."

"I didn't figure that telling you was going to change anything."

Mrs. Atkins thought this over. "So what do you want from me?"

"Some answers, and a promise."

"Maybe I can give you some answers. What's the promise?"

"Raymond Boyce is an extremely dangerous individual. Bad things happen to people that cross him. He currently has two purposes in life: to figure out who's responsible for his daughter's death, and to find his wife. It would be a good idea for you to stay out of his way."

"He's the person responsible for Patty Boyce's death."

"I doubt he'll see it that way, and it's not going to take long for him to figure out you're involved."

"No, it won't take him long at all, because I plan to make sure he knows exactly what happened and why."

"So I don't suppose you'd promise to get on the next plane to Nebraska?"

"No, but you might have better luck with your questions."

"Do you know where Alicia Boyce is right now?"

"No, detective, but I wish I did."

"Would you tell me if you knew?"

"Yes, I would. For someone, anyone, to find her now, before her husband does, is her only hope. Even if it's that gum-popping DEA agent, who thinks I'll tell him everything I know if he just smiles at me and acts like he doesn't think I'm senile."

"Who was Alicia's next contact with the Underground here?"

"I've already told you I don't know."

"If you knew, would you tell me?"

"No."

"That's called obstruction of justice."

"I serve a higher justice."

"That's what Dowling would tell me, and maybe Boyce, too."

Annika Atkins stood up. "If you don't find Alicia Boyce very, very soon, all of these discussions are going to be very, very theoretical."

Alvarez could think of one other thing Annika Atkins could tell him. "Let me know if Dowling chews gum while he eats," he said.

Alvarez wanted to find Alicia Boyce, Dowling wanted to interrogate her, Annika Atkins wanted to reunite her with her daughter, and Raymond Boyce was chomping at the bit to get his hands on his missing wife before any of the rest of them. Unfortunately, to the El Paso Police Department, she was just one missing person, just one part of an investigation which involved another woman dead under circumstances that couldn't be tied to Raymond Boyce.

A hurried meeting with the Chief of the Special Case Force resulted in a grudging assignment of three uniformed cops to canvass motels for someone matching Mrs. Boyce's description, and a technician ordered to look for credit card charges that might indicate her whereabouts. It wasn't the best Alvarez could have hoped for, but it wasn't the worst, either. His request for a tail on Raymond Boyce was turned down. No matter how hot the DEA was for Boyce, he hadn't broken any laws during his brief stay in El Paso.

Alvarez took one call when he heard that Scott was on the line, so he could bring his partner up to date with recent developments. Scott listened carefully. "I can't see the connection between Boyce's women and what happened to Lenora Hinson," he said at the end of Alvarez's recitation. "But if s-s-something doesn't break pretty soon, my bet is that Boyce will start leaning on anyone associated with this c-c-case. I'd look for him to shake down K-Keaton and Ryan next."

The idea of Boyce leaning on Keaton wasn't a pleasant one, although Alvarez could envision him talking to Ryan without any mental wincing.

"We're officially in a reactive mode, as usual," he told

Scott. "Until Boyce leans on someone, we can't do anything about it. Keep your eyes open, and I'll tell Tory to watch her step. Her name already came up in our conversation." He thought about telling his partner that Boyce had mentioned Scott's wife and son, but decided against it.

After their conversation, Alvarez realized it was later than he thought. It was going to be tight if he wanted to talk to Father Sanchez and Rodney Kiepper before the day was over. He grabbed his coat and headed out, thinking his grandmother would have been pleased to see him properly dressed for a visit with a priest, even if Father Sanchez was Episcopalian instead of Catholic.

The secretary tried again to hand him his phone messages on his way out, but he eluded her. "Places to go, people to see," he said.

"There's a woman on the line for you right now," she pleaded. "She's called two times today already."

"Who is it?"

"She says her name is Tory Travers."

He thought about taking the call, but he was running out of time in more ways than one. He had a feeling that if he and Scott couldn't figure out the connection between Lenora Hinson's death and the suspected felon who intended to dog their every step, things were going to blow wide open, and Alicia Boyce might not be the only casualty. The sooner he could get Boyce, Dowling, Mrs. Atkins, Mutt, Jeff, and their missing colleague on a plane back to Nebraska, the happier he would be. Although maybe it had better be separate planes.

"Give her a message for me. Tonight, seven-thirty, red and slinky. No deviations allowed."

The secretary shrugged and did as she was told. It was not even close to being the most unusual message she'd been asked to relay while working on the second floor.

CHAPTER NINETEEN:

TRACKING THE MASTER BUILDER
El Paso, Texas:
Tuesday, January 3, mid-afternoon

Tory hung up the pay phone and looked at Jazz. "He wouldn't take my call," she said, dismayed.

Jazz stomped his feet and blew on his fingers. Waiting for Tory's call to go through various police operators had not improved his mood, not to mention the fact that if his boss had remembered to recharge her cell phone, they wouldn't be standing at a pay phone outside a convenience store.

"It's taken me more than a day to track this guy down," he said shortly. "I don't think he's gonna wait around for you to get some damned cop to take your call." He looked sourly at a group of Hispanic teenage boys in a low rider, swilling beer, playing the car radio at a pulsating level, and gunning the motor in time to the music. "Maybe if we hang around here a while longer, those *cholos* will mug us, and then someone at the police department would talk to us."

Tory looked at the low rider. It wasn't what was bothering her. "Alvarez is never going to believe that I called first thing to tell him about tracking down Scav Herrero," she said. "The one morning he doesn't come into the office."

"Typical government employee."

"Then, when you called and told me you'd found someone to talk to, I called him again. I even called before I got in the car and drove down here, but they told me he was in some kind of meeting. And now he won't take my call. I should have told him last night."

"Last night?" asked Jazz, keeping his eyes on the low rider.

"I talked to him last night, but I got distracted and forgot to tell him about the column and Scav Herrero. I guess I can just tell him tonight."

"Tonight?" This time Jazz took his eyes off the low rider.

"Well, yes. I'm having dinner with him tonight. It wasn't my idea, it was part of a game that he and his partner play ..." she trailed off.

"*Eso tiene más razón*, Tory," said Jazz. "I know I gave you a hard time about getting into trouble on your own. But it's Tuesday, right?" Tory nodded. "So, we saw your Detective Alvarez on Sunday. Then you talked to him Sunday night, you talked to him again last night, and now you're having dinner with him—tonight?" Tory nodded again. "I'd say you're doing a good job of keeping in touch. Do you think maybe he's not taking your phone calls because he feels like the guy in, what was that movie, *Fatal Attraction*?" Tory stared at him. "Close your mouth, boss. I was just kidding. So are we going to do this or not?" Jazz looked at his watch. "We've got two hours before I have to be at the airport."

"Tell me again why I agreed to let you take annual leave."

"Because you and the dragon lady you call a secretary are always on my case about me seeing my family, so when my sister in Boulder called and asked me to come visit after the first of the year, you thought it was a great idea."

"Well, it seemed like a great idea at the time. But that was three months ago."

"That's what you always say whenever I want to take time off."

"Isn't it nice to feel needed?"

"You're wasting time, and I'm freezing my ass off. Are we going to do this or not? It's your call."

"What's the plan again?"

"Scav Herrero's nephew is supposed to be working today at an apartment complex off Dyer street."

"I knew a girl in college who was from El Paso. She said mothers always warned their daughters to stay away from Dyer Street because that's where the enlisted men from Fort Bliss hung out. Aren't there a lot of bars and massage parlors there?"

"There's an apartment renovation project off Dyer Street, which is where we can find Scav's nephew. Besides, what does it matter what their mothers told them?"

"What?"

"Whether they hung out on Dyer Street or not, they'd still be Texans," said Jazz with the disdain that native New Mexicans reserved for the residents of their neighboring state.

"It's always nice to be reminded you're such a liberal, caring kind of guy," said Tory. "Dyer Street, here we come. So how do we do this?"

"You follow me to the apartment complex and stay in your car until I convince this guy to talk to us."

"You don't need my help?"

"No, boss, I don't need your help."

"Then how will you convince him to talk to us?"

"Boss, some things you're not too smart about. Do you really want me to pull my wallet out in front of these guys?"

Tory followed Jazz's car to a gutted apartment complex a few blocks off Dyer Street. Jazz disappeared into the building, and Tory had almost half an hour to question why she was parked there, and why she hadn't remembered to recharge her cell phone. She was so deep into contemplation of these questions that she jumped when Jazz tapped on the passenger window of her white RX. He had a large young man in tow, who was sweating in spite of the cold and looked like a Hispanic version of the Pillsbury Dough Boy. Tory unlocked the door and Jazz got in the back seat, while his companion reluctantly climbed into the passenger seat.

"This is Ricky Herrero, Scav's nephew," said Jazz in way of introduction.

"*Te digo que no me llamo Herrero, por el amor de Dios,*" said the young man pleadingly. "*Me llamo* Ricky Acosta. Acosta, *por favor.*"

"Our friend here seems to have more than one name," said Jazz, "depending on what's convenient. Right now he's working with a guy who's not too fond of his uncle, so for this job he's Ricky Acosta. But back when he was working with Scav, he was Ricky Herrero."

Ricky looked none too pleased with Jazz's explanation, but he didn't say anything.

"*Hablo Inglés?*" asked Tory.

"No," said Ricky shortly.

"*Donde esta* ... your uncle?" Tory asked, unable for the moment to come up with the Spanish word for uncle.

"*No sé.*"

"Ricky says his uncle is dead," explained Jazz.

"I'm sorry to hear that," said Tory.

"Don't be too sorry. Before Ricky found out what we wanted to talk about, when we were still on friendly terms, he told me his uncle went happy. Died in the arms of some hooker."

"No hooker," said Ricky emphatically. "*Esa no es más que una pica palos mira.*" It seemed the ill-fated Scav Herrero had died in the arms of someone who was no more than a prick teaser, if one translated Ricky's description literally.

"*Con mucha calma,*" said Jazz immediately. He had a low tolerance for certain profanities in Tory's presence.

"He means *esa es una pura chiflada,*" said Tory quickly, softening Ricky's description of the nameless woman to a mere tease. "Since I understand everything you say, and so does Jazz, why don't we speak English, Ricky? What do you say?"

"Okay," said Ricky, but he didn't sound too happy about it.

"We want to talk to you about a house your uncle worked on, a house owned by *Señora* Hinson on Rim Road," said Tory.

"I don' know nothing about that," said Ricky immediately.

Jazz smacked him on the back of the head. "That's not what you said earlier, *pendejo*. You remember, fifty dollars earlier?"

"I don' remember too well," Ricky whined.

Jazz pulled a $20 bill out of his wallet. "You better remember now, *cabrón*. Or I'll go tell your foreman what your last name was before you started using Acosta."

Ricky looked nervously at Tory, but he slowly reached out his hand to take the money Jazz was holding. He looked at the bill, folded it carefully, and put it in his shirt pocket. "Whatchu wanna know, man?"

"Did you work on the job she asked you about?"

"Yeah, I work on it. Chuss me and my uncle, 'cause no one else supposed to know."

"What kind of job was it?" asked Tory, trying to think what Alvarez would have asked.

"A basement room, right?" he replied nervously, like he was afraid of giving the wrong answer and getting hit on the back of the head again. "Why? Someone do some other job there?"

"Ricky here isn't into current events," Jazz said to Tory, which she took to mean that Ricky hadn't seen the recent newscasts. "Did the column in the basement room come from the old All Souls Episcopal Church?" he asked Ricky.

"Hey, man, I don' know where the column come from," said Ricky. "I chuss help my uncle. He was in charge." Ricky looked at Tory and licked his lips. "Did my uncle steal the column? Is that whatchu guys so hot about?" Tory noted that he didn't ask what column they were referring to.

"Why did Scav put the column there?" asked Jazz, ignoring Ricky's questions. "He was a real son of a bitch, but he didn't do sloppy work."

Ricky reached out and started running his fingers along the door handle, as if the action reassured him. "Because of *La Bruja Blanca*," he said. "That's what my uncle called the woman who own the house."

"Was her name Lenora Hinson?" asked Tory eagerly. "The White Witch" certainly fit the descriptions of Mrs. Hinson that Tory had heard so far.

"I don' know her name," said Ricky. "But my uncle, he call her other things besides *La Bruja Blanca*," he added helpfully.

"What about her?" asked Jazz.

"She fought with my uncle alla time, tell him what to do. She wanted everything chuss so, but it no make sense. We needed bigger beams in the ceiling, man, but she no want us to. So my uncle, he put the column there."

"Did he tell her that if someone pulled the column out, it would cause a collapse?" asked Tory.

Ricky looked at her in amazement. "How'd chu know that?"

"She didn't," said Jazz shortly. "It was just a lucky guess. So did Scav ever talk to anyone about pulling the column out?"

"Yeah. He and *La Bruja* fight alla time over money. My uncle hated her. He tole me she live where his family used to live, and she had no right to be there."

"*No me fregas*," said Jazz. "Your uncle's family never got closer to Rim Road than taking some hot little *muchacha* up to the Scenic Drive overlook. So who talked about pulling the column out?"

"My uncle. He told *La Bruja Blanca* if she did no pay

him, he come back some night and pull the column out and everything fall down."

Jazz looked at Tory triumphantly. She wondered where a tape recorder was when you needed it. "Did you know what the room was used for?" she asked. Ricky shook his head. He had started caressing the door handle again, which Tory took as a sign that the interview was coming to an end. "Was there anyone with Lenora Hinson—" Ricky looked at her dubiously and she rephrased her question. "Was there anyone else with *La Bruja Blanca* when you worked on the room with your uncle?"

Ricky Acosta made a terrible face, which Tory took as a sign of concentration. "Coupla times," he said slowly, "another man there."

"What did he look like?" asked Tory.

"You know, chuss a man."

Jazz smacked Ricky on the back of the head again. "I bought more than that," he said.

"An old white dude, a big man," said Ricky, looking back at Jazz reproachfully. "I don' know more than that. I only see him once or twice."

"What color hair?" asked Tory.

"I don' know. Dark."

"Do you remember anything else about him?"

Ricky Acosta made a terrible face again. "Yeah," he said suddenly. "I know somethin' else. My uncle call him *Padre*."

"Why, did he wear priests' clothes?" asked Jazz.

"No," answered Ricky.

"Then why did your uncle call him *Padre*?"

"I don' know," Ricky whined. "I tellchu all I know. I gotta get back to work now, or I gonna get fired."

"Would you tell this to the police tomorrow?" asked Tory.

Ricky Acosta looked at her like she had just sprouted wings. "No man, this don' buy me talkin' to no police. I never seen you two before, I don' know nothin'." He jerked the door handle up and climbed out of the car, but before he closed the door behind him, he bent down and looked in at Jazz. "My uncle, he say that his family lived where *La Bruja Blanca* lived, and he did no lie about thins like that." Apparently feeling like he had sufficiently defended his family's honor, Ricky Herrero Acosta trotted back to the apartment building, patting the shirt pocket that held his interview fee.

"Well," said Jazz after a moment. "I guess that's better than nothing."

"I think Alvarez will want to talk to him," said Tory.

"I wish him luck. I don't think Ricky Acosta is gonna want to be found again, boss."

"I know," said Tory dismally.

"Will you do something for me when you get back to the office?"

Tory looked at her watch. "If it doesn't take a lot of time."

"Why? Is there something going on back there I don't know about? Do you really need me to stay?"

Tory realized that Jazz was as reluctant to go visit his sister as she was reluctant to have him leave. "No, there's nothing going on. I just need to get back in time to get something done."

"What?"

"Find something red and slinky to wear to dinner with Alvarez, so he doesn't bite my head off when I tell him I think we just took his one shot at Ricky Acosta."

Jazz cocked his head thoughtfully. "Somehow, I can't picture you in something red and slinky, boss."

"Am I supposed to take that as a compliment? I wasn't born in a dress-for-success suit," she snapped.

"Christ, boss, I don't care what you wear to dinner. But if you really think it matters, I'm sure Sylvia could lend you something."

"God help us if it comes to that," said Tory. "So what is it you want me to do for you in the office?"

"Put in an expense voucher for me."

"For what?"

Jazz looked at her quizzically. "You better be faster on your feet than that tonight, boss. I need you to put in an expense voucher for seventy dollars out-of-pocket expense, what else?"

CHAPTER TWENTY:

CLERICAL CONTACTS
El Paso, Texas:
Tuesday, January 3, late afternoon

Rodney Kiepper lived in Summit Heights, an older residential area of modest but well-kept homes, about a fifteen-minute drive from both downtown and Rim Road. It would be more efficient to visit Father Sanchez first, but the priest had sounded more accessible than the headmaster, so Alvarez would have to drive out to Summit Heights and then back downtown again. Police work was like that. Alvarez thought about calling Kiepper before heading out to his house, but decided against it. Sometimes it was better to show up unannounced, and if he didn't call ahead, Kiepper couldn't tell him that he wouldn't be available.

The streets in Summit Heights were all named after presidents, although the subdivision dated itself by the names that were missing. Rodney Kiepper's house was a red brick, ranch-style home located on Tyler Street. Alvarez wondered if those with strong political ties had a problem living on streets named after presidents from opposing parties.

Kiepper answered the door not twenty seconds after Alvarez rang the bell, but instead of looking like he expected him, he regarded Alvarez like he didn't recall who he was. Alvarez tried to prod his memory by showing his badge and reintroducing himself. Kiepper continued to look at him doubtfully through the screen door, making no move to invite him in. "And why do you need to talk to me?" he asked.

"We're still trying to determine what happened to Lenora Hinson," said Alvarez patiently. "And so we're talking to everyone who knew her." He wished he could say "We can do this here, or we can do this down at the station," like on TV, but in reality, unless he had cause to arrest someone, he had to rely on people's willingness to help or their intimidation by authority figures, whichever worked best.

"Will this take long?" asked Kiepper.

"Not as long as it will take if I have to stand out here."

Rodney Kiepper reluctantly unlatched the screen door and held it open. Alvarez stepped inside. "The living room is to your left," Kiepper said. Alvarez found it with no problem and sat on a brown-striped armchair. Kiepper sat on a couch across from him, perched on the very edge, like he expected the interview to be a short one.

Alvarez pulled out his notebook to make this look official. "Thanks for taking the time to talk to me," he said. "I'd like to get a little more information about you. I know you're the headmaster at St. Michael's Episcopal School for Girls. How long have you been in that position?"

"Fifteen years."

Alvarez looked up in surprise. "And you are how old, Mr. Kiepper?"

"I'm forty-two."

"You must have come into the position relatively young." Kiepper simply continued to look at him, making no comment. He certainly didn't seem as talkative as he had at Keaton's house, where he had offered to identify himself before anyone even asked. Alvarez wondered what was responsible for the change in attitude—being interviewed directly by the police, inheriting a quarter of the Hinson estate, or something else. "How long did you know Lenora Hinson?" Alvarez asked.

"I met her when Keaton transferred to St. Michael's during her freshman year in high school," said Kiepper.

Alvarez did some mental arithmetic. Keaton had told him she was twenty-eight years old. "So that means you've known her for about fourteen years?" Kiepper nodded. "And you didn't know her husband?" Kiepper shook his head. What Alvarez needed was a question that couldn't be answered with a simple yes or no. "Why did Keaton transfer to your school in the middle of a year?" he asked, fishing.

"Because she was expelled from Radson," said Kiepper shortly.

"Why was she expelled?"

Kiepper continued to give him a dubious look, as though he wasn't sure if it wouldn't have been a better choice to have closed the front door and left Alvarez standing on the porch. "I can't see what any of this has to do with Lenora's death," he said finally.

"Please just answer the question, Mr. Kiepper," said Alvarez.

"Radson is a very exclusive private school. They have very high standards of behavior for their students, and Keaton didn't meet those standards."

"I understand that St. Michael's is also a very exclusive private school," said Alvarez. "Why don't you save us both a lot of time and just answer the question?"

"She was expelled for organizing a telephone ring," said Kiepper shortly.

"A what?"

"A telephone ring."

Alvarez continued to look at Kiepper, his pencil poised in the air, in order to convey that he needed more information to understand what the headmaster was talking about. After a lengthy pause, Kiepper continued. "She recruited certain class-mates at Radson to talk dirty on the phone to boys. She sold phone numbers and a time that they could call, like those nine hundred-number adult phone-sex businesses."

Alvarez didn't think it would help his rapport with Kiepper to grin at the thought of an enterprising teenaged Keaton, so he made an effort to keep a straight face. "I can see where that would get her expelled from Radson," he said. "But is that the kind of student that would be accepted at St. Michael's?"

"Not usually. But we all felt that Keaton had potential, if only she was taught to focus it properly."

"Would Keaton have been accepted at St. Michael's if her mother hadn't been wealthy and influential?"

Kiepper sighed. "Unfortunately, the real world involves compromises. Tuition to St. Michael's only covers about half our operating costs. We depend on donations to cover the rest, and to fund scholarships for students whose parents couldn't send them otherwise."

Kiepper had successfully avoided directly answering Alvarez's question. "So did Mrs. Hinson make contributions to St. Michael's?" he asked.

"Yes."

"How much?"

"I don't know. I don't keep track of those things."

"Make a guess."

There was that sigh again. Kiepper did not appear happy for someone who'd had a wealthy benefactor. "Maybe two million dollars over the last fourteen years. Spread out over that amount of time, it's not really that much," he added.

Bullshit, thought Alvarez. He tried to imagine how ecstatic the nuns at Horizon House, where his sister Anna lived in Las Cruces, would be at the prospect of receiving more than $100,000 a year. The thought prompted an unbidden recollection of his own Catholic grandmother, to whom tithing had been a religion unto itself. He realized he'd have to come to terms with his own recent inheritance and earmark an amount for good works in order to keep his indomitable grandmother from haunting his dreams. "Shit," he muttered to himself.

Kiepper said, "I beg your pardon?"

"Sorry, I was just thinking. Was Keaton a problem at St. Michael's?"

Kiepper sighed again at the recollection. "The first two years were horrible," he said bluntly. "Sometimes I didn't think I'd be able to persuade the rest of the Board to let her stay. Keaton didn't just get into trouble by herself, she could convince the other girls to do the most outrageous things. But by her junior year, she settled down, and things weren't so bad."

Because by then she had another outlet for those wild impulses, thought Alvarez to himself. True love, not to mention hot, forbidden, illicit teenage sex. Enough to keep anyone occupied for a while, even Keaton. "Did you know that she had a boyfriend, a Gary Cabrioni?"

"Yes. He was older than Keaton, and Lenora worried about the influence he might have on her."

Once again Alvarez managed to keep a straight face. He figured Keaton had been about a hundred light years ahead of Cabrioni in the matter of one influencing the other. "So after Keaton graduated from high school, did you stay in contact with Mrs. Hinson?"

"Yes. She was a member of our Board of Directors," said Kiepper uncomfortably.

"And when did that happen?"

"When Keaton was admitted to St. Michael's."

So the headmaster had at least one ally in his efforts to keep Keaton in school, reflected Alvarez. "That's quite a bequest you received today," he said. "Was it a surprise, or did you know that Mrs. Hinson intended to leave you part of her estate?"

"Is this the real purpose of your visit, detective? To see if I knew Lenora was leaving me a lot of money? Does this make me a suspect?"

"I'm just trying to get information, Mr. Kiepper. To be honest, if you killed Mrs. Hinson in order to get your hands on her money, you don't appear too ecstatic about your success."

"I'm not," said Kiepper. "Ecstatic about the money, that is."

"And why is that?"

"It raises certain ethical questions."

"And those would be?"

Kiepper regarded Alvarez in silence for a moment. "I don't know what you've been told about Lenora," he said finally, "but she could be a very difficult person."

"So we've gathered."

"I had no idea that she was leaving money to me personally. I had hopes, of course, but my hopes were that she would leave a bequest directly to the school."

"And the fact that she left the money to you personally poses a problem?"

"Yes. Being involved with Lenora was like being mired in quicksand. She wanted very specific things, and she was fully prepared to manipulate, bribe, and threaten to get them."

"And what did she want from you?"

"St. Michael's needs to move forward. We have plans to expand our facilities and admit boys, making the school co-educational. Lenora emphatically opposed those plans."

"So that's why her will charged you to continue your work in the way she would have wanted, or however it was phrased?"

"Exactly."

"I don't see the problem. As soon as the will is probated, the money will be yours, free and clear. You can use it however you see fit. You don't even have to use it for the school."

"I told you you wouldn't understand. Headmasters for Episcopal schools aren't exactly recruited off the street. I am a devout, committed Episcopalian, which means that I am a man of God, and as such, I must follow my conscience."

"Speaking of men of God, how are you associated with Father Sanchez and All Souls Episcopal Church?"

"Father Sanchez is a friend of mine. Many of our students' families attend his church, but there's no direct connection between All Souls and St. Michael's."

"Have you ever heard of the Underground Railroad, Mr. Kiepper?"

"Isn't that an organization that helps shelter abused spouses and children?"

"Sort of. Did you have any reason to suspect that Mrs. Hinson was involved with the Underground Railroad?"

"No, not at all." Kiepper paused for a moment. "Is that what the basement room was for?"

"That's what it looks like. Does the name Raymond Boyce sound familiar to you?"

"No, who is he?"

"He's the father of the other woman who was found with Mrs. Hinson." Kiepper continued to shake his head regretfully. "What kind of relationship do you have with Lenora Hinson's children?"

"I hope they regard me as a family friend. I've tried to help with Keaton's various problems."

"Did you know that Gary Cabrioni is the father of Keaton's daughter?"

Kiepper stared at Alvarez. "Are you sure?" he asked.

"Pretty sure."

Kiepper put his hand to his temples and began to rub like he was trying to stave off a headache. "Those poor kids," he said. "Lenora spent every waking moment trying to figure out how to run their lives, and this is what it comes to. Ryan hates being an accountant. He spent his whole life trying to please his mother and never succeeded. Keaton was pushed into a marriage she didn't want, and she's never learned how to stand on her own two feet. Maybe it's a blessing that Lenora didn't live to find out that her only grandchild is illegitimate. She hoped Hero would turn out differently."

"Speaking of Lenora's children, did you know that she manipulated her husband's attorney in order to tie up their inheritance, and place it under her control until they each turned thirty-five?"

Kiepper looked as though he was becoming weary of the conversation. "One could hardly know Ryan Hinson and not be aware of it, although I never knew if it was true, or merely Ryan's suspicions."

"How did Keaton feel about the trust funds?"

"I don't think she cared. Keaton doesn't appear to care about a lot of things that concern normal people."

"Why do you think Mrs. Hinson named Father Sanchez as the trustee of her children's funds?"

"I really don't know. I can't tell you what was in Lenora's mind from one day to the next."

"What do you think Father Sanchez will do with the funds?"

"I don't know, detective. I don't think you can expect me to know what other people are thinking, or what they plan to do. Are there any other questions that you have for me? I would really like to spend some time alone."

"Where were you on New Year's Eve?"

Kiepper did not look pleased with the question, but he answered it. "I don't go out a lot. I was here."

"Alone?"

"Yes."

"Do you have children, Mr. Kiepper?"

"No."

"Are you married?"

"I was, but my wife died."

"I'm sorry to hear that."

Rodney Kiepper stood up, indicating that the interview was at an end. "You don't have to be sorry; it happened a long time ago. And now, if you don't mind, I'm going to see you to the door."

And he did.

It was after five when Alvarez reached All Souls Episcopal Church downtown, so he went to the parsonage directly behind the church, like he'd been told. No one answered his knock, and he was beginning to feel foolish when he noticed there were lights on in the administrative building attached to the new, modern sanctuary.

The door to the building was unlocked, and Alvarez went down the hall, peering into empty offices and rooms, until he came upon one that was occupied. Father Sanchez, deep in concentration, sat in front of a computer screen. Before Alvarez could knock on the door to announce his arrival, he heard the priest say plainly, "Goddamn it to hell, you spawn of the Devil. I've followed all the directions in the user's handbook, so I *command* you to work, in the name of God and all his heavenly hosts!"

Alvarez cleared his throat.

Father Sanchez looked up, startled, and then smiled. "Oh, hello. Do you happen to know anything about networking computers?" Alvarez shook his head. "That's too bad," said the priest, disappointment plain on his face. "There are all these controversies about modernizing the Church. Do we ordain women, do we accept homosexual unions, do we sanction abortion, and if so, under what conditions? Me, I just want the Church to name a patron saint for those of us over sixty who have to use computers."

Alvarez dug into his dusty memory of saintly matters. For the life of him, he couldn't remember the patron saint of lost causes. "How about St. Christopher," he suggested, "because you're trying to cross uncharted waters?"

Father Sanchez looked thoughtful. "Theologically sound," he said, "but not too original. I would hazard a guess that you are churched, but lapsed. Roman Catholic?"

"Aren't we all?"

This brought a smile to the priest's face. "God works in mysterious ways, my son. He even calls some Hispanics to be Episcopalians, as strange as that may seem."

Alvarez smiled in spite of himself. "Can I sit down?" he asked.

"Certainly," Father Sanchez answered. "I obviously need a break. I am guilty of being one of those who prays for patience, but just not right now. What can I do for you? I'll answer whatever questions you have, to the best of my ability. Even theological ones, if you are so inclined."

"I think I'll stick to secular questions today. No one is waiting for you at home?"

"No. I have two grown daughters that live here, but they have lives and families of their own, and my wife died of cancer three years ago."

"I'm sorry to hear that."

At least Father Sanchez wasn't one to immediately shake off condolences like an embarrassment. "Thank you. It was an enormous loss to everyone who knew her. My Emma was truly a wonderful woman. She would have had some refreshment to offer you, where I'm terribly lacking in that regard. Shall I find a cup of coffee for you?"

Alvarez shook his head. "How long have you been the rector here?"

"For twenty blessed years."

"So you knew Rodney Kiepper when he became the headmaster at St. Michael's Episcopal School for Girls?"

"I certainly did. He's a very dedicated young man. Rodney is one of the best things that ever happened to that school."

"How long have you known Lenora Hinson?"

"Twenty years. The Hinson family belonged to this church before I became rector. Keaton and her family still come sometimes, Easter and Christmas, but I haven't seen Ryan or his wife at Church for years. I married both the children, and years before, I conducted the burial service for Harold. It was terrible, a man with a family dying suddenly like that, in the prime of his life." Father Sanchez looked saddened at the memory of it. "And now, I'll be conducting Lenora's service on Friday," he added soberly.

"What did you think of Lenora Hinson?"

"She was a terribly unhappy, controlling person. She was very destructive to almost anyone who came within her sphere of influence."

"You don't mince words, do you?"

"I didn't think you came to hear me mince words, my son."

Alvarez wasn't about to argue with that. "Were you involved with the Hinson family other than being their priest?"

"If you think about that question, detective, I'm sure you'll realize how foolish it sounds."

Alvarez conceded the priest was right. "Was Lenora Hinson actively involved with All Souls Church?" he asked instead.

"Oh my, yes. She bounced from one group and committee to another, depending on how quickly she came to loggerheads with other parishioners. How do you like our sanctuary?" asked Father Sanchez suddenly.

"It looks a lot different than the old one."

"Yes, well, have you ever heard the saying that God so loved the world he didn't send a committee?" Alvarez shook his head. "When our old church burned down, a Building Committee was appointed to oversee the construction of a new sanctuary. Because of her monetary contributions, Lenora ended up chairing the committee, and what you see is the result. We must have lost a score of parishioners because she railroaded her own personal vision in over the desires and opinions of other members of this church."

Alvarez wondered if driving away parishioners might provide a priest with a motive for murder. "Do you know anything about an organization called the Underground Railroad?"

Father Sanchez looked confused. "Wasn't that what helped southern slaves escape to freedom in the north?"

"Today, it's an organization that helps non-custodial parents kidnap their own children."

"And why in heaven's name would they want to do that?"

"Because they believe that the courts have awarded their children to an abusive parent."

Father Sanchez thought this over. "And that's what the room in the basement was used for? I try not to listen to gossip, but I do watch the local newscasts." Alvarez nodded. "And you think Lenora was involved in this organization?" Alvarez nodded again. Father Sanchez sighed. "Unfortunately, that makes a lot of sense. Lenora would have a lot of power in a group that couldn't raise funds through conventional means. And she wouldn't be above threatening people with exposure to get her way, either."

"Do you think either of her children would know about her involvement?"

Father Sanchez shook his head. "Both of Lenora's children hated her. Their family structure failed to prepare Keaton and Ryan for adult life, and not because of a lack of attention or money, which are the usual excuses. Lenora used her wealth and her will to tie her children to her, and thereby warped and stunted their development."

"Which obviously brings us to the trust funds," said Alvarez. "Why did she select you to be the trustee of her children's funds?"

"Why not? It's not like she had a large number of close friends to choose from."

"Good point. So what are your plans, as trustee of the funds?"

"In Ryan's case, that's a moot question, and I plan to turn Keaton's fund over to her as soon as I can figure out how to accomplish that. It's about time the poor child had some adult activity to occupy her. I see no advantage in having one adult oversee the material goods of another."

"And what about the money you'll inherit? What do you plan to do with that?"

Father Sanchez laughed. "I suppose the fact that I'm inheriting a great deal of money from Lenora makes me a suspect of some sort, detective, and to remove suspicion, I should tell you that I'll donate all the money to the Church. But that wouldn't be the truth. I have five grandchildren, and one of them is a Downs Syndrome child. This money will be a godsend to her parents. I plan to set up trusts for all my grandchildren, trusts that their parents can manage and access. Lenora Hinson's money will send four of my grandchildren to college, and will provide care for the fifth one after her parents are dead. When I've accomplished all that, I'll probably do-nate the balance to various charities."

"Did you know that Lenora Hinson was leaving you a quarter of her estate?"

"No, I didn't," said Father Sanchez. "And if this had hap-pened while Emma was alive, it would be a different story. I would have bought her a house that wasn't a parsonage, for once in her life, and I would have taken her wherever she wanted to go. But Emma's dead now, so what's the point? If you wanted to count me as having a motive to kill Lenora, detective, you should have come three years earlier."

"Can you tell me where you were on New Year's Eve?"

"Certainly. I was here conducting a midnight Mass."

"You can't be serious. People don't come to church to celebrate New Year's Eve."

"Oh yes, they do. You should try it yourself, detective. We start about nine, with a pot-luck buffet, and we visit and so-cialize until eleven, when we have the Eucharist. It allows our parishioners to go somewhere families are welcome, where the party doesn't get out of hand, and where they can start the New Year in communion with God."

Alvarez couldn't argue with that logic. "And where were you before nine o'clock on New Year's Eve?"

"Here, preparing for the service, but before you ask, there was no one else here until about eight-thirty. That's when the Church Women start setting up the buffet."

Alvarez closed his notebook. "So the Church is moving toward modernization, but the Church Women are still the ones who set up the buffet? Who does the clean-up afterward, Father?"

Father Sanchez beamed at him as if he had said some-thing brilliant, and leaned over to write something on a desk blotter that was already covered with indecipherable scribbles. "What a wonderful observation, detective. I will suggest that next year, the Men's Group do both the setup and the clean-up. Maybe you'll join us?"

Alvarez stood. "Stranger things have happened," he said, stretching. It had been a long day, and the beds at the Shady Lady weren't the best. "Rodney Kiepper mentioned that he lost his wife a long time ago. He looks kind of young for that."

Father Sanchez frowned. "Yes, there was some sort of trag-edy. I think that was one of the reasons he came here, to put it behind him. I'm embarrassed to say that I can't remember what it was, but I talk to so many people about the tragedies in their lives. You'd be amazed how seldom people think to share anything joyous with their priest."

"Kind of sounds like being a police officer," said Alvarez.

"I'm sure it does. My secretary, Sally, would know. Sally keeps track of things like personal tragedies," said Father Sanchez, then winced. "I didn't mean for it to sound like that, but I'm sure you understand what I mean."

"No problem," said Alvarez, looking at his watch. It was going to be tight to pick up sirloin for Carumba Cotton Candy, get showered and dressed and to the State Line by seven-thirty. He didn't want to think about Tory's response if she thought he'd stood her up.

"Would you like me to call you tomorrow after I talk to Sally, or will you be talking to Rodney again?"

"Not unless something else comes up. He didn't seem too pleased to be talking to me the first time. So, if Sally remembers anything about the circumstances that brought him here to El Paso, I'd like to hear about it." Alvarez gave the priest his card.

"Do you pray, my son?" asked Father Sanchez.

"Sometimes," admitted Alvarez. He hoped he wouldn't be

questioned about the nature of his prayers, which in the last
two decades had tended to be along the lines of "Holy shit—
please don't let him have a gun, God."

"Then," said Father Sanchez, "since I've taken the time to
answer your questions, I'd be very grateful if you'd do something for me. Could you stop in the sanctuary and say a quick
prayer that my installation of this damned network program
is successful?"

Since Father Sanchez put it that way, Alvarez figured the
least he could do was oblige.

CHAPTER TWENTY-ONE:

LIPPING THE STEAKS
El Paso, Texas:
Tuesday, January 3, early evening

Carumba Cotton Candy was at Alvarez's front window, looking out, when he drove up. He could have taken it as a sign of canine devotion, but he'd seen her look out the window the previous evening, before he left for Anthony, after he'd closed the shades. He figured she could see about as much with the shades closed as with them open.

He had thought about what to call the dog, especially now that he knew her full name. When Alvarez suggested that maybe Lenora Hinson was more unbalanced than they thought, giving a dog three names, Scott patiently explained that purebred registered dogs were like actors, and no two of the same breed could have the same name. Candy was no improvement over Cotton; Carumba was out. The only other derivation of her name that he could come up with was CeeCee, and he'd be damned if he'd have a dog named CeeCee, trust fund or no trust fund. So Cotton it was.

"Hi, dog," he said when he walked in the door. Cotton ran to meet him, making the little mewling noises he had come to interpret as welcoming sounds. Behind her she dragged a wooden magazine rack, the magazines falling everywhere.

"What the hell?" he said, and bent down to see what was going on. Somehow her strong, tightly-curled tail had wrapped around the narrow handle of the magazine rack, and she was dragging it after her. She stood patiently while he liberated the wooden rack.

"I brought you something," he said, keeping up his end of

the one-way conversation. Cotton sat at his feet, her newly freed tail swishing back and forth on the floor. Alvarez opened the package of sirloin steak, placed the meat on a cutting board, and cut about a third of the steak into bite-sized chunks.

"Why not?" he said, getting a plate out of the cabinet. It wasn't like it was family heirloom china. He put the meat on the plate and set it in front of the dog. Then he filled a glass with tap water, lifting it to the dog in a toast. "Here's to a long and healthy life, " he said, as Carumba Cotton Candy's dinner disappeared in less time than it had taken him to fix it.

The phone rang. "This had better not be my date calling to cancel," he told the dog, who was watching him like she expected a second course. "Dinner with you is not what I had in mind for tonight."

He picked up the phone on the second ring and said, "Alvarez."

"It's Scott. I need to t-t-talk to you."

Alvarez groaned. "Not now," he protested. "I've got a heavy date, and for once it's not someone handpicked by Donna." There was silence on the other end, which wasn't their normal conversational pattern. Alvarez quickly switched gears. "Hey, man, what is it?"

"I'd have c-c-called sooner, but I've been trying to c-c-calm Donna down," was Scott's oblique reply.

"What's going on? Is Donna okay?"

"She's shut herself and S-S-Scotty up in the b-bedroom. She thinks the phone c-c-call is my fault."

"What phone call?"

"Right before f-five, she got a phone call from a m-m-medical lab, c-calling to t-t-tell her that Scotty's AIDS test was negative."

Alvarez was still looking at Cotton, but he wasn't seeing her. "And Donna didn't have Scotty tested for AIDS, did she?"

"No."

"So what did you do?"

"I d-drove down there, p-p-pounded on the d-door and m-made them open up and talk to me. The results were right there, on a computer print out, with Scotty's b-b-birthdate and social security n-number and his pediatrician's name."

"What does the pediatrician say about it?"

"Their office was already closed. I have a call into him, but he hasn't c-called back yet."

"Sounds like Boyce is serious about finding out what we know," said Alvarez after a pause.

"He's s-serious about finding his wife," said Scott. "Mine's in the b-bedroom and I don't know if she's ever c-c-coming out again."

Marital advice was not Alvarez's strong point. Surely Donna was not so naive as to think that Scott's work would never touch her. Or maybe she was. Maybe that belief was a prerequisite for everyone who married a police officer. "Why don't you send them out of town for a few days?" he asked.

"I already thought of that," said Scott. "But what if they're t-tailing her? She might be safer here than somewhere else without me."

It was interesting that Scott chose not to include his son's name in this discussion. "Then I'd suggest you sit tight," said Alvarez. "Lie low for the next few days, work the inheritance angle of the investigation. If nothing breaks, Boyce will collect his kid and get out of town, then the rest of the circus will follow him back to Nebraska. I think he's just flexing his muscles for show."

"Yeah, m-maybe," said Scott glumly. "Meanwhile, I'll be flexing my muscles on the c-c-couch again. Hey, we got a c-c-call from the morgue late this afternoon. A woman was asking if anyone had identified the second c-corpse from the Hinson house, b-b-but she got spooked and left."

"Damn. What happened? Did the mouse woman hiss at her?"

"No, they p-played it just like we asked them to. Told her s-s-someone would be happy to talk to her and see if they could help. She still split."

"Do we think it was Alicia Boyce? What did she look like?"

"Scarf and d-dark glasses, that's what."

"Maybe she was scoping it out, and she'll show up again tomorrow. We still got a lid on the fact that the second corpse is Patty Boyce?"

"So far so good. But we can't control who Boyce talks to."

"No shit," said Alvarez, thinking of conversations with pediatricians and medical laboratories.

"You b-better watch your b-back," said Scott grimly. "But have a nice time at dinner," he added, in an effort to finish on an upbeat note.

"Yeah, I'll do that," said Alvarez. "And if it doesn't work out, at least I've got some leftover sirloin." Cotton cocked her head disapprovingly at him as he hung up, as if she understood every word.

There was no sign of Tory or her white Mazda RX when Alvarez arrived at the State Line, which had only a modest dinner crowd on the Tuesday night following New Year's Day. He'd called ahead for reservations, so he was seated immediately. He ordered a bottle of chilled champagne, had the waiter fill both glasses, and sipped his while he waited. He saw Tory walk in, and he saw the head waiter remove her coat. She was wearing a burgundy dress with a high draped neckline, but as she turned to help the waiter free her from her coat, he saw that the back of her dress was cut almost to her waist. Donna had once called something similar an "exit dress."

When the waiter gestured to his table, and Tory started walking toward him, he saw that the seemingly demure dress also had a slit up the side. It was promising, but he estimated the slit ended about four inches below where Keaton Crandell's red dress had started.

Alvarez stood wordlessly and pulled out Tory's chair for her, seating her with a flourish. She bumped into the table, dangerously jostling the champagne glasses. She was obviously nervous; she certainly wasn't smiling.

He resumed his seat, put his elbows on the table, his chin in his hands, and enjoyed looking at her. "You look absolutely beautiful," he said frankly.

"Well, thank you," she replied, looking everywhere but at him. She spied the iced champagne bottle and started. "Good heavens," she said. "Do you have any idea how expensive that is?"

"We're celebrating."

"What are we celebrating?"

"Many things, starting with the fact that you're sitting across the table from me. We're not at a crime scene, you're not engaged in breaking and entering, and no one is shooting at us. I'd say this is real progress."

She frowned at him. "I can't do this," she said suddenly.

"Why? I haven't talked dirty yet, or told you what to do. What's the problem?"

She continued to regard him solemnly with those incredibly blue eyes of hers. "You're going to be really angry," she said shortly. "I can't let you buy me dinner when I know that you're going to be absolutely furious later on."

He looked at her regretfully. "You just couldn't let it wait, could you?" She shook her head no. "You've been messing in my case, haven't you?" She nodded. "Have you killed anyone?"

"Of course not," she said indignantly.

"Kidnapped anyone? Stolen anything?" She continued shaking her head. "Threatened anyone?"

"Not exactly—" she started, but he held up his hand to stop her.

"Skip that one. Broken any laws?" She shook her head again. "Good," he said. "We can get through this. One step at a time, and this is the first step." He picked up his champagne glass, drained it, and reached over to refill it. Tory watched him like she would a coiled rattlesnake. He lifted his glass. "I propose a toast," he said. "Bottoms up."

"You don't say bottoms up for champagne that costs this much," she told him. "And what are we toasting to?"

"Carumba Cotton Candy," he told her. She looked at him like he was crazy. "This is how it works," he continued. "You drink a glass of champagne, and I'll tell you about Carumba Cotton Candy. Then we order dinner. We drink some more champagne. Then we talk about the case a little, then we drink more champagne. When we've started on the second bottle, and not a minute before, then you can tell me what it is that I'm going to be so furious about."

She continued to look at him dubiously. "Are you sure you can afford a second bottle of this?" she asked.

"That's the least of my worries at this point," he said frankly. "How about it?"

She looked at him a while longer, and then nodded. "If you can do it, I can," she said. She lifted her champagne glass to meet his. "To Carumba Cotton Candy," she said, and drained the contents.

The appetizers went well with the champagne, as did the main course, and dessert. Alvarez chronologically worked his way through telling her about his day, from the morning will-reading to the identification of Patty Boyce, and finally, to his conversations with the Episcopal headmaster and priest. He got her to laugh over the trust fund for Cotton, but her eyes darkened with concern when he told her about the fate of Raymond Boyce's elder daughter. He meant to tell her about his phone conversation with Scott and its implications, but he got sidetracked describing his interviews with Rodney Kiepper and Father Sanchez. At the mention of All Souls Episcopal Church, Tory practically started squirming in her seat.

"Do you need to go to the Ladies Room?" he asked. "If you do, it's okay. I can handle that sort of thing."

"I think it's time to order the second bottle of champagne," she said, so he did. The waiter brought it quickly, uncorked it, and refilled their glasses. "I think you better have one more glass," she said, so he did.

"Well?" he asked, setting his empty glass carefully on the table.

"Part of it's your fault," she started out. "There wouldn't be a problem if you would have taken just one of my phone calls today."

"Skip the justifications. Just tell me what you've done."

"All right. But you can't interrupt me, or start yelling at me."

"I never yell at you."

"No, you don't," she admitted. "Your voice gets all quiet and hard, and you sound like you want to kill me with your bare hands. So you can't do that."

"Or what?"

"Or I'll get nervous, and after all this rich food and champagne, I'll might get sick at the table. I don't think you should count on me to be as talented as Keaton. I'd probably throw up all over both of us."

"You make a convincing argument," he admitted, refilling his champagne glass. "So tell me."

And she did. She followed his lead, telling him chronologically the events that led to the interview with Ricky Herrero/ Acosta, starting with Jazz's comments the night after they had inspected the Rim Road residence. Alvarez was as good as his word, not interrupting her, simply drinking two more glasses of champagne during her recitation. At one point he did start drumming his fingers against the table, but when she asked him to stop, he did.

When she was done, she asked him if he had any questions.

"Of course I have questions," he said shortly. "If you hadn't gone and done this, would you have worn this dress tonight?"

"What a strange question. Does that mean you're not angry?"

"Of course I'm angry. But the dress and the champagne help. Some. Enough for me to resist putting my hands around your throat, at least for now." And then he took her through the whole interview again, word for word, as close as she could remember it.

Then he started asking her the questions he would have asked. What did "old dude" mean? Thirty, the age Ryan Hinson would have been five years ago, or Kiepper's thirty-six, or Cabrioni's mid-twenties, or even Father Sanchez's late fifties? How old was Ricky Acosta, and how old had he been five years ago? How had that affected his frame of reference? How dark-skinned was he? Could dark hair have meant medium-brown, or did Acosta mean dark in comparison to his? Was Acosta really sure that his uncle had called the man "Padre," or could he have it mistaken for the respectful title of "Patron"? Had the mystery man been present when Acosta's uncle threatened to return and pull the column out? Had Ricky or his uncle ever done any work at St. Michael's Episcopal School for Girls? Did Ricky Herrero/Acosta know either Father Sanchez or Rodney Kiepper?

"I don't know, I don't know, I don't know," said Tory, her own chin resting in her hand now as she looked glumly at Alvarez from across the table. "He didn't want to talk to us at all, and some of the things he said didn't make sense. He told Jazz some story about his uncle resenting Lenora Hinson because she lived where his family used to live. Now are you going to tell me that I should have asked him questions about that, too?"

Alvarez felt that chill go down his spine that he got when things were starting to fall together, when he was closing in on a story that would make sense. He started to tell Tory about Stormsville and the Hispanic community that had existed where the Rim Road residences now stood, but he never got a word out.

Raymond Boyce pulled up a chair and sat down at their table.

"Detective Alvarez, Mrs. Travers," said Boyce pleasantly. "How convenient to find the two of you together."

Tory sat up straight in her chair. "Do I know you?" she asked.

"No, but you're going to," said Boyce. "I'm Raymond Boyce, and I'm pleased to make your acquaintance." Tory simply looked at him, ignoring the hand which Boyce smoothly withdrew.

"I don't recall inviting you to sit down at our table," said Alvarez, scanning the room for Boyce's companions.

"No, no," said Boyce, reading his mind. "Hector, Enrique, and Alfonso are all otherwise occupied, and I won't take but a moment of your time. I've been watching you, and you both seemed so immersed in your conversation. Trading information, are you?"

Tory didn't say a word. Alvarez was watching Boyce's hands, which so far remained on the table. "Information is what I'm interested in," said Boyce, "and I don't care where it comes from." He turned to Tory. "I'm a simple man, Mrs. Travers. I want to find my wife. Is there something wrong with that?"

"Yes," said Tory succinctly, keeping her eyes on Boyce's face. Alvarez wished that if she was going to be sick from nerves, she would do it now, but she gave no indication of it.

Boyce narrowed his eyes, the way he had at the morgue when someone said something that surprised him, but he kept his tone light. "I want to find my wife, and I'll make it well worth the while of anyone who helps me. I'll also make it very difficult for anyone who stands in my way." He turned to Alvarez. "You're a man with few family ties, Mr. Alvarez, but I learned something interesting today. You have a sister, don't you?"

"If you've done your research," said Alvarez, matching his tone, "you know that she's a retard, and I've had to provide for her my whole life. Are you proposing something that will change that?"

Boyce turned back to Tory. "I've already talked to Emmett Delgado, Mrs. Travers. But the people who know anything about this case tell me that you're the engineer of the hour. When would it be convenient for you to discuss your findings with me?"

"When hell freezes over," said Tory pleasantly.

"Ah, well," said Boyce regretfully. "I'll leave you to your evening then, whatever recreational activities you and Detective Alvarez have planned for afterward. Let me know when you change your mind. I'm sure you'll both come to realize that it's really a simple thing I'm asking." Boyce stood up and walked out of the restaurant.

Tory started to say something to Alvarez, but she was cut off by the arrival of another visitor to their table. "Howdy, home boy," said Derek Dowling, taking Boyce's vacated seat. He chewed his gum for a moment and then asked, "How're you holding up?"

"Jesus Christ," said Alvarez in disgust, throwing his napkin down on the table. "Where's Mrs. Atkins? She's all we need to complete this party."

"We had an early dinner; she's resting. She's got a hell of a lot of energy for an old lady, but she's not up to following Boyce around at night. She followed him all day, and I followed her. She's making some pretty wild threats, talking about giving that tape to the press. I think she's getting to him." When Alvarez didn't answer, Dowling turned to Tory. "I'm Derek Dowling," he said, offering his hand. "Sorry to break up your dinner party, but I wanted to check on your boyfriend here."

Tory ignored Dowling's hand, too. "He's not my boyfriend," she said.

"Whatever," said Dowling dismissively. He looked back at Alvarez. "I hope you can take the heat," he said. "I'd hate for your investigation to develop leaks that lead Boyce to his wife before we can get our hands on her."

"I think I can handle the heat," said Alvarez evenly. "It's the uninvited dinner guests that are getting to me."

"I hear you got a nibble at the morgue today."

"Maybe," said Alvarez noncommittally.

"If you and I and the people at the morgue know about it, someone else may know about it, too," said Dowling pointedly.

"Maybe," said Alvarez again, clenching his jaw. "But it's not something I can do anything about right now. Did I hear you say you were just leaving?"

Dowling looked regretfully at the remaining champagne on ice. "I don't suppose you'd like to invite me to share an after-dinner drink," he said.

"Not even close," said Alvarez.

"Well," said Dowling, standing up, "watch your back."

He was the second one to tell Alvarez that this evening, when all Alvarez really wanted to be watching was Tory Travers's bare back. "And if I were you, I'd keep the civilians out of the line of fire."

"What about Mrs. Atkins?" asked Alvarez. He didn't want to postpone Dowling's departure, but he couldn't resist.

"Hey, home boy, Mrs. Atkins is a player. There's nothing civilian about her." Still chewing gum, Dowling gave Alvarez a thumbs-up signal, then duplicated Boyce's exit.

Alvarez look at Tory. "Are you okay? Feel like you're going to throw up?"

She shook her head. "I always thought dating was horrible," she said, "but I never remember it being this bad."

Alvarez signaled for the waiter. "Two coffees," he said.

"What's our plan?" asked Tory immediately.

"It's being rapidly revised, even as we speak," he said. "You're now in the middle of things up to those baby blue eyes of yours. I need to find Ricky Acosta, and since Jazz isn't available, I need you to help me find him. Think you're up to that?"

Tory nodded. Their coffee arrived, and Tory played with hers. "Did you mean what you said?" she asked.

He replayed their recent conversation. "That your eyes are baby blue?" he asked. "Not really. That's just a figure of speech. They're more cobalt—"

"Not that. Did you mean what you said about your sister?"

Alvarez looked at her in exasperation. "Okay," he said. "I'll answer that one question. Then I'll walk you to your car, you'll drive straight home, lock yourself in with Tango the Transylvanian Hound, and show up tomorrow at ten to help me find Ricky Acosta. Deal?"

"At ten? Do you always start so late?"

"I need some time to go over things with Scott."

"Do I get deputized?"

"Yeah, Tory, sure. That means you're my deputy, and you have to do whatever I say."

"What else is new? Are you going to answer my question about your sister?"

"Anna is at Horizon House in Las Cruces. The nuns and I have an agreement. Their records show that I visit her twice a year."

"But that isn't the case, is it?"

"No, that isn't the case."

She looked at him for a moment and then nodded her head. "Okay, then," she said. "Let's get out of here. This was a nice idea and all, but ..."

"Give me a chance to pay," he told her. "Getting apprehended for walking out on this check would really top off the evening."

Alvarez enjoyed the experience of helping Tory into her coat. However, he was distracted from the pleasure of watching her walk in front of him to her car by the Hispanic man leaning against the vehicle, smoking a cigarette. He was not someone Alvarez recognized, but he had a bad feeling about it all the same.

"Mrs. Travers," the man said without question, throwing down his cigarette. "Mr. Boyce asked me to give you this." He handed Tory something before Alvarez could get between the two of them. As Tory stood frozen, Alvarez saw over her shoulder that she was holding a snap shot of a dark-haired teenaged boy. The picture had been torn in two and taped back together.

Alvarez went around Tory and lunged for the man. He grabbed him with a variation of the moves he had used the night before, only instead of bringing his arm around the intruder's throat, he shoved him face first against the wall of the restaurant. "Hey, man," the Hispanic said, his words muffled against the wall, "this is police brutality. I ain' broke no law."

Alvarez gave him another bone-crunching shove while he patted him down with his free hand. He suspected his search would be fruitless, and he was right. "I'll show you police brutality," he said into the Hispanic's ear, and proceeded to tell the man in his native language what he could expect if he ever approached *Señora* Travers again. Before he could go into the desired detail, Tory came out of her trance, and started pulling at Alvarez's jacket.

"Do you have a gun? Where's your gun, David?"

"It's okay," he told her. "I've got the situation under control."

But she continued plucking frantically at his jacket. "Where's your gun? Where is it?"

Thinking maybe it would calm her down, he said, "It's in my glove compartment, Tory. But it's okay."

"Where are your keys?"

"They're in my pants pocket," he said, wondering why they were having this insane conversation while he was trying to immobilize a hired thug. Tory stopped plucking at his jacket and started trying to reach into his front pants pocket. While this was mildly erotic, it didn't help him at all in keeping control of the situation. "What the hell are you doing?" he yelled, startled in spite of himself. Her hands were cold, and now his shirt had come untucked, so she was touching his bare skin.

"I want to get your gun," she said frantically, doubling her efforts.

"It's okay, Tory. He's not going to hurt you. He doesn't have a gun." He managed to stop yelling, but he couldn't help flinching away from her touch. Next thing he knew, he was going to get ticklish.

"I'm not worried about him hurting me, you idiot," she practically screamed at him in frustration. "I want to get your gun so I can kill him."

The Hispanic suddenly got concerned. "Keep her away from me!" he yelled. "Keep the crazy *puta* bitch away from me! I no do nothing."

Alvarez had seen his share of physical situations, but keeping a grown male immobilized by sheer force while a grown female tried to get in his pants pocket was not something that had come up in any training exercises before. Where were evasion techniques when you needed them? "What did you call the lady?" he hissed, smacking the Hispanic into the wall for a third time.

"I said to keep the crazy lady away from me, man!"

"I can't hold her off much longer. If I let go, you disappear at a dead run. And if I ever see you again, *pendejo*, I'm going to hand her my gun and close my eyes. *Comprende* that, you *hijo de puta?*"

The Hispanic nodded as much as he could with the side of his face mashed against the wall. Alvarez gave him one last shove for good measure, and then stepped back, finally free to catch Tory's hands and hold them down at her sides. The Hispanic looked at them like they were both crazy, straightened his coat, and took off running. Blessedly, no one had come in or gone out of the restaurant through the whole episode. Alvarez let go of Tory's hands.

"You should have let me shoot him," she said, obviously still on an adrenaline high.

Alvarez shook his head regretfully while he tucked in his shirt. "I was tempted, but then I would have had to arrest you, and you, I have other plans for."

Tory looked at him in disgust. "This is not the time, or the place," she said ominously.

"You're supposed to help me find Ricky Acosta tomorrow, remember?" She nodded slowly. "Tory, where is Cody?" he asked softly.

"With my father in Florida."

"Where in Florida?"

"I don't know. He was at my father's home outside of Ocala, but when I talked to him this morning, they were going to travel around the state some."

"Who else knows where he is?"

"Sylvia, Lonnie, Jazz, the rest of the people in my office, probably, Cody's friends, and that girl."

Alvarez shook his head. "Too many people to control. You need to call them, Tory, and tell them not to let anyone know where they're going for the next couple of days. That's all it will take. Boyce will be out of our hair one way or another by then. It's probably just a precaution, but you'd feel better about it, and I would, too."

Tory reached inside her purse for her cell phone. Alvarez shook his head. "That's how the royals got in trouble," he said.

"I'll call when I get home," Tory replied, itching to take some kind of action since he'd kept her from homicide. He shook his head again. "Your house—" she started and trailed off.

"It's too cold to stand outside at a pay phone. Get in your car and follow me."

"I can hardly wait to see what you come up with next," she said, but she did as she was told.

Tory waited in her car while Alvarez got the key to Room 10 at the Shady Lady from the ever-accommodating Slam. Alvarez opened the door and turned on the lights for her. "Bet you never thought you'd be a frequent visitor here," he said. She just looked at him. "Dial direct, wherever you need to call. It's taken care of."

Without taking her coat off, she sat on the bed and pulled

a small notebook out of her purse. "This will not be cool," she said, mostly to herself. She looked up at him. "It's after midnight in Florida." Alvarez shrugged.

Tory dialed a number and waited a long time for an answer. Then she spent an even longer time persuading the person on the other end that she really was Senator Wheatley's daughter, and that she urgently needed to get in touch with him no matter how late it was. She ended by giving the number at the Shady Lady and hung up in disgust. "The asshole won't give me the number," she said. "He said he'll have my father call me back." Alvarez shrugged again. They sat in silence for another ten minutes, Tory hovering over the phone. She picked it up on the first ring.

"Yes, it's Tory. Yes, everything is okay. Well, some things aren't okay. I need to talk to Cody ... Yes, I know you'll have to wake him up. He's young, he can handle it, take my word for it. Just put him on the phone."

Tory tapped her foot impatiently until her son got on the line. "Where are you? ... Why Gainesville? ... What do you mean, he's showing you the University of Florida, and it would be a neat place to go to school? Never mind, we've got a problem here ... No, I'm okay."

Tory gave him a much-laundered version of events in the Lenora Hinson case, emphasizing how the police needed her to help them locate Ricky Acosta because of her construction background, and how Raymond Boyce was putting pressure on everyone involved with the case, even if it was just for show. She ended by asking Cody not to let anyone, even his grandfather's staff, know where they were, and to call her on her cell phone twice a day, but not to tell her where he was when he called.

Then it must have been Cody's turn to talk, because Tory

was silent for a while. "No, she said finally, "I don't need you to come home. Detective Alvarez is taking very good care of me." She looked at Alvarez and rolled her eyes like she was having to lie through her teeth to reassure her son.

"You're doing what tomorrow?" she asked. "My father? Are you sure that it's him, and not just someone pretending to be my father?" She said a few more motherly things, reminded Cody to be careful, repeated her instructions to him, and told him again that she would be fine. She ended with, "No, Cody, I haven't seen Kohli lately, but I've been busy. If I see her I'll be sure and tell her hello for you." She started to end the conversation and then obviously thought better of it. "Cody, if you call that girl, you better not tell her where you are, no matter how much she wants to know. If I hear that you've told her where you are, I'll ground you for the rest of high school, do you understand me?" She allowed Cody a brief time to reply before she hung up.

She looked at Alvarez. "They're traveling around the state, no plans, no agenda. They ate lunch at someplace called the 43rd Street Deli, and the owner told them he cooked the best barbecue in the South. My father took exception, so now he and Cody are staying over to help cater some barbecue event tomorrow, and my father and the guy are going to have some kind of barbecue cook-off. Does that sound nuts, or what? My father, the senator, slinging barbecue."

"People change," said Alvarez simply. He had other things besides barbecue on his mind. "I don't suppose you'd consider staying with me tonight? You could tell yourself it was for security reasons."

"You just never give up, do you?"

"Perseverance is an important part of a detective's job."

"What are you suggesting, that we stay here?"

"No," said Alvarez regretfully. "We can only have the room for a little while. You might not think so, but you have to call ahead to get a room here for the whole night. We could go to my place."

"Surely Boyce is more concerned with pressuring you than he is with threatening me. So I wouldn't be any safer at your place than I would be at home. Which is where I'm going now, thank you very much."

"Half the population to choose from, and I end up with a woman who has an unerring sense of logic," Alvarez muttered. "Let me walk you to your car."

"Been there, done that," said Tory, standing up.

"Yeah, but this time, we're going to do it right," said Alvarez, closing the distance between them. He slipped his hands inside her open coat on either side of her waist. The burgundy dress felt just as smooth and silky as he had thought it would, he noted, just before he kissed her. She went absolutely still. He leaned back and looked at her. "This is an inclusive sport," he said. "You're allowed to participate."

She didn't open her eyes. "Yeah," she said softly, "but will you still respect me in the morning?"

"Oh yes," he said. "I'll respect the hell out of you in the morning. Especially when you find Ricky Acosta for me." He kissed her again, and this time she put her arms around his neck and kissed him back for a period of time that was much too short. Then she stepped back, and as she did so, she put her hands on his and firmly removed them from her waist, clutching her coat around her after she did so.

"I thought there was a policy against fraternization between detectives and deputies," she said, trying to keep it light.

"You're not a deputy yet," he answered, looking at his watch. "Not for almost twelve more hours, which leaves a lot of time for fraternization." He leaned toward her again, but she put her hands on his chest and pushed him away.

"I have to go," she said firmly.

He took her hand and led her out of the room, checking for unwanted visitors as he did so. Finding none, he maneuvered Tory up against her car and kissed her thoroughly one last time. Pushing him away, she fumbled in her purse for her keys. He liked the fact that his proximity seemed to make her clumsy. "They're easier to keep track of in your jeans pockets," he observed.

"Don't I know it," she said, unlocking the door. "Tomorrow will be a jeans type of day, just in case I have to make a quick get away." And without any more goodbye than that, she got in and drove off. Alvarez stood in the cold night air and watched the little white car as it headed toward the access ramp to the interstate.

He returned the room key to Slam, asked him to be on the lookout for Raymond Boyce and his cohorts, and headed his own car toward home, humming to the radio. When he unlocked his door and stepped inside, he slid on something on the floor, something wet and sticky.

"Shit," he said, fumbling for the light. He relived every conviction he'd ever had about not providing hostages to fate, fully expecting to see a mutilated canine corpse, or something worse, when he turned on the light. It took him a moment to realize what he had stepped in, and for an instant, he was actually relieved. Tory Travers had gotten through the evening without giving into nerves, but Carumba Cotton Candy had regurgitated recognizable chunks of sirloin steak all over Alvarez's kitchen floor.

CHAPTER TWENTY-TWO:

SYSTEM FAILURES
El Paso, Texas:
Wednesday, January 4

Scott was in promptly at eight, looking the worse for wear, but he perked up when Alvarez told him about Ricky Herrero/Acosta. They kicked around new versions of old stories, but kept coming up against the same problems. Was Lenora Hinson's death related to her involvement with the Underground Railroad, or did someone else know about the concealed room?

Scott wondered aloud if the regional organizations of the Railroad had turf wars, but Alvarez pointed out that the end result wasn't exactly the same as the cash payoff that came with running prostitutes, drugs, or guns. What Scott really wanted to do was go after Raymond Boyce, and Alvarez knew it. Instead, they both agreed that Ricky looked like an important lead to track down. Tory Travers appeared promptly at ten, clad in jeans and a plaid flannel shirt, making Alvarez feel overdressed.

Kissing a prospective deputy the night before did not ensure smooth investigative procedures the morning after. Tory immediately objected to using Alvarez's car in their search for Ricky. Alvarez replied that he didn't think a Corvette would stand out any more at a construction site than a white Mazda RX, or Tory herself for that matter, and besides, he'd be damned if he was going to chase after someone in a car he wasn't driving. It gave the wrong message about who was in charge.

Tory was heatedly pointing out the fallacy of his reasoning when Alvarez's phone rang. It was Karen, calling to tell him that Boyce had been busy at the hospital. She had no choice but to release his daughter to him; the best she could achieve was holding her one more night for observation. Frankly, she said, the hospital administrators were anxious to discharge the little girl. Not only had Boyce and his companions been haunting the hospital halls, Annika Atkins had put in an appearance and was offering to play her video tape for anyone who would talk to her. They both agreed there was no more need for the plainclothes guard. Then Alvarez thanked Karen for her help and hung up.

Tory immediately asked, "Did she?"

"Did who what?"

"Did your friend Karen watch the video tape?"

"Of course not."

"Why of course not?"

Alvarez sighed. This was not a discussion he wanted to have right now. "Because it's not part of her job," he said.

"I don't think that's the real reason," Tory replied.

"And what do you think the real reason is?" He tried to keep his voice even and impatience out of his tone.

"Because she doesn't have control over how the situation would be affected by the information on the tape, so why bother?"

"That makes it sound like she doesn't care, and she does." Alvarez didn't know why he felt compelled to defend Karen. "She's already hot that Boyce hasn't spent any time with his daughter. All the kid has is still what the hospital workers rounded up for her the night she was brought in—toys from the lost and found and a damned leftover rattle with someone else's initial."

"I didn't mean she didn't care," said Tory. "I'm just finding it hard to understand why that little girl will be turned over to someone like Raymond Boyce tomorrow morning."

"No system is perfect, Tory, including your own judgments about what's going on. If Lenora Hinson had cared more about her children than about controlling them, they wouldn't have grown up hating her. If Annika Atkins had worked with the system instead of outside it, maybe Dowling could have found another way to bring down Boyce."

"None of that changes the fact that someone should do something," said Tory firmly.

Why did Alvarez feel the need to defend his own actions? Why did Tory have to keep bringing up the kid? Alvarez much preferred to think of this case as one of those locked room mysteries. "You're entitled to your own opinions, but you're not entitled to your own facts," he said. "Right here, right now, Boyce is untouchable. And if that changes, it will probably mean another casualty." Alvarez considered telling Tory about the phone call to Donna Faulkner, but decided not to. He stood up and grabbed his jacket. "Ready to go?" he asked instead.

She started to say something else and then obviously changed her mind. "So which car are we taking?" she asked.

"Do you have a gun?"

"No."

"Then we're taking my car. The person with the gun gets to choose."

That earned the barest hint of a smile as they went off to search for the elusive nephew of Scav Herrero.

Trying to find Ricky Herrero/Acosta involved endless rounds of identifying the person in charge, waiting to talk to him, and then finding out that the person they really needed to talk to was on break, off to get supplies, or at another site. Alvarez decided that it was a wonder anything ever got done at any of the construction sites they visited.

By their fourth stop, he would have traded one of Cotton's monthly maintenance payments for Jazz Rodriguez. If he had to stand on one more construction site and endure the cat calls, ogling, and propositions coming Tory's way, he was going to have to hit someone. Tory remained cool through it all, refusing his offer to flash his shield, doggedly extracting bilingual information from grinning foremen and leering construction workers, and firmly refusing to respond to all types of creative theories about why the *gringa* was so set on finding *gordito* Ricky. The final result of their efforts was locating the site where Ricky Acosta was supposed to be doing some carpentry work, only to find he was a no show.

"Let's go get lunch," said Alvarez through clenched teeth.

"What's bugging you?" asked Tory.

"That this is taking so long. I'll bet Jazz could have tracked the guy down in half the time."

Tory glared at him. "This is the thanks I get?"

"If you hadn't gone off like the Lone Ranger and talked to this guy, we wouldn't be chasing him down for the second time," said Alvarez shortly. "I'm just making an observation."

"Well, why don't you just make silence?" asked Tory, stalking back to the car.

So he did, briefly checking in to see if there had been any new developments, then selecting a nondescript Mexican-food restaurant for lunch. They entered the restaurant in silence, studied their menus in silence, and ordered without speaking to each other. Alvarez figured he had the advantage in the situation, as he was perfectly satisfied to spend lunch looking at Tory Travers, but even that simple activity was interrupted by the arrival of another meal-time visitor.

The minute Alvarez noticed that Dowling wasn't chewing gum, he had a bad feeling. "Hiya," said Dowling.

Alvarez had never known anyone before who actually said "Hiya," but then he'd never had the chance to meet any of his midwestern relatives, his mother being effectively disowned before he was born. "How'd you find us?" he asked Dowling. Alvarez had been checking all morning to see if they were being followed by one of Boyce's men, and if he'd missed Dowling on their tail, he was really slipping.

"Called your office," said Dowling, as he slid into the booth next to Tory. "They said you'd checked in from this part of town, and after that it wasn't much of a challenge. Not too many bronze Corvettes parked in front of restaurants."

A pleasant, middle-aged waitress put down two steaming plates of red enchiladas, and looked expectantly at Dowling. When Dowling turned down her offer to take his order, Alvarez suddenly didn't feel very hungry any more. Tory must have felt the same, for she didn't make a move to touch her food.

"So what brings you here?" asked Alvarez.

"I asked them to let me tell you the news myself, home boy."

"I was thinking just this morning," said Alvarez, "that maybe we should have been looking for people staking out the morgue."

"Could you have gotten authorization for that?"

"Maybe, maybe not," said Alvarez truthfully.

"Then don't second guess it," said Dowling, almost kindly. "It's an old story. Boyce has more manpower, more money, and more time. He could have gotten access to airport surveillance tapes. He could have had his Cuban goons scoping out all the single women checking into El Paso motels in the last few days. He could have tracked her through a rental car."

"So what's your news?" asked Alvarez in resignation.

"A maid at a motel over by the airport went in to clean a

room this morning. The door was unlocked, but it looked like someone was still staying there."

"And was someone?"

"Well, the occupant of the room had left all right, by way of the balcony, probably in the wee hours of the morning."

"I take it that this was not a ground-level room." Alvarez glanced at Tory, who had paled. It was probably a good thing that Dowling was recounting his news before she'd eaten her enchiladas.

"Not a chance. Try sixth floor, overlooking a deserted frontage road with a bunch of vegetation grown up along the sides. If the maid hadn't gone out on the balcony and looked down, it could have been days before someone found the body."

"And our only hint would be Boyce leaving town," said Alvarez evenly.

"You got it," said Dowling, matching his tone.

"I don't get it," said Tory. "Are you saying the dead woman is Alicia Boyce?"

"Was there a suicide note?" asked Alvarez, ignoring her.

"You betcha," said Dowling, using another phrase that Alvarez didn't encounter too often. "Half a sheet of paper, torn off, with her signature at the bottom. The note was typed, all about how she couldn't live with the lies that she'd spread about her husband, and how Patty had died trying to keep her from running off with the kid. It's a real piece of work, that suicide note. Tied up all the loose ends. About the only thing it didn't do was tell us what happened to the old lady who owned the house."

"That's a shame," said Alvarez.

"Raymond Boyce is bound to have access to papers his wife had signed," interjected Tory.

"Got to leave something for you home boys to do, to justify your existence," continued Dowling, as if Tory hadn't spoken.

"*Es verdad*," agreed Alvarez gravely.

"And who types a suicide note, for heaven's sake?" continued Tory. "She'd either write it out long hand, or use a computer. Nobody uses a typewriter any more."

Dowling turned to look at Tory, and then back at Alvarez. "That's not half bad," he said. "There any more like her where this one came from?"

"No," said Alvarez, "and believe me, one is enough." Tory kicked him under the table, but he ignored it. "Will it hold as a suicide?" he asked.

"It will hold," sighed Dowling. "Her neck was broken, they'll say from the fall. If there's one thing Boyce isn't, it's sloppy. He's already identified the body. The signature will be genuine, no doubt about that. He'll probably say that his wife came to town bringing her suicide note with her. No need to find a typewriter after she got here."

"I thought you were keeping an eye on him," said Alvarez.

"I was," said Dowling shortly. "You're looking at Raymond Boyce's airtight alibi."

"So do I expect to be scraping Mrs. Atkins off the pavement later this afternoon?"

"Hey, home boy, we're staying in a motel that has all ground-floor rooms. I wasn't born yesterday. She's still at the hospital, seeing if she can get someone there to intervene about the kid, but she asked me to book her a ticket back when I book mine. I'll see if we can get out on something early in the morning. You don't exactly have a lot of flights heading to Omaha from here."

"That's a frequent complaint," conceded Alvarez. "If something does turn up about the other aspects of this case, you'll get in touch with me?"

"You betcha," Dowling assured him, standing up and shaking hands with Alvarez. "You've got him all to yourself now," he told Tory. "Hasta la vista and all that shit," he added, and was gone.

One of the advantages of Mexican food served on metal platters is that it stays hot a long time. Alvarez realized that he was hungry again. Tory looked at him in amazement as he dug into his enchiladas.

"Is that it?" she asked.

"Is what it?"

"Is that the end of it? Alicia Boyce is declared a suicide, Boyce claims his daughter, they go back to Nebraska and you forget about it?"

"Eat your enchiladas."

"I beg your pardon?"

"Eat your enchiladas. It's going to be a long afternoon, and we won't be stopping for dinner."

"Exactly what is it we're going to do?"

"We're going to find Ricky Acosta, if he's anywhere to be found. I've still got an open case, and I'm going to investigate it until I decide I'm at a dead end or someone in charge tells me to stop."

"And how do you plan to find Ricky Acosta?"

"Go back to every damn construction site until we find someone who knows where he lives. I wasn't concentrating this morning. I was watching you and looking out for Boyce's men. We didn't cover all our bases, we just tried to find out where he was supposed to be working today. Now we go back and try something else, and for that, I still need you."

"Even if I run second place to Jazz?"

"Even so," agreed Alvarez, shoveling a fork full of enchiladas into his mouth. He swallowed. "Even if you screwed with my best lead so far, I still need you. It gives you a chance to undo some of the mess you've made."

"Why all of a sudden is everything my fault?"

"Because you're here," said Alvarez shortly. "It's convenient."

"So now you're mad at me?" she snapped.

"Why not?"

"Because you weren't mad last night, not very, and it's not fair to start all over and get mad now," she retorted.

"Do you have any idea how inane you sound?"

"Well, it's true. You weren't that angry last night ..." Obviously she remembered why she thought he hadn't been that angry.

"I'd be an idiot to be mad last night. Last night, in case you don't remember, you plied me with liquor and you wore a dress cut down to here and up to there ..." Alvarez leaned over the table to graphically illustrate what he was talking about. Tory pushed his hand away. "I've been meaning to ask," he continued, "what do you wear under a dress cut to the waist?"

"Sit down," Tory hissed. "People are looking at us. You are so bad," she continued in the same tone she had used to talk to her son the previous evening.

"No," Alvarez said distinctly. "I'm very, very good." At least he'd succeeded in getting her mind off the Boyce family for the moment. "And that's what bothers you," he added for good measure.

"My dress was cut to the waist in the back," she continued, frowning. "Not in the front. It makes a big difference."

"I still have the same question," he said.

Tory ignored him. "If we're going to work together, there's going to be some ground rules. I won't criticize how you're handling this case, and you won't go on about how I shouldn't have talked to Ricky Acosta, and how you wish Jazz was here instead of me. Deal?"

Alvarez looked at her. She looked ready to walk out on

him if he didn't agree. "You betcha," he said. Tory glared at him. "Eat your enchiladas," he added. "If there's one thing I can't stand, it's girls who can't eat what they order."

Tory picked up her fork. "The term is 'woman,'" she said, "and I've never ordered an enchilada yet that I couldn't handle."

"You may think you're tough," said Alvarez, "but those blue eyes and freckles indicate weakness where I come from."

"Yeah?"

Alvarez picked up the bowl of hot sauce. He poured half of it on his plate of enchiladas, setting it down with a smack between them. Tory looked straight at him as she picked it up and poured the remaining half on her plate. In spite of how rotten the day was turning out, Alvarez was tempted to grin. Instead, he signaled to the waitress. "When you bring the check," he said, "we'd like two large Cokes to go."

As they painstakingly retraced their steps from construction site to construction site, Tory asked what they were going to talk about. "Dogs," he said, saying the first thing that came into his head.

It turned out that Tory knew a lot about dogs, especially about Hungarian breeds, since she owned one herself. She told Alvarez that Puli's were sheep dogs, light-boned so they could run on the backs of sheep to herd them. Their eyes were supposed to remain hidden, genetically programmed never to see direct sun light. If the dog's facial hair was cut to expose the eyes, they'd get infections. She told him that some people wove the Puli's unruly coat into dreadlocks for dog shows, but she didn't recommend that, since it required frequent trips to the groomer. That Cotton's upkeep would require monetary outlay was not information Alvarez was pleased to learn.

And since it was Tory Travers, she couldn't just leave it there. "How old do you suppose Cotton is?" she asked.

"I don't know," he said, suddenly concerned, turning to look at her as he stopped at a stop light. "You don't think she's about to keel over, do you?"

"No," said Tory, "she didn't look like an old dog to me. You're sure she's female?"

"Why?" he asked, accelerating into traffic. "Is there something I was supposed to check out? Scott told me she was, but hey, look who he ended up with, right?"

"You're horrible," said Tory, and punched him in the arm.

"Are we back to that?" he asked. "Frankly, I liked it a lot better when you were trying to put your hands in my pants last night. You were jumping up and down with excitement, remember?"

"I remember exactly what I was excited about," said Tory firmly. "If Cotton is a female, and if she hasn't been spayed, maybe she could have puppies."

"Christ, Tory, I don't know how to put this to you, but I'm not much of a family man. One dog barfing on my kitchen floor is enough, thank you."

"Because there's the trust fund to be considered," she continued.

"What about the trust fund?"

"Well, if the lawyers could be persuaded to finagle one set of trust funds, maybe they could be persuaded to finagle this one."

"You sound like a criminal, talking like that." He tried to leave it there, but he couldn't. "So what do you have in mind?"

"If there's an allowance for Cotton, why not continue the allowance for Children of Cotton? Puppies, I mean, but Children of Cotton has a nice ring to it."

He looked at her in frank admiration, visualizing himself deep in conversation with a veterinarian about options for reversing canine sterilization procedures. Then his beeper went off.

Alvarez refused the offered use of Tory's cell phone, preferring to use a pay phone instead. "You can't still be worried about Boyce monitoring my calls," she said.

"Better safe than sorry," he replied as he pulled over, and just then her cell phone started to ring. He left Tory in the privacy of his car to talk over the great barbecue cook-off with her son, while he dialed the number showing on his pager from a phone booth.

"All Souls Episcopal Church," was what he heard on the other end.

"This is Detective Alvarez," he said. "Someone at this number called me."

"That would be me," the voice said briskly. "I'm Sally Handleson, Father Sanchez's secretary. Father said that I should give you a call."

"Thank you, Mrs. Handleson."

"That's Ms.," she told him firmly.

"Sorry," said Alvarez, trying to keep his teeth from chattering in the wind that had kicked up and was finding its way into the phone booth. Score two points for modernization of the Episcopal Church. "And you were calling about?" he prompted.

"Father said you wanted to know about that poor boy, Rodney Kiepper, and what happened to his wife before he came to St. Mike's. We here at All Souls call it St. Mike's. Makes it sound more contemporary, don't you think?"

"What happened to Rodney Kiepper's wife?" asked Alvarez patiently.

"It was terrible, a real tragedy. His wife drank, you see, but they never like to talk about things like that."

"Who doesn't like to talk about things like that?"

"Well, the clergy, of course. Who else would I mean?"

Alvarez looked at the receiver in his hand. He considered going back to the car to warm up and coming back and trying again. "Why would the clergy be talking about it?" he asked carefully.

"Well, they wouldn't, of course, that's just the point," said Ms. Handleson briskly. "So the poor girl took the baby ..."

"There was a baby?"

"Of course there was a baby. Are you going to let me tell this or not?"

"Certainly, Ms. Handleson, go ahead."

"She took the baby out one night, and she was drunker than a skunk, as my daddy used to say. She ran head on into a light pole. Killed her and the child instantly, bless their souls. No wonder the poor boy left."

"Left where?"

"I don't know where. I think maybe it was Ohio, but I'm not sure. Do you want me to check?"

"You said he left."

"He left the priesthood, poor dear. Said he couldn't minister to others when he still couldn't bring himself to forgive his own wife."

"Rodney Kiepper was a priest?"

"Well, yes, what else would he be? Ordained just six months before it happened, never got to the church that had called him, just came here and took over St. Mike's instead."

"Father Sanchez never told me that Rodney Kiepper was a priest."

"Well, did you ask him?"

Alvarez hung up and placed a call to have Kiepper picked

up and brought in for questioning. As an afterthought, he asked for Officer Kurita to make the pickup if he was available. By the time Alvarez returned to the car, Tory was done talking to her son.

"I told him that it looks like everything will be back to normal tomorrow," she said. "Do you think that's okay?"

"I try not to use the word 'normal,'" he told her honestly. "But yeah, I think after Boyce leaves town, he won't bother you any more."

"Cody said that the barbecue cook-off was declared a tie," Tory said as Alvarez pulled back into traffic. "And he and my father are planning something else, but they want to wait until this blows over to tell me what it is." She frowned. "God, I hate surprises," she said earnestly.

"I'll try to keep you informed of all my intentions as we go along, then. How many more people do you think we'll have to talk to before we get a line on Ricky?"

She guessed ten and he guessed two. It was actually five before Tory slipped someone a twenty and they were rewarded with Ricky's home address, which turned out to be the second floor of a small, rock building on Piedras Street. The ground floor was an interesting combination hardware store and adult magazine shop. The proprietress, a tiny, wizened Hispanic lady with blackened teeth, let go with rapid-fire Spanish when Alvarez asked about the apartment above the store. She was the landlady, and she disapproved heartily of recent events involving her renter.

She talked so quickly and with such vehemence that even Alvarez had to ask her to repeat herself. She told him that when she was closing the store the night before, she heard footsteps going up the outside staircase that led to the second-story apartment. She didn't think much about it until she heard pounding and yelling overhead, and language that wasn't tolerated on the premises, no matter what kind of magazines she sold. Then Ricky came running down the stairs, hopped onto his motorcycle, took off, and hadn't been seen since. And he owed her rent on Friday, she said in disgust, and spat into a soda can next to her, solving the mystery of her blackened teeth.

Alvarez asked carefully if she had seen Ricky's visitor. "*No te haces tan bobo,*" she informed him. Tory was fascinated to hear Alvarez called "ninny." The landlady went on to tell him in great detail that she made it a practice to mind her own business, how else did the *bobo* detective think that she had managed to live so long? And the *policia* were no friends of hers, trying to keep a poor old woman from earning an honest living. She spat into her soda can again for emphasis.

"*Abuela,*" said Alvarez politely, "*yo quiero dos revistas aquí.*" He pointed at two of the less lurid selections. "*Y no quiero cambio,*" he added, handing her a twenty. Only after the transaction had been made, and he had the magazines firmly in hand, did he ask her to go over her story.

She adamantly refused to admit that she had seen Ricky's visitor, but she did tell Alvarez that he "cussed funny." It took all of Alvarez's persuasive powers to convince her to tell him what the man had said after Ricky came running down the stairs. "*Me cago en el coño de Maceo,*" she finally said shortly, ducking her head, refusing to repeat it. She was willing to give them the key to the apartment, especially if it meant that Alvarez was done with his questions.

"Why did you buy the magazines from her?" asked Tory curiously as they stepped outside. "Jazz and I just out and out bribed people."

Alvarez shook his head as he started up the steps two at a time. "I don't think I want to keep giving you pointers on what I do," he said. "It's getting to be dangerous."

"Tell me," she insisted.

He paused to look down at her. "The old lady has been hassled by the police about selling to minors. When I bought the magazines, she knew I wouldn't be bothering her."

Tory trailed behind Alvarez as he went up the stairs. "But that reduces the value of the bribe," she said.

Alvarez turned to look at her again. "Do you ever stop thinking about how to optimize things?" Tory shook her head.

Alvarez didn't draw his gun, just pushed open the door cautiously, which wasn't locked. Then he told her that if she didn't stand outside until he said it was okay, he would shoot her himself.

Tory decided not to point out that Alvarez was the only person who had ever actually threatened to shoot her. Other people just did it, or sent her anonymous threatening notes, or handed her torn pictures of her son, or other things she refused to think about right now. When he finally motioned her inside, it was apparent even to her untrained eye that the place had been tossed.

"Don't touch anything," he told her immediately. "Sit down on one of the kitchen chairs, and stay put."

There wasn't much to the apartment, just a bedroom, bathroom, and small kitchen area. It was in the bedroom that Alvarez found what he was looking for. He came back into the kitchen, grabbed a paper towel, and opened drawers until he found a box of plastic bags. He took one, went back to the bedroom, and returned with a nasty looking switchblade in the plastic bag. It had something dark and dried on it, but Tory chose to focus on its other unusual attributes. It had wire hooks that had been attached to the metal casing of the knife. Two rubber bands were suspended from either hook.

Alvarez used the paper towel to lift the receiver from Ricky's phone and called in a request for CSU. He gave them the address, told them that he would wait for them, and then dropped into the chair across from Tory. "This may take a while," he said, "but there's no help for it. After we're done I'll take you back downtown and you can pick up your car and head home."

"Aren't you going to try to find Ricky Acosta?" asked Tory.

Alvarez looked tired. "If you were Latino and had someone after you, where would you head?"

"Across the border," she said immediately.

Alvarez nodded. "And once someone crosses the border," he said, "our chances of finding him are zip."

"Are you going to tell me what's going on?"

"What do you want to know?"

Tory tried to think of where to start. "What is that?" she asked, pointing to the knife in the plastic bag.

"It's called a band blade, not be to confused with a band aid," he said. "You don't see them much any more, now that guns are so popular, but they used to be commonplace when I was in high school. You rig the blade so it's held against your forearm in tension between two rubber bands, so if you flick your hand just so, the knife comes into it, blade out, ready to go. The beauty of it is that it's so primitive. I'll bet Boyce's guy never thought to look for a weapon on Ricky's forearm, and that probably saved Ricky's ass."

Tory looked at the knife more closely. "I don't see how you rig the rubber bands," she said, pushing up her shirt sleeve to look at her own forearm.

Alvarez leaned over to grasp her wrist. "Like this," he said, stopped to think a moment, and then pushed her arm away. "You almost had me there. Since you're along for the ride, and up to your eyeballs in this case, I'll answer your questions, but I'm not so stupid that I'm going to tell you how to rig a band blade. Next thing I know, you'll come up with some innovation to improve them and we'll be seeing them all over town again."

Tory sighed. She really did hate to leave a problem unsolved, but she decided there wasn't much chance in changing his mind. Besides, if she thought about it enough, she could probably figure it out by herself.

"You think one of Boyce's men followed Ricky here, and tried to find out what he knew," she said slowly.

"You got that right."

"But you can't know that," continued Tory. "Not for sure. This could have absolutely nothing to do with Boyce."

Alvarez just looked at her. "How likely do you think it is that someone of Cuban descent coincidentally happened to visit Ricky a few hours after you talked to him?"

"How do you know his visitor was Cuban?"

"Remember that the landlady told us he 'cussed funny'? She said he yelled '*me cago en el coño de Maceo.*' Want to translate that for me?"

"Would you believe me if I told you I didn't know what it means?"

"No," he said flatly.

"I shit the hell over someone or something called Maceo?"

"Colonel Antonio Maceo," said Alvarez. "He's a big Cuban hero, pre-Castro, fought against the Spanish."

"How do you know this?"

"I had a friend in high school from Cuba. Used to go around saying things like '*Bueno, Maceo en becicleta.*' I remember laughing so hard over that, I got thrown out of study hall."

"Maceo on a bicycle?" asked Tory dubiously.

"You had to be there," said Alvarez.

"How would one of Boyce's men find Ricky?"

Alvarez looked at her. "You sure you want to know?"

"Have you ever heard me ask a question I didn't want answered?" she countered.

"No," he admitted. "But I don't think you're going to like the answer to this one. Boyce told me at the morgue he brought three men to town, but there were only two with him at the time. I think the third one was already tailing you. You and Jazz led him to Ricky. He didn't want to talk to Ricky with other people around, so he waited, followed him home."

Tory swallowed. "So what do we do now?"

"We wait here for CSU. Then you go home, and try to stay out of trouble."

"And what happens to your case?"

Alvarez shrugged. "Unless Scott turns up something, the only lead I have right now is Rodney Kiepper. What I found out about him fits the profile of Underground Railroad supporters, but it doesn't prove anything."

"But you're forgetting that he's a priest, and Ricky said his uncle called the man with Lenora Hinson *Padre*," said Tory eagerly.

"I'm not forgetting anything," said Alvarez. "Right now, that's just hearsay," he added pointedly.

Tory chose not to pursue it. She looked down at the knife in the plastic bag on the kitchen table. She bet if she could pick it up and look at it, she could figure out how to rig a band blade.

"It takes a lot of practice to do it right," Alvarez said, reading her mind. "The next time I see you I'm going to check your arms for knife cuts, and it won't be suicide attempts I'm worried about."

"So what do we do while we wait?" she asked.

Alvarez grinned. "I just happen to have some reading material with me," he said.

Alvarez relented and bought them both dinner after they finally left the apartment—a greasy cheeseburger on their way back downtown. "Do you always eat like this?" she asked, licking her fingers.

"Why, you want Twinkies for dessert?" he countered.

It was almost nine when they got back to his office, and he let her hang around while he talked to Scott. It wasn't encouraging. Rodney Kiepper's house had been staked out since late afternoon, but he hadn't shown up. Scott hadn't unearthed anything of interest while investigating the other recipients of Lenora Hinson's will, except for the fact that they still hadn't located one single individual who had liked the woman.

"Pretty soon, someone will decide it's just possible that Lenora Hinson discovered Patty using drugs, and Patty fought with her before she OD'd," said Alvarez dejectedly. "Hell, I'm starting to think that's what happened myself." He seemed to suddenly remember that Tory was still sitting there. "Let's get you home," he said. "I'll walk you to your car."

Before they got to the staircase, Tory found the nerve to turn around and look at him. "There's something I want to tell you," she said determinedly.

"What?" he asked. "You've decided that you want to borrow my magazines after all?"

"No," she said doggedly. "I want to say that I'm sorry. If I kept you from solving this case by talking to Ricky Acosta, I'm really sorry about it, and I'll try not to get in your way again."

Alvarez clasped his hand to his chest. "My God," he said in mock agony. "It's the big one. Where's a wire when you need it? I have a feeling that I could use a tape of you saying that."

"I'm not apologizing for everything," she said quickly. "Remember, I was the one who set you straight about the column."

"And one of the things about you that really stands out is your humility," he said, reaching out, catching her arm and pulling her toward him. "I'm about to violate policy," he said into her ear. "We don't allow any DOAs at police headquarters."

"DOAs?" she asked, faintly alarmed. Surely she had heard him wrong.

"Displays of Affection," he said before he kissed her.

She pushed him away. "You need to make up your mind, whether you're mad at me or not," she told him.

"Oh," he said easily. "I've made up my mind, and it doesn't have anything to do with that."

He led her out to her car and got her settled inside. "There are still too many loose ends for comfort," he said seriously, looking down at her. "Boyce is still in town with his goons, Ricky Acosta is on the run, and Rodney Kiepper is out there somewhere. So that means no more solo investigating, Tory. You lock your door, drive straight home, and try to stay out of trouble. I'll call you tomorrow."

"Right," said Tory. She was, of course, referring to his last statement.

CHAPTER TWENTY-THREE:

SALVAGE OPERATIONS
El Paso, Texas:
Wednesday, January 4, late evening

As she started toward the interstate, Tory was still trying to determine exactly what she meant to cover with her apology. She would admit that tracking down Scav Herrero's nephew and interviewing him might not have been state-of-the-art investigative technique. But no matter how much she thought about it, she couldn't come up with a scenario where Ricky Acosta provided information which prevented Raymond Boyce from taking custody of his daughter. And the fact that the little girl would be turned over to a known criminal and alleged molester bothered her more than the unsolved aspects of the case.

Tory had to respect Alvarez's approach to his investigative work, the way he pulled out all the stops to entertain any hypotheses, no matter how farfetched, but was unwilling to make value judgements about the justice system he served. In her mind, it was kind of like designing to mandated codes and ordinances, even when you knew that for a particular project you could decrease the safety margin and no one would ever know. David Alvarez was a police detective, so he refused to bend the law. Tory Travers was a dedicated engineer, so she followed codes and ordinances to the letter. But *she* wasn't a police detective, as Alvarez kept reminding her...

Tory considered herself to be a law-abiding person, but there was still enough of the rebellious teenager in her, the one who had driven her politician father to distraction, to question if she was morally bound to follow the letter of the law in any and all circumstances. Alvarez liked taunting her about her burglary escapade. What would he think about kidnapping, she wondered, and then resolutely banished the thought from her head.

That didn't mean that she was giving up, though. Surely someone could do *something*. Maybe there were other relatives of Hannah Boyce who would be willing to intervene. Now that was a pretty good idea, she told herself, and wondered why no one else had come up with it.

Mrs. A might know about Alicia Boyce's family. Dowling had mentioned she was still trying to get the hospital authorities to delay releasing Hannah, so maybe Annika Atkins was still at Mt. Franklin General. Even if she wasn't, maybe Tory could go in and hold the little girl and rock her for a while. It was the least she could do right now.

She could hear the roar of disapproval from Alvarez in her head, so she told herself that she would be very responsible in her actions. First, she would make sure she wasn't being followed. To that end, Tory took a detour through a residential area, feeling more than a little foolish. Certain she was the only one driving down the deserted streets of the small subdivision, she headed for the hospital.

The lobby was deserted; the few people around seemed to be hospital staff, intent on their nighttime duties. No one looked at Tory as she crossed the lobby. One of the two elevator doors had an OUT OF ORDER sign taped to it. Tory didn't want to stand around in the lobby any longer than necessary, so she took the stairs.

She had just reached the third-floor landing when someone opened the door to the stairwell. Annika Atkins, holding a baby in her arms, stepped onto the landing. It took Tory a moment to realize what was out of place—Mrs. Atkins was attired in a nurse's uniform.

"Mrs. Travers, you are one of the few people who would recognize me here," Annika Atkins said regretfully in her grandmotherly voice. "How unfortunate." Then, unlike any grandmother Tory had ever seen, Mrs. Atkins reached into her pocket and pulled out a gun.

"Twenty-two," said Tory automatically. "That's a really small caliber for a handgun."

"But at close range, it gets the job done," replied Mrs. Atkins. "And you don't really want to try to stop me, do you, my dear?"

"Stop you from doing what?"

"Isn't it obvious?"

"You're kidnapping the baby?"

"I prefer to say that I'm helping Hannah start a new life, one where she has a chance to grow into a happy, productive adult."

"But you'll be the first person they'll suspect," said Tory.

"I won't be around," replied Mrs. Atkins. "I'm taking Hannah and disappearing, so we need to get moving. I have a rendezvous outside in five minutes, and you're coming with me, Mrs. Travers."

"I can't come with you," said Tory in a panic. "I have a son, a business ..."

"I don't mean that you're coming with me into hiding," said Mrs. Atkins impatiently. "I'm meeting someone outside who's taking me to our next contact point. You're coming along, and then we'll decide what to do with you."

Tory didn't like how that sounded, but when Annika Atkins gestured impatiently with the gun for her to start back down the stairs, she did. "I don't think you'd shoot me," she said cautiously, without turning around. "It wouldn't be in character."

"Well, my dear," said Mrs. Atkins close behind her, "I'd try very hard not to kill you. But I've gone too far to turn back now, and as I'm sure your detective friend can tell you, I'm very set on having my own way. So if you give me any trouble, I will shoot you, and I don't imagine that I'll have any problem slipping away in the confusion."

"So do you know what happened to Lenora Hinson?" Tory asked. If she was going to be stuck at the wrong end of a gun in this mess, she sure as hell wanted some answers.

"It's not important," said Mrs. Atkins. "Stop when you get to the door. When we walk out into the lobby, I want to be very, very close to you. As a matter of fact, wait, turn around."

Tory turned to face Annika Atkins, her pulse pounding in her ears. She resolved never to get into another situation where one person was holding a gun on another, unless she was the one with the gun. She remembered Alvarez telling her earlier that the person with the gun got to make all the choices. That conversation seemed a lifetime away.

"Here, you hold her." Annika Atkins placed the sleeping, baby in Tory's arms. A detached part of Tory's mind noted that the woman had efficiently gathered up the little girl's playthings and bundled them in the blanket with her. "Now, that will leave me free to make sure you do what I tell you to do," said Mrs. Atkins, jamming the gun into Tory's side. "We're going to walk out this door and straight through the lobby. Don't make eye contact with anyone. Go outside, to your left. Around the side of the building is an alcove with picnic tables. That's where we're meeting someone. Got it?"

"But what about the person you're meeting?" asked Tory. "Once I see who it is, how can you let me go? It would be better if you let me walk away right now."

Annika Atkins looked at Tory and sighed. "You do have a

good mind, I have to say that for you," she said. "But I don't trust you. I can't afford to, there's too much at stake. You'll go with us to our next point of contact. Then I'll let my local person deal with you however he sees best."

That sounded less than comforting to Tory, but Mrs. Atkins didn't give her a chance to debate the issue. She poked the gun into Tory's side again and gestured with her chin at the door. "Let's go. Right through the lobby, no eye contact, out the door and to the left." Tory paused instinctively to make sure the blankets were pulled tight around the sleeping Hannah, and then did as she was told.

Once they went through the front doors and stepped away from the lighted area, it was pitch black. Tory followed a narrow walkway to her left, going slowly so she wouldn't stumble. When the walkway turned at the corner of the hospital building, she followed its path, trying to remember what she could from her former visit. She would have given anything to have seen a site plan of the place. If there was only somewhere dark and sheltered close by, she might be able to make a run for it. She wondered if Annika Atkins would risk shooting if there was a chance she might hit the baby.

Then all such thoughts ended when they reached a deserted alcove. Tory could make out the dark form of a man, bundled in a coat and leaning against the wall in the shadows, waiting for them.

"Who's she?" he asked anxiously, pushing himself off the wall. "This wasn't part of the plan." He looked down at Annika Atkins hands. "And neither was a gun," he added.

"Sometimes plans have to change," said Mrs. Atkins cheerfully. "She's someone who recognizes me, but she doesn't know you. She's going to come with us to the contact point. Then you can drop her somewhere."

"But what if she recognizes me later?" asked the man urgently. "I've had enough trouble. I want out."

"Fine, get out," snapped Annika Atkins, no longer the cheerful grandmother. "I don't care what you do, as long as you cover your tracks and get me to the next contact point. You do know how to do that, don't you?"

"Yes, I know how to do that," the man said, still staring at Tory. She hoped that if someone was going to shoot her, they would at least have the decency to let her hand off the sleeping baby before they did. She was beginning to have a healthy respect for David Alvarez's opinion of people who worked outside the law, and she only hoped that she would have the opportunity to tell him that.

"So where's your car?" asked Mrs. Atkins impatiently. "I hope you did like you were told, and didn't park in the hospital lot."

"I did exactly like I was told," said the man. "That's what's gotten me into all this trouble, doing what I was told. The car is a couple blocks down the street. Come on, I'll show you."

"That won't be necessary," said Alvarez, stepping into their midst from behind one of the alcove walls. He was so unexpected that there was no challenge to his taking control of the situation. He relieved Annika Atkins of her gun with one smooth movement and pushed her up against the wall next to the man.

"Tell me you're not part of this," he said without pausing to look at Tory as he efficiently patted down her two companions. The twenty-two disappeared and then he was holding a serious-sized gun on the pair against the wall as if it was part of his daily routine. Which maybe it was, Tory reminded herself.

"Use your detecting skills," she said, trying to keep her voice from shaking. "If I was part of this, would she be holding a gun on me?"

"Just checking," said Alvarez pleasantly. "Good evening, Mr. Kiepper. We've had several officers out looking for you."

"I never meant for any of this to happen," said Rodney Kiepper.

"Shut up, Rodney," said Mrs. Atkins. "You don't have to tell them anything. If Mrs. Travers can be persuaded to keep her mouth shut about this evening, it will be his word against ours about what happened." Tory wondered how Mrs. Atkins planned to explain the sleeping baby in her arms. Was she going to claim they all showed up at the same time and decided to take Hannah Boyce on a late night walk around the grounds?

"Mrs. Travers does some things exceptionally well," said Alvarez, "but keeping her mouth shut has never been one of them."

Tory had had it with being talked about like she wasn't there. "Do you know how uncomfortable it is, standing around in freezing weather, holding a sleeping baby while you all figure this out at gun point?" she asked. She was beginning to shake, and she suspected it wasn't all from the cold.

"Just hang in there," said Alvarez, never taking his eyes off the two people in front of him. "I'll be happy to warm you up later."

"How about it, Mrs. Travers?" asked Annika Atkins. Her voice was back to being grandmotherly again. "Are you willing to testify that what we're doing is a criminal activity? How would you sleep with that at night?"

"She could do worse, maybe has," said Alvarez in the same pleasant tone of voice he had been using since he showed up. Tory didn't know who she wanted to slap the most, him or Annika Atkins. She wondered fleetingly if she could ask the man Alvarez called Kiepper to hold the baby.

"It doesn't matter," Kiepper said suddenly, anguish in his

voice. "I can't live this way, it's worse than before. I never meant for it to happen." Tory might be new to investigative work, but she could figure out that this wasn't the time to ask the man if he would hold the baby.

"You never meant for what to happen?" asked Alvarez.

Tory wondered if this was going to be one of those long, drawn out confessions. Would anyone notice if she simply took Hannah and returned to the warmth and relative safety of the hospital lobby, she wondered.

"I never meant for Lenora Hinson to die," said Rodney Kiepper. "It was an accident."

"What happened?" asked Alvarez.

"It went bad from the beginning," said Kiepper miserably. "From almost the moment they got to the house, Lenora was on the phone complaining to me. The mother wasn't polite, she wasn't grateful, she didn't know how to keep the baby quiet. I didn't pay a lot of attention. No one ever measured up to Lenora's standards."

"So no one knew she wasn't the kid's mother?" Alvarez asked.

Even being held at gunpoint, Kiepper had a tone of righteous indignation in his voice. "It never occurred to us to check the IDs of people coming to us for the express purpose of losing their identity," he snapped.

"So then what happened?" Alvarez asked Kiepper again.

"Lenora called me in the afternoon, told me she had decided they were going to have a proper New Year's Eve dinner at her house, and that she was going to have Mrs. Boyce help her cook it. She thought the baby's mother was sleeping too much. She was going to wake her up and put her to work, and give her some parenting pointers while she was at it."

"But she couldn't wake her up, could she?" asked Alvarez.

"No, Lenora called me about five o'clock, hysterical. I got over there by six, and the minute I saw her I knew what had happened—I'd done work with homeless shelters before I was ordained. There wasn't any point in calling an ambulance."

"So did you tell Mrs. Hinson her guest died of a drug overdose?"

"Yeah, and that was a big mistake. Lenora was hysterical, blaming me for all of it—and I was just their next contact—I didn't have anything to do with taking them into the system." Kiepper shot Annika Atkins an accusing glance. "Lenora said she was going to call the police, tell them everything, and she would never go to jail because she had money and all these contacts."

"And what did you say?"

"I told her to calm down so I could think. I told her she didn't have anything linking me to the dead woman or the baby, but they were in her house, so she was the only one implicated. That enraged her. She picked up a poker and started swinging it at me. I grabbed her arms to keep her from hitting me and she slipped. She fell over backwards and hit her head on the hearth." Kiepper shuddered. "It was an awful sound. And then her eyes fluttered, and ..."

"She was dead," Alvarez finished for him. "So then you had two bodies instead of one."

"Yes," said Kiepper desperately, "and a baby. What in God's name was I going to do with the baby? Then I remembered that old carpenter threatening Lenora about pulling the column out so everything would fall down. It was all I could think of. So I carried the baby upstairs, made sure the heat was on, and then I got some rope, tied it to the column ..."

"And stood outside the door and pulled it out of place," Tory finished for him, forgetting her previous resolve to stay out of the interrogation. "Then the end of the column was close enough that you could reach in, untie the rope, close the door, and leave."

Kiepper looked at Tory as though she was the personification of some all-knowing avenging angel.

"Then you made the nine-one-one call, but you couldn't leave it alone," continued Alvarez, "because of the kid. That's why you showed up at Keaton's house. You knew we'd be notifying the next of kin, but you had to make sure we'd found the baby. But we weren't telling anyone about the kid—all we did was ask Keaton if her mother had any visitors with small children."

"I thought your question meant that you'd found the baby, but I couldn't be sure. I called *News Now* as soon as you left Keaton's house," said Kiepper. "I thought if anyone could ferret out more information, it would be them."

"I wondered how they got there so quick on New Year's Day," said Alvarez. "But we still weren't saying anything about the kid."

"I know. I couldn't think what to do next, so after the newscast, I called in an anonymous tip that the police found a baby in the house where the collapse occurred," continued Kiepper.

"They can't run stories based on an anonymous tip," Alvarez said automatically.

"I figured you'd decided not to say anything for a reason. I told the reporter to try checking with the emergency medical personnel to verify what I was telling her. The next day I heard it on the news, so I knew the baby had been discovered and taken care of."

"Pretty cagey for a priest-turned-headmaster of a girls' school," was Alvarez's comment. "Maybe associating with Keaton taught you more than you realized."

"So where's the crime, Detective?" asked Annika Atkins impatiently. "Is anything he did worse than turning this child over to Boyce? And you can put away your gun, Rodney certainly isn't any threat to you, and now I'm not, either."

Alvarez thought about it for a moment, then slowly complied, returning his gun to a shoulder holster underneath his jacket. "I was just getting to you, Mrs. Atkins," he said, and if Tory had not already been shivering, the tone of his voice would have been enough to make her start. "So far I have you down for kidnapping and assault with a deadly weapon. I don't think you want to know how I feel about finding you holding a gun on Mrs. Travers. I heard you leave her welfare up to Mr. Kiepper here. How do you know she wouldn't have come to harm?"

Mrs. Atkins shrugged impatiently. "Rodney wouldn't hurt anyone. You know that as well as I do. So don't keep us in suspense, detective. What are you going to do?"

"I'm going to return the kid to her room, take Kiepper in, and let you go," Alvarez said shortly.

Tory wasn't any more surprised than Annika Atkins herself.

"Why? Why are you letting me go?"

"Because Boyce murdered his wife in my backyard. Because I caught up with you before you got away with the kid, and because you're the person most likely to be able to get to Boyce. Just make sure you do it somewhere else."

"I don't suppose you'd settle for taking Rodney in and give me Hannah?" Mrs. Atkins asked. "I can guarantee you that we'd disappear so quickly no one would ever find us."

"Don't even think about it," said Alvarez. "And if you leave me much time to consider what I'm doing, I may change my mind. Do you have a car here?" Annika Atkins nodded. "And a plane ticket back to Nebraska?"

Annika Atkins nodded again. "It was the only way to convince that idiot DEA agent that I was giving up and going home."

"Then I'd suggest you leave now, and make sure you're on the plane in the morning," Alvarez said. Mrs. Atkins looked disappointed, but she didn't stay to argue. She started toward the deserted parking lot that was adjacent to the alcove.

Alvarez turned his attention back to Kiepper. "What I'd suggest, Mr. Kiepper, is that we let Mrs. Travers return the baby to her room and go on her way. If we say you found me and turned yourself in, it might go easier for you."

"Whatever you say," said Kiepper, seemingly disinterested in Alvarez's offer.

"Think you can handle that?" Alvarez said, finally turning to look at Tory. "Getting the kid back into her room?"

"Yes, I can handle that," she snapped, her nerves shot. "What I want to know is what you're doing here."

"Christ, Tory, I rescue you from being held at gunpoint and you want to know what I'm doing here? I was following you to make sure you stayed out of trouble, and sure enough, you didn't."

"But I checked to make sure I wasn't being followed," she said doggedly, determined to hang on to some shred of dignity, even if she was the one holding the baby through all the excitement.

"Tory," he said gently, "do you know anything about traffic engineering?"

"What has that got to do with anything?"

"That's one of the few engineering things I know about," continued Alvarez patiently, as if he was talking to a remedial student. "Those new subdivisions are constructed to have one access, to cut down traffic and reduce crime. You turn into one of those neighborhoods, you have to come out the same way. If someone is following you, all they have to do is pull over and wait for you to come out the same way you went in."

Any possible reply was lost in a deafening explosion and blinding flash of light from the parking lot, and time stood still.

"Oh my god," said Kiepper, pressing his hands to his mouth, "It was Annika Atkins. I watched her open the door to her car, and ..."

"Jesus H. fucking Christ," said Alvarez.

"They'll never pin this on him, will they?" asked Tory, the words out of her mouth before she knew she was going to say them. She instinctively turned away from the glare to shield the baby, who had been startled awake. She didn't need a second look to know that no one near that conflagration could have survived.

Alvarez grabbed Kiepper by the shoulder. "You've got ten seconds to make a choice," he said.

"What choice?"

"Shut up and listen. You can stay here, take your chance on beating a manslaughter charge and inheriting millions of dollars. Or you can take Annika Atkin's place, walk off with the kid and disappear forever."

To his credit, there was no hesitation. Rodney Kiepper wordlessly held out his arms for the baby, and Tory started to hand the screaming child to him. "Not like that," said Alvarez roughly, pushing her back. "Take off your coat," he said to Kiepper. Kiepper quickly pulled off his coat and held it out to Alvarez, who ignored him. Alvarez turned to Tory and dug the screaming baby out of her bundling, leaving Tory holding the blanket and toys. He placed the baby in Kiepper's out-stretched arms. "Go," he said tersely. He didn't have to repeat himself. Kiepper wrapped the screaming baby in his coat and ran into the night.

Alvarez took the blanket and toys from Tory. "You came here to say goodbye to the kid," he said. "You saw Annika Atkins, followed her down to the parking lot, saw her get in the car with the kid, saw the explosion. Can you handle it?"

There was no time for discussion. Tory sensed, rather than heard, people pouring out of the hospital's front doors. "Yes," she said.

Alvarez turned away from her, toward the parking lot. "What are you doing?" she asked, suddenly panicked.

"I'm a fucking law enforcement officer," he said, "so I'm fucking going to act like one." He turned and ran toward the flames.

There were now a few people at the edge of the parking lot, but Alvarez had a lead on them. The explosion was burning so brightly that it was hard to see anything else, and if Tory hadn't been straining her eyes to watch him, she would have never seen him throw the blanket containing Hannah Boyce's hand-me-down toys and rattle toward the flames. Then there was a secondary explosion, lifting and knocking Alvarez back. Then Tory started running too, but there were people in white coats ahead of her.

Somewhere in the distance she heard sirens, but they weren't for Rodney Kiepper or Hannah Boyce.

CHAPTER TWENTY-FOUR:

AFTERMATH
El Paso, Texas:
Wednesday, January 4, late evening

The first thing Alvarez said when he opened his eyes inside the hospital where he had been carried was, "Fucking convenient place to get injured." The second thing he said was about ten seconds later, when, without opening his eyes again, he muttered, "There's no way I'm staying here."

Tory had stuck to him like glue from the moment she reached his side. No one questioned her statement that the injured man was a detective with the El Paso Police Department, and she was working with him. One of the uniformed officers who showed up after they got Alvarez inside offered to call Scott Faulkner, and Tory didn't object. She wanted as many friendly faces around as possible.

It had been years since she had to concoct cover stories, and she would have liked a little more preparation for this one. There were holes in her story that could blow the whole thing wide open, her analytical mind told her, and how in heaven's name did Alvarez plan to make his version coincide with hers? That question was answered when the officer came back to take her statement, and Alvarez, who was now having his right forearm dressed for second-degree burns, reached out with his good hand and caught hers.

"Mrs. Travers has been through quite an ordeal this evening," Alvarez said, his voice steady while the nurse cut away burned cloth and skin so the injury could be cleaned and treated. A doctor had given Alvarez a mild pain killer, explaining they didn't want to medicate him more until they were sure about the extent of his injuries. "She'd be more comfortable talking to you with me present," Alvarez continued.

Tory decided it was for the greater good if handholding with Alvarez looked more like he was comforting her instead of the other way around. She told the police officer that she'd come to say goodbye to Hannah before returning home. She related how she had been standing in the lobby waiting for the elevator when someone in a nurse's uniform, looking a lot like Annika Atkins and holding an infant, exited the stairwell and walked out of the hospital. Tory followed her outside to ascertain if it really was Annika Atkins. When the woman got in a car with the baby, Tory started to return to the lobby to alert the proper authorities. That was when she ran into Alvarez, but before she could tell him what she had seen, there was an explosion, and Alvarez immediately ran toward the car to see if he could save anyone. Which she thought was very brave, by the way.

When Tory got to the part about meeting up with Alvarez and interpreting his actions and intentions, his grip on her hand became downright painful, but she ignored it. She was on a roll. It had been years since she had experienced the exhilaration of concocting an airtight alibi. She had forgotten how easy it was to get caught up in your own story, if it was a good one, and she thought hers qualified. She intended to point out to Alvarez later how she had structured her tale to cover the possibility of someone seeing her cross the lobby in close proximity to Annika Atkins.

Scott Faulkner arrived in time for the conclusion of her story, concern for his partner stamped across his face. The doctor assured him that the burns on Alvarez's arm, though painful and likely to scar, would not, with proper treatment, affect the use of his arm. Scott and Alvarez both seemed to

relax somewhat after this pronouncement and Tory realized
with a jolt that it was Alvarez's shooting arm which was being
discussed. The doctor went on to say that Alvarez had a minor
concussion, and needed to be under observation for the next
twenty-four hours.

"Not here," said the patient immediately.

"I'll stay with him," said Scott and Tory in unison.

"Well, you'll have to pick," said the attending doctor. "I
don't think he's up to having company."

"Golly, what a hard choice," said Alvarez.

Scott ignored him, looking at Tory. "Would you? This is
the f-f-f-first chance I've had to sleep in my own bed in three
nights."

"And I thought being a doctor was rough," muttered the
attending physician, starting to bandage Alvarez's arm.

A second uniformed officer came into the room to report
on the scene outside. "The fire's out, and the firefighters say
that no one near the car could have survived when the bomb
went off," he said specifically to Alvarez. "There's not much
left, but we found this a few feet from the car." The officer
held out an evidence bag containing a blackened metal object.
Tory could tell from where she sat that it was the metal baby
rattle Annika Atkins had bundled up with Hannah Boyce.

Alvarez broke the silence. "Any other casualties?" he asked.

"No," replied the officer, relieved to move on to a brighter
subject. "We were really lucky. The parking lot was pretty deserted, and the car that blew was parked in the outer-most area.
The only other casualty was a red Jaguar parked beside it."

"What did you say?" asked the doctor, peering around
Alvarez.

"There was a red Jaguar parked next to the car that ex-
ploded," repeated the officer.

"Holy shit," the doctor said. "I park out there because I thought it would be safer. Here," he handed the end of the bandage that he was securing around Alvarez's arm to a nurse. "You finish this." He disappeared from the room at a dead run.

"That got his attention," remarked Alvarez drily. "Lucky I'm not bleeding to death."

"What do you need?" asked Scott.

"Whatever you can do that might tie Boyce to this," said Alvarez, grimacing as the last part of the bandage was taped into place. "I'd really like to nail that bastard. Figure out when the car was parked here, and see if we can turn up someone who can place one of Boyce's men around the car."

"You got it."

"Track down Dowling, let him know what happened. He hasn't been worth shit so far, but maybe he'll have some ideas on how to handle this. Someone needs to be there when they break the news to Boyce, see if he lets anything slip."

"Sir," said the nurse, valiantly stepping into the absent doctor's shoes, "I need to read you your patient's rights."

"You're kidding," said Alvarez.

"No sir," the nurse informed him earnestly. She proceeded to read a long list of dire things that might occur because of Alvarez's injury, the medication he was given, and the treatment he had received.

"I think I feel worse already," he said when the recitation of possible side effects finally stopped.

"I'm not finished," the nurse told him, then proceeded to read a long disclaimer in which the hospital, doctor, and entire staff disavowed any responsibility or liability for Alvarez's future well-being.

"That's pretty impressive," said Scott.

"Yeah," concurred Alvarez. "Maybe we can work something like it into Miranda. I especially like the part that says 'we, collectively and individually, disavow any and all responsibility ...'"

"And here's a prescription for pain killers you can use after the first twenty-four hours," interrupted the nurse, pressing a paper into Alvarez's hand.

"What the hell do I do in the meantime?" he asked.

"Try to distract yourself, as much as possible," was the reply, and the nurse was gone.

"Excuse me," said the first uniformed officer to Alvarez, "but I need to get your statement."

"It's just like Mrs. Travers said," replied Alvarez. "Mrs. Travers was threatened because of her part in the investigation, so I followed her when she left our office to make sure she got safely on the interstate. She came here instead, and I assumed she had come to visit the infant involved in this case. I saw Mrs. Travers leaving the lobby and followed her outside to the parking lot. She was returning to the lobby when the explosion occurred."

"How could you have s-s-seen her leaving the lobby, and not noticed Annika Atkins?" asked Scott curiously. "There's only one entrance." Tory could hear her heart beating in her ears for the second time that evening. Maybe calling Scott hadn't been such a good idea after all.

"And the door to the men's room is directly off the entrance," said Alvarez without missing a beat. "I really needed to take a piss when I got here, so that's where I headed. Annika Atkins must have gone out to the parking lot by the time I came out of the men's room. The only person I saw was Mrs. Travers walking through the front door toward the parking lot, and I followed her."

Scott looked like he was about to ask another question.

"There are some other details about the case I need to clear up for you later," added Alvarez pointedly, and Scott shut his mouth. The officer taking the statement looked at the three of them expectantly, but no one offered anything further. He flipped his notebook shut.

"Thanks, Detective Alvarez," he said. "You need to get home and get some rest. If we have any other questions we'll get back to you." He left the room and Alvarez pushed himself off the examining table with another grimace.

He took a hard look at Tory. "Are you okay?" he asked. "You don't look so good."

"I think I look damn good, considering the circumstances," she replied.

Alvarez gave her another hard look but didn't say anything else about it. "Let's get out of here," he said. "The keys to my Corvette are in my pocket."

"I'll get them," said Scott quickly.

"You make a hell of a partner, but you're really dense sometimes," muttered Alvarez, which Scott ignored. "You drive," continued Alvarez. "We need to talk."

"Are you sure you don't mind staying with him?" Scott asked Tory, after successfully fishing Alvarez's keys out of his pants pocket.

"Of course she's sure," answered Alvarez for her. "I'd hate to think I went through all this for nothing."

"I'll get an officer to follow us in a squad car," Scott told Tory. "Then he can drive me back here."

And that's how they did it, three cars in a row, so that when Tory Travers finally drove to David Alvarez's house to spend the night, it was a parade.

Scott unlocked the door and turned on the lights, then

helped Tory feed an elated Cotton, who was filled with joy at the unexpected company. Alvarez went straight to a kitchen cabinet, pulled out a bottle of Tequila, sat down in the living room and started drinking out of the bottle.

"I don't think you're supposed to do that," said Tory.

Alvarez looked at her. "They said I couldn't take pain pills for the next twenty-four hours," he said. "They didn't say anything about getting drunk."

Tory couldn't think of anything to say to that, so she followed Scott and the other officer to the door. Scott waved him on and hung back to talk to her.

"David's m-m-mother was shot to death in a hospital parking lot," said Scott without preface. "It was a drive-by shooting that was never solved."

"That's awful," said Tory.

Scott handed her a business card. "I put my home phone number on the b-b-back," he told her. "In case he gets out of hand, or you need something."

Tory put the card in her jeans pocket. "I'm going to try to get him to bed," she said.

Scott grinned. "He'd get a k-kick out of hearing you say that," he said.

"But I'll wake him up every few hours to make sure he doesn't go into a coma, or anything like that," she continued serenely.

"I don't think there's going to be any k-kind of retaliation," said Scott after a moment. "There's no reason f-f-for Boyce to think that you were helping Annika Atkins. But call me if you need me."

Tory was doing a pretty good job of not thinking about Annika Atkins and what happened to her, but it seemed as though someone brought her name up every five minutes or so. No one had mentioned notifying anyone of her death, but surely that was something the police would address.

"Thanks," she said simply.

"Lock the door behind me," Scott admonished her, and then he was gone.

Tory went back into the living room to check on Alvarez. He was sitting exactly as she had left him, drinking steadily. He didn't look too much the worse for wear, except that he was grimy and one sleeve of his shirt and jacket had been cut away and replaced with bandages. "We might as well get your jacket off," she said briskly, "and for that, you'll have to put down the bottle." Cotton, lying at Alvarez's feet, thumped her tail softly when Tory spoke.

Alvarez looked at Tory balefully but complied. After she helped him ease the remaining portion of his jacket off she asked if she could get him anything. Surely Florence Nightingale herself couldn't have presented a more helpful demeanor, she thought. Maybe Alvarez had an afghan in a closet that he would like tucked around him.

"Beer, as a chaser, would be nice," he replied.

Tory wasn't sure what Florence Nightingale would have to say to that, but she decided to save her energy for more important confrontations. The refrigerator was well-stocked with beer, so she helped herself to two. She handed one to Alvarez and sat down on the couch next to a phone. She took a sip from hers. "May I use your phone to make a call?" she asked.

"Grammatically correct to the end," he replied, studying her from across the room. "Are you checking in with someone?"

"No," she said. "I don't have a dog door. I thought I'd call Sylvia and ask her to go over and let Tango out."

"Go ahead," he said, raising his beer in a toast to her proposed call. "This should be good."

Tory couldn't argue with that. She called Sylvia, trying hard to stick to the basic fundamentals of her story without digressing to answer Sylvia's myriad questions. Finally, she ended up hissing into the phone, "I can't talk about that right now. He's sitting right here. Yes, I'll see you tomorrow. Goodbye."

Alvarez continued to drink and to study her from across the room. "This is ironic. Here you are, you've even given your Girl Scout promise to spend the night, and I'm too damned depressed to do anything about it."

"Drunk, you mean."

"Depressed," he insisted.

She took a deep breath. "Okay, maybe you're depressed. Someone died out there, and that's pretty awful. But it's not your fault."

"If I had taken her in, played it by the book, she'd still be alive," he said.

Tory had thought about this. "She drove a rental car, right?" Alvarez nodded. "So it makes sense that at some point, someone would have to go pick up the car, right?" Alvarez nodded again. "And who would it be?" she wondered out loud. "A police officer, or someone from the rental car agency?" Alvarez shrugged, indicating that he didn't know the answer. "Whoever picked up the car, they would have died. And if it happened during the day, a lot of other people might have died, too," she concluded.

"If Boyce found out she'd been picked up, he might have disarmed the car bomb."

"Give me a break," she said. "How often have you heard of a hired thug disarming a car bomb he's rigged?"

Alvarez shrugged. "Could happen," he said.

"Sometimes there are problems that don't have answers,"

she said carefully. "This was a situation that didn't have a good outcome. I think you did good. You need to leave it there."

"And you wouldn't just be saying that." He didn't make it a question.

"As you've pointed out so many times before, I don't say things I don't mean," she said. "Did you tell Scott what happened?"

"Yeah," he said after a moment. "There are some things you can't keep from your partner, or pretty soon, you aren't really partners any more."

She nodded her understanding of this. "And what did he say?"

"Pretty much the same thing you said."

"I guess you'll just have to take it on good authority then."

"You think I should tell Karen?"

It took her by surprise, both the question and the fact that he was asking her opinion. "I don't know," she said honestly. "But you don't have to decide that tonight."

Alvarez looked at her a while longer, like he was thinking something over. "I think I better go to bed while I can still get there under my own speed," he said finally. "I don't suppose you'd care to join me?"

"You never give up, do you?"

"You never ask, you never know," he replied, looking down at Cotton. Tory wondered if he was studying the dog or trying to figure out how to get up out of the chair. "Ah, Carumba Cotton Candy," he said finally. "You're not so particular, are you?" He put down the bottle, snapped his fingers at the dog, and got up quite ably for a man who had consumed as much tequila as he had in the last half hour. Tory trailed after him down the hall to the master bedroom, which was amazingly neat and tasteful, with a king-sized bed that took up a good portion of the room. Alvarez turned and caught her looking at it.

"Is it the fact that I make my bed, or that it's so big, that surprises you?" he asked.

"Neither," she said quickly.

"Well, I toss and turn a lot when I sleep," he said, "so I need a lot of room."

"Can I get some pajamas out for you?" she asked.

He shook his head. "You really don't get out a lot, do you? I don't wear pajamas. I'm not nearly as drunk as you think I am, and I'm not in any danger from myself or my injuries. I appreciate the gesture, but why don't you just go home?"

She stood her ground. "And have to tell Sylvia Maestes that I didn't stay, when I already told her I would? You may think you're scary, but you're not nearly as scary as that. It would ruin my reputation. No one would respect me anymore."

That brought a slight smile to his face. "Point taken," he said. "So what do you suggest?"

"Go in the bathroom and brush your teeth," she said. "That's always a good idea. Then take off your shoes and I'll help you off with your shirt, and you can sleep in your pants."

"Do I get to remove my belt?"

"We'll see how it goes," she promised.

Alvarez disappeared into the bathroom, and Tory busied herself turning down the bed. She heard the water go on, which wasn't part of the deal, but she didn't have the nerve to intervene. She was beginning to wonder how she could judge whether he had passed out in the shower when suddenly the water went off, and soon after he came out of the bathroom wearing a pair of sweat pants. His wet, tousled hair made him look younger and more vulnerable than he'd looked sitting in the armchair and drinking tequila. "What?" he asked, when she kept looking at him.

"I'm just glad you're okay," she said. "I was worried about you passing out and drowning in the shower."

He grinned at her, which was the second smile since the car bomb had gone off, so Tory figured they were making progress. "I've had a lot of experience taking care of myself," he said, getting into the turned-down bed. Cotton clambered up on top of the covers like it was a nightly routine. "You were right," Alvarez said wryly, "about her getting the upper hand."

Tory pulled the covers up over him. "I'll be coming in and waking you up every so often," she told him.

"The nurse said to try to distract myself from the pain."

"That was what the tequila was for."

"If you insist on sleeping on the couch," he said in resignation, "there's extra blankets and pillows in the hall closet."

"Thanks," said Tory. And because Detective David Alvarez of the El Paso Police Department Special Case Force looked so incongruous tucked into bed next to Carumba Cotton Candy, she leaned over and brushed her lips over his temple before she turned out the light and left the room.

It was strange walking around in his house. She explored the guest bathroom, and was not surprised to find a supply of new, unused toothbrushes, one of which she commandeered for herself. She looked longingly at the shower for only a few moments before giving into temptation. If Boyce's cohorts came calling, Cotton would simply have to hold down the fort for a while, she decided.

After Tory got out of the shower, she couldn't bear the thought of putting on her sooty clothes again, so she wrapped a towel around her and went in search of the utility room, where she threw her clothes in the washing machine. She didn't have to look farther than the front closet to find another set of sweats, which were too large, but warm and comfortable.

Tory made sure that all the doors were locked, and then started turning out the lights. She paused at the door to the bedroom that obviously served as an office, then gave into temptation and walked in.

Two of the walls were covered with bookshelves that went from floor to ceiling, packed with books. There were reference books on criminology, pathology, psychiatry and ballistics interspersed with mysteries, and titles that fit in neither category. Tory was especially fascinated to find a large volume of short stories titled *Bitches and Sad Ladies* next to Susan Faludi's *Backlash*. Lonnie had given her a copy of *Backlash* several Christmases ago, she remembered, but then her investigation of Alvarez's reading habits was interrupted by the phone. Tory had to look around for a moment before she located a phone on the desk. "Hello?" she said tentatively, hoping she wouldn't have to explain her presence to someone on the other end.

"Where have you been?" demanded Sylvia breathlessly. "I called earlier and the phone rang and rang."

Shit, thought Tory, hoping it hadn't disturbed Alvarez. "I was in the shower," she said.

"The shower?" exclaimed Sylvia. The phone practically vibrated in Tory's hand. "What were you doing in the *shower*? I thought you were staying with him because he's injured."

"I was in the shower getting clean," explained Tory, "and yes, he is injured, and I put him to bed. Why are you calling?" she asked, before Sylvia could formulate another question.

"Cody called, looking for you. He said he couldn't get you on your cell phone."

"Why did he call?" asked Tory. Damn, she thought, she hadn't turned her cell phone off all day, the battery must have run out again.

"He called to let you know that they've decided to drive

back. It seems your father has gotten this idea into his head that he needs to come check up on you," said Sylvia. Tory's mind went blank. "Tory, are you still there?" Sylvia asked.

Tory was looking at the receiver in her hand. "Yes, I'm still here," she said faintly. Seventeen years later and her father had decided to come check up on her.

"Well, it wasn't any picnic either, explaining where you were," said Sylvia briskly, "but I did the best I could."

"I'm sure you did," agreed Tory. The cheeseburgers that she and Alvarez had shared seemed a long time ago; she didn't have the fortitude to hear the explanations that Sylvia had made to her father and son.

"Tory, are you okay?" asked Sylvia. "What are you going to do?"

"I'm okay," said Tory, "And I don't know what I'm going to do." She made reassuring sounds, promising Sylvia that she really would return in the morning, while she promised herself that she wouldn't make Ricky Acosta her role model by disappearing across the border. Finally she was able to hang up the phone. She walked into the kitchen and ate potato chips while she thought about her father on the road to visit her. That meant she had to go back to the hall bathroom and brush her teeth again. She decided to look in on Alvarez before she made up the couch.

He seemed to be sleeping soundly, but she couldn't sneak up on Cotton. What the dog lacked in visible eyes, she seemed to make up in keen hearing, for she thumped her tail when Tory approached the bed.

"Good dog," whispered Tory. "How would you like for me to move in for a few days? If I decide to go into hiding, could I count on you to keep it a secret?" The dog just thumped her tail harder. "Guess not," said Tory. "You heiress types are all so irresponsible." The dog looked awfully comfortable curled up next to Alvarez.

He had on clothes, so did she. She was tired and cold. How radical could it be to simply lie down next to someone for bodily comfort? Impulsively she turned back the covers and slid in, turning her back to him. She pulled his good arm over her and then pulled the covers back over both of them. He shifted to accommodate her, pulling her back more firmly against him. She was shocked at how familiar and comfortable it felt to lay like this. She wondered if it was too late to change her mind and retreat to the couch.

"You're not asleep," she said.

"Not while you're wandering around my house, not a chance," he said quietly next to her ear. "Leave you on your own, and God only knows what might happen. How were the potato chips?"

"How do you know I ate potato chips?" she asked, feeling foolish.

"You want to keep what you're doing secret, choose a quieter food the next time you're nervous," he advised.

"I was hungry, not nervous. You listened in on my phone call." She didn't make it a question, since she was staring right at the phone on the bedstand.

"I'm a detective. What do you expect?" She could hear the smile in his voice.

"I don't know what to do," she said. She didn't elaborate on exactly which topics she was addressing.

"Think about it in the morning," he whispered. She closed her eyes and decided for once to do what she was told.

EPILOGUE

Chimayo, New Mexico:
Thursday, January 5, early morning

Upon waking, it took Rodney Kiepper a moment to realize where he was. He'd never traveled in northern New Mexico, so his kindly host had explained the night before that the Indian name for the town was pronounced *Chee-my-o*. As the man made up the bed in the small adobe guest house that would serve as their residence for the next two days, he went on to tell Rodney that Chimayo was considered a place of spiritual healing by both the native Americans and the Catholics who came afterward. At the southeast end of town stood El Santuario de Nuestro Señor de Esquipulas, an adobe chapel built by a visionary farmer in 1816. This chapel contained an earthen pit with supposedly curative powers, which was lined with various crutches, braces, canes, and walkers left as testimony to the miracles that had occurred there.

Rodney had no need to visit the chapel. His miracle had already happened.

Two more days. Two more days and he and Amanda would travel to Abiquiu, another small New Mexican settlement, pronounced *Ab-eh-cue*, his host coached him. There, Rodney would be provided with new identification papers, and a résumé showing his extensive teaching experience in small, rural New Mexican schools. He and Amanda would spend a few weeks in Abiquiu, practicing their new identities while they openly posed as visitors there. Then they would be provided transport to Los Angeles. With the teacher shortages and his glowing recommendation letters, Rodney doubted he would be without a job for very long.

He had been worried about taking care of Amanda, but his worries were unfounded. Taking care of a baby was just like riding a bicycle, you might get rusty, but you didn't forget the fundamentals. Rodney's hands were steady as he tended to Amanda's needs, and she basked in his attention. He could already tell that she would be an easy baby. He would have liked to name her Christina, after his dead daughter, but his host discouraged anything that could be interpreted as a tie to his former life. So together they settled on Amanda, which meant "beloved," and seemed appropriate.

Rodney was surprised at how little thought he gave to his former life. St. Michael's Episcopal School for Girls would have to start the spring semester without a headmaster, and he supposed the police would surmise his disappearance proved his implied connection with the Underground Railroad. He didn't know what the official conclusion would be regarding his involvement with Lenora Hinson's death, and he found he didn't care. He wondered what would become of Keaton and her marriage, and how the attorneys would dispose of the portion of Lenora's estate that had been willed to him, but these musings were theoretical, devoid of any real emotional involvement. Rodney wished he could let Father Sanchez know what had happened, but he decided not to think about that right now. God could provide the means to address that in His own time.

For the first time in many years, Rodney could feel God working in his life again. The prior events in his life had prepared him to be the one person who was available in Amanda's hour of need, the one person who could prevent the child from becoming the property of a monster named Raymond Boyce. And it must surely be God's hand dealing divine justice, that Raymond Boyce would believe his last remaining blood descendant died at his own hand.

Rodney walked over to the crib to look at the sleeping Amanda. Amanda meant everything. Amanda meant more than his past life, his aspirations to the priesthood, even more than his all-consuming rage at his dead spouse. Rodney could be brave for Amanda, for Amanda he could start a new life. For Amanda's sake, beginning today, he would pray for the soul of his poor deceased wife.

For the first time since tragedy robbed him of his family, Rodney looked toward the future with anticipation, without the burden of either crippling regret or hatred. Tomorrow, he and Amanda, free.